In the Land of the Everliving

TOR BOOKS BY STEPHEN R. LAWHEAD

In the Region of the Summer Stars
In the Land of the Everliving

EIRLANDIA ✤ BOOK TWO

IN THE LAND OF THE EVERLIVING

Stephen R. Lawhead

A TOM DOHERTY ASSOCIATES BOOK

NEW YORK

IN THE LAND OF THE EVERLIVING

Map by Jon Lansberg

A Tor Book
Published by Tom Doherty Associates
175 Fifth Avenue
New York, NY 10010

www.tor-forge.com

Tor® is a registered trademark of Macmillan Publishing Group, LLC.

Library of Congress Cataloging-in-Publication Data

Names: Lawhead, Stephen R., 1950– author.
Title: In the land of the everliving / Stephen R. Lawhead.
Description: First Edition. | New York : Tor, 2019. | "A Tom Doherty
    Associates Book."
Identifiers: LCCN 2018045771| ISBN 9780765383464 (hardcover) |
    ISBN 9781466891814 (ebook)
Subjects: | GSAFD: Science fiction.
Classification: LCC PS3562.A865 I5 2019 | DDC 813/.54—dc23
LC record available at https://lccn.loc.gov/2018045771

Our books may be purchased in bulk for promotional, educational, or
business use. Please contact your local bookseller or the Macmillan Corporate
and Premium Sales Department at 1-800-221-7945, extension 5442,
or by email at MacmillanSpecialMarkets@macmillan.com.

First Edition: February 2019

Printed in the United States of America

9 8 7 6 5 4 3 2 1

In Memory of My Mother
Lois Lawhead

GREAT SEA
Robogdí
Venceni
Erídani
Dúnaird
Darini
Concani
Voluntí
Nagnati
Ulaid
Cauci
Hill of Tara
Coriondi
Auteini
Brigantes
Laigini
Dead Lands
Bréifne
Cruithne
NARROW SEA
Lands the Scálda Stole

In the Land of the Everliving

Eamon

Like many another fella, I remember where I was when word of Lord Brecan's death came my way. I was about joining the younger lads at their weapons on the field below the ráth. I like to keep my arm strong and help with the training whenever I can. Seghan is a spruce hand with the spear, and a shrewdy with feints and backhand thrusts and such. Everybody likes the pretty flowers, so they say—but sometimes I think a warrior should tend to the roots of our craft as well. I know I do.

Ach, well, I had collected my sword from the hall and was heading across the yard when visitors came clopping through the gates. I knew them on sight—a party of seven Coriondi warriors with their lord, King Cahir, at the head. Cahir is a good friend to us and our king's closest ally. Still, he had not been seen at Dúnaird since the shameful incident at that disastrous Oenach when our Conor went and got himself mixed up with that mad druid, Cadoc, or Mádoc, or whatever was his name.

By the sword in my strong right hand, I never believed Conor a thief. Neither thief nor liar is our Conor. If a fella ever wanted to see what honour on two legs looked like, all he had to do was catch a glimpse of Conor mac Ardan and he'd know it right enough.

I still ent got to the end of it all, but the long and short was the trouble got Conor exiled from the tribe and made outlaw, so he did.

We lost Conor, sad enough, but we also lost Fergal and Donal, and that is a bitter blow, I can tell you. Those two would not be separated from him and so they followed him into exile. Nor have they been heard from since—any of them.

And now, here was Cahir, come nosing around. I stood aside as they rode into the yard and watched them dismount, but I did not go to see what had brought them here. Truth, I begrudged Cahir for his part in Conor's exile. He could have stopped it and he stood aside and said not a word.

I went on to join the lads at practice, but could not keep my mind on the task. Like a nervous sparrow, my attention kept flitting back to Lord Cahir and that lot and wondering why they had come and what news had brought them.

Ach! What news it was. . . .

King Brecan mac Lergath, Lord of the Brigantes, was dead. Murdered!

That was the word from the wider world and it was on everyone's lips the moment we strolled back into the yard. 'Is it true?' I shouted up at Braida, the young lad on guard duty that morning. 'Brecan dead?'

'That's what they're saying,' he called back from his place on the walkway above the gate. 'Slaughtered like a pig by the Scálda.' Wiping the sweat from my face, I thought, *Aye, and there's a fox put among the geese for sure.*

Braida was talking to me. I glanced up, squinting in the sunlight. 'Say again?'

'If you go to the hall, will you send word back?' He gestured to the gate. 'I'm here the whole day long.'

'I expect you've heard the best of it,' I told him. 'If there's anything more to be said, you'll find it out soon enough.'

I hurried to the hall then and entered to find the lords already on their second or third welcome cup. A few of Ardan's advisors, including Liam, our battlechief, occupied one end of the long board, with my lord Ardan, and Cahir and Dara, the Coriondi king's battlechief, at the other end. Dara I knew from previous meetings at gatherings and such, and reckoned him a good man with a blade.

Hanging my sword and spear on the wall, I started toward the table. My lord Ardan saw me and hailed me, saying, 'Here, now! Eamon, to me. Friend Cahir has news for us.'

'Sit with us,' said Cahir. 'Have a drink to wet your tongue.' He shoved the cup across the board to me as I lowered myself to the bench across from him. Ardan, jar in hand, sat in his chair at the end of the table. He poured more mead into the silver welcome cup.

'Brecan Brigantes is dead,' Cahir announced. I noticed he could not keep the smile long from his face. He was enjoying the chance to tell us something we did not know.

'Scálda killed him?' I raised the cup to my lips and took a long draught of the cool, sweet liquor. 'What was it—a raid on Aintrén?' I took another drink, handed the cup back, and wiped my mouth on the back of my hand.

'Nay, nay,' replied Cahir. 'I'm hearing it was Balor Evil Eye himself did the deed.'

My eyes must have grown wide to hear this, for both Cahir and Ardan shared a chuckle at my expense, and my lord said, 'It appears that Brecan was on his way to a secret meeting some little way beyond the southern border.'

'A meeting with Balor Berugderc?' This did not make sense to me. I shook my head, trying to think what that could mean. 'How do you know this?'

'Ach, well, the dog-eaters sent his poor dead carcass back home on his horse.' He gave me a knowing look. 'And that brute of a battlechief of his—'

'Cethern,' I said. 'His name was Cethern.'

'Aye, that's the fella,' confirmed Cahir. 'Him they killed, too, and him they sent back in little pieces scattered along the road.'

'Bastards,' huffed Ardan. 'Puffed-up gloating bastards.'

'The Brigantes are outraged, as you might expect. Demanding an honour price and all.'

'How much?' wondered Ardan, lifting the cup to his lips.

'Twenty pounds of gold, forty pounds of silver, a hundred horses, and fifty hounds,' Cahir said, shaking his head at the audacious amount.

'You might as well ask for the moon and the stars and all the fish in the sea,' concluded Ardan, swirling the mead in the cup, 'for you will never see so much as a shrivelled bean from the black-hearted Scálda scum.'

'Too right,' agreed Cahir, taking the cup Ardan offered.

'I suppose,' I ventured, 'fixing the honour price at such a ridiculous sum is just to show how grieved and angry they are.'

'A hundred horses . . . ,' muttered my lord, shaking his head; he poured more of the sweet golden nectar into the cup before passing it back to me. 'Or,' he suggested, 'they mean to impress everyone with how great a king was Brecan Big Brócs.'

'Big Brócs!' hooted Cahir. 'I like that.' He leaned his sturdy bulk forward and put his arms on the table. 'More likely that fluffy little chit of a queen set that absurd high amount in order to disguise the simple fact that their top-lofty lord, for all his grand ways, was not well loved.'

'Either by his wife *or* his people. They say even his dogs avoided him!' added Ardan, and lofted the cup in mock salute.

We drank in silence for a moment, passing the cup hand to hand, listening to the low murmur of voices from the other end of the board and sounds from the yard outside: women talking, laughing, shouts of children running around. Occasionally, a horse would whinny, or a dog would bark.

'Mark me,' said Cahir, growing sly, 'there is a stink to this that festers in the nostrils.' He wrinkled up his face as if that stench got up his nose just then.

'Have you ever known Scálda raiders to return our dead to their tribes?' I said, feeling the liquor spreading its warm, soft fingers through me. 'They have never done that before. You are right, lord'—I lifted the cup to Cahir— 'there is more to this than we know.'

'Aye, I'm right. I know it,' said Cahir, taking a long pull at his cup, then wiping his moustache on his sleeve. 'I'm thinking there's legs to this rumour that Brecan and Balor had a secret meeting of some sort and a fight broke out. That's what I'm thinking.'

'Now we'll never know,' concluded Ardan, gazing into his cup. Then, glancing up, he said, 'Will you stay the night? I will have Aoife sing and play for us. We can talk some more.'

'Ach, well, that is tempting,' replied Cahir. 'But I will move along down the road. I just came to tell you the news and see if you had any word from your Conor.'

'Neither peep nor cheep,' I said. 'Though there are those among us who wish otherwise.'

'Ach, don't tell me,' said Cahir ruefully. He gazed into the depths of his cup. 'Accusing your Conor of the crime—that was all part of old Mádoc's cockeyed plan, I am embarrassed to say.' He looked to Ardan. 'I'm sorry I had any part of it. Believe me, it was a mistake I regret. I only hope to make it right one day.'

'What's done is done,' replied Ardan. 'Are you sure you won't stay— have something to eat at least?'

'Ach, nay,' said Cahir, rising. 'I thank you for the drink, my friend. But I have one more stop to make. Lord Sechtan will want to hear the news.' He paused, rubbing his chin as he reconsidered his plan, then said, 'I don't suppose you would care to send a messenger to him?'

'Stop here tonight and we will go together in the morning,' suggested

Ardan. 'I have not seen Sechtan since the Oenach, and the Robogdi were that close to joining Brecan. It would be good to sit down together and see where their loyalties lie now.'

Cahir smiled and accepted the offer. 'Maybe I am getting old,' he said, 'but a dry bed and a tight roof are too appealing to resist. Very well then, I will stay and we will ride out together tomorrow.'

The Coriondi lord went out to inform his men, and I took up my sword and begged leave to return to my weapon's practice. Lord Ardan walked with me from the hall and called a boy to go fetch his stable master to prepare a place for his visitors' horses. As the lad raced away, my lord murmured, 'How I wish Conor was here.' He turned to me. 'Where do you suppose he is now?'

I shook my head. 'By my shield, if I knew I would go and bring him back.'

Conor stood at the water's edge with waves lapping at his feet. The late sun threw his shadow across the glistening slate shingle. A solitary seagull soared effortlessly in the clear blue sky, dipping and gliding high overhead, and a light landward breeze lifted stray wisps of his light brown hair—grown longer now in the months of his slow and painful recovery—long enough to wear it in a tight braid gathered at the side of his head like one of the ancient kings whose exploits the bards turned into song.

Indeed, dressed in his splendid new clothes he appeared the very image of a prince of Eirlandia's noble line. Thanks to his host's generosity, he now possessed a siarc of gleaming scarlet edged in heavy gold thread; brown breecs the colour of oak leaves on the turn; fine brócs of soft deer leather that laced halfway to the knee; and a wide black belt studded with tiny gold rivets in the pattern of sea waves, and a cloak of tiny blue-and-black checks. This magnificent attire, like the healing care given him in the last many weeks, was a gift from a grateful benefactor: Gwydion, King of the Tylwyth Teg and Lord of the House of Llŷr, whose daughter Conor and his friends had rescued from the Scálda.

Just now, Conor paused in his stroll along the water's edge and gazed out across the green-grey water of the Narrow Sea, suddenly overcome by the realisation that time was passing in the wider world. How much time, he could not say. Here, in the Region of the Summer Stars, time behaved differently. He did not know why and understanding, much less any explanation, remained just beyond his grasp. Tír nan Óg, and the island realm the faéry folk called Ynys Afallon, was part of, and yet somehow separate from, the wider world beyond its shores.

Conor stood on the strand, his dark eyes searching the shimmering horizon, in the hopes of catching a glimpse of Eirlandia lying out on the rim of the sea. All the while, he massaged his arm and shoulder with his free hand. The wounds that had laid him low for such a long time were almost healed; he could move his arm freely and strength was fast returning. His side no longer ached every time he moved, nor sent a pain stabbing through him when he stooped or ran. According to Eurig, chief of the faéry physicians, his feet were on the path to health restored and he would soon be able to travel freely once more.

He felt more than ready. Although, curiously, as strength returned, the homeward pull diminished. Each day that passed, it seemed to Conor that he forgot a little more the cares and concerns of his homeland: the war with the Scálda, its ever-present urgency, its towering importance, receded a little more; even his memories seemed to grow more distant—as if they belonged to another Conor in another time and place. Lately, he had begun to fear that if he and his friends did not go soon, they would never leave.

As he looked out across the gleaming silver sea, he reminded himself once again that, as pleasant as life among the faéry was for him and Fergal and Donal, they could not stay. He told himself that the Land of the Everliving was not their home and they were needed in Eirlandia. *He* was needed in Eirlandia. The thought conjured an image of Aoife, long hair streaming in the wind as she, like him, stood on the strand gazing out to sea. She was waiting for him; his beloved, his betrothed was waiting, willing his return. If not for Lord Brecan, that devious and deceitful schemer, the two of them would be married by now.

But the fatal intrigues of the arrogant and ambitious Brigantes king had set Conor's feet on a different path. Perhaps, Clíona, that fickle and flighty daughter of destiny, had decreed they would forever remain apart. Conor cringed from the thought, and felt a pang of longing pierce him to the marrow. *Aoife, dearest heart of my heart, how cruelly you have been treated. I will come back for you.*

Hearing a crunch of footsteps approaching over the strand, he tensed. No doubt it was his physician come to fetch him and chide him for his errant ways. A moment later, a voice called out, 'Here you are, brother—and me looking for you half the day.'

'Aye,' agreed Conor without turning around. 'Here I am.'

'Did Eurig say you could come out?'

Conor gave vent to a resigned sigh as Donal came to stand beside him. 'Ach, well, good Eurig did not say I *couldn't* go out.'

'They are wonder workers, these faéry healers,' Donal observed.

'They are that,' agreed Conor. 'If they could mend *you*, I suppose they could put anyone back together.' He turned to his friend. 'It is that good to see *you* up on your two hind legs—a sight I never thought I would see again.'

'Was I that bad, then?' wondered Donal in a matter-of-fact tone.

'Worse—at least, worse than me.' Conor put out a hand to grip Donal by the shoulder. Despite his friend's recent ordeal, he seemed much his old self: his broad good-natured face glowed with good health; his long, thick moustache was neatly trimmed, his jaw clean shaven. Certainly, his solid, well-muscled frame—clothed now in the fine brown breecs and splendid siarc, and a cloak of faéry weave that combined blue and brown and violet in a check pattern—had never looked better. But his pensive black eyes hinted at new depths of knowledge or understanding that Conor had never noticed before. The observation prompted Conor to say, 'I am sorry you had to suffer so. If only—'

Donal shook his head. 'It was not *your* spear that caught me. You brought me here and that was the saving of me. You have nothing to feel sorry about.'

Conor accepted this without comment. Bending down, he selected a small, flat bit of slate, hefted it, and gave it a quick flip that sent it flying out into the bay. The stone skipped four times before sinking.

'Not bad,' observed Donal. 'But is that the throw of the fella who used to win all the contests when we were sprouts?'

'I did not throw with my left hand then,' Conor told him, lifting his injured right arm slightly. He rolled his shoulder and swung the arm to loosen it.

'A good warrior would be able to throw with either hand,' Donal reminded him. 'A *good* warrior can skip a stone seven times at least.'

'Seven times?' Conor challenged. 'Go on then, let's see how a good warrior skips a stone.'

Grinning, Donal picked up a round, flat sliver of slate from among the countless small stones at his feet. He stood, hefting it in his hands for a moment, squinted his eyes and said, 'Six.'

With that, he drew back his arm and, with a whipping motion, released the stone. It flew low over the water before dipping and skipping six times over the surface.

'Six, is it?' said Conor, searching for a stone. 'Six is fair, but it is not seven.' He bent and chose another stone, then prepared to let fly.

'Three,' said Donal, squinting his eyes and looking out into the bay.

'Seven,' Conor insisted. He threw again, awkwardly, and the stone sank after the third skip. 'Ach, well, you distracted me.'

'Then by all means, try again. Find a better stone this time.'

Conor did and, as before, just as he was about to let fly, Donal said, 'Five.'

The stone made five equal skips before plunking into the water some little way out in the calm water of the bay. This process was repeated six more times: with each throw Conor announced a number, Donal countered it with another—sometimes higher, sometimes lower—and each time the stone skipped the number of times Donal predicted.

After the seventh throw, Conor regarded his friend sharply, and was about to comment on this uncanny run of predictive luck when the expression on his friend's face stopped the words in his mouth.

Donal stood with eyes squeezed shut, his features clenched tight. After a moment, Donal's features relaxed, and Conor said, 'Is it your injury? Are you in pain?'

'Ach, nay,' he said, averting his eyes and lowering his head. 'Well, maybe—maybe we've both been a little too brisk just now.' He gave Conor a fishy, hesitant smile—which did nothing to allay Conor's concern.

'We should go before they come to drag us back.' Conor turned and started back up the strand toward the path leading to their house at the little lake the faéry called Llyn Rhaedr. Donal, however, remained gazing out to sea. 'Coming?' called Conor and, with a shake of his shoulders, as if he had been doused with cold water, Donal turned and quickly followed.

The two walked easy in one another's company as they crossed the strand; they had just reached the greensward when there came a shout from the linden-lined path directly ahead. 'Conor! Donal!'

Both men glanced up to see Fergal standing in the middle of the trail, hands on hips, waiting for them. Conor raised a hand in greeting. 'Fergal!' he called. 'How goes the battle?'

Fergal hurried to meet them. 'Does it never occur to either of you to tell anyone where you're going? What were you doing out here?' This last was directed at Conor.

'Well, you know me and the sea,' Conor replied. 'Try as I might, I cannot stay away from it. I have the ocean in my veins now.'

'Seawater for brains, more like.' The tall fair-haired man arranged his long face in an unsuccessful frown of disapproval.

Like the other two, his sojourn among the faéry-kind had made a new man of him. He seemed both taller and broader, Conor thought, his hair longer, and neatly braided into a thick hank that, like his own, hung at the side of his head, making his face and bearing seem more regal. In his splendid new rust-coloured siarc and breecs he looked every inch a lord of wealth and stature. Adjusting the flawless cloak of yellow and green checks across his well-muscled shoulders, Fergal rested his hand on the pommel of the gold-hilted knife the faéry king had given him and shook his head. 'You should be in bed resting, you know. You look terrible, Conor.'

'Ach, well, that is a matter of opinion.'

'Nay,' said Donal. 'It is a plain fact. You *do* look terrible.'

'But better than before.'

'*That* is a matter of opinion,' replied Fergal, falling into step beside Conor. 'Lord Gwydion is asking for you. He says he has news.'

'Has he now?' said Conor. 'As it happens, I would like to speak to him, too.'

Donal raised a questioning brow.

'Brothers, it is time to go home. I mean to ask our gracious host to take us back to Eirlandia.'

'Soon, aye,' agreed Fergal, 'but you are nowise ready to travel. For all you're only just up from your sickbed—and you probably shouldn't even be out here at all.'

'Ach, Eurig says I have exhausted his art. I am full ready to travel.'

Fergal gave him a long, scornful look to show what he thought of that idea and pulled on the corner of his moustache. 'Exhausted his patience, more like.'

'As pleasant as it would be to stay on this most favoured isle and while away our days among the faéry folk,' said Conor, 'we are needed elsewhere. King Brecan's death is bound to create problems for everyone. We are needed at home.'

'To do what?' demanded Fergal testily. 'What do you think we can do that would make any difference to anyone at all?'

'For a start, we can tell them what we know.'

'Who will listen?' said Fergal. 'I will tell you, shall I? No one. No one is going to listen to us—three exiles, cast out of our tribe for our crimes. Will anyone even deign to receive us? I think not. And if they do, it will be only to hold us to blame for Huw and Mádoc's deaths—maybe that swine Brecan's, too, for all I know.'

Donal saw the dangerous look in Conor's eye, and said, 'Enough, Fergal. You've said enough.'

'Too much,' muttered Conor.

Fergal sighed. 'I am sorry, brother. I meant no disrespect to Mádoc or Huw, or anyone else. But we must try to see how things stand now. You are injured and Donal is still recovering, and whatever you imagine is happening across the water in Eirlandia has most likely happened already and without us.'

'For once, Fergal is right,' offered Donal. 'You should rest and fully recover the strength of that arm of yours. Let Eurig and his helpers take care of you so that when we *do* go back, you will be fighting fit again.'

'I am fighting fit already,' Conor insisted. He looked at his two friends and a slow smile spread across his pale features. 'Thank you for your wise counsel. I know you intend it for my good.'

Fergal threw a cautious glance at Donal. 'Does that mean you will abide?' he asked.

'Nay,' replied Conor. 'I am still going to ask Gwydion to take me back to Eirlandia as soon as possible.'

2

Lord Gwydion sat with his long hands beneath his chin, his large dark eyes glinting in the bright golden flame burning silently in the expansive hearth of the great hall of Caer Raedr, his palace carved from the living stone of their island home. The enchanted fire splashed dancing shadows across the rough-hewn walls of the great cavern. In a far corner, sunlight from a fissure in the ceiling showered down upon a silver cage; tiny birds of yellow, blue, and green twittered pleasantly, mingling their song with the tinkling sound of water burbling up from a perpetual fountain in the centre of the enormous room. Few of the faéry remained in the hall; the day was bright and with the season on the change, most wanted to enjoy the last of the sun before winter wrapped their island in blankets of mist and snow for months on end.

Conor stood before the king and though he itched for an answer to his question, he held his tongue and waited for his reluctant patron to make up his mind without further urging or argument from him. Finally the faéry king raised his head and, offering a kindly smile, replied, 'I can well understand your eagerness to return home. I myself was in a similar position not so very long ago—and it is thanks to your skill and courage as a warrior that I was able to make my return at all. For that, I am grateful and forever in your debt.'

Conor accepted the praise, but said, 'There can be no debt between friends.'

Gwydion spread his hands as if to indicate that Conor's response only confirmed his own high opinion. 'Be that as it may, I have a charge to lay upon you and I hope you will honour it.'

'Ask what you will, lord king, and if it is in my power to fulfil, then trust it will be done.'

'It is, I think, well within your command,' the king replied. 'For I ask only that you remain in Ynys Afallon a little longer. Allow your healing to be completed so that you will be well equipped to meet the demands of your return. I have no doubt those demands will be many.' Gwydion saw or sensed the objection rising within Conor and quickly added, 'I am confidently informed by Eurig that you are well on the path to full recovery of both strength and health, but that destination is still some way distant. It is my understanding that taking on too much too soon will undo all his good work— and that, you will agree, is not the best outcome either of us would care to see.' Gwydion smiled again, rose, and came to stand before Conor. He put his hand on Conor's shoulder and said, 'Abide but a small while, my friend. The world will wait a little longer.'

At this, Conor's heart sank; nevertheless, he had to admit that the king made a fair point and that it would be ill mannered to refuse. 'You are most gracious, lord king. I will allow your wisdom and that of your physician to be my guide. But please know that I will welcome his release as soon as possible.'

Gwydion raised an eyebrow. 'You are that anxious to return to battle?'

'So long as my people suffer the cruel ravages of a wicked and relentless enemy, my duty is clear. I have no other choice.'

The faéry king released his hold, signalling the end of the audience, but said, gently, 'Spoken not like a warrior,' he said, 'but like a king.'

Conor left the cavern and returned to the lake house he and Fergal and Donal had made their home, and where the next days were spent much as the days before. Conor dutifully followed the care and direction of Eurig, the chief physician: he rested, slept, and ate well; he took walks along the strand, or in the surrounding woodland, or swam in the lake and bathed in the sweet-water stream below the waterfall. Taken this way, each day was a simple delight. Yet, each day also brought its own torment because, beguiling as the Isle of the Everliving was, there was someplace else he wanted to be. And, as enchanting as the faéry could be in all their grandeur, there was someone else he wanted to see.

He missed Aoife, ached for her. She was his first thought every morning and his last thought every night. Through the day he would find himself wondering what she might be doing at that moment, or wondering whether she thought of him. Did she miss him as much as he missed her? In his most abject moments he wondered if she even knew he was still alive.

The thought that Aoife might think him dead tortured him. He yearned to send word to her, to reassure her, to let her know he was alive and thought of her daily, that he had not forgotten her, that one day they would be together, that their long betrothal would be over and they would be married and never parted again. All this, and more, he burned to tell her. But each day ended the same: Aoife away in Eirlandia over the sea, and he in the Region of the Summer Stars.

Fergal and Donal also missed their homeland, but Conor sensed that longing diminishing, weakening as time went by. Like him, they enjoyed the easy splendour and luxury of Gwydion's court, and the fine company of the elegant and graceful inhabitants of the House of Llŷr; unlike him, they enjoyed it a little too much—or so it seemed to Conor. Together with their guide, Nodons, they explored the length and breadth of Tír nan Óg and returned, sometimes days later, with reports of the various wonders they had seen in the faéry strongholds and dwellings they visited: a magical vat that served up mead, or ale, or wine, or sweet water according to the desire of whoever dipped a cup . . . or a harp that played of its own accord whenever music was requested . . . or a cauldron that would quickly boil the meat of a champion, but would cast out the meat of a coward . . . a tree that produced both blossoms and ripe fruit at any time of the year . . . of a grain hamper that could not be emptied so that whatever grain was placed in it, however much was taken out, that much more remained . . . of a knife with a blade that could never be dulled . . . a small green plant, the leaves of which, when applied to any cut or bruise, instantly healed the injury . . . of a sparán made from the feathers of three hundred larks that multiplied by three any gem or coin placed in it . . . and many other weird and wondrous objects and artefacts besides.

They visited dúns located inside mounds and caverns, and strongholds on crannogs in the middle of lakes, and ráths so high up on the hilltops they seemed to float in the clouds; and in each of these settlements they were received like noble kinsmen and royalty. They visited Caer Ban where Cynan Eiddin, a kinsman of Gwydion, kept a palace to rival the king's: an enormous dwelling that contained sixty rooms and seven halls—rooms for sleeping, for working, for storing food and drink; and halls for eating, for dancing, for gathering in solemn assembly. Twenty pillars held up its walls, each one cut from an elder oak of the Great Forest of Orobris that once covered all of Albion. The walls themselves were covered in tiles that shone like polished gems. The roof was high-pitched, and covered with slates of seven different colours. There were nine doors, each wide enough and tall enough to admit a warrior on a horse, and each carved with runes of enchantment so that no one who entered could disturb the peace of anyone dwelling within.

The two mortals spent their nights in chambers sleeping on beds lined with cushions and pallets stuffed with goose down and soft feathers, and woke to music that drifted in from open wind holes set high up in the wall. Wherever they looked, they saw the intricate, sweeping lines of faéry design that adorned the brooches and torcs, buckles, bracelets, and rings. And it was everywhere: woven into clothing and engraved on cups of silver and platters of gold; enticing patterns were carved into doorposts and lintels, on beams and rooftrees, chiselled on pediments and columns and arches; it adorned the walls of their halls and was set into the paving stones on the floors of homes and courtyards. The cunning interwoven lines, at once so lithe and flowing, dazzled the eye and lifted the heart of the beholder, lending an air of grace and refinement to all of faéry life.

Everywhere they cast their eyes, they glimpsed something of the beauty that was part of the nature and character of the faéry race—so much so that travelling through the Region of the Summer Stars became a continual delight. The sights they saw and later described were the objects of stories and songs long familiar to druid bards, tales told and sung at festivals and gatherings of every kind in Eirlandia; the very things the Dé Danann marvelled at as children and dreamt about at night were commonplace to the faéry. Even the humblest items of everyday use—a chair, a bowl, a lampstand, a spoon, a stool, a cooking pot—would be treasures anywhere in the world of mortals; but here, in this otherworldly realm, the objects of daily life were not the stuff of dreams or the fancies of singers and storytellers. Here, in Tír nan Óg, in the Region of the Summer Stars, those dreamt-of things were real.

Conor listened to his friends recount their travels and marvelled—just as he had when he was a boy sitting with his brothers at the Lughnasadh fire. He admitted it would be a fine thing to remain in a place where such wonders of splendour and magnificence were not only possible, but common occurrences. Even so, the greater part of him knew that could not be; they could not remain in Tír nan Óg while the evil Scálda infested his homeland. He was needed elsewhere.

When the day finally came that Eurig declared himself satisfied that Conor's healing was complete, Conor embraced his physician and thanked him for his unstinting care, and then ran off to find Fergal and Donal to tell them the good news: they were going home!

3

Three large stone-and-timber houses overlooked Llyn Rhaedr, the small, fern-lined lake fed by the waterfall concealing the entrance to the faéry caverns. The houses were used by visitors during gatherings and celebrations—which, like everything else, the faéry seemed to enjoy in abundance—as well as for the very rare visitors who were not allowed beyond the guarding waterfall into the stony heart of the faéry realm.

The caves, on the other hand, were the sole domain of the faéry themselves, and those few deemed worthy of the honour. For instance, the Aessídhe faéry that Conor had rescued from the Scálda and who had been transported to the island along with Conor had not been admitted to the caverns. In fact, Lord Lenos and his Kerionid had not cared to remain the guests of the Tylwyth Teg any longer than they could suffer the humiliation of having been saved by their sworn enemies. Thus, the day after their arrival King Lenos had demanded to be taken home to Eilean Ceó, an island in the northern seas within sight of the shores of Albion—a wish granted without hesitation. When Conor asked about their swift departure, he was told only that too much had happened in the past to believe the two tribes could be reconciled in a day.

Neither Lord Gwydion, nor anyone else Conor asked, cared to make any further comment on their troubled history; not even would Princess Rhiannon speak of it. As for Conor, Fergal, and Donal—the Dé Danann warriors were welcomed as champions and given the best private chambers and principal places at elaborate celebratory meals. Extravagantly decorated and appointed with every luxury the faéry could command—rich wall hangings and colourful-woven coverings for the floor, high wooden beds, candle trees of burnished bronze and silver with candles that never burned out, enormous washbasins in the shape of giant seashells and silver ewers shaped like seahorses—the cave chambers, like the great hall and other magnificent rooms, did require a certain temperament to fully appreciate. That is to say, splendid though they were, the caves were not to everyone's taste because of the subterranean nature of the place. So it was for the three Dé Danann: after a few days residence inside the mountain, Conor, Fergal, and Donal had moved down to more familiar dwellings at the lake where they felt at home.

And it was here that Conor found Fergal, sitting in a chair on the gallery platform of their lake house, eyes closed, his feet propped on the rail and his face turned toward the sun. He opened his eyes when he heard Conor's footsteps on the wooden stairs leading up to the gallery. Seeing Conor's expression, he said, 'You look like the bear that found the honey tree.'

'Eurig says I am healed.' Conor dropped into the empty chair beside his friend.

'Good news that.'

Fergal closed his eyes again, and Conor sat for a while gazing at the placid waters below them and the swans gliding serenely over the glassy green surface of the sun-bright water. 'It is so very peaceful here.'

'Aye, so it is,' agreed the lanky warrior. 'I expect that means you're working up to leaving.'

'I like it here as much as anyone, but we are needed at home.'

Fergal nodded and sighed. 'Have you spoken to Gwydion yet?'

'Not yet. I wanted to tell you and Donal first.'

'I mean,' corrected Fergal, 'have you asked him to join us in fighting the Scálda?'

'That is still to do,' Conor told him. 'I'm waiting for the right time.'

'And if he refuses?'

'Ach, well,' sighed Conor, 'then I reckon we are no worse off than before.'

'But the faéry have a stake in this, too. They know that, do they not?'

'I will tell him.'

'See that you do.'

Conor shoved back in his chair and put his feet on the rail, too. 'An alliance between the Tylwyth Teg and the Dé Danann could defeat Balor Evil

Eye once and for all—I know it. Together we would win such a victory that the Scálda would never trouble us again.'

'Even if we were to convince the faéry folk to join us, do you think it would be that easy?'

'Easy? Nay, but I believe it would end the deadlock and tip the balance in our favour,' Conor replied firmly. 'Aye, and I'm not the only one who thinks so.'

'Who else?'

'Balor Berugderc.' Conor spat the name. 'Why do you think that vile creature has been trying to capture as many of the faéry kind as he can find? He would force them to join him. Failing that, he's capturing as many as he can get his bloody hands on and torturing them to reveal their secrets. It is only a matter of time before he succeeds.'

Fergal was quiet for a long moment, and Conor sat gazing out over the lake and the surrounding greensward with its scattering of wildflowers. The honeyed light of a westering sun sparkled in the tranquil water and the autumn reds and yellows and chestnut browns of leaves of the trees and plants along the borders of the glade. Dragonflies flitted among the reeds, their iridescent bodies glinting like wing-borne jewels.

'I hate the thought of leaving,' said Fergal, his voice at once wistful and resigned. 'I like it here. Even the air smells better, sweeter.'

Conor drew a breath and admitted that Fergal was right. Everything about the Isle of the Everliving was as perfect as the faéry could make it. Little wonder then that the Tylwyth Teg had fled Eirlandia with all its shocks and alarms, calamities and strife. Their island paradise was a haven and a refuge, a fortress protected not by timber walls and warriors, but by a multitude of charms and deft enchantments.

'Aye, I know it,' Conor sympathized. 'I know it here.' He placed a hand over his heart. 'And it grieves me full well.'

'Aye, but I think Donal will hate leaving most of all.'

'Then he can stay,' Conor decided. 'You stay, too, if that is your desire. Leaving is my decision, I do not mean to make it yours.' He paused and then added, 'I never said either of you must accompany me.'

'What? And are we to remain here without you?' blurted out Fergal. 'Ach, nay—not Fergal mac Caen. You should know me better than that.'

'Listen to me, brother, and think about it,' Conor insisted. 'You and

Donal must decide for yourselves. If you choose to remain in Tír nan Óg— if it is in your heart to abide—then so be it.'

'Aye, and then who would save your poor, poxy hide next time you get yourself into a scrape, eh?' Fergal hooted. 'It is not *if,* mind, but *when.* I know you, Conor mac Ardan—trouble follows you like a faithful hound.'

'I cannot disagree,' Conor granted. 'But do consider what I said. While you are considering, I will ask Gwydion to ready a ship to leave as soon as possible.'

'There is no need to decide anything. We were with you from the beginning and we are with you still. If you go, we go with you.'

Having said what he came to say, Conor leaned back and closed his eyes. The two sat together in silence for a time, content in one another's company, enjoying the sun and warmth—until they heard the singing: the lilting sound of a pleasant female voice. Conor opened his eyes and glanced around, spying Rhiannon on the path leading around the lake and down to the harbour. Conor's breath caught at the sight of her and his senses quickened. Dressed in a scarlet gown with a girdle of pale yellow adorned with golden spiral disks, and a long white tunic that glistened in the sun like quicksilver, it was pure pleasure to observe her lithe form as she stepped lightly down the path toward the water. She sang as she walked, unaware that she was being observed by the two men on the platform above.

After a moment, Conor, grown uncomfortable staring, called down to her. 'Good day to you, Lady Rhiannon. What is that song?'

She halted and glanced up, smiled, and then turned and came to join them. 'I might have guessed you would be taking the sun,' she said, climbing the steps to the platform. 'In these last bright days, we must store up in our hearts light and warmth enough to last us until the spring. Winter can be so dark and cold—even in the Region of the Summer Stars.'

She greeted Fergal, smiled, then said to Conor, 'My father says Eurig has declared your healing complete.'

'Aye, so he has,' replied Conor. Though he had hoped to avoid an awkward conversation, it appeared to have found him anyway. 'I mean to ask the king for a ship to take us home—' He glanced at Fergal, who said nothing. 'We'll leave as soon as the ship can take us.'

The cheerful light went out of her eyes and Conor suddenly felt moved to explain. 'I am sorry, but I cannot wait. The winter seas will make the voyage difficult and dangerous. I think it best to go now while a good sailing is still possible.'

Rhiannon studied him with eyes the colour of the sky and, sensing as there was nothing she could do to make him change his mind, she said, 'And will you also ask him to join you in the war against the Scálda?'

'I intend that very thing,' Conor replied. Then added, 'Though I do not expect him to agree.'

'Nor do I,' she admitted. 'But do not resent him for his refusal, Conor.'

'Never say it, my lady. You and your people have been nothing but kindness itself to us. . . .' He glanced at Fergal again and saw his friend was watching them, but staying out of the discussion. 'More than kind to all of us. As for myself, I would be food for worms even now if not for you.'

Rhiannon looked away, then bowed her head and folded her hands. 'You must understand that our race is neither as great nor as powerful as it was in the past.' She looked up and her gaze took on a faraway aspect as if gazing into a glorious sunset now fading from view, or a grand treasure now beyond recovery. 'Once we were masters of land and sea. We ruled over all that passed beneath our gaze, and thought we would rule always. Alas, it seems the Great Mother has decreed that our walk in this worlds-realm is drawing to an end. Though we live long, the days of our supremacy are gone. We diminish so that mortals may ascend.'

'Must it be that way? Broad as it is, this world must surely have room for both our tribes.'

'Room enough, perhaps, but not the nature, I think. Everything has its season—people and animals, to be sure. They are born and thrive, then fade and die. That is the way of the world—for all races and empires, too. Our kind ruled and now will pass away to allow the next to have its day in the sun. But while we still live, we will pass the time that remains in peace and plenty, in harmony and the enjoyment of the Great Mother's wealth of gifts. My father understands this, but the memory of all we once were, all we once possessed haunts him and will until he dies.'

'I thought the Tylwyth Teg lived forever,' said Conor softly. A heavy sadness had settled on his heart.

She offered him a forlorn smile. 'Nothing lasts forever, Conor.'

The wind gusted just then, rustling the dry leaves on the trees round about.

'Winter thoughts, to be sure,' Rhiannon said with a sad smile. She uttered a little laugh and shook her head, her black hair shimmering in the golden light. 'We can be a morose and sullen folk—especially with the change of seasons at the ending of the year.'

Conor rose to stand before her; he lifted a hand and rested it on her shoulder, feeling the slight tingle in his fingertips. 'I would stay if I could,' he said. 'Nothing would please me more than to spend all my days here in the Land of the Everliving. But I must return home. My people need me. If they do not know it now, they will realise it soon enough.'

Rhiannon, her head bent once more, nodded. 'Will you come back one day?'

'If you will have me,' Conor replied.

'Do you have to ask?'

'Then, nothing preventing, I will return,' Conor replied. 'On that you have my solemn vow.'

4

The night before they were to leave Ynys Afallon, Lord Gwydion held a feast to honour the three Dé Danann who had risked their lives to save not only his daughter and her handmaid, but Kerionid lord, King Lenos of the Aessídhe and more than a dozen of his people as well. For this celebration, the Gwydion had invited all the noble faéry tribes and clans to send representatives to Caer Rhaedr, that they might pay homage to the departing warriors. The palace halls and corridors fairly heaved as final preparations were made and guests began arriving from across the island and one or two provinces on the mainland as well. With the setting sun, one of the king's servants appeared at the door of the great reception hall to summon the guests of honour. Conor, Donal, and Fergal, scrubbed and brushed and dressed in all their faéry finery, were conducted to the king's great reception hall where they were hailed and welcomed to almost deafening acclaim. The cheers and salutations broke over them in wave upon wave like the waters of a noisy sea as they processed to the foot of King Gwydion's throne.

The throne, like the hall itself, seemed carved out of a single stone and polished until it gleamed in the light of a thousand torches that lined the walls of the enormous room. Lord Gwydion rose as they came to stand before him; he raised his hands for silence until the cheering hushed. Then he said, 'Tonight we honour the courage and sacrifice of true friends. In doing so, we surround ourselves with still more friends—some we know, others we have not yet chanced to meet. I trust that in the short time we have together, we will take full advantage of this occasion to heighten the resolve to achieve a new and better understanding of our Dé Danann friends, and to strengthen the ties that bind true hearts together.'

Stepping down from his circular dais, the king moved from one to the next, resting his hand on each in turn: Conor first, then Donal, then Fergal, pausing to lean close and whisper a private word. When he finished, he stepped back and summoned his chief steward to attend him; a tall, dour-looking faéry with eyes pale as ice, he took his place beside the king, head erect, body straight.

'My people,' said Gwydion, lifting his voice once more to carry across the crowd, 'here stand before you three warriors without peer, the finest of their kind to be found in this worlds-realm. Yet, as skilled in their craft as they may be, a craftsman can only work with the tools he has been given. With this in mind, I have commissioned implements suitable for the warrior craft to be made by our finest artisans that our friends may have the finest tools.'

The faéry king nodded to his court steward who made a wide flourish with his hand and nine bearers came snaking through the crowd. The first three carried shields: long, narrow oblongs slightly wider at the top and bottom and half curved to fit close to the body. The colour and lustre of heavy bronze, yet light as a bird's wing, each shield was adorned with a cunning faéry mark incised into the metal and traced in silver.

Taking up one of the shields, the king said, 'When the battle rages around you may this serve as your refuge.' He handed the shield to Conor and, again, leaning close whispered into his ear, 'Your shield is called Pared, it will be a stout wall around you. No one but you is to speak its name.'

Moving on, the king repeated the gifting ceremony with Donal and then Fergal in turn. Then, while he still stood before Fergal, the steward summoned another bearer; this one held a long, slender-shafted spear with a thin, leaf-shaped blade that tapered to a lethal point. Like the shield, the spear appeared to be solid bronze with a design etched in silver at the base of the blade. The king presented the weapon to Fergal, saying, 'When you attack the enemy may you find this a true and trustworthy companion, quick to the fight and unerring in flight.' He placed the weapon in Fergal's right hand, leaned close and whispered the weapon's name. He did the same with Donal, and then presented a spear to Conor, saying, 'Your spear is called Pelydr, for it is a staff of great value. No one but you is to speak its name.'

Conor thanked the king and took up the spear; though lighter in weight than any he had ever hefted, he sensed a lively strength, a quickness barely contained within the weapon coursing through the shaft from the butt to the head.

The chief steward summoned the last three bearers to attend the king. Each of these stepped forward carrying a sword across his palms. Taking up the first sword, the king raised it high so all could see. 'When in the heat of battle your enemies swarm around you, may you find this blade swift to strike and swifter still to defend.'

He gave the weapon into Donal's hand, bent low to whisper its name and provenance, then moved on to Fergal and then Conor. The moment Conor's hand closed upon the hilt, he felt a sudden vitality; more than a blade to wield, the weapon seemed part of him, a supple extension of his arm. 'Your sword is called Eirian,' whispered the king, 'for it will be a bright blaze in your enemy's eyes. Let no one but you speak its name.' Gwydion dismissed the bearers and the chief steward withdrew with them; Conor stole a sideways glance at his friends and saw that they were as surprised as he was and just as pleased. Like him, they recognised the worth of the gifts they had been given. The spears, swords, and shields were both like and un-like any they had ever known: light in weight, but robust; responsive and quick, but firm in the hand; keen-edged as razors. But the faéry king was not yet finished. Taking his place on the dais once more, he said, 'Since your time among us has been well spent, you will recognise something of the quality of the gifts you have been given. But you may not so readily appre-ciate that each of these weapons has been bound to a particular charm.' Reaching out, he brushed his fingertips over the intricate silver design cut into the shield on Conor's arm. 'The shields will withstand blows that would shatter lesser defences and will not be dented.' Indicating the spear and sword, he said, 'These blades will neither bend nor break; moreover, they will remain true and maintain their lethal edge in the blinding heat of the fiercest battle.'

Knowing the inestimable value the faéry placed on such items, Conor understood the significance of what he was being given, and the honour being paid them. At once thrilled and humbled by the faéry king's largesse, he found himself at a loss and struggled to find words adequate to convey his gratitude. 'Lord king, we are beggared by your generosity as much as by your compassion. Weapons to a warrior are life itself, and we have received both from your hand. Your servant thanks you.'

Fergal and Donal repeated similar sentiments to the noisy acclaim of the faéry looking on. Gwydion accepted the warriors' gratitude, and said, 'My friends, I commend these weapons to your best and highest use. They are given in the hope that you will employ them in your struggle to free Eirlandia from the Scálda curse.'

'Trust in it, my lord,' replied Conor. 'Touching on the Scálda, I would speak to you further about that.' It was a clumsy attempt and Conor knew it, but it was the only chance he had seen and he had taken it.

The king, aware of all the eyes on them, merely smiled and inclined his head, saying, 'Of course. In the morning, perhaps, before you leave. I will send for you.' Then, raising his hands and voice to address the throng, he commended the three Dé Danann heroes to his people and the hall rang with their chorused shouts of commendation and applause.

Next it was Rhiannon's turn to give a gift, but this gifting took place after the conclusion of the ceremony when the guests were being led to their places at one of the seven long boards set up in the great dining hall. As Conor crossed the threshold into the enormous carved-cavern room, he felt Rhiannon's light touch on his arm as she glided into step beside him. 'I also have a gift for you, my friend,' she said, her voice low so those around them would not hear.

'You and your father have already given us so much, I do not think I can bear to accept anything else.'

She smiled, her shapely lips curving in a sweetly secretive smile. 'I think you will not find this gift too difficult to bear,' she said. 'Indeed, you have borne it admirably well for some time already.'

Conor regarded her with a quizzical look. 'I have?'

Stepping from the long line of guests entering the banqueting hall, Rhiannon pulled him into a nook behind one of the many pillars lining the perimeter of the great room. 'My gift to you is to renew the charm I bestowed when first we parted,' she told him, taking his hands in hers. 'Do you remember?'

Whether by suggestion or through her touch, into Conor's mind sprang the memory of that moment when the two of them stood on the shore moments before the faéry ship carried Donal away to Tír nan Óg where he might find healing for his wounds. For an instant, Conor could almost hear the restless wash of the waves and the mournful cry of the seagulls as Rhiannon placed her right hand over his heart and said, 'I have only to speak your name to know where to find you.' Lightly touching her left hand to his forehead, she leaned close and whispered, 'You have only to whisper my name and I will be there.'

Conor felt his throat grow tight, choking off any reply he might make. There was more than magic in that touch, and Conor felt it: there was also love. He was saved having to make a reply by the abrupt summons of Gwydion's chief steward calling all the guests to take their places.

Conor's name was announced and Rhiannon released him to join Donal and Fergal at the king's right hand; Conor took his place in the chair beside the golden-haired beauty, Queen Arianrhod. While the other guests were ushered to seats at other tables, Conor and the faéry queen exchanged a few mild pleasantries. Those were soon exhausted and the queen moved to the matter that was uppermost in her mind. 'I hope you know how much we value your friendship, my lord—'

'I am no lord,' Conor corrected lightly. 'Merely a warrior whose curiosity is as boundless as his ignorance is profound.'

The Lady of the House of Llŷr favoured him with a look of mock astonishment. 'I do not believe that,' she said, 'not even for an instant.'

'I assure you it is true,' Conor insisted. 'How else can it be explained? Ask Fergal there'—he nodded in the direction of his friends who were just then sharing a cup with the king—'or Donal; it will be his sole delight to tell you all the many ways my wayward nature has plunged us all into deep and troubled waters.'

'And yet, here you are!' laughed the queen. 'Many a mortal has longed to sit where you sit now and grew old with that desire unfulfilled.'

'Luck,' suggested Conor. 'Nothing more.'

'I think there is far more to you than you allow yourself to believe.' Growing suddenly solemn, she added, 'Until you do so believe, you will remain that unfortunate plaything of ignorance and curiosity that you describe.' Her deep green eyes took on a far-off look—as if viewing the world from a vast distance—as she added, 'And your war with the Scálda will never end.'

Conor did not know what to say to that, but was saved having to reply by the arrival of a serving boy with a jar to fill their cups with mead. 'I drink to you, Conor mac Ardan,' said Arianrhod. 'May good fortune find you and follow you forever.'

They drank then, and talk turned to their time in the Land of the Everliving and the memories the three mortals would take with them to

Eirlandia. While they talked, the cups were filled and refreshed and soon the food was served: enormous platters with slabs of roast pork and root vegetables—most of which Conor had never seen—and whole partridges, grouse, and quail stuffed with boiled oats flavoured with sage and other herbs and spices. There were bowls containing the drippings from the roast into which chunks of stale bread were sopped, and sour compotes of red and black currant, and fifteen or twenty more dishes containing items Conor had never tasted before. While the bowls were being ladled full by the serving boys, the musicians entered to fill the great hall with music, and the feast became more lively as the guests drank and ate and talked long into the night.

As much as Conor enjoyed the food and song, and he truly did, some portion of the delight he might have felt had been leeched from the celebration by the queen's inauspicious comment regarding Eirlandia's never-ending war. Before he had finished eating, and long before the guests began creeping away to find other entertainments or beds for the night, Conor found himself wishing he was already at the rail of Lord Gwydion's ship, watching the misty green hills of Eirlandia rising in the west.

5

The sun was a mere rumour in the east when Conor rose, ready for the voyage home. Thoughts of Aoife and himself wrapped in a warm, welcoming embrace had banished sleep from his bed and in his eagerness to be off and on his way, he got up and carried his clothes out onto the platform outside the front door, dressed there, and then settled himself in one of the chairs to wait for Fergal and Donal to rise. He was still there, and still waiting, some time later when one of the king's serving boys appeared with the message that the king wished to speak with him before their departure. Donal and Fergal emerged from the house to hear Conor tell the lad he would be pleased to attend at once.

'What's this then?' wondered Fergal.

'Lord Gwydion has summoned me to an audience,' he explained. 'Wish me luck.'

Donal glanced at Fergal. 'We're going with you.'

Fergal gave a curt nod and Conor, seeing that it would be a futile waste of time to argue, said, 'Then let's go see the king.'

The three Dé Danann made their way up the path and joined the serving boy who was waiting for them at the waterfall that hid the entrance to the faéry king's palatial cavern abode. The boy led them through the waterfall, into the grand entrance corridor and delivered them into the chief steward's hands; the steward led them through the great hall to the king's private quarters in a chamber at the far end of the hall and ushered them into the king's presence.

Lord Gwydion, dressed in a long, loose tunic of shimmering blue that looked like sunlight on water, his long dark hair swept back and held by the thin band of a gold circlet, rose from his large, thronelike chair to welcome them and invited them to join him at the nearby board, which was laden with food to break their fast—an unnecessary nicety since they were still replete from the feast the night before. But the three took their places at the board and, at the urging of their host, picked from the platters before them while they waited for him to begin the discussion to which they had been summoned. The faéry lord took his time, warming to his purpose with expressions of friendship and hope for continued rapport in the future.

'I would like that,' Conor told him. 'Indeed, it is my most fervent hope that our two peoples can become better friends than ever we have been in the past. I believe we have much to teach one another—and,' Conor said pointedly, 'much we can do to help one another find peace in this hostile worlds-realm.'

Gwydion's eyes narrowed. 'You are speaking of your present conflict with Balor Berugderc.'

Conor answered forthrightly. 'I am.'

'That would explain your impertinent petition last night,' said the king. He raised an admonitory finger and tried to make light of the incident. 'Not the time or the place, I think.'

'No one has ever accused our Conor of being subtle,' said Fergal.

'But, know also,' added Donal, 'that he would not have risked such an affront to the dignity of the occasion if need were not so pressing.'

Gwydion accepted the apologies, and said, 'Spoken like the good and faithful friends you are. Such loyalty shows my trifling slight for the unworthy thing it is.' Then, arranging his elegant features in an expression of solemn sympathy, he said, 'How long have the Dé Danann been at war with the Scálda?'

Conor did a rapid calculation. 'Thirteen at least.' He glanced at Fergal and Donal for confirmation. 'Thirteen years or so. But you will know that as well as I.'

'A long time,' said the king. 'So, unless I am much mistaken, I believe you have it in mind to ask me to become entangled in a war that has sputtered along in fits and starts for more than half your life without any sign of resolution and—'

'Lord Gwydion, if you—'

'*Without any sign of resolution* and which your people have no realistic hope of ever winning.' The faéry lord placed his hands flat on the board before him as if establishing a known truth. 'Would you call that a fair summary of your request?'

'Fair enough, but with all respect I would merely remind you that you and your people have suffered the cruel brutality of the Scálda, too. Your daughter Rhiannon will have told you about her ordeal at the hands of Balor Evil Eye. She was not the first of your race to fall into the hands of the enemy and, unless the Scálda are stopped, she will not be the last. How many of your people has Balor caught? How many of your people has Balor killed?' Conor let the question hang in the air a moment, before concluding. 'Lord king, I am not lying when I say that the Scálda now endanger the faéry as much as the Dé Danann. The war has held us in its grip far longer than anyone could have foreseen, that is true—and, believe me, no one regrets or hates it more than I do. Yet, the Dé Danann still cling to every hope of victory. Would we have lasted this long if we had no hope?'

The king unfolded his long-limbed body from his chair, rose from the board, and circled it thoughtfully, before speaking again.

'My friends, your endurance *is* legendary,' allowed the faéry king with an airy wave of his hand. 'I will grant that, unlike us, you and your people may harbour some vague hope of eventual triumph, but this fighting could easily go on for another fifteen or twenty years, and another twenty or thirty after that.' He fixed Conor with a stern, almost fierce, expression—as if daring him to deny it.

'Aye, it could,' allowed Conor. 'But it need not. This is why I ask your aid. If the Tylwyth Teg joined us in the fight, the balance of power would shift in our favour. Indeed, victory would be transformed from a faint and distant hope to a swift and present certainty.'

'Spoken like a true warrior,' the king stopped pacing, returned to the table and rested his slender hands on the back of his chair. 'If I listened to any more of your smooth speech I might even find myself persuaded.' Before Conor could pounce on this tiny opening, the king shook his head. 'But no. I will not allow myself to be so persuaded. Despite what you may think, the Tylwyth Teg are not schooled in the brutal arts of combat which is the glory of your race. We learned long ago that warfare offers no lasting solutions, only despair and death. Thus, we lack both the skill and temperament for war, and I cannot with good heart pretend otherwise. Neither will I commit the lives of any more of my people to this hopeless struggle of yours.'

Conor heard the finality of Gwydion's decision and his heart sank. 'I understand, my lord king. But, I trust you will not think ill of me for asking,' he said, masking the true depth of his disappointment. 'For the sake of Eirlandia, I had to ask.'

'I will never think anything but the best of you, my friend,' Gwydion reassured him. 'Of all of you.' He gave a nod to include Donal and Fergal. 'As you have reminded me—if I ever needed reminding—you are the men who rescued my daughter from the cold embrace of death and returned her safely to her home. There are not many who could, or would, have done what you did—in this, at least, I *am* persuaded.'

Conor was tempted to turn Gwydion's gratitude to his advantage—but only for a moment. The king, and the faéry with him, had their way of walking on the earth, just as the Dé Danann had theirs. In that moment, he did not see how he could change that.

'You are more than welcome here,' the king continued. 'You and your friends may come and go as you please, and it will remain my continuing pleasure to celebrate your presence. In short, Conor mac Ardan, Fergal mac Caen, and Donal mac Donogh,' he said, letting his benevolent gaze rest on each of them in turn, 'you have a home here on Ynys Afallon for as long as you live—and the undying friendship of people who hold you in the highest regard.' Conor and his companions shifted uneasily under the faéry lord's blandishments, but thanked the king for his gracious words.

The king moved around the table and came to stand behind Conor. He raised his hands and rested them on Conor's shoulders—a fatherly gesture that Conor found slightly disconcerting. 'It is because of this shared friendship that I would offer you three a bit of advice. May I?'

Conor allowed that few men would be bold enough, or fool enough, to gainsay a king in his own hall, and invited the king to speak his mind freely.

Gwydion accepted this with an indulgent smile. 'My advice is this,' he said, growing serious again. 'Make peace with your enemy.' Seeing the startled expressions of his guests, he continued quickly. 'I urge this most sincerely. It seems too obvious to me that if neither side has prevailed in this struggle, despite all these years of strife, then neither side is destined for victory. Therefore, the wisest course would be to arrive at a mutually agreeable resolution and learn to live together.'

The naivety, the *audacity* of the suggestion stole Conor's breath away; the red birthmark that marred his face tingled and burned. 'Make peace with the Scálda,' he repeated, his voice growing thick and flat. 'Make peace with those who invaded our shores, stole our lands and slaughtered our people. Make peace with the creatures who will kill you and all those you love without a moment's thought or hesitation. Make peace with those who destroy everything they touch, who will not be appeased until they have exterminated every last living child of Danu.' His eyes sparked dark fire as he continued, 'I ask you, my king, how do you make peace with an enemy who will not be satisfied with anything less than your complete and utter annihilation?'

'You are angry,' observed Gwydion blandly. 'I understand that my advice is not what you expected to hear.'

'I confess it was not.'

'Even so,' said the king, 'I hope that in time you will come to accept that the course I recommend has considerable merit. The slaughter and destruction you speak of can cease. Only peace will bring an end to the war.'

'On that we agree,' replied Conor evenly. 'But if the faéry will not help us, I fear it will be the peace of the grave.'

The king turned away sadly and walked to the hearth where he stood gazing into the bright flames. 'Think about what I said—that is all I ask.' He looked sideways at Conor, who had not moved. 'I think we must leave our discussion there,' continued Gwydion. 'The ship is ready and waiting to take you back to Eirlandia. It is yours to command whenever you would like to depart.' He smiled, trying to recover the friendly fellowship they had previously enjoyed. 'I will meet you at the dock and make my farewells there. My servant will see you back to your lodging to gather your things.'

The three rose from the king's board, thanked him for his care, and departed. But the royal audiences were not finished yet. On their way back through the hall, they were met by Queen Arianrhod who had, apparently, been waiting for them to finish with the king. As Conor drew near to greet her, she motioned him to step aside. He indicated to Fergal and Donal that they should go on without him, and the queen led him to an alcove just inside a passageway leading deeper into the warren of interconnecting rooms of the faéry cavern.

'A brief word, Lord Conor, if you please,' she said, leading him into the passage and out of sight of the hall. After a few steps, she stopped, turned and, clasping her hands before her, said, 'I hope you will not take offense by what I am about to say.'

'How could I possibly find offense in anything the wife of my friend and benefactor may say or do?'

Queen Arianrhod dashed aside the comment with a quick lift of her chin. 'Do not imagine you can sway me from my self-appointed task with flattery and blandishments,' she replied lightly, and Conor heard a note of stony resolve under her winsome tone. 'I will not be swayed. I mean to speak to you about your benefactor, as you call him—my husband.'

'Is something wrong?' he asked, searching her eyes for a clue to her secretive and ominous behaviour.

'Nothing that cannot be helped by a friend who is willing,' replied the queen.

'Then I hope you will consider me that friend. Whatever a friend can do, trust that I will do it.'

'Thank you, Conor. I would not ask at all, but . . .' Her voice trailed off and she bowed her head.

'My queen, you have only to speak it out and it is done,' Conor told her after a moment.

Conor thought he saw the glint of tears, but when she raised her head again to answer, her eyes were dry and her voice steady as she replied, 'Do not allow him to involve himself in this hopeless war with the Scálda. He will, if you ask it of him.'

'But I—'

'If you ask it of him he will,' she insisted. 'He will become entangled in a trap from which there is no escape and that will be the death of him, and likely the death of us all. The debt of honour he feels that he owes you is so very great that he will be unable to resist your request. So, again, I beg of you, please, if you have any regard for him or any of our race, do not ask us to side with you in this endless, hopeless war.'

'But I have already asked that very thing,' Conor blurted out, confused. 'The deed you dread is done.'

Arianrhod stared at him, nodding slightly as if in confirmation of some inner voice. 'I see,' she said, her voice grown cold. 'And he has armed you for the fight.'

'It is true the king has given us a very great boon of charmed weapons,' Conor told her, 'but I can tell you in all honesty that my lord Gwydion heard my request for aid in the war and he refused.'

'He did? Truly?' she said, the coldness melting in an instant. She sighed with relief. 'Ah, then it seems I must seek your forgiveness. The ceremony last night—the gifts of weapons, the feast, your meeting this morning before you leave—all this led me to believe the two of you had come to some agreement. I am sorry—'

'There is nothing to forgive,' Conor interrupted. 'It is the duty of a wife to care for her husband—all the more so when that husband is a king. I understand and I bear no hard feelings. And I hope you understand that it is a very poor warrior who would shun any useful weapon in a fight. And the struggle with the Scálda is a fight we must win—for the Dé Danann, aye, and for the Tylwyth Teg as well.' Now Conor's glance became stern. 'I *will* take exception to one thing, if you will permit me—you call our struggle against the Scálda hopeless, aye?'

The queen bit her lip and nodded uncertainly. 'I did.'

'It is not hopeless to *me*,' Conor replied, feeling the strawberry blotch that disfigured the left side of his face begin to burn—as it always did when anger or battle roused him. 'To me it is a battle for survival and thus a battle in which the Dé Danann must, at any cost, win. We do not have the luxury of simply refusing the fight, or stepping aside—as the faéry have done. Now then, it may well be beyond all reasonable hope—time will judge. But while I live and breathe in this worlds-realm, I will pursue the fight and I will not rest until the evil invader has been defeated and the lands they stole made safe and returned to our tribes.'

In a heartfelt gesture of empathy, the queen reached out and took Conor's hand. Though her touch was cool, which was normal for the faéry, Conor sensed genuine compassion in the gesture. 'I fear I have offended you . . . ,' she said, gazing at him earnestly—as if willing him to believe her. 'Truly, that was the last thing I wanted and the last thing my husband would have wanted—especially on the day of your leaving. In a little while you will depart and I will not spoil your final moments among your friends with my poor manners.'

She made to withdraw her hand, but Conor held it firmly in his. 'You are a queen in your own palace,' he told her. 'What manner of world would it be if you could not speak your mind within the walls of your own stronghold?'

She offered a gracious and regal smile. 'Then when we meet again, we will speak of more cheerful things and banish all unpleasantness from within these selfsame walls.'

Donal

I was never anyone's favourite. Not the least bird in the flock, nay, but never highest in the roost. No maiden's smile ever comes my way when I enter a hall or ride through the gate of a ráth. The female eye does not linger long in my direction. My body is a little too thick and my hands a little too rough, perhaps, my ears poke out a little too much to turn a fair lady's head, much less melt a maiden's heart. I know this. I have always known—and if I am ever liable to be forgetting, there are always plenty folk around ready to re-mind me.

Feel no pity for Donal mac Donogh. Save that for some sad wretch who needs it the more. In Fergal and Conor, I have a bond of trust and affection closer than blood. I would walk through fire for them. Aye, I would—and never ask why.

And now . . . now I think I must include Rhiannon and her folk in that tidy number as well. They saved my life, pulled me back from the grave the Scálda dug for me. Besides the healing, the faéry folk have given me a gift granted only a few. I think this was an accident, mind. No one intended me to have it. In fact, Lord Gwydion's faéry healers were as surprised as any-one that I should be the one to own it, but own it I do.

Against any expectation—and maybe even nature itself—I now possess the Second Sight of a seventh-generation druid. Lest you be tempted to cry up this ability or hail it too highly, let me say that this rare gifting is not at all what common folk imagine it to be. At least, it is nothing like *I* thought it when hearing of such things. For one, I cannot gaze into the future—like some gatekeeper up his perch peering out across the dim and misty distance to tell you what is coming down the road from far away. Nor can I tell what you or anyone else will do two days from now. I cannot even say with certainty if it will rain or snow tonight.

What I *can* see, when I use what I call my *inward* eye, is a very clear view of how a thing before me—a battle, say, or a chase, or any kind of action at all—will play out, how a matter will end, which of the many possible outcomes of a thing will likely prevail. I have only to close my earthly eyes, look inside, and I see the thing unfold before me—much, I imagine—as the hawk in the sky sees the field below him and knows where the mouse track leads and where the mouse sits cowering under the leaf. Like the hawk hovering over the corn, I see the field with its hidden tracks, and I see the mouse.

Eurig, one of Lord Gwydion's physicians, is a healer and druid of some high rank, and he tells me that this gift of mine may be improved over time with practice and determination. I am not so sure. That is, I'm not convinced that I *want* this Second Sight improved. But, Eurig tells me this gift came to me by way of my walk with the goddess in the fair and sunlit meadows of Mag Mell. He also says there is nothing I can do about it now but make the best of it.

Making the best of things, I tell him, is something I have been doing all my life.

He also tells me that I cannot return to my warrior ways. I am blind to very little that passes before me, but I can in no wise see why this should be so. Not be a warrior?

I tell you the truth: the day Donal mac Donogh lays aside his spear is the day they lay him in the tomb. And that is all I have to say about that.

6

Riding ahead of Fergal and Donal, Conor had been listening to the grumbling and muttering since coming off the ship a short time ago. He paused on the trail and lifted his head to the freshening breeze. He smelled rain on the way. Búrach, Conor's grey stallion smelled it, too, and jigged in place, chafing to move along. Conor reached down and gave the grey a firm pat on the neck. 'Be easy, friend,' he murmured. 'We'll stop soon enough.' Looking back along the trail, he called, 'It's going to rain. We'll stop next good shelter we see.'

A moment later, Fergal and Donal reined up beside him. 'Why not stop here?' suggested Donal, looking around. 'Before it gets too dark, is what I'm thinking.'

Fergal glanced at the sky, low and menacing overhead. The bracken-covered hills round about glowed in the dwindling light like burnished copper and the birch trees in the near distance etched white lines against the greens and greys of the wood beyond. The air was cool, damp, and heavy. 'But it's not dark yet,' he pointed out. 'And we're due to find a holding of some kind soon. I say we push on. We might get a little wet, but we're sure to find a friendly fire and ale to warm us.'

Ale and a fire sounded better than a wet night under a dripping tree, so they rode on and the sky grew more threatening and the land more strange. In truth, the region had seemed odd from the moment they set foot back on Eirlandia's soil. Though it was not something any of them could put a word to, each felt it in his own way: an uneasiness, a vague sense of menace—as if they had entered a land where unseen dangers lurked to ensnare the unwary. And although this was familiar territory with the same hills and trees and streams and marshes—the same they had known since old enough to walk—it appeared altered somehow. Indeed, since leaving the faéry ship, they had continually floundered, finding themselves on unrecognised paths, losing the trail, or discovering that the river or hill or holding they expected to see around the next bend was not there, or that it was a different river or hill or farming settlement entirely.

The sense of peculiarity and uncertainty made them feel as if they were intruding, as if they had entered a foreign land, or a territory beset with taboos they did not know, a place where they were not welcome. Conor, who had grown used to being treated as an outcast, sensed this most acutely. He felt like a man returning to his home only to find he no longer knew it.

'It is not Eirlandia, it is us,' mused Donal as they sat on their horses gazing at wide lough populated by numerous little tree-bound islands—in a place where there should have been a broad valley sown with Volunti fields and farms.

'Us?' wondered Fergal. 'You maybe. I'm the same as all I ever was.'

'Nay, brother,' countered Conor. 'Donal's right; we're the ones changed, not the land.'

Fergal gave him a sideways look and shook his head. 'I haven't changed,' he maintained halfheartedly. 'We just took the wrong trail, that's all. Could happen to anybody.'

Conor agreed with Donal. Some alteration within themselves would seem to explain the way he felt: ill at ease and nervy—much as he had as a boy stealing into the bake house for a bit of honey cake or loaf still warm from the oven. Or, as if he had awakened from a dream to find the world had changed around him while he slept and he no longer recognised it.

Despite their current disquiet, the journey aboard the faéry ship had been swift and smooth, and accomplished, like the previous sailing, with an almost effortless ease. Following their audience with King Gwydion, they had gathered their things and trooped down to the waiting ship where they made their final farewells. The royal family, along with the physician Eurig, a few servants and some of the maidens who had taken a liking to the mortals, assembled on the wooden dock to wave them away with branches from a laurel tree. This was a traditional faéry farewell for a departing nobleman or beloved family member embarking on a long, perhaps arduous, journey. The simple ritual represented a hope for good fortune and a swift return.

It was then that Conor had sprung his surprise. Taking Pelydr, the charmed spear Gwydion had given to him, Conor took it and, holding the shaft across his palms, approached the king as if to present it to him. At the king's questioning glance, Conor had drawn himself up and said, 'Your gifts were genuine expressions of your generous spirit and that of your people, and for this, Lord Gwydion, I thank you. But our need is such that—useful though these weapons would surely be—we cannot accept them.'

The king, startled and amazed, glanced at his wife and daughter as if to make certain he had heard Conor correctly. 'Cannot accept them?' he echoed. 'Why?'

'Victory in the war with the Scálda is life and death to us. Every day we are attacked, our settlements burned, our herds of sheep and cattle and horses stolen, our people tortured and killed. Every day, Balor Evil Eye plots how to lay waste to our land and bring our people to destruction. And every day, the Dé Danann marshal our forces and stand against the Scálda scourge. We fight, but the enemy is numerous and they are strong. We fight, aye, but we cannot prevail. At best, we can only hope to forestall the inevitable collapse, the destruction that will condemn our race to oblivion.

'Know you, my king, when the Dé Danann go, the Tylwyth Teg and the Aes-sídhe will go, too. And Cymru, Prydain, and Albion will be no more. How long do you imagine you will survive when the fierce tribes of Eirlandia are no longer able to stand as a wall between you and the ravening hordes of blood-lusting Scálda? Not long, I think. And then all that is good and true and worthy in this worlds-realm will follow you into the darkness of everlasting night.

'Your art, your craft, your mystical charms of song and magic, your elegance and grace have long given us mortals a taste of higher things and inspired a will to imitate and champion the most noble qualities in our own way and in our own world. These qualities have not only shaped all that is best in us, they have become to us as the shining stars that guide the storm-wearied seafarer to the sweet haven of better shores. That these great and worthy ideals should pass away does us a grief beyond contemplation.

'Nevertheless,' Conor concluded, 'if that is your decision, so be it.' Lifting the spear a little higher, he said, 'At risk of causing further offense, I feel that we must return these gifts. For, if we cannot depend on your support to fight the Scálda, we will not depend on your weapons.'

The King of the House of Llŷr stiffened at these words and the light in his eyes grew cold. 'What was given was given to help you in the fight you describe. I will not take back the weapons.'

Conor nodded, then stooped and placed the charmed spear, Pelydr, lengthwise at the faéry king's feet. Then, with a gesture, he motioned Donal and Fergal to do the same; taking up their weapons, they added them to Conor's; next they brought the swords and shields the king had given them and added them to the pile at the king's feet.

'What will you do now?' The question came from Queen Arianrhod who, from her expression, appeared troubled and deeply moved by Conor's words.

'We are Dé Danann,' replied Conor, rising from adding his sword to the little heap of charmed weapons. 'We are the Children of Danu, warriors descended from a race of warriors. We will do what we have done these last many years. We will fight. We will fight until the last breath of the last man. And if, after all our striving, we are destined to go down to the Hag Queen's hall, we will go down fighting.'

It was Rhiannon who intervened to break the tension between them. 'Dear friends,' she said, raising her hands in a mollifying gesture, 'there is something you do not understand.' She went on to explain, to the obvious discomfort of those looking on, that among her people it was well known that to refuse a faéry gift, or to return one, not only renders the giver powerless, but foredooms the recipient to certain disaster. 'So, I implore you to reconsider your decision,' she pleaded. 'If not for the sake of our friendship, then for the sake of your people who long for your safe return.'

Conor, humbled by the princess's appeal, regretted his decision. 'Please know, it was never my intention to insult you, my king, much less cause you harm. Accept my apologies.'

'Your loyalty to your people is laudable, Conor. I suspect your desire to help them has, perhaps, overthrown your better judgment. There is no fault to forgive,' replied Gwydion. 'Go in peace.'

With a simple nod of assent, Conor stooped to retrieve his weapons. Fergal and Donal did likewise and the three offered a final, if slightly stilted, farewell.

Nothing more was said after that; there was nothing more to say. The horses and sacks of provisions were already aboard the ship now, so the Dé Danann boarded the ship and the king's servants pushed the craft away from the stone wharf. The sleek, low-riding vessel moved out into the bay—as serenely as a swan gliding across the glassy surface of a lough. Upon reaching the open sea, Eraint, the ship's pilot, set a westward course. The triangular green sails bellied out and the craft took on speed, the high, sharp prow slicing easily through the wave swell. Within moments, they were fairly skimming over the wind-stirred sea.

After a time—Conor was never able to say how long—a great, thick bank of mist and fog rose up before them. Eraint held a steady course into the fog. The dense clouds of mist and fog cut off all sight and sound save the splash of the waves sliding by the hull. Shortly after that—again, it was impossible to say how long after—the heavy fog wore thin and they heard the crackling sigh of the waves sifting the pebbled shingle of a near distant shore. The ship emerged from the mist with Eirlandia's rock-rimmed eastern coastline in full view and the day far spent.

Eraint made landfall on a deserted northern beach at a place Conor judged to be somewhere near Volunti territory. The Volunti were a fair-sized tribe of the northeast whose lands bordered the Brigantes to the south and the Darini to the north—which, Conor reckoned, would place them out of reach of the Scálda, but still a day or so away from Dúnaird. After bidding farewell to Eraint and his crewmen, the three had travelled inland—and into a land all but abandoned by summer. The woodland hills were adorned in autumn colours; the breeze that rattled the bracken and scattered the dry leaves across the trail was cool and smelled of damp, dying vegetation.

Now, as the light faded in a darkly threatening sky, the travellers merely hoped to find a dry place before the storm broke and the rain set in. They guided their restless mounts around the lake and saw, in a sheltered curve of the low surrounding hills, a small farm holding. Little more than an earthen rampart surrounded by a ring ditch, it contained a handful of dwellings, a barn or two, and several storehouses; a series of pens for pigs and cattle lay just outside the settlement and recently harvested grain fields beyond these.

'There!' shouted Conor as he caught sight of a thread of smoke drifting up into the lowering sky. 'Brothers, I do believe we will sleep dry tonight.'

'Not a moment too soon,' said Fergal as, even while he was speaking, the first drops of rain began spattering down. By the time they reached the settlement, they were well soaked but welcomed by the chieftain and his young son who met them outside the palisade gate at the end of the plank bridge across the ditch.

'Noblemen, is it?' he said, eyeing their exquisite clothes. 'Well, you best come in and get out of this wet. It looks like settling in for the night.'

Fergal thanked the fellow and introduced himself and his companions, saying that they were travelling home to Dúnaird and would be moving on in the morning. 'I am Gobnu,' the chief said, 'and this is Ródri, my son. He'll show you where to put up your horses.' He nudged the lad, who had not stopped staring at the splendid clothes and weapons since the riders entered the yard.

The three dismounted and followed the youth into one of the barns where they removed the horse cloths and rubbed the animals' coats with dry straw. While they were drying their mounts, Ródri and one of the farmers fetched water and oats for the beasts, and then they all went to join Gobnu in the big house. The genial chief had already summoned a few of the holding's men and was pouring cups of ale from jars set on the board. 'Here now, get this in you—good ale to warm your cockles,' he said, passing the cups around. 'My wife brews it, so she does, and I'll put a cup of hers against any you care to pour.'

'A fella can't ask better than that,' agreed Fergal happily; he swirled the frothy liquid, gave it a sniff, and sighed with contentment.

Conor accepted his cup and thanked the chieftain for his hospitality. The three travellers drank then, watched by the farmers. When they lowered their cups and declared the brew the best they'd had all summer, the farmers smiled and nodded and then drank themselves.

'Am I right in thinking we are on Volunti land?' asked Conor as Gobnu refilled the cups.

'Aye, so you are,' he replied, waving Conor and his friends to seats at the board. They sat and the farmers filled in places around them. 'I'd a'thought a true-born Darini would know that.'

'And you would be right to think it,' Conor told him. 'But we've come in from the coast, you see, and lost ourselves on the trail when the daylight gave out.'

'Well, that can happen, I suppose—to those who don't know the valleys hereabouts.'

'Is it far you have come today?' asked one of the farmers, speaking up. He received a dark look from the chief, but ignored it.

'Far enough,' said Fergal. 'Truth to tell, we have been away from home for some little time. Maybe you fellas could tell us what all's been happening hereabouts—'

'If it wouldn't trouble you overmuch,' added Conor.

'Nay, nay,' said Gobnu quickly, 'you'll hear it soon enough anywhere else, you might as well hear it here first.' He licked his lips and looked down the board, deciding where to start.

The farmer next to Conor leaned over and whispered, 'Your man there'—he indicated Donal—'he don't say much.'

'True enough,' replied Conor, 'but he thinks deep thoughts.'

'Ach, does he now?'

'I suppose you know,' said Gobnu, speaking as if making an announcement to a grand Oenach assembly, 'that the Scálda scum killed that big king Brecan Brigantes. Killed him in ambush and sent him home tied to his horse like a gutted hog.'

'We might have heard something of that,' remarked Fergal, glancing at Conor.

'Worse for that fella Cethern,' chirped another of the farmers. 'Him the dog-eaters chopped up in little pieces and left for the birds along the trail.'

'That is low,' muttered the man next to him. 'Even for Scálda that is low.'

They all nodded and took a sip of sweet ale from their wooden bowls.

'Has anyone said who is to be the Brigantes king now?' asked Conor.

'Nay, nay,' replied Gobnu, with a slow shake of his head. 'That is, if they have a new king, they ent said yet who it is—not that we've heard.'

'Great pity that,' observed one of the men, 'killing the high king like that. And him just getting ready to drive the whole stinking lot of Scálda vermin into the sea.'

'Brecan was not the high king,' blurted out Conor, unable to prevent himself.

'Aye, he was,' insisted the chief.

'He only *thought* he was,' said Conor. 'There's a very great difference.'

Fergal gave Conor a warning glance and quickly asked, 'When did this happen?'

'Not so long ago,' answered Gobnu. 'Near the end of summer, I think.'

'We had'na begun the harvest yet,' offered one of the farmers.

'A few weeks maybe,' added another. 'Not more.'

'Ach, aye,' said Gobnu. 'We heard he was out hunting and was ambushed by a Scálda raiding party.' He nodded, and the others nodded with him. 'The king tried to fight them off, but there were too many.'

'Aye,' confirmed the farmer next to Conor. 'That's what we heard.'

They talked a little more and then Ródri returned from looking after the

horses, together with Gobnu's wife, one of the farmstead's hounds, and three
women bearing baskets and platters of food: small loaves of heavy dark barley bread and thin slices of succulent smoked pork, and some fire-roasted
root vegetables and a soft new cheese. Ródri pulled up a stool to the table
near Fergal; his father poured him a cup and the lad settled in to listen to
the men talk while the women busied themselves with serving up the food.

They ate and talked, and the food and ale and travel began to tell and
soon travellers were yawning in their cups. Seeing his guests begin to nod,
Gobnu declared that there was work to be done in the morning and so
begged his guests to allow him to go to his rest. The farmers rose and filed
noisily out; Conor, Fergal, and Donal were given rush pallets covered with
fleeces in a dark corner of the little hall and left to themselves. 'Weeks only,'
whispered Conor. 'Did you hear that? Brecan's murder happened before
summer's end.'

'I heard that,' Fergal allowed. 'Yet we've been gone . . .' He tried to esti-
mate their absence, could not, and gave up, saying, 'I don't know—the better part of a year, at least. Longer maybe.'

'Weeks only,' said Conor, still trying to reconcile the difference.

'Aye, for Eirlandia,' Donal said. 'But things are different in the Isle of
the Everliving. Time and the seasons, to be sure.'

'Everything is different,' mused Fergal.

They talked like this awhile longer and fell asleep listening to the rain
pattering on the roof thatch and the yard outside. Next morning, the three
rose early, washed in the basin that had been left outside the door, and then
went to feed the horses. After breaking fast on warm bread and fresh milk,
they thanked their host and took their leave. The night's rain had cleansed
the air and scrubbed the clouds until they glowed bright and white in the
cool morning breeze. Refreshed and rested, the three rode out into a land
that seemed newly made. Indeed, it seemed to them that the night's rain that
still glistened like tiny gemstones on the leaves of grass and trees only heightened the uncanny feeling they were seeing an old familiar world for the first
time.

7

Conor led Búrach to the top of the hill overlooking the rockbound eastern coast of northern Eirlandia. In the distance, he could see the lead-coloured sea stretching to the flat horizon and, just a little nearer, the faint grey-blue smudge of smoke that hung over Dúnaird in pale yellow light of a late autumn day. He had stood on this selfsame knoll countless times, yet, once again, he had the feeling that he was viewing a place he knew well, but for the first time; and the strangeness of the sensation made him queasy: as if he stood not on solid ground, but on water trembling under his feet. Indeed, it had been so long since he had seen his home—and so much had happened in the interval—the place no longer appeared as he remembered it: the unassailable stronghold boldly facing a shining sea. Now it seemed diminished somehow, the fields smaller, the ráth scruffier, shabbier and, though he hated to admit it, much poorer than the fortress of his memory.

He released the grey's halter and allowed the stallion to nuzzle the long grass on the windy hilltop; then, wrapping his cloak more tightly around himself, he sat down to wait for Donal and Fergal to catch up. As he sat filling his eyes with the newly familiar sight of his childhood home, he imagined Aoife there, standing on the walkway over the gate, scanning the hills for a glimpse of him, or perhaps stirring a pot over a fire in the women's house, or beating flax into fibres, or stroking the thick neck of a fat yearling calf—any of a hundred of the small tasks that made up her ordinary day.

Down there, behind those walls his beloved waited for him—and that alone covered a multitude of shortcomings. He was relishing the thought that soon he would be holding his loving Aoife in his arms when a voice called out behind him. He glanced around to see Fergal and Donal toiling up the hill. He turned back to the view of Dúnaird and waited until the other two caught up with him.

'Are you that anxious to face the executioner's blade that you have to run, now?' said Donal as the two reined up beside him.

'They won't kill me, you know,' replied Conor. 'Mádoc's lame deception is known for the ruse it was. My banishment ended when he died.'

Donal glanced at Fergal, who said, 'That is your opinion, brother. But what if your father does not share it? What then? He'd be duty-bound to honour the ban with the edge of his sword—or give up his kingship.'

'He wouldn't—'

'Ach, aye,' countered Donal. 'He would, you know. He'd have no choice.'

'See here, Conor. You must allow us to go on ahead,' said Fergal. 'We will judge how things stand there and send back word.'

'They will have heard about Mádoc's mad plan by now. They will welcome us home with music and a feast.'

'A grand thing to be sure,' agreed Donal. 'We can hope they do that very thing. But what if they have not heard the truth of Mádoc's plan, and Brecan's death, and the rest of it? What then?'

'I'll tell you,' put in Fergal, 'music and feasting will be the last thing they'll be thinking.'

'Which is why you must let us go first. If all is well, then we will trip over ourselves in our haste to bring you home.'

Seeing his friends so determined to protect him, Conor relented. 'If that is the way of it, why are you sitting there looking at me? Go—that you may return that much sooner.'

The two rode on together, working their way down the rocky hillside to the coast path and on to Dúnaird. When they came within hailing distance of the walls, they stopped and dismounted, then continued, leading their horses to the gate on foot. Conor watched this and, when he could not contain his impatience any longer, he took up Búrach's reins and rode down to join them.

He was still some little way off when he heard Fergal shout, 'Ho, there! Watchman! Who is guarding this gate?'

Conor moved in closer.

Fergal shouted again and his call brought a response in the form of a young warrior appearing on the walkway above the gate.

'Braida! Is that you, lad?'

The gateman looked down at the two standing before the entrance. 'Aye, it is Braida,' the youth called back. 'And is that Fergal mac Caen? Who is that with you?'

'It is Donal mac Donogh,' replied Donal, stepping forth. 'Open the doors and let us in.'

'Wait there!' Braida disappeared from view, returned a few moments later with another warrior wearing a helmet and carrying a spear.

Conor, judging he had come as close as he dared, dismounted and stood by his mount.

'Fergal! Donal!' came the shout from the walkway. 'Have you returned then?'

'Aye, we have—as you can plainly see. And who is that talking to us?'

'It is Gamael here,' the man called back, removing his helmet. 'Do you not know me?'

'I know you now that I can see you,' said Fergal. 'Open the gate, man. We've been travelling all day and we are tired.'

'A welcome cup would not go amiss,' added Donal, 'if Lord Ardan still serves such to weary travellers.'

The two guards conferred with one another for a moment. Fergal cast a worried glance at Donal—and then at Conor some little distance away. Donal shook his head, warning Conor to stay back and whispering to Fergal, 'Here is a strange thing. I do not think they're going to let us in.'

Fergal dismissed the idea. 'Well, perhaps they have good reason to be cautious.'

Finally, Gamael called down to them. 'Full sorry I am, but we cannot let you in just now.'

'Why ever not?' demanded Fergal. 'You can see it is us.'

'Aye, we see you right enough,' said Braida. 'But it is more than our lives are worth to disobey our duty.'

'Far be it from us to ask anyone to disobey anything,' said Fergal growing impatient. 'But Dúnaird has always welcomed our clansmen and, I might add, valued members of the king's warband.'

'That may be true,' considered Gamael. 'But we have orders not to let anyone in just now.'

'Who has given such a stupid command?' demanded Fergal, growing angry as well as impatient.

'The order was given by our warleader himself,' replied Gamael. 'Liam has decreed that the gates shall remain closed to all strangers.'

'But we're *not* strangers!' cried Fergal, losing whatever was left of his patience. 'Go tell the king who it is that seeks admittance.'

'That we cannot do,' answered Gamael. 'Our king is away just now. He will not return for many days. Lord Liam is in authority while his father is gone. That is why the gates remain closed.'

Fergal opened his mouth to swear a curse up the stubborn pigheadedness on display before him, but Donal laid a hand on his arm and called up to the two on the walkway, saying, 'Friends, it is indeed a shame and disgrace to us both for you to be made to stand here and argue with your swordbrothers over such a trivial matter. If you could go and tell Liam that we have returned and seek entrance to the ráth of our youth, then we will be in your debt.'

The two guards seemed pleased with this solution to their unwanted problem and the elder Gamael sent the younger Braida on the run with the message for Liam.

'Where have you been that you are so long away?' asked Gamael as soon as Braida had gone. 'And who is that you have with you?' He pointed across to Conor, who stood with his face all but obscured by his cloak. 'That is for the king's ears alone, I think,' replied Fergal. 'If he chooses to tell you, then so be it. But where has Lord Ardan gone?'

'Well,' sniffed Gamael somewhat put out by the rebuff, 'that is for the king to tell, I think. If he chooses to tell you, then you'll know.'

'Come down here and say that to my face, dog breath,' shouted Fergal. To Donal, he said, 'Have they gone mad here in Dúnaird since we've been away?'

'Calm yourself, Fergal. All will be answered soon enough.' He glanced back at Conor and shook his head again in warning.

The wandering warriors stood before the gate trying to rein in their runaway frustration; having to wait before the gates they themselves had often guarded in earlier times seemed a needless humiliation. Finally, Liam appeared on the walkway and Donal whispered, 'Keep a humble tongue now, I warn you, or we will be standing here all night.'

'We've been standing here long enough already,' muttered Fergal under his breath. Then, turning to Liam, he put a smile on his face and said,

'Greetings, Liam. I have just been told that the king is away and you are in authority here just now.'

'That is true,' replied Liam. 'What are you doing here?'

'Why,' said Fergal, his veneer of civility already wearing thin, 'our sojourn is over, we have returned to our hearth and home as you can see.'

'And where have you been that it took you so long to come back?'

'As to that, the answer is simple enough,' said Fergal, still smiling. 'We were not in Eirlandia.' He glanced at Donal, who nodded his encouragement. 'We were with the faéry in Tír nan Óg.'

Liam glanced at the gatemen, who only gazed back. 'Do I look like a nursling child that you think I would believe a tale like that?'

'No one would make such a regrettable mistake, lord,' replied Fergal, his smile fading rapidly. 'But I might think it strange if, hearing such a tale, a fella would not care to know how such a claim might be explained—all the more if it came from someone wearing such clothes as Donal and I are wearing now.' He plucked at his rust-coloured siarc and adjusted his splendid cloak. 'That I would think strange, so I would.'

'I don't care what you think, Fergal Faintheart,' said Liam, sneering. 'The fact of the matter is you abandoned your rightful lord to run after Conor the Outcast. You chose a criminal over Ardan, and in so choosing forfeited any rights of kinship with the Darini. I can only think that Conor must now be dead—killed with scheming Brecan, I expect. Otherwise you would not dare to return.' He shook his head. 'Pathetic. What have you to say to that?'

'Conor is not dead,' said Donal. 'He is with us—waiting for word . . .' He gestured vaguely to the crags behind him. 'He wants to come home.'

'Waiting for word, is it?' replied Liam, glancing at the mute figure standing just out of reach but within earshot.

'I care little enough for what Conor wants,' replied Liam. 'But if he still lives and breathes under this sky, at least he knows enough to stay away—which is more than I can say for his false-faced friends.'

'My lord battlechief,' said Donal, trying again, 'you wrong us when you call us false-faced and fainthearted. Moreover, you wrong Conor, the son of your own mother and your father Ardan, who is lord over all Darini. Nevertheless, I am certain this grave misunderstanding can easily be cleared up once we sit down together and discuss it like honest and reasonable men. Allow us to summon Conor and let all of us meet together over a welcome cup in the king's hall. You will find there is much we have to tell that is worth your hearing.'

Liam drew himself up. 'No. I will hear nothing you have to say. You and your friend Conor have no place here. If you wish to continue the life you have chosen, then you will leave at once.'

'At least,' called Donal, 'let us speak to Aoife so that we can give her a greeting from Conor.'

'Conor has caused that good lady nothing but pain. His leaving was the best thing to happen to her and Aoife is better off without him. You can tell Conor that.' Liam waved them away and turned to go.

Fergal drew breath and shouted after him, 'This is an outrage! When the king—'

Donal grabbed him by the arm and pulled him back. 'Say no more, brother. Nothing good will come of it and will only make matters worse.'

Fergal frowned, his mouth a firm, hard line, and Donal called up to the men on the walkway, 'We are going—for now. It may be our lord Ardan will take a different view. We will wait for the king to return and discuss it with him another day.'

'Then you will grow old in waiting,' shouted Liam without turning back, 'for that day will never come.'

8

'I have not come this far to stare at the barred gates of Dúnaird,' growled Conor when Fergal and Donal joined him. He gained the top of the hill once more and started toward his mount.

'Conor, what are you doing?' Fergal, breathing hard from his fast climb, cast an urgent glance at Donal, who said, 'Conor, wait! Before you do something foolish, let's talk this through.'

'Liam thinks I am dead does he?' Conor muttered. 'Aye, well I will show him what death looks like, so I will.' Four quick steps carried him to Búrach's side; he took hold of the stallion's halter and vaulted up onto its broad back. 'I am going to see Aoife, and if Liam thinks he can command me to stay away, I will soon show him for the fool he truly is.'

'Hear me and heed me well,' Donal told him. 'Liam is in authority now and he has declared that you are outcast. There is neither hearth nor ale cup waiting for us within those gates—only a harsh rebuke and sharp sword. You cannot force your way in—and by trying, you only give Liam all the reason he needs to summon the warband to fight you and kill you.'

'Listen to your wise counsellors,' said Fergal. 'If there was a way to force Liam to pay you the respect you deserve, I would be first in the very long line to make him do it. But until your father returns your brother is in authority and, whether we like it or not, he will be obeyed. We cannot storm the gates and that is that. I say, give it a few days and we will try again when the king is here to speak sense to that hotheaded son of his.'

'What about Aoife?' said Conor. 'She is waiting for me—most likely thinking me dead if she has been listening to Liam. What am I to do about that?'

'There is nothing to be done about that now,' Donal told him bluntly. 'Come away and we will think what to do.'

Indeed, the bright day had grown overcast and a stiff breeze was blowing misty rain over the hills from the west. Donal wrapped his cloak more tightly around his shoulders and moved to Conor's side. 'This day has turned against us in every way. Even the weather has betrayed us. Let us accept our defeat and go find shelter.'

'Aoife thinks me dead,' Conor intoned coldly. He gathered up the reins and turned Búrach's head toward the track leading to the ráth. 'I'm going to see her—if only to tell her otherwise. You two can stay here and whimper like beaten hounds, or you can come with me and reclaim our rightful place in the tribe.'

'Would you raise a killing blade against your own kinsmen and sword-brothers?' said Fergal.

Conor glared at him. 'It would never come to that.'

'Aye, it would. With Liam as angry as he is right now, that is exactly what would happen. You would not even reach the gate before the blades were drawn.'

Donal took another step forward and, in a voice neither Conor nor Fergal had ever heard before, said, 'Climb down from that horse, Conor mac Ardan. There will be no bloodshed this day.'

He did not shout or raise his voice, but the note of command and authority was unmistakable and so uncharacteristically powerful that Conor halted and Fergal looked around to see if it really was Donal who had spoken and not a druid from Carn Dubh.

Conor stared, regarding his friend with an expression of astonishment. 'What did you say to me?'

'I said for you to climb down—'

Conor gazed at him for a long moment, then sighed and, throwing his leg over the stallion's neck, slid to the ground. He raised his eyes to the bleak overcast sky and drew his hand over his face. The day was not getting any brighter and the clouds were low, thickening on a cold wind driving in from the west and bringing a thickening mist with it. 'Aye, truly, this day has turned against us.'

'That it has,' agreed Fergal. 'But we live to fight another day. Let's find shelter.'

With great and grudging reluctance, Conor submitted to the will of his friends. It was possible, he realised, that whatever changes the death of King Brecan had wrought in the land the resulting scramble to fill the void the Brigantes lord left behind only heightened the upheaval. Conor took one last look at the timber walls of the ráth he had once called home and his heart moved within him. Aoife was there, locked behind those gates, and he could do nothing about it. There would be a day of reckoning, he vowed; old debts would be settled.

Then, snatching up the halter strap, he turned away from the settlement and started back down the track leading away from Dúnaird. His friends returned to their horses and followed. They had not gone far when Fergal said, 'There was a little rock hollow at the foot of that line of hills to the west—if I remember. Maybe we—' Fergal found he was talking to himself. He stopped and turned around.

Donal was standing in the track with his spear over his shoulder, leading his horse. 'Someone's coming,' he said in reply to the question rising to Fergal's lips.

'How did you know—' began Fergal, but Donal was already moving away. Fergal called to Conor who was riding a little ahead. 'Someone is coming!'

Conor wheeled his horse and rode back to where Donal was waiting on the hilltop. 'How many? Can you see?'

'Only one.'

Fergal joined them. 'I don't see anyone.'

Dropping the reins, Conor slid off the stallion and pulled his spear from its leather sheath under the horsecloth and trained his gaze toward the ráth; through the mist and murk in the fading light, he could barely make out the dim shape of a figure toiling up the trail. 'Who is it?' he asked. 'Can you see?'

The other two shook their heads.

'I don't know how he saw anyone at all in this wrack,' grumped Fergal. 'I truly don't.'

The three waited, leaning on the shafts of their spears, suggesting to one another who it might be. Eamon? Gamael? A member of the warband? Who? Finally, Donal turned to them and said, 'It's Aoife.'

'Aoife!' said Conor. '*My* Aoife?'

'Aye,' Donal told him. 'Unless you know any others at Dúnaird.'

Conor gave Donal a wondering look and then started down the track at a run. Fergal poked Donal on the arm with his finger. 'How did you know that?' he asked. 'Have you weasel eyes now that you can see in the dark?'

'We cannot let him go down there,' Donal replied.

Fergal sighed. 'I'll go.' He ran after Conor and caught him just as two more figures emerged from the ráth below. Fergal snatched Conor by the arm and held him firm. 'Wait, brother. See what happens.'

'I must go to her.' Conor pulled his arm away and started forward again.

'Conor! Wait!'

Down at the entrance to the ráth, the second two had caught up with the first lone figure; a brief conference took place and then all three turned around and retreated into the stronghold once more. Conor's steps faltered and he stood looking until the gates closed once more; then, he slowly turned around and trudged back to his horse.

'I guess it was not Aoife, after all,' suggested Fergal as he passed.

'I guess not.' With a last glance down the hill, he turned his back on Dúnaird. 'Let's find that cave of yours and get a fire started. I'm cold.'

The three outcasts made their way to the place Fergal thought he remembered: a shallow bowl-shaped depression, or coombe, enclosed on three sides with an overhanging rock ledge at the far end that formed a recess in which they could make their camp. The open end faced the south, so the wind and rain would not be blowing in upon them. 'This is better than I remembered,' said Fergal as they stood in the entrance to the hollow.

'It will do,' Conor told him, passing Búrach's halter strap to him. 'We need firewood. We should be able to find some in the copse we passed through back there.'

'Stay here,' Fergal said. 'I'll fetch it.'

'I'll go with you,' offered Donal.

The two went off together, leaving Conor to set up camp. He tethered the stallion and the two mares just outside the ledge overhang, and then tossed loose stones into a heap to be arranged in a circle for the fire ring. Then he began arranging the stones into a fair-sized ring. He was putting the last stone in place when there came a low whistle signalling Fergal and Donal's return with the firewood. 'We could have got more,' explained Donal, throwing his armful into a pile a few paces from the ring of stones, 'but it got too dark to see.'

'At least, it is still dry,' observed Fergal. 'No sign of your rain, then?'

Donal cocked his head to one side as if listening to something only he could hear. Then he replied, 'It is coming on the wind. It will be here before nightfall.'

'It's almost nightfall now,' Fergal pointed out, grinning smugly. 'Maybe we should better consult your horse, no doubt—'

He did not complete the thought before the first spattering of rain began to fall.

'There it is,' Conor said, 'just as Donal promised. Light the fire and warm this place. I'll fetch the faéry sparáns and see what's left to eat.'

'Is there any of that mead still?' called Fergal, arranging some of the smaller sticks in a lattice from which to kindle the campfire. 'I'm parched and this looks to be a long, wet night.'

Aoife

I had my hand on the beam ready to lift the bar and open the gate when Lord Liam climbed down from the guardsmen's walkway. I had heard him talking to Fergal and Donal and my first and only thought was to let them in so I could see my beloved at last, and all Dúnaird could welcome our brave wanderers home.

Alive! I was thinking. *Conor is alive and he is home!*

After so many days and weeks of watching and waiting, never knowing which rumour to believe: Conor was killed in an ambush. . . . Conor betrayed King Brecan. . . . Conor killed Brecan. . . . Brecan killed Conor. . . . Conor has sold himself to the enemy. . . .

All lies, I know. All of them rank and wicked lies. In my heart, I know my Conor could never have done what they said of him. Still, I heard the rumours and could not help wondering. But now he was here and I could not contain the joy I felt. Conor was here and we would be together once more and soon married. My dearest heart had returned and we would never be parted again!

'What are you doing?' demanded Liam, his voice a slap in my face. 'Stop that.' He slammed the beam down into its slot. 'You know this gate is not to be opened.'

'Braida here,' I nodded to the man on the other end of the beam, 'brought word that Donal and Fergal have returned—and Conor is with them.' Even speaking the name of my beloved aloud made my heart beat the faster.

'Get back on watch,' Liam told the young warrior. 'Now!'

Braida all but fell over himself to disappear. Stung, I turned to Liam. 'Why?'

'Conor was not with them,' he muttered. 'Leastwise, if he was he dared not show his face to me.'

'Ach, well, I am opening the gate to receive them.' I made to lift the beam once more. 'Let us welcome them home.'

'There is no need,' said Liam curtly, putting his hand to the gate bar and slamming it back into place yet again. 'They are not to be staying.'

'My lord? I don't understand.' I searched his face for a reason and saw only a hardness like a clenched fist.

'I sent them away.'

Liam turned abruptly, and stormed off. I cast a glance at Gamael and Braida up on the walkway; both shook their heads in dismay. I hurried after our esteemed warleader, falling quickly into step beside him. 'Forgive my asking, lord, but why? Why did you send our kinsmen and friends away?'

Liam, obviously angry, stopped and turned on me. 'I suppose you are against me, too?'

'Nay, lord, I merely—' I began, then stopped and started again on a different path. 'But should we not listen to what they have to say? It might be that—'

'I would not credit a single word those traitors said.'

'Traitors?' I blinked at him in confusion and dismay, the joy curdling in my breast. 'Why do you call them traitors? How have they betrayed us?'

'You would gainsay your king?' he demanded. 'Ardan has decreed them exiles and outcasts. He has said that—' He gave a growl of frustration and made a chop of his hand to halt further discussion. 'I need explain nothing to you.'

But I could not let Liam's unreasoning dislike of his brother cloud his better judgement. 'Again, I beg your forgiveness, but we know that Conor is no criminal. We do know that.' I stated this as firmly as I could. 'The theft of that gold bracelet was a ruse perpetrated by the druid Mádoc to remove Conor from danger and ensure his aid in helping discover the extent of Brecan's treachery. Rónán told us that much—you will remember.'

'Aye, Rónán told us—and we only have Rónán's word for it.' He strode off again.

'The word of a druid,' I called after him. He did not stop, so I hurried to catch up with him once more before he reached the hall where others would hear us arguing. 'The word of a druid and, if I say it, your own brother.'

'Rónán always takes Conor's side,' Liam growled. 'Always has. Always will.'

That was not true, but I let it go. 'We know that Lord Brecan was conferring with the enemy, and we know that he was killed because of it. Mádoc was right after all.'

'Ach, so he was right was he?' mocked Liam. 'We'll never know because he is dead now, too.' He jabbed a finger at me. 'Mádoc, Brecan, and Cethern—all three dead and how many more besides? And Conor was involved. One way or another, Conor is always involved in the worst crimes and calamities.'

That stopped me in my tracks. 'You blame Conor for King Brecan's death. What about the raids this summer—you blame him for those, too?'

'Who else?' snarled Liam, his face grown ugly with the venom boiling inside him. 'His betrayal has opened a flood tide of death.' He spat in the dirt. 'Conor is an outcast. Fergal and Donal likewise. They chose him, not us. They are not welcome here anymore.'

'Your father would not be so harsh and uncaring. If he was here, he would listen to reason.'

Liam stared at me, his eyes cold. 'But he is not here and I rule in his place. I say they are outcasts still.' He turned on his heel and walked away.

I could but stare in rage at our false, audacious warleader. Brecan's death unleashed a summer of calamity, that is true. The enemy pressed us hard all along the borderlands and beyond and everyone to the south suffered. But I never imagined Liam would find a way to lay that at my Conor's feet. Absurd as it was outrageous—yet Liam seemed to believe it.

Liam stalked across the yard to the hall, and I watched him go—wishing I had a whip in my hands just then, or a bowl of burning coals. I was still standing there when Aillil, my dearest and closest friend among our womenfolk, came running to me. 'They are saying Conor and the others have returned,' she said. Her dark eyes swept past me to take in the yard and hall behind. 'Where are they? Have they gone to the hall?'

'Aye, they returned,' I muttered darkly. 'And our battlechief has sent them away again.'

Aillil looked into my eyes and—ach, I saw light of her joy extinguished. For, I think she kept that flame alive for Fergal, though he was not to know it yet. 'But I don't understand.'

'Fergal and Donal came to the gate seeking entrance. They said Conor was with them and that they wanted to come home.'

'And they went to get your Conor?' Hope leapt up again in an instant. 'They'll come back soon—all three of them, aye?'

My heart moved within me for the pity of what I had to say. 'Liam refused. He sent them away. Conor and his friends are outcasts still,' I told her, my voice breaking on those hateful words.

Aillil's eyes narrowed and she looked to the barred gate. 'I thought the king was to allow them to return.'

'But Ardan is not here,' I said, my voice full of hurt and hopelessness. 'Liam rules in his father's place, and what is more, he holds Conor to blame for Brecan's death and everything that has come after.'

'He said that?' she gasped. 'Liam said that?'

Almost rigid with anger, I spat, 'He said it, aye—but I will never believe it!' I turned on my heel and started toward the hall.

Aillil came after me. She caught me by the arm and pulled me around to look at her. 'Do not go in there, Aoife. Anything you say or do will only make things worse—for yourself, if not for Conor, too. Wait just a little. We can but hope Liam will see reason when he has had a chance to think more clearly. In any case, Ardan will soon return and then all will be made right. You'll see.'

I pulled away, took two steps, and then halted, my mind filled with death and destruction raining down upon that hall.

'Think you now,' she said, 'how best to help Conor.'

She was right. I must think of Conor and how best to help him. I turned around and made for the gate.

'Where are you going?' Aillil called. 'Aoife, answer me. Where are you going?'

'I'm going after Conor.'

'You can't.'

'Watch me.' I kept walking.

'Aoife, think what you're doing. If you leave now, Liam will count it betrayal and he will not allow you to come back.'

'Why should I wish to return?' I replied, tears beginning to well in my eyes. 'If Conor no longer has a home here, then neither do I.'

9

The night passed. Despite the wind and rain, the rock shelter in the little coombe remained dry and the sleepers warm, wrapped in their fine faéry cloaks. For Conor, however, the relief of sleep came but slowly; long after Fergal and Donal had settled into slumber, he lay awake gazing out into a night sky where moon and stars were concealed by cloud and mist and no light could be seen—like his own bleak, sorrowful mood that no light of joy could penetrate.

Time and again, the appalling thought rose in his mind like a tormenting ghost: he was outcast. After all he had done, all he had endured and survived, all he knew of the enemy's intentions—all of it counted for nothing. He remained an outcast, turned away by his own people . . . by his own brother.

This gloomy thought cast him in a hopeless, helpless mood. What was he to do? Why was this happening? What had he done to deserve such a fate? The whole world seemed to be against him, mocking his efforts. Try as he might, he could never seem to get quit of the swamp of muck and mire that only deepened with every attempt to free himself. Everything he tried went against him somehow. He was indeed the most unfortunate of men.

Misery took him and he embraced it, wrapping himself in it, wearing it like a second skin. He wondered whether to do as Donal suggested and try again in a few days. Perhaps when his father returned from his travels, he would hear Conor out and change his mind. Surely, that was the wisest course. But, just as surely, that would go against him too; in some unforeseen way, his little cup of hope would only be dashed away by an unseen hand.

Well, he would not do it. He would not beseech his father to return to a place that loved him not. After the way he had been treated today, to return now bore the taint of begging and that stuck in his gullet like a scraggy bit of gristle. Moreover, he could in no wise return under suffrage of the insufferable Liam who would never forego an opportunity to revile him. Liam would hold it over him forever after. That he could not stomach.

Slowly, the resolve grew within him to turn away from Dúnaird and abandon any hope of returning. That did not mean he would forget about Aoife. Never that! But he must establish himself first and then send for her when he was free and able to do so.

By the time sleep found him, Conor, in the grip of unrelenting desolation, had decided only when he was implored by the very people who turned him away would he consent to ride through the gates of Dúnaird. He would arrive, not as a supplicant, but as a champion of his people.

By the time the sun kindled in a dull, overcast sky, Conor was determined to move on and seek his future elsewhere. He lay awake thinking of this and when he rose a short time later, he was resolute in heart and mind. He woke the others with his stirring and as they broke fast on a bit of bread and smoke-dried salmon from the provisions the faéry had given them, Conor told Donal and Fergal he was resigned not to force another confrontation, but to bide his time. As soon as the horses had been fed and watered, the three moved on. During the morning, the heavy cloud cover began to wear thin. Soon pockets of bright blue sky could be seen in the west, and by midday they were far beyond the borders of Darini territory, heading south. They travelled in silence for the most part, speaking only rarely, each lost in his own melancholy thoughts, pausing only to rest the animals or drink from the streams and burns they crossed. By nightfall they arrived on the shores of a long, narrow clear-water lough that stretched from one end of a pinched valley to the other. A flock of grey geese had settled on a near shore; their raucous squawking echoed across the still water, disturbing the tranquillity of the place.

'I think that is Lough Tass,' mused Fergal. 'And look over there'—he pointed to a smudge of smoke rising above the trees on the western side of the lake—'a settlement, maybe?'

'A fishing camp, more like,' replied Donal.

'More likely than a ráth?' wondered Fergal. 'Why would you think that?'

'It seems plain enough to me.'

'Not to me.'

Conor gave an impatient snort and said, 'Listen to the both of you. Why stand here squabbling when we can go there and end all dispute?'

Quitting the shelter of the trees, the three rode on, skirting the lakeshore and arriving at the smallholding a short time later—a rough little steading consisting of nothing more than a cluster of round, reed-thatched huts and outbuildings huddled around a single large round house; there was a small pen for animals, of which they saw only a few goats and sheep, and a long, raised wooden walkway leading to the lough. The holding was surrounded by a simple palisade of ashwood stakes held together by woven willow branches. Although the travellers saw smoke from a fire drifting up through the roof of what they took to be the main house, there seemed to be no one about.

The three stood off a short distance, shielded by the low brush that lined the banks of the lough, to observe and see what they might learn of the place. 'If that is Lough Tass,' mused Donal after a time, 'then we are in Ulaid lands, I think.'

'Who is king there now?' wondered Fergal. 'Lord Tamlaigh? Is that his name?'

'Dalaigh, I think.'

'Nay, brother, I'm sure it is Tamlaigh.'

'Does it matter?' snipped Conor. 'Ask instead if they have food and shelter for travellers.'

Fergal and Donal exchanged a look of concern, but said nothing. They continued to watch awhile longer and, seeing nothing to alert or alarm, proceeded to the holding where they were met by two old men and three old women who greeted them warily, explaining that they were maintaining the place for use by the tribe's fishermen and hunters. 'I commend your diligence,' Fergal told them. 'May I be so bold as to ask if you have a roof and a meal to spare for hungry wayfarers?'

'We do,' replied the stout white-haired man who seemed to be the spokesman of the group. 'And, since we are being bold, perhaps you have a little gold or silver to spare for some poor caretakers on a damp and lonely lough?'

The travellers stared at the audacity of the fellow—asking for payment in exchange for food and shelter. Fergal, ready to chasten the lout for his rudeness, glanced at Conor who only shook his head slowly. Before either of them could reply, one of the women pushed forward. 'Get away with you,

Obhar!' she cried, shoving the man aside. 'That is no comely way to treat with strangers—and right noble lords, too, by the look of them. Get you off and make up the fire.' The old man shuffled away, muttering. Turning to Fergal, the woman said, 'We do not see many visitors here, lord. But we will do our best by you, never fear. What we have we will gladly share, and welcome to you.'

The old woman and her two companions hurried off to begin preparing the meal, leaving the visitors in the care of the remaining old man. 'Noblemen, is it?' he said, casting a watery eye over their obviously rare and expensive clothing.

'Warriors,' corrected Conor, 'from Lord Ardan's warband—all three of us.'

'Wayfaring, eh? You're not so very far from Darini lands,' he observed. 'But I expect you know that.'

'Aye,' agreed Donal, 'we've just come from Dúnaird. We're heading south.'

'Well, you best come along in, then.' He turned and, motioning the visitors to follow, led them into the little circle of dwellings and outbuildings that formed the holding. They were shown to one of the huts used by the hunters. 'You can sleep there,' he told them. 'It'll be tight enough. And there is a barn just behind for the horses—fine animals that they are. You can put them up in there and I'll fetch a bit of fodder in time.' He glanced around the hut as if to satisfy himself that all was as it should be, then took his leave, saying, 'Rest yourselves here the while. Calla will bring you some embers to start the fire.' He nodded. 'I'll come back when I've opened the barrel and poured the ale. I'm Dalaigh, so you know.'

'Like your king.'

'Aye, just like.' He grinned, showing a smile with two missing teeth. 'Shout for me if you need anything more just now.' He pushed open the door, paused, and added over his shoulder, 'Pay no heed to Obhar, now. Greed gets hold of him from time to time, but he means no ill.'

Donal thanked the man for his care, and told him they would enjoy speaking to him more about recent events in the region over their cups.

'Good man,' observed Donal as the door closed leaving them alone.

'For an Ulaid, you mean,' added Fergal.

'For anyone at all.' Donal looked around the room and, seeing four sleeping pallets piled with furs, sat down on the nearest one. 'This will do.'

'Let's see to the horses,' Conor said. Stepping out the door, he disappeared into the yard outside.

Fergal watched the door close, then said, 'Conor is hurting. Should we be worried?'

'The wound to his pride is still fresh,' Donal pointed out. 'Allow him a little time to heal.'

That night in the round house the visitors were treated to a simple meal of stewed hare flavoured with fennel and mustard greens, fresh bread and salted butter, and sweet brown ale served in cedar cups. They sat cross-legged on the floor or reclined on rolled-up fleeces and ate while the women fluttered around, serving them dishes and filling cups and bowls. Ferga, licking his fingers, commented on the savoury dish. 'Three cooks at the hearth,' observed Dalaigh sagely. 'Always delicious.'

'And never dull,' added Obhar, drawing the ire of Calla, who was just then ladling stew into his bowl.

'Ach! And if I hear another word like that, you miserable man, you will be cooking your thin gruel all on your own.'

Old Obhar hunched his shoulders at the rebuke, but glanced up as she moved on. 'So it is,' he whispered.

'A man of my own heart!' Fergal laughed and, lifting his cup, declared, 'I drink to you, Obhar the Forbearing. May your endless vat of patience never run dry.'

Conor and Donal raised their cups to the grumpy old fellow, shouting, 'Obhar Foditiu!' The epithet made him smile; Dalaigh roared with laughter, and all the women tittered behind their hands. Conor invited the women to join them, with mannerly protests over the impropriety, they happily settled in among their cordial guests.

The simple meal became a revel then. Conor roused himself from his lethargy and gloom and, when the ale had sufficiently loosened everyone's tongue, he began to enquire into what they knew about the Scálda attack that had taken King Brecan's life. 'You heard about that, have you?'

'Ach, well,' Dalaigh made a sour face, 'nasty doings—that's what we heard. The Scálda are always making trouble. Know you, they mean to kill us all—those dog-eating . . .' His mouth worked into a curse, but words failed him. 'Nasty doings.'

'Too true,' said Obhar, swirling the ale in his cup. 'It was that—ambushed on his way home from a hunt. And on his own lands as well!'

'You weren't there!' Calla pointed out tartly.

'I was not,' Obhar agreed. 'And glad of that, I should be.' He turned a woeful face to his guests. 'Beastly thing it was, too, from what I hear—'

'Which is little enough,' one of the women said.

'Enough to know that it was a right roguish and hateful affair,' he maintained.

'So it was, too,' confirmed Dalaigh. He took a long draught of his cup and the refilled it, emptying the jar. He handed the empty vessel to Calla who rose and went to refill it. 'Obhar is right. They are saying that the Scálda attacked the hunt—swooping out of the wood. Killed the king and his champion with him.'

'Anything about being betrayed by one of his own warriors?' asked Conor. Fergal and Donal leaned forward to hear the answer.

'Ach, now,' said Obhar, 'now that you mention it, there may have been something like that. Aye, I think so.' He nodded sagely and sucked his teeth.

'We had it that poor Brecan was taken in a raid while out hunting,' confirmed Dalaigh. 'If there was more to it than that, I never heard it.'

'And I the same,' said Calla. 'We all heard the same.'

'Do you stay here all the time?' wondered Donal. 'All of you?'

'I mostly stay here,' said Obhar. 'Me and Binne mostly.' He nodded to the grey-haired woman next to Conor. 'Someone has to keep the place together for when the fishers and hunters come. The others stay or go as they will, bringing supplies and that.'

'Not the winter, though,' the woman called Binne replied. 'Nay, nay, not the winter. We'll abide here a moon or two longer then go back to the ráth.'

'Is your ráth far?' wondered Fergal.

'Half a day to the west,' Dalaigh told him. 'That and no more. Are you thinking of going there?'

'We are going to Dún Cruach to speak to Lord Cahir,' said Fergal. At Dalaigh and Obhar's uncomprehending gaze, he added, 'Cahir of the Coriondi.'

'Ach, that is some days from here,' said Dalaigh helpfully. 'The Coriondi we know.'

'I'd have thought you were going to the Brigantes,' said Calla. 'They are without a king for all that and you being noblemen. All spears welcome— that is what they are saying now. For men like you, I'd have thought that made sense.'

'What do you know about it, woman?' muttered Obhar.

'I heard what you heard,' she replied crisply. 'Word for word—same as you. So, do not come all puffed up and proudy with me, Obhar Foditiu!' Everybody laughed again, including Obhar.

'I expect they'll be about choosing a new high king,' said one of the women. 'All the lords, that is.'

'Lord Brecan was not the high king,' said Fergal after another drink.

'Was he not?' said Dalaigh in mild surprise.

'He was not,' Fergal told him firmly. 'As much as he wanted folk to think he wore the golden torc, he had in no way earned that honour.'

'You say the kings are to be summoned to decide what should be done about Brecan's death?' said Conor, steering the conversation back on course. 'When is that gathering to take place?'

The question drew vacant looks all around the table. 'I don't think we ever heard that at all,' offered Calla at last. 'If anyone said as much, we didn't hear it.'

'Soon I expect,' remarked Obhar. 'What with the dog-eaters pressing everyone so hard. We need a new high king to drive them out.'

'Exactly what we need in these dark days,' agreed Dalaigh, and Obhar nodded sagely. 'A right worthy high king.'

He raised the jar and offered it to Conor. 'Your cup is dry, friend. Fill it and let us drink to better days to come.'

'A grand idea,' said Conor, lifting his cup to be filled. 'Let us all drink to better days.'

10

The three travellers left the lough-side holding the next morning with the best regards of their elderly hosts who saw them on their way with supplies of dried bósaill—the strips of salty, sun-dried beef favoured by warriors—flat, fragrant stacks of smoked trout, a couple rounds of hard cheese, and black bread in fist-sized loaves, twice-baked for eating on the trail. 'Sprinkle a little water on them and they'll soften, so they will,' Calla told them as she handed the bundle to Donal. The provisions were wrapped in grass cloth, packed into the fine kidskin travelling bags the faéry had given them, and strapped to the horses.

Fergal pledged to remember the kindness shown them and to repay it one day. 'Just drive out that Balor Evil Eye,' Dalaigh replied. 'That is all the reward anyone could ask.'

'That is the sole aim of my life,' Fergal told him. 'Aye, and that day cannot come soon enough.'

The three resumed their journey and the sun had scarce quartered the sky when they came to a crossing of the ways: one track led to the west, the other wound down a long range of hills to lower land in the south. Here, Conor halted. Fergal riding a few lengths behind, saw him stop. 'What—have you heard something?'

'Brother, I have just been thinking.'

Fergal called to Donal who was a short distance in the lead. 'Hold up!' he called. 'Conor here has had a thought.' To Conor, he said, 'Dangerous occupation, thinking—at least when *you* attempt it.'

'You say that only because you are so much out of practice,' Conor told him, a flash of his former humour returning. The short time spent with the simple fisher folk had salved the pain in his heart. 'But with a little effort, you might soon acquire the skill.'

'What is it?' asked Donal, joining them just then. 'What are you thinking, Conor?'

'I am thinking that it is to Aintrén we should be going, not Dún Cruach.'

'To the Brigantes?' said Donal. 'Not Lord Cahir?'

Fergal glanced at Donal and frowned. 'It is as I feared,' he said. To Conor he said, 'Why ever would we want to go among the puffed-up Brigantes—especially now when their king is dead and their warband ruined?'

'But this is the best time of all to go to them,' answered Conor, his voice taking on confidence as he spoke. 'Remember what the fishwife told us back there?' He gestured vaguely in the direction of the holding behind them.

'All spears welcome,' replied Donal, a slow smile spreading across his broad face. 'They are needing warriors, and we are needing a warband.'

'That is as may be,' allowed Fergal mildly. 'But how is it to look when, after all that has passed, you show up hale and whole when the last time anyone saw you was with Brecan on the night he was murdered? How is that to look?'

Conor stared at him. 'You mean that they will think I was the one who betrayed Brecan? Go ahead and say it, brother. That's what you are thinking.'

'I am that,' Fergal said, nodding. 'But never mind me. What if that is what the Brigantes are thinking? That is the lie they are telling everyone. A friendly welcome is the last thing they will be giving you. A blade through the ribs, more like.' He let that sink in a moment then added, 'Better by far that we should be going to Dún Cruach—and maybe Lord Cahir could be convinced to intercede for us with Liam.'

'As you know, that was my first thought, too,' Conor allowed. 'But I have been asking myself if I can live at Liam's beck and call until I grow too old to lift a blade?' He shook his head. 'For all the gold in Eirlandia—and love of the world into the bargain—I cannot bring myself to spend a single day under his rule.'

Fergal glanced at Donal for help in this debate, but Donal only shrugged.

'Ach, but with the Brigantes now,' Conor continued, his face brightening as he spoke, 'we have a chance at something much greater.' Fergal opened his mouth to object, but Conor cut him off, saying, 'Hear me out. The Brigantes lost a king, but they also lost their champion and chief of battle—that heavy-handed brute Cethern—and with him Mog Ruith, the king's chief advisor.'

'I remember this Cethern,' Fergal mused. 'And that grim old disagreeable druid, too.' He regarded Conor with a shrewd expression. 'And is it your plan to worm your way into the battlechief's empty place at the king's board?'

'That very thing, brother.'

Fergal frowned, but Donal nodded thoughtfully.

'Well?'

'Even if they allow you inside the gates in one living piece, what makes you think anyone at Aintrén would let you sit in the battlechief's place?'

'Because, my doubtful friend, I bested their best in a single contest when I first joined Brecan's host. That was the test the king set before me, and I won through. Because of that, the warriors know me and there are those among them even now who would support me.'

'If, by some wild leap, what you say is true,' allowed Fergal, 'it does not change the fact that the new king—whoever he may be—is sure to have other ideas. He will name his own man to lead the Brigantes warhost.'

Conor's smile grew into a grin. 'That is where you're wrong, brother. There will be no new king—at least, not for a season or two, I expect. The Brigantes have a queen. And,' he added, with a guilty glance at his friends, 'that queen has a certain fondness for me.'

'Ha!' cried Fergal. 'You think *every* female in a girdle and shawl has a certain fondness for you.'

'Ach, well, perhaps not *every* female. But I do know this one well enough,' Conor assured him. 'Lady Sceana did think warmly of me, and gave me reason to believe it—whether *you* believe me or not.'

Fergal, shaking his head, replied, 'At last I begin to see the shape of your delusion, Conor mac Ardan. You imagine that this besotted queen will throw open the doors to the hall and make you her champion and battlechief, and we will be embraced to the Brigantes bosom as long-lost kinsmen come home.'

'Who better?' said Conor. 'I tell you they trust me. And there are those among the Brigantes who know I am no traitor. On the other hand, who knows what Cahir and the Coriondi have heard or believe?'

The horses, having grown impatient with all the talk, snorted and chafed the damp ground, eager to be moving again. 'There! You see?' said Conor. 'Even Búrach agrees with me.'

'That settles the question, then. We'll let the horses decide.'

'We could do worse,' suggested Conor. He reached out and patted his mount on the broad forehead. 'Wise Búrach knows a thing or two about the ways of the world.'

'Which is more than can be said for his rider,' sighed Fergal.

'Hear me,' said Conor, growing solemn. 'We will not do this if everyone is not agreed. I have told you my thoughts, but you must both make up your own minds. We go together, as one—or we do not go at all.'

Donal, gazing steadily at Conor, said, 'Our friend makes a good case. Lord Cahir may have been Ardan's friend, but he owes nothing to us and might well hold that Conor is the traitor the rumours would make him out to be. But see now, Conor has good and valuable experience with the Brigantes and knows how things stand there. Since we are about making the best of a bad lot, I say the Brigantes offer our best hope of changing our fortunes. I am satisfied.' To Conor, he said, 'I am with you, brother, whatever may come our way.'

Fergal regarded his swordbrother with an odd expression. 'Have I said otherwise?' he complained. 'I was about to say the very same, so I was.'

'You are with us then?' asked Donal.

'I am wounded that you would ever think otherwise,' replied Fergal rolling his eyes. 'Sorely wounded.'

'Then it is decided,' declared Conor. 'We go to the Brigantes and make a place for ourselves in Queen Sceana's court.'

'And then?' wondered Fergal.

'And then,' said Conor, turning his eyes to the south. 'We work to win back our homeland from the enemy.'

11

Two days of wet and blustery travel over rain-drenched hills and through wind-scoured valleys brought the exiles to the gates of Aintrén. Unlike the rough, rock-rimmed lands around Dúnaird, the country of the Brigantes was softer, rounder, and liberally seamed with rivers and streams abounding in trout and freshwater clams.

The three travellers had paused to rest at Tara, but did not linger long. From a distance, the hill was as mysterious and majestic as ever, but bleak and lonely without the Oenach camps to populate the surrounding plains. Since the passing of the last true high king of Eirlandia, no one had possessed Tara or settle there; instead, it was used as a place where kings and lords of all Eirlandia's tribes could gather to discuss matters of mutual concern in both formal and informal councils and gatherings. Out of respect for the ideal of sovereignty it represented, Tara Hill was considered sacred and left alone. So, after a drink and a bit of hard bread and cheese, the travellers journeyed on, arriving at the Brigantes stronghold as the damp day gave way to evening.

Aintrén's high timber walls had been renewed and enlarged under the late Brecan's rule to form an impressive crown atop an imposing steep-sided hill. Below the palisade and encircling the hill were four concentric ring ditches—three containing brambles and nettles, and one filled with putrid water—to help stifle the enthusiasm of any would-be attackers. The fortress commanded clean views both ways along two broad valleys that contained the numerous fields and grazing lands that supplied the realm with grain and cattle. The chief stronghold of the Brigantes, Aintrén was impressive as it was intimidating.

'It is a bigger place than I thought it might be,' Fergal said as they stood observing from the foot of the hill on which the stronghold had been planted. 'I knew them for a wealthy lot, but never so much as this.'

'All you see and more,' Conor told him. 'Their tribe numbers eight clans, and each have a ráth or dún—along with many farms. They have more pigs and cattle than the two next biggest tribes combined. The warband is larger than any hereabouts so that other kings are paying tribute—at least they were paying while Brecan lived.'

'To judge by what I see'—Donal's hand made a wide sweep taking in the hill and both valleys—'it does appear Lord Brecan was well down the road to the high king's throne. Had he lived, I do think he could have made it.'

'Ach, well now we'll never know,' said Fergal. 'Nor, will we ever know whether they'll be giving us food and lodging though we stand here flapping our tongues all night.' To Conor, he said, 'Lead the way, brother, and we shall soon discover if you are as highly esteemed within those gates as you imagine yourself.'

'That we will.' Conor gazed at the high walls on the hill rising above them, but made no move to proceed.

'Today at all?' asked Fergal after a moment. 'Or is it second thoughts you are having?'

'Nay, nay, never that. I was only thinking how best to present myself.'

'Try the truth of the matter,' suggested Donal. 'That has sometimes been known to work wonders.'

Conor gave him a raw look and, lifting the reins, urged Búrach up the long ramp to the gates, where they were met by a single guard wielding a sword and shield. A young man with a dark shag of hair, he was wrapped in a green cloak against the coming evening chill. 'Greetings, friends,' called the man. 'Stand easy and declare your intentions.' He moved forward a step or two, then stopped. 'Conor? Is it you?'

'Ach, Galart, do you not know me, friend?'

The guardsman stared and the shield slipped down a little. 'It *is* Conor!' He stared. 'But, they . . . they said you were dead.'

'Nay, but not for lack of trying,' Conor told him. He slid off the grey and strode boldly up to the young warrior. 'But it is good to see you, my friend.' He nodded toward the settlement inside the walls. 'How are things within?'

'Not happy—nay, not at all. I am not lying when I say they have rarely been worse.'

'Well, worry not.' Conor gave him a friendly swat on the shoulder. 'We are here to help.' Indicating his friends, he said, 'Fergal, Donal—this is Galart, a right worthy spearman and foremost of the warriors of the rank.'

'We were sorry to hear about the murder of your king and champion,' offered Fergal, and Donal added, 'I expect they will be sorely missed.'

'That is not the half of it,' replied the young warrior glumly. 'The tribe and clans have been in turmoil ever since—and there is no end to it.'

'Will you let us in?' asked Conor. 'We have come to pledge our swords to the aid of your queen.'

Galart hesitated, his good-natured face creased in thought.

'Why this reluctance?' asked Conor after a moment. 'Is something amiss?'

'I am under instruction not to let anyone pass.'

Conor glanced at his friends. 'Is it that my friends are strangers to you?'

Galart offered a reluctant nod. 'Aye, to be sure.'

'Even friends of the court?' wondered Conor.

'Ach! *Especially* them!' cried Galart. 'You have hit on it there, brother. These past weeks we have had so many so-called friends and well-wishers that our lady Sceana's store of hospitality is fair exhausted. She craves a day of peace and quiet without the siege of suitors. She asked that no one be admitted from sunrise to sunrise this day.'

'Suitors?' echoed Conor.

'Noblemen of one clan or another who believe she will be needing a king to rule here,' explained Galart. 'Not a day goes by but that someone doesn't come thinking to claim the prize.'

'That is not seemly,' Conor replied. 'Not seemly at all. But, see now, if you let us in my friends and I will promise not to make any demands on the queen or her hospitality. What do you say?'

'Are all gates everywhere to be closed against us now?' muttered Fergal to Donal. 'I begin to think so.'

Ignoring him, Conor continued to press his case. 'You know me, Galart. And, as I think you also will recall, she held me in good favour when I lived among you. I was her chosen champion, remember?'

Still the young warrior hesitated, chewing his lip, wavering, but holding firm to his queen's command.

'Also, I can tell you now,' Conor leaned close to confide, 'I was with Lord

Brecan when he was killed. One day soon, your queen may like to hear what
I can tell her about that dreadful night.'

'Then it is true? You were there? I heard as much.'

'I was in the thick of the fight. And I alone escaped—sorely wounded
and unable to return until this very day.'

Galart regarded the three men before him, looking from one to the other,
shifting from foot to foot with indecision.

'If I know the queen at all, she will want to hear that her husband died
with a sword in his hand,' Conor said softly. 'And she will want to learn his
last words.'

Galart nodded. 'Do you promise not to make any untoward demands?'

'You have my word,' said Conor, 'and that of my friends.'

'My word is pledged,' offered Fergal.

'And mine,' said Donal. 'No demands.'

The young warrior looked from one to the other and back again. 'Then
wait here,' he sighed and, turning to the gate, rapped on it with the butt of
his spear. He called to the gateman on the other side and was admitted a
few moments later.

The three travellers waited in the growing twilight, listening to the wind
as it freshened from the west, driving cold, damp air before it. 'Early winter,' remarked Donal. 'I see snow before Samhain.'

Fergal grunted. 'What is taking so long?'

Finally, the gate opened once more and Galart poked his head through
the gap. 'You can come in,' he told them. 'And you can explain to Médon
how it is you got past me.' At Conor's wondering glance, he said, 'Aye,
Cethern's kinsman is battlechief now.'

'Is he now? Well, do not worry about Médon,' Conor told him, placing
a hand on the young man's shoulder. 'He will be more than happy to see
me, I will make sure of that.'

With this final assurance, Galart disappeared and the heavy timber door
opened a little wider to admit the travellers and their horses. Conor thanked
his young friend for allowing them in, and then led his party into the great
yard. Galart followed them through and commanded the gateman, 'Help me
bar the gate. No one else gains entrance tonight.'

The three entered the stronghold without attracting much notice and
paused to take in the place. Twilight had fallen and there were but few people
about. Smoke from the various hearths and cooking fires of the ráth drifted

low across the stone-paved square in pale, many-stranded ropes. 'The hall is there,' Conor said, pointing across the open, empty yard to the large steeply roofed building confronting them. He indicated another, smaller house to the left of the hall—thatched with river reed and with painted doorposts, a small iron brazier burning outside, it appeared a much more convivial place than the king's hall. 'That is the queen's house,' Conor told them, then pointed out the slate-roofed Bards' House to the right of the hall and the foremost of the warriors' house across the yard.

'Is there a guest lodge, then?' asked Fergal.

'There is,' replied Conor. 'And that is it over there.' He indicated a tidy house with a blue-painted door. 'For visitors—though I never saw any.'

'Did you never stay there?' wondered Donal.

The memory of his delightful reception by the queen floated into his mind. Conor smiled and shook his head. 'That particular pleasure was denied me.'

'But other pleasures were not, I reckon.' Fergal took in the expanse of the yard and the situation of the houses and whistled quietly under his breath. 'Tidy place, this. I like it.'

'Brecan ruled it well,' Conor allowed. 'Whatever else you may hear, he did not neglect his people.'

They stood taking in the mood of the place. All seemed quiet enough, if somewhat bereft of the usual activity Conor remembered. The one or two folk they saw hurried about their business with heads down and shoulders hunched. Galart rejoined them and led them across an empty yard and, after tying their horses to a post outside the hall, they climbed the low wooden steps to the entrance of the hall. Unlike the times when the king was in residence, there was no guard on the door, nor could they hear any sound from within.

Galart pulled aside the oxhide covering and pushed open the wooden door, leading them into the Brigantes king's hall. A bare handful of warriors sat in near darkness along the board. Galart clapped his hands for attention and shouted, 'Brothers! Look who has come to cheer us!'

Half the board rose as one and three hurried from their places, hailing Conor, gripping his arms in welcome and pounding him on the back; others called out to be recognised.

'They seem glad to see him,' observed Donal, watching from a few paces away. 'That's a good sign.'

'With any luck, there may be a jar or two in it yet.' Donal glanced away from the glad reception and took in the expansive room. It was at least twice the size of Ardan's at Dúnaird, with large rooftrees made from pine trunks and painted red and green. A long low table lined one side and benches ran the length of it. There were booths and ranks of fleece-covered pallets for sleeping, and a generous hearth, now lit only with a barely sputtering flame, in the centre of the room and, above it, a large round smoke hole; a few smoky torches fluttered from iron sconces affixed to nearby rooftrees and at either end of the great rectangular room. These did little to dispel the heavy shadows of the place; gloom seemed to come seeping out of the corners. 'At least it is warm,' he concluded, 'and dry.'

'At least,' agreed Fergal, eyeing the long board where large platters of meat and bread and bowls of broth sat waiting beside numerous jars and beakers of ale.

Then, among the little group of welcomers, there appeared a warrior who stood a bit taller than the others—almost as tall as Fergal—and slightly older than Galart and the others by two or three years. He was dressed in a dark brown siarc and breecs, and wore his hair short, but for a long braid at the side of his head; around his throat he wore a torc of twisted copper strands. Conor saw him as the crowd around him parted to allow the newcomer to join them. 'See here!' called Galart. 'Conor is back from the dead.'

'So I see,' replied the newcomer. There was neither smile nor welcome on his face or in his tone.

'Greetings, Médon,' said Conor, squaring his shoulders to meet the man face-to-face. 'I have returned.'

'Like a dog to its vomit,' said the haughty warrior with a toss of his head. 'Here you are again—and I ask myself why.' He pushed his mouth into a frown and looked at Conor from head to foot. 'You should have stayed dead. But here you are and I must ask you where were you on the night our king and warleader were killed?'

Galart made to intercede. 'This is no place—'

Conor put out a hand to silence him and said, 'I was there. I saw them die.'

'Because you betrayed them into the hands of the enemy.'

This declaration caused an immediate cooling of their warm reception; the Brigantes warriors looked to Conor to challenge the allegation made against him.

'There goes our ale portion,' moaned Donal.

'And our warm bed,' commiserated Fergal. 'I knew this was too good to be true.'

Médon, staring in stark defiance at Conor, lifted an imperious hand and said, 'Well? You've heard the accusation. What do you have to say for yourself?'

Conor looked his accuser in the eye and answered, 'I was there, aye, and I saw them fall. And I can tell you that your king was struck down by the hand of Balor Evil Eye, and Mog Ruith died by the same knife. Cethern, your uncle, fought bravely and well, but was overcome and died trying to protect them. Even so, thanks to Cethern, I was able to make good my escape.' He looked to the warriors around him. 'Had it been in my power to save them, I would have spared nothing. On my honour, I would not have left the fight without them.'

'Hear him!' shouted someone from among the ranks.

But Médon was not finished. '*If* you escaped as you say,' he scoffed, 'then where have you been all this time? It should have been you who brought us word of the murder. And yet, we had to learn of it from the Scálda filth who returned the body of our lord tied to his horse—and that of our warleader chopped into crow bait and left in pieces along the trail.'

'As to that—' Conor began, then hesitated.

'Well?' demanded his accuser. 'Was it cowardice? Knowing you had deserted your lord in the hot blood of battle? Or, were you his betrayer?' A slow, superior smile slid across Médon's smooth face. 'What was it then? Coward? Or traitor?'

At the utterance of the hateful word, all eyes turned to Conor and his mouth went dry. He had to say something. Yet, anything he said would only make his position more precarious: to tell the truth could not but offend the memory of the king and incite the rancour of those whose goodwill he was trying to win. But, say nothing and his silence would serve to further impugn his integrity.

'Answer!' called one of the warriors. The word rang in the hall like a judgement. Another shouted, 'Tell us the truth!'

Silence descended upon the hall in a stifling fog of doubt and distrust.

12

'The truth is, Conor was not the only one to escape the enemy's trap that night.' It was Fergal who came to Conor's defence, his voice loud in the fraught silence. 'He saved others and was sorely wounded defending their retreat. He shed his own blood to save them and they walk the land of the living today because he put his life at risk to save them.'

This bold declaration caused an outcry. 'Show us the wounds!' shouted some. 'The wounds will tell.'

Médon allowed the shouting to continue a moment, then raised his hands for quiet. When he could be heard again, he fixed Conor with a fearsome gaze and demanded, 'Your man here says you were sorely wounded. Is this true?'

'It is that.'

'Who were these others?' called someone from the ranks. 'What tribes?'

'They were fa—' began Fergal.

But Conor cut him off. Turning to address the warriors, he said, 'You asked to see the wounds—I will show you.' With that he drew back the sleeve of his siarc and turned his arm for all gathered there to see the puckered red skin of a fresh scar. He then pulled the hem of his siarc from his belt, raised it, and displayed the ugly crease in his side—despite his lengthy convalescence with the faéry the wound was still livid and with a virulent appearance to match its colour—a testament to his continuing recovery. The sight brought some gasps from the warriors who knew well enough that such injuries were not easy to heal, much less survive. Conor raised the siarc higher to reveal the long, ragged gash on his chest—shallow, true, but impressive enough in light of the others.

Dropping his siarc once more, he said, 'Now I have a question for you, Médon. And it is this—if you were so concerned about the safety of your lord and battlechief why did you not go with them to meet with Balor Berugderc that day?'

Médon gazed back at him coldly. 'How could I?'

'That is no answer.'

'I was forbidden to go,' the warrior spat. 'As were you.'

'Yet, you knew your lord and king was meeting with the Scálda—and that this was not the first time,' continued Conor, pressing his point. 'Even so, you knew your king and battlechief were meeting with Balor Evil Eye and yet you let them go into an enemy fortress alone and unprotected.'

'Is this true?' asked Galart. 'You *knew* our king was holding council with the enemy?'

Médon opened his mouth to object, but before he could find the words to counter Conor's assertion, someone else said, 'You knew, brother, and you said nothing?' The question still hung in the air when someone added, 'If *I* had known about this I would have done something. I would have—even if I was forbidden.'

This sentiment was swiftly taken up and soon everyone was clamouring for Médon to explain the secret meetings between Lord Brecan and the Scálda king and warleader. Conor watched as the Brigantes battlechief twisted this way and that, looking guilty as a thief with a stolen pig under his arm. The shouting grew more strident and swiftly rose toward the point of blows; Médon, trapped in his guilty knowledge, looked to Conor for help.

'Let him speak!' shouted Conor, stamping on the floor. 'Let us hear what he has to say.' To Médon, he said, 'Go on. There are no brehons here to judge you—only your swordbrothers, eager to hear your explanation.'

The words had an immediate effect and not only did the shouting cease, but the anger, so quickly heated, began to cool. Médon cleared his throat and, turning to his warband, said, 'What Conor says is true. I knew that Brecan and Mog Ruith were meeting in secret with the Scálda. By the time I learned this, they had already attended several such meetings over many months.' The clamour verged on erupting again, but Conor quelled it and nodded for Médon to continue. 'No one told me this,' he insisted, 'not outright. But Cethern let slip a word or two in my hearing on occasion. I never learned why the king agreed to these meetings, or what was discussed at them. Like Conor, I had suspicions—only that, nothing more.' He put out a hand in appeal. 'Twice, as you will all remember, as a member of Brecan's tiranam, I accompanied the ardféne and the king—as did you Comgall, and you Nuadh, and Aedd, and Calbhan, Dearg, and Tagdh. . . .' He appealed to each of these young warriors in turn before continuing. 'Look to your hearts and tell me that you did not suspect our king was placing himself in great peril. We all had our misgivings, did we not?'

The men named shuffled their feet and mumbled that Médon spoke the truth. At last, Médon looked to Conor, who said, 'Well, it seems to me that none of us should be throwing accusations at another. Perhaps if you had spoken openly of your suspicions something could have been done.' Turning to the others, added, 'The same can be said for the rest of you who stood by nursing your suspicions instead of speaking up.'

The young warleader shook his head. 'Nay, the king demanded secrecy— as you well know. Whatever he and Mog Ruith discussed with Balor Berugderc has gone with them into the tomb.' He extended a conciliatory hand to Conor. 'I am sorry I doubted you. But hard times have come to Aintrén and, as things stand, I had to make certain you and your friends could be trusted.'

'And is there now any doubt?' Conor searched the young warleader's face for any hint of misgiving.

'I have none,' he said, shaking his head.

Then Conor took the offered hand and, gripping it, pulled Médon into a hearty embrace. 'In your place, I would have done the same. It is forgotten and we will speak of it no more.'

The sight of the two men putting aside their differences to embrace one another as brothers cheered the Brigantes warriors and they renewed their welcome of a favoured member of their warband. Immediately, the cheerless atmosphere of the hall brightened; men all talked at once, recalling better times when Conor was one of their number; they greeted his friends with laughter, welcome cups appeared, and even the fire in the hearth seemed to burn with a brighter, fresher flame.

The three newcomers were led to the board and given places on the bench. Their bowls were piled high with choice morsels and their cups filled time and again. Though every man among them longed to hear what had happened the night their king was murdered, to ask outright would violate the hospitality of the hall and table, and none dared raise the subject.

Later—many cups later—the three Darini, claiming weariness from their day's journey, rose from the board; yawning and a little unsteady on their feet, they asked to be allowed to retire. Galart conducted the travellers to the guesthouse and bade them a good night's rest. As soon as the door closed on them and they were alone once more, Donal observed, 'That ended better than it began.'

'Still, it was a close-run thing,' added Fergal. 'It could easily have gone against us.'

'Aye, and would have,' granted Conor, 'if not for you, brother.' Draping his arm around his friend's shoulder, he said, 'We have you to thank for saving our necks tonight.'

Fergal grinned. 'I was only saving our supper.'

'The Brigantes lay an enviable board,' said Donal. 'I give them that.' He glanced around the room; a fire had been lit in the hearth to warm the empty room. Unfastening his cloak pin, he tossed the cloak onto a nearby pallet. 'Tell me, brother—how did you know that your man Médon knew about the secret meetings?'

Conor likewise drew off his cloak and put it aside. 'In all truth, I only suspected. I knew he often rode with the king's ardféne and might have been included of a time. That, and his persistence in holding *me* to blame—as if I was responsible for Brecan getting himself killed—strengthened my suspicions. I reckoned he might be trying to ease his guilt—something like that.' He glanced around at Fergal, who was standing at the hearth rubbing his hands at the fire. 'I had to curtail your explanation, but you were about to tell them about the faéries.'

'Aye, so I was. It is the truth and it was the truth they wanted to hear.'

'To be sure, but I'm thinking there might be a few particulars we should best keep to ourselves for a while. Also, I did not wish to confuse things overmuch by adding another strand to the story that would require a lengthy explanation—'

'And would likely defy belief,' added Donal. 'Conor is right.' He lay down on his pallet and pulled his cloak over him. 'We should foreswear all talk of the faéry. That is a secret best held close. It may be of better use to us later.'

'What happens with us now?'

'A warm and peaceful sleep, I hope,' replied Conor. 'And then tomorrow, I will ask the queen's permission for us to join the Brigantes warband.' He smiled and stretched out on the pallet. 'After all that has happened here these past days, I expect she will be heartily pleased to accept our blades into her service.'

'What is she like, this queen of theirs?' asked Fergal. He placed another chunk of wood on the fire, and added one more for good measure, then crossed to an empty pallet and sat down. 'Well? What is she like?'

Conor drew his cloak over him and replied, 'What do you imagine the wife of Lord Brecan mac Lergath should be like?'

Fergal thought for a moment. 'A bloated old matron with a face like a pig's rear end and grandiose delusions of ruling the world?' he suggested. 'In other words, much like her husband, I expect.'

'You must know the lady intimately,' observed Conor. 'For you describe her with uncanny skill.'

'Truly?'

'You'll see for yourself tomorrow,' Conor told him. He yawned and closed his eyes. 'Aye, so you will.'

13

Early the next morning, the three Darini trooped out with a few of the Brigantes warriors to bathe in the shallow river to the north of the stronghold—a common ritual for Conor who, contrary to Fergal and Donal's moaning, had grown to welcome such a bracing start to the day. As a rose-coloured dawn lightened the sky, they tromped through the stubble fields accompanied by a few dogs from the valley farm holdings. The day broke fair, but chill, and a veil of fog rose from the surface of the water to hang in a slow-drifting cloud above the river course.

Shedding their clothing on the bank, the men splashed into the stream and began swimming and sporting in the cold water. After the first, quickening splash, they washed, passing fist-sized lumps of tallow-and-ash soap to one another. Leaving his two friends to their muttering, Conor sought out the company of Galart. 'Are the others not joining us?' he asked, having marked how few bathers had turned out.

'What others do you mean?' wondered the dark-haired young man. He yawned and glanced down along the bank of the stream.

'The warriors of the other houses,' replied Conor. The Brigantes boasted three houses of warriors, and on most days men from all three houses would join in the daily ablutions. 'Are they out riding the borders?'

Galart rubbed the soap on his face and hair and, returning the lump to Conor, began scrubbing vigorously. 'There is only the one house now,' he answered finally.

'Only one . . .' Conor stopped himself asking what had happened to all the others. He realised with an empty feeling in the pit of his stomach that he already knew. 'Has it really been so bad this summer?'

Galart nodded, then ducked his head in the water.

'I am sorry to hear it,' said Conor when the young warrior resurfaced.

'You have nothing to be sorry about, friend,' replied Galart, shaking water from his face and hair. Turning his gaze to the wood across the stream, he said, 'The Scálda have been pressing us hard on the borderlands all summer—little battles here and there, picking away at us piecemeal. We make good account of ourselves, mind—'

'I'm certain you do,' Conor sympathised.

'Even so,' Galart admitted, 'as many as we kill, they always send more and those we lose stay lost to us.' Glancing around at his swordbrothers, he added, 'Now we barely have enough to protect the ráth.' He glanced at Conor. 'I am glad you came back. . . .' He paused as if he would say more, and then decided against it.

'What is in your mind? Tell me, Galart. Nothing you say will offend me.'

'Ach, well, it is only this. . . .' He faltered again.

'I will take no offense,' Conor coaxed.

'*Why* did you come back here?'

'Why not go home to Dúnaird—is that what you mean?' Conor guessed. 'As to that, I am an outcast as you might remember. My brother Liam is battlechief and warleader, but he has taken against me and clings to the ban.' Conor felt a pang of regret twist through him when remembered Aoife waiting there.

Galart nodded as if he had suspected as much. 'That is hard.'

'Hard as it may be, that is the way of it.'

One of the nearby bathers called for the soap and Conor rubbed the chunk in his hair, then tossed it to the next in line.

'What about your friends?' asked Galart. 'Are they outcast, too?'

Conor looked around to see Fergal and Donal kneeling in the stream, laving cold water over themselves to rinse away the soapsuds. 'Nay, nay—only by choice.'

The young warrior nodded appreciatively. 'They must be good friends, then.'

'Ach, aye, they are all that and more.'

They finished bathing and waded back to the riverbank to retrieve their clothes. They dried themselves as best they could with their cloaks, dressed, and then hurried back to the stronghold to break fast and warm themselves in the hall. They ascended the long ramp to the gate and trooped into the yard. Some of the women had set up a great cauldron and were heating water for boiling clothes. 'They'll wash your clothes, too,' Galart told him. 'But I think they won't have seen anything so fine as what you are wearing.'

'Ach, well, I think that now we are here we will dress less like lords and more like warriors—if you can spare a siarc or two and some breecs.'

Just then Conor heard his name called from across the yard. Glancing around, he saw Lady Sceana standing on the steps of the king's house. She was dressed in a drab green mantle and pale yellow cloak, but under the mantle Conor saw she wore men's rough-woven breecs; no doubt she meant to convey the message that she was now ruler of the tribe. Conor put on his best smile and lifted a hand in greeting as he hurried across the yard to meet her. Fergal and Donal saw him go and paused to watch how he was received.

'So, it is true,' she said as soon as he was close enough not to have to shout. 'My champion has returned.' There was no warmth in her tone, but much cold judgement.

Conor pressed the back of his hand to his forehead in the customary sign of respect and waited for her to speak again.

'They also said you had brought others with you.' She glanced beyond him to where Fergal and Donal waited. 'Are those men just there your friends?'

'They are, lady.' Conor raised his arm and summoned the two to join them, presenting each in turn to the queen. 'I give you Fergal mac Caen and Donal mac Donogh of the Darini—swordbrothers of mine for many years. My friends,' he said, 'I present you to Lady Sceana, Queen of the Brigantes.'

Both men made the sign of obeisance to nobility, and Fergal coloured slightly, impressed by her comeliness and grace. 'My lady,' he said at last, and lowered his gaze. 'We are indebted to your hospitality.'

'You are welcome here,' she told them. 'You will know by now that we stand in sore need of warriors. Our brave warband has borne the brunt of maintaining the borderlands and the raiding this summer has cut the very heart out of our warhost. I am happy to accept all who will pledge loyalty to me.'

'Our blades are yours to command,' replied Fergal. And Donal echoed the sentiment, adding, 'We will do all we can to avenge the death of Lord Brecan.'

The queen thanked them and dismissed them, saying, 'You will tell Médon that I have accepted you into my service and that you are to be treated as valued members of the warband. Serve me well and you will be well rewarded.' Turning to Conor, she said, 'Stay here, a little. I would speak to my champion alone.'

Fergal and Donal bowed and, with a last sneaking glance at Conor, withdrew. When the others had gone, the queen said, 'Sit with me, my friend. I have asked for food to be brought that we may break fast together while we talk.' She smiled quickly. 'I will also summon a maid to shave you. It seems you have misplaced your razor.'

'Too true,' replied Conor lightly. 'That and much else besides.'

The queen turned and led him through the door to the main room where a small fire burned on the central hearth; a low table had been placed beside the hearth and fleeces spread around. Sceana indicated a place at the table; Conor sat and, after summoning one of her handmaids, the queen took the place across from him. She folded her long legs beneath her, and gazed at him for a time without speaking.

Conor felt himself growing uneasy beneath her unrelenting gaze. Finally, she cleared her throat and said, 'We thought you dead—along with the others—the night my husband was killed.'

'I survived—alone, it would appear.'

'Galart has told me you were wounded in the ambush. He told me he saw the scars and that healing is not yet complete.'

'Complete enough,' Conor said, 'or I would not be here. As it is, my injuries prevented me from coming sooner.'

Before he could say more, one of the queen's companions appeared with bronze basin, a cloth, and a razor. At the queen's bidding, she invited Conor to take the chair in the corner of the room and to lean back. He did as he was told and was quickly and expertly shaved with deft, sure strokes of the bronze razor.

The handmaid then wiped the soap from his face and dried him with the cloth. She untied the thin leather strap that bound his long hair and combed it out with an ox-bone comb, braided it, and replaced the strap to hold it in place. Then, with a little bow, she departed—quickly to be replaced by another serving woman bearing a large platter of cold roast pork and fresh radishes, and a basket of brown bread in loaves the size of goose eggs; a second attendant brought a bowl of butter, and one of salt. The two withdrew without a word, and one returned with two wooden cups filled with buttermilk.

'Please, eat,' said the queen. 'I know you must be hungry after your travels.'

'After you, lady,' replied Conor.

'You will excuse me, I hope,' she said diffidently, 'but I have little appetite these days.' Conor helped himself to a loaf of bread, broke it, and began spreading butter with the gold-handled knife from his belt. She watched him for a moment, then said, 'That knife seems very well made. May I see it?'

Conor handed her the blade. The queen examined it, turning it this way and that. 'A most clever design,' she observed, handing it back to him. 'And your clothes—your cloak and siarc—I do not believe I have ever seen anything so wondrously fine. Certainly not in this part of Eirlandia—or any other that I know of.' She frowned and bit her lip. 'They are not Scálda clothes?'

'Never that, my queen. If they were, I would sooner burn them and go about the earth naked than allow anything so vile to touch my flesh.'

'If not Scálda then . . .' She gazed at Conor, waiting for an answer to her unspoken question.

Conor relented, saying, 'After escaping from the Scálda ambush that night, I helped some faéry escape as well. My cloak and breecs and all the rest,' he plucked at the siarc, 'were a gift of gratitude from their king.'

'This was not in Eirlandia, I think.'

'Nay, lady, it was in Tír nan Óg.'

'The Land of the Everliving,' the queen said thoughtfully. 'A place only spoken of in druid tales.' Sceana's eyes narrowed for a moment as she weighed his words. Then, abandoning the attempt, she looked away. Conor brought the buttered loaf to his mouth, took a bite, and chewed thoughtfully, trying to assess the queen's attitude toward him—which was not easy owing to her much-subdued demeanour.

'Did he suffer?' she asked. 'My lord and husband, I mean—was there much pain in the end?'

'There was not. Indeed, I do not think he fully knew what had happened.' This last part was not completely true, but near enough. 'I heartily wish I could have saved him—and Cethern, too. I tried. You must believe me, lady—I did try. We were but two blades against a dozen or more. There were just too many against us. I believe Balor intended to murder us all from the beginning. There was never to be any survivors that night.'

'Balor?' she asked, her voice flat with disbelief. 'Balor Evil Eye? He was there, you say?'

'He was. For a fact, he was,' affirmed Conor, regarding her curiously. 'Did you not know that?'

Sceana gave a slight shake of her head and turned her face away. 'There were many things I did not know, it seems. I know the rumours . . . still, I dared hope . . .'

After a moment, she looked back again and Conor saw not displeasure scrawled upon her features, but desperation. Moreover, her tone and deportment had changed utterly. 'Conor,' she said softly, almost pleading, 'what am I going to do?'

The change was so sudden, it took Conor aback.

'My husband has left us in such turmoil,' she continued, lowering her head to gaze helplessly at her lap, 'and I don't know what to do about . . . about any of it.' Her voice quivered on the edge of tears. 'Each day that passes, I learn of some new charge or allegation, some fresh condemnation to lay against my husband's name.'

Conor did not know what to say to this, so merely offered, 'He was a man of great ambition, to be sure.'

'Ambition?' she scoffed angrily. 'We both know better. He was a prideful and self-serving fool, a bully with grandiose notions of his own eminence and importance. And where has it led? Where? It has led him to an early grave and his people to ruin.' She thrust out a hand to Conor. 'I set an honour price for his murder—did you know?'

Conor shook his head. 'I heard nothing about it.'

'Twenty pounds of gold and forty pounds of silver,' she said, disdain making her voice harsh, 'a hundred horses, fifty hounds, and ten young hostages. Honour price? Call it a *dis*honour price for that is closer the mark.'

'A high price, indeed,' mused Conor, 'even for a king. Why set such an exalted value if that is the way you feel?'

The queen tossed back her head. 'Look around you, friend. This fortress, this Aintrén is looked upon by many as the jewel in the ring of Eirlandia. But our tribe is large and we have long lived beyond our ability to supply our needs through our own efforts. In short, we depend on the tribute of our client lords—and the costs grow ever higher.'

'A large warband to supply the protection you have promised,' said Conor.

'That, to be sure—but also the endless gifts and bribes required to keep all those greedy clients content,' replied Sceana bitterly. 'Believe me when I tell you, there is much I never knew and more I learn every day.' She sighed ruefully. 'I set the honour price for my husband's death so high because that is what Brecan would do to show his underlords that he would not be shamed or humiliated by the Scálda.'

'You did it for show?'

'I thought it a good idea,' she insisted. 'Not that I believed even for an instant that debt would ever be paid. I merely want the client kings to know that here in Aintrén we valued our king—as they must continue to do.' Folding her hands in her lap, she stared down at them a moment, and then said, 'But now that Brecan is gone, I fear they will turn against us, desert us, or worse—attack us to seize the kingship and lay claim to Aintrén because they see me as a weak and pitiful woman.' She thrust out a hand to Conor and said, 'Again, I ask you, what am I to do?'

'That is not for me to say.' Conor rose and moved around the table to kneel beside her and, taking her offered hand in his, he said, 'But, I will stand with you and help you in any way I can and to the utmost of my power. I pledge myself and my sword to your service. I am yours to command how you will.'

Queen Sceana gazed at him forlornly and pressed his hand; then, as if on a sudden impulse, took it up and kissed it. 'I accept your pledge, my friend, and I have a request of you.'

'Speak it out, and it will be done.'

'I would that you become my champion,' she said.

'I am that already, if you will recall—'

She raised a finger and stopped him 'There is more I would have you hear. I want you to be my chief of battle as well.'

Conor straightened. 'My lady, Médon is more than able. He is—'

She shook her head. 'Médon serves me now, that is true—but only until a new battlechief can be chosen. I have delayed these last weeks in order for him to prove himself a worthy leader and advisor. But, he is young yet and possesses little experience—as even he will tell you. And, now that you have returned, I see I have a better choice. Conor mac Ardan, I choose you.'

'He knows this? Médon knows?'

'He knows the torc has not been given,' replied Sceana. 'I expect he has entertained the hope that the place would fall to him. But he understands that his position is provisional at best.' The queen saw Conor's hesitation and said, 'Hear me. Médon is an able warrior—and a fair teacher for the others—but he is not the warleader we need just now. Men do not leap to his command, much less anticipate it—at least,' she added, 'not as they do for you.'

Conor regarded her thoughtfully. The ruby birthmark on his cheek began to tingle as he imagined himself, a Darini from the wild north, leading the vaunted Brigantes warband in battle. What would Liam say to that? What would his father say?

The queen continued in an earnest, almost pleading tone, saying, 'You have the most battle experience against the enemy, and even Médon cannot deny that you are the most skilled warrior among us.' A ghost of her old smile played upon her lips. 'You bested Cethern, as I think *you* will recall.'

Conor realised then that she had been considering this since she learned of his return. In any event, it suited his purposes—such as they were. Still kneeling, he put his right fist upon his chest over his heart and, bowing his head, replied, 'My queen, I will be the warleader and battlechief of your choosing. Further, I will do all that may be done to build up the warband, increase its strength and numbers, and do my best to instruct others in all the skills I have acquired in battle. On this, you have my promise.'

She smiled and Conor saw the light come up in her eyes; her old spirit surfaced briefly in that smile and then, as if remembering the awful weight of authority she must bear, the light faded again, smothered by grief and care. 'Thank you, Conor. I place my trust and the protection of my people in your strong hands.'

So saying, she summoned her handmaid who brought out a fine silver torc made of three braided strands, and bade Conor to lower his head before her. He did so and, spreading the ends of the torc apart, the queen slipped the ornament around his throat, then closed up the ends again. 'There,' she said, resting her hands on his shoulder and gazing at him with an expression of relief and satisfaction. 'It is done.'

Conor, fingering the torc, returned to his place and, as they finished eating, he told her what he knew of the agreement between her husband and Balor, as well as what he had learned from her husband about the reason for the secret meeting and the king's lofty plans for the future. 'He told me he was acting in the best interest of Eirlandia and all its tribes,' he concluded.

'And did you believe him?' asked Sceana. There was no suspicion in the question, merely a hope for confirmation.

'In truth, I did. I truly believe Lord Brecan despaired of the continual squabbling among the smaller tribes and lords and thought that if he could gain the high king's throne, he could unite all the warbands under one command and in this way build a force strong enough to drive the Scálda from our lands.'

'But he was meeting with the enemy.'

'Only to gain enough time, I think—time to make his vision possible. He seemed to think an alliance with the Scálda, or at least some kind of treaty, would give him space enough and time to accomplish his ambition.' Conor nodded. That was what he thought at the time, and largely what Conor still believed lay at the heart of Brecan's disastrous plan.

'Would it have worked?' asked Sceana.

'Perhaps,' Conor conceded, trying to soften the blow. 'But, knowing the Scálda, I fear the scheme was doomed. Balor Berugderc has his own aims and ambitions. When Brecan was no longer of use to him, he killed the king without a moment's hesitation.'

The queen sat for a time, pondering what Conor had told her. At last, she said, 'Do you believe me when I say I knew none of this?'

'No one but the king's druid and battlechief knew it, my lady—not even the warriors that rode with the king that night knew of this plan. I only learned it because I was there and he had to find a way to win me to his side.'

'Even so, I *should* have known,' she said adamantly, pressing her hand to her chest. 'I was his wife and queen! I should have known. I should have taken more of an interest in the affairs of the realm. I should have made it my work to know what was in my husband's mind.' She paused, then asked, 'Would that have made a difference, do you think?'

Conor returned her doleful gaze with a light shake of his head. 'I think not, lady. The king was at pains to conceal his affairs—this one most especially. No one save Mog Ruith and Cethern knew of it. As I say, he only told me because I blundered into it.' He went on to explain how he had followed the king and his men when they rode out that day, and had then been captured and taken by the Scálda to the meeting place. 'As I think on it now, I do believe the king saw the prize within his grasp and was willing to risk everything to achieve it. I doubt anything anyone could have said or done would have guided him into a different path.'

Sceana accepted this and thanked Conor for telling her. She then concluded the audience saying, 'I will think about all you have said, and we will talk again soon.' She gazed on him with warmth and affection renewed. 'I think this is but the first of many such discussions we will be having.'

Conor bowed his head. 'My lady.' He stood and begged leave to begin organising the warband. 'I will speak to Médon. He should be told right away so that I can make a fresh start.'

'I will tell him,' Sceana said. 'It is my decision. I will tell him in a way that he can accept. You need fear no difficulty from him.' She reached out a hand to Conor and he took it. 'I thank you, my friend. I am in your debt. Is there anything I can do for you?'

'Nay, lady, I—' he began, then hesitated as he changed his mind. 'Ach, well, there is one small thing I might ask.'

'Ask and, small or large, it is yours.'

'These clothes—as you have noticed,' he said, smoothing his hand over his fine faéry siarc, 'are the clothes of a king—not those of a battlechief or warrior. My friends and I will need something more suitable to our work.'

Queen Sceana put back her head and laughed. 'You shall have them, all of you—and gladly. Although, I shall be sorry not to see you so splendidly arrayed. I will speak to Galagar, the chief steward, and he will give you everything you require.'

Conor thanked her and went out to begin assessing the strength and capability of the beleaguered and much-reduced Brigantes warband.

Rónán

By the time I reached Dúnaird, almost an entire season had passed since I had heard the devastating news of Conor's death. I confess it was a blow that hit me hard—it did not seem so very long ago that I had last seen him. Now, he was no more. Never would I see Conor again, hear his voice, nor see the light in his clear eyes. Murdered . . . the hateful word rolled like thunder through my head, resounding again and again. Murdered . . . my brother was dead.

That he had been killed along with King Brecan of the Brigantes and both cut down by the great and terrible Scálda king, Balor Berugderc, Lord of the Fomórai, while in the act of treason made his death not only grievous but profoundly shameful. Like a captive beast in torment, my conscience writhed with the torture of that knowledge. I could barely imagine my father's humiliation. To have a son known to one and all as a traitor, not only to his tribe but to Eirlandia entire, is a blow few men can endure, and fewer still survive with dignity and honour intact.

I would have gone at once, but Talgobain, our Wise Head, prevented me. 'Let time pass,' he counselled. 'The storms of grief will cloud your reason.'

'But my father—my people will have need of me in this time of mourning and upheaval.'

'What will you give them?'

'Comfort, Wise One. Comfort and solace.'

'Comfort out of your own misery, and solace from your turmoil? Go now and your judgement will be impaired. Any help you hope to bring will be tainted as a fountain poisoned at the fountainhead.'

'I should be there.'

'You will go when you can offer some healing—not add to the suffering around you.' Talgobain smiled sadly. 'It is a hard thing, I know. But if you master this trial, you will be proof against any like it that come your way. Trust me, for it is so.'

Reluctant as I was to accept this harsh judgement, I could not go against it. Thus, the season passed, and in truth I did find the clouds of grief cleared for me and reason returned. When I discerned that I was ready, I went again to our brehon and requested permission to go to Dúnaird; this time consent was granted. Thus, I set out with little Tuán for it was he who had first brought word of Brecan's death to me at Clethar Ciall. Although he was as dismayed by the delay as anyone—for he had known Conor very well—at my request he agreed to accompany me. He had word of Conor's last movements with Lord Brecan and I thought that this might be of some use to my father and brother. We travelled on foot so that took a few more days, but I used that time to compose a funeral song for my brother, commemorating his short life. Alas, owing to the shameful nature of his death with the treacherous Brigantes king, there was little to celebrate and, I fear, it was a bitter, cheerless song I made.

My travelling companion did his best to allow me time and solitude for thought. He made our camp each night and prepared our food and sometimes, when night closed around us, he sang one of the songs about the heroes of old who became gods in Eirlandia. He sang 'The Voyage of Bran mac Febail and the Silver Branch,' 'Conchobar and the Battle of Ros na Ríg,' 'The Feast of Bricrenn and the Exiled Princes,' and others that awakened my heart to the deeds both high and low of our island race from the time of our first arrival in this green land.

I listened to his gentle voice and let the tears flow as they would. The songs renewed the grief, aye, but they were also a balm for my bruised heart. As one day gave way to the next and one woodland to another, I felt my battered heart revive and I once again turned my eyes to the future and how I might best help my father and brother to weather this dreadful storm.

To be sure, this was another reason I wanted Tuán with me. Hard words are never welcome when spoken by blood kin, and I feared that the Darini would have to face hard truths about Conor and his despicable alliance with King Brecan. Tuán, a cheerful spirit, possessed the ability to confront without rousing anger as well. Perhaps his dwarfish size and sprightly manner made him seem less a threat to men of greater physical stature. His counsel, however sharp or unwanted, was never viewed as a challenge to anyone's rank or authority. And despite his odd, creaturely appearance, his mind was quick and ready and keen as a well-honed knife, able to pierce to the heart of a matter with such skill that it often seemed effortless—all the better when a reluctant listener must be persuaded to a difficult or distasteful course.

I hoped in the few days afforded us at Dúnaird that together we might ease some of the pain of Conor's betrayal and perhaps guide my father and Liam's shame to a more helpful outcome. Truly, that was my most fervent hope.

Sadly, Liam did not share this view.

The king was not there when I arrived. He was away to the Robogdi to see Lord Sechtan, and Liam was left in authority. Liam received us with a great show of respect and, I believe, genuine brotherly regard. He poured out a generous welcome cup with his own hand and gave me his bed in the great hall our father had built to replace the squalid hovel that the father of Eochaid Tight-Fist had erected and his wastrel son neglected. Over our cups and meat that first night Liam told us what he knew of how Conor met his death.

'It appears Brecan was so ambitious and anxious for the high kingship that he courted an alliance with the enemy to achieve it,' he said. 'So I have heard, and so I believe.'

'Did anyone ever suggest how this thing was to come about?' asked Tuán. He had said much the same thing and I was happy the two accounts matched.

Liam shook his head glumly. 'Not that I heard. But it hardly matters. The great fool should have known the Scálda cannot be trusted. They know only death and destruction.'

'Conor would have known that, surely,' I suggested. 'How did he come to be persuaded to join in this alliance?'

'Who knows?' Liam lifted his shoulders. 'Brecan probably promised him a share in the spoils. That's all it would have taken to turn Conor's head.'

Seizing on this remark, Tuán leaned forward. 'Do you hold your brother in such low esteem that you believe he would betray his people for wealth?'

Liam gave the little bard a dark, hateful look. 'You little know him if you think him above that. In truth, he has always yearned for wealth and status. Look what he did at the Oenach—stealing old Mádoc's gold brace-let just because he wanted it.' He shook his head again. 'Risked his honour and that of the Darini for a mere bauble, so he did. *That* is how little he cares about such things as truth and honour.'

Could I believe what I was hearing? I could not.

'But that was a sham,' I replied, trying to keep my tone even. 'That was a ruse dreamt up by Mádoc in order to secure Conor's aid and protection.'

'So you say,' muttered Liam. 'But you weren't there. I was.'

Silence claimed the near-empty hall then. We sat for a time in solemn thought. Finally, Tuán looked around and said, 'Is it always so quiet here now?'

'Quiet enough,' Liam told him, also looking around. 'It is quiet here to-night because Eamon is riding the southern border—he and the greater part of the warband. The rest are with my father. I was out the night before with the few left here in the ráth.'

'Is this something you are doing often?'

'Ach, aye, it is that. Since Lord Brecan's murder, the dog-eaters have become more persistent and more daring. They are raiding ever further into our territories—thieving and burning, then running away.'

'Even here in the north?' I asked. I had not heard things were so bad.

'Even here,' Liam assured me. 'The Brigantes and others have it worse, to be sure. But we see raiding parties up here from time to time. They come by ship and make landfall at night on the empty coastal watches south of here. If we can catch them before they are fully assembled on shore, they flee rather than fight. So, we watch the coasts most nights when the weather is good.'

Our talk moved on then to the funeral ceremony I had thought to perform for Conor.

'For Conor! That traitor?' said Liam. 'That is not necessary—I can as-sure you of that!'

A dark and sombre cloud settled over Liam's countenance then, so I said, 'I would speak to Aoife, too. I thought she might be here to play for us to-night.'

'No doubt she would have been happy to see you,' Liam replied. 'But, as it happens, she is not well just now.'

'Aoife ill?' I said, half rising from my seat on the bench at his table. 'Per-haps Tuán and I should go and see what we can do for her.'

'Ach, nay,' said Liam, waving aside the suggestion. 'It would be best if you left it until tomorrow or the next day.' He poured more of the good sweet mead into our cups, then leaned forward and confided, 'Women's troubles, you see.'

I left the matter there and talk passed on to other things. Then the mead and hearth and food began to tell against us and, seeing as we had travelled far and our fatigue was heavy upon us and that we were yawning over our cups, we begged our host's leave to go to our sleep. Liam obliged and with good grace, offered me his bed in the hall; Tuán was given a pallet in one of the side chambers and Liam, bidding us a fair rest, went to the Warriors' House.

After Liam left, Tuán lingered a little. 'Your brother is not so much like you or Conor,' he said. 'Though I see the family resemblance. Is he more like your father, then?'

'So I believe,' I told him. 'But I do not know my father all that well. I was that young when Morien took me. . . .' I lapsed into silence, remembering.

'Do you regret your life as a druid?'

'Nay, nay,' I told him quickly. 'Well, perhaps, a little at first—what else did I know? But after a year or so, I would not alter a day, nor trade it for any other.'

Tuán's wide mouth framed a cheerful, froglike grin. 'Nor would I,' he said. 'I was abandoned as an infant.'

'Truly?' I said, surprised at this information. For though I knew well enough that such things did often happen, it still appalled me that any mother would do that to her newborn child.

'Ach, well, the tribe took my birth—the way I am, you see—as an evil omen and forced her to give me up. But, luckily for me, she did not place me on the dung heap as the old wives advised, but carried me to Carn Dubh instead. I think it must have been a surprise for the learned brothers to find a baby in a grain basket at the gate.' He laughed. 'I have never known another hearth, but that one—nor would I trade it for any I have seen since then.'

Well tired, we slept long and rose the next morning to find that Liam and the remaining warriors had ridden out to hunt in order to provide extra meat for his visitors. But Eamon and his scouting party had returned just after daybreak. The woman serving us in the hall said, 'They are sleeping now, so they are. But they will waken soon enough if you care to wait.'

Tuán finished eating and went off to view the land round about Dúnaird, leaving me alone. With nothing else to do, I decided to go see if I might be of some aid to Aoife in her illness. For, although I did not choose the physician's path, all bards know much about the healing herbs and such for various ailments and diseases.

Taking up my bard's oversized sparán and my staff, I went to the Women's House. The door was opened to my knock and I told the maiden there that I had come to visit Aoife and see if I might be of service to her. The young woman—who could not have been more than twelve summers—regarded me with wide, wondering eyes—for all she had not seen many druids, I think. 'My lord bard, Aoife is not here.'

'That is well,' I replied. 'Kindly tell me where she is and I will go to her.'

She gave me a sly glance—as if she did not trust me with this knowledge. I hastened to reassure her. 'Fret not, child, you can trust a druid to behave with honour.'

She swallowed and glanced away, then regarding me with some trepidation, leaned close and whispered, 'Aoife is in the cattle byre.'

I thanked the maiden and, assuming Aoife had recovered her health, I hurried off to the little barn our tribe used for the birthing of calves and the care of sick cattle. Following the lanes and narrow paths between the houses crowding the curved walls of the ráth, I came to a small pen and a collection of outbuildings: a grain store, a brewing hut, and the byre. The door was slightly ajar and I paused before entering and gave a little cough to announce my presence. The invitation from within was forthcoming. 'Enter.'

I put my hand to the door and pulled it open. There, on a floor strewn with clean reeds and rushes, sat Aoife, stroking the swelling belly of a young cow.

'Aoife, I—'

At the sound of my voice she turned and the change in her appearance made me stifle a gasp. Her skin had a sickly pallor, her lustrous dark hair, unbraided, hung limp and dull, and her eyes had the lifeless sunken aspect of the grave.

Such was her illness, then. Of this I had no doubt. My first thought was to go find Tuán and determine if, between us, we might find a remedy for our poor, suffering sister.

'My lady,' I said, stepping into the byre, 'I would not intrude, but—'

'Rónán!' she cried, leaping up. 'You're here!' She rushed to me and threw her arms around me in glad welcome. 'Deira said some druids had come, but I did not think . . . but here you are.'

'I am here, aye, and Tuán is with me. Come, sit, tell me what ails you and we will do our best to find a remedy.'

Confusion creased her brow. 'What ails me?' she said—as if this should be well known to one and all.

'Your illness, lady,' I said. 'Do pardon me for speaking of intimate matters, but Liam told me. And I am here to help.'

'I am not *ill*,' she said, all but spitting the words. 'Except, perhaps, for the love of my betrothed.'

I nodded as understanding dawned within me. 'Conor—' I said, my voice heavy with sorrow. 'His death brings a burden of grief difficult to bear. It must be all the harder for you.'

Confusion creased her brow. She pulled away. Her red-rimmed eyes searched mine as if looking for something that was not to be found. Finally, she said, 'But Conor is not *dead*.'

'No?' It is sometimes the way with folk to deny the dear one's departure from this worlds-realm. 'But Aoife, my heart, he was murdered by the Scálda in the fight that killed King Brecan.'

'Conor is not dead,' she said again, strength returning to her voice. 'He is banished.'

Her conviction was many things, perhaps, but it was not denial. She was both adamant and defiant. I sat back on my heels and pondered what she said, and in the end could not decide what to make of it. 'I do not understand.'

She tossed her head and something of her customary fire returned, flushing colour to her pale cheeks. 'Aye, Conor is banished. Exiled by Liam,' she spat, 'and I—I am made hostage here.'

Fergal and Donal were in the yard with the other warriors. Having eaten well from the warriors' table, they were beginning the day's weapons training, warming cold muscles by sparring with wooden swords and blunted spears. They quickly abandoned their halfhearted swordwork and hurried to meet Conor the moment he emerged from his audience with the queen.

'Here you are—looking like the cat that caught the cow,' observed Fergal. 'What is her queenship's pleasure?'

'Will she have us in the warband at all?' asked Donal.

'Ach, I expect she will,' replied Conor with a grin. Touching the silver torc at his throat, he said, 'But, since I have been made chief of battle for the tribe, the question you must ask is whether *I* will be having you?'

'Battlechief!' exclaimed Fergal, rubbing the back of his neck.

Donal, eyeing the torc, merely whistled.

'Do not pretend such amazement,' Conor said. 'I bested Cethern—'

'As you never tire of telling us.'

'And I was the queen's champion,' Conor continued, unperturbed by Fergal's derision. 'Lady Sceana has asked me to resume that service and, since Cethern is no longer with us, she has asked me to take up his position as well. But, cheer up,' he added, giving Fergal a pat on the back, 'she has agreed to give you two new clothes.'

'I like what I am wearing,' Fergal replied, spreading his arms and looking down his own long length.

'Just you wait until you get Scálda blood all over them,' Donal told him, 'and then you'll be singing a different song.' To Conor, he said, 'What will friend Médon think about being taken down a peg, I wonder?' mused Donal.

'Not much, I'll wager,' said Fergal. 'I know it would chafe me raw, so it would.'

Conor looked beyond his two companions to where a young woman was even then speaking to Médon. 'I expect we will be finding out soon enough. The queen said she would tell him her decision and I think he goes to receive the news even now.'

The three watched as the queen's handmaid led Médon to the King's House where the queen stood waiting before the door. She held her audience then and there, in full view of everyone looking on; the talk was short and, judging from the warrior's reaction, amiably concluded: he simply gave a nod of acknowledgement and, taking a step back, touched his forehead with the back of his head in a gesture of fealty and respect. Then, he turned and strode to where Conor and the others waited.

'Our queen has told you her decision,' intoned the former battlechief, gazing directly at Conor without expression.

'Aye, that she has. I want you to know that I did not seek—'

'Lady Sceana is our queen and sole ruler now,' Médon said, forestalling the need for further explanation. 'For the good of the tribe, it is our duty to help her in any way we can to ensure our safety and restore our fortunes. It is my fervent hope that you will serve her well and consider me a loyal and trustworthy warrior.' He allowed himself a sly smile. 'And remember this—I will be watching you, Conor mac Ardan. Put a foot wrong and that silver torc you now wear around your throat is mine.'

'Fair enough,' Conor told him. 'I will rely on you for guidance.' Placing a hand on the warrior's shoulder, he said, 'As your battlechief, I am making you a member of the queen's ardféne.'

Médon appeared somewhat bewildered by this designation. 'A queen's advisor . . . but I cannot—'

'Why not? As you say, it is our duty to help her in any way we can. Besides that, you know the mood of the tribe as well as anyone and better than some—including me. Also, you have earned the trust of the warriors,' Conor replied. 'Now, let us inform the rest of the warband of the queen's decision.'

All four walked to where the warriors now stood watching; aware that something of some moment had taken place, they leaned on their spears waiting to be told what had happened.

'My friends, the queen has—' began Conor as he came to stand before the assembled warband.

Médon put out a hand to stop him, saying, 'If you would allow me, Conor, I would they heard this from me.'

Conor glanced at the faces gathered around him and surrendered the field. Médon took half a step forward and, fixing his fellows with a steady gaze, he said, 'Since losing king and battlechief, friends and swordbrothers to the enemy, we have been stumbling about in a daze of grief and fear—grief for all that was lost, and fear for what is to come.' There were muted sounds of agreement all around. 'But not all is lost,' he continued. 'If we doubted—as I think many here doubted—then Conor arrived to remind us otherwise. He survived the attack that killed our lord and his champion, and he is here to show the rest of us how to survive as well.'

'Hear him! Hear him!' said one of the warriors, to a rattling of wooden swords on shields. It was Galart and, beside him, Aedd and some of the younger men.

'For this reason, our good queen has chosen Conor mac Ardan to be her chief of battle and our warleader. . . .'

This news received a mixed reception: smiles and nods of encouragement in some quarters, questions in others, and a few frowns here and there.

'As for myself,' Médon continued, 'lest you think me hard done by, I tell you I welcome her choice—all the more since most of you will know how I have struggled in these last days to maintain order and confidence within our ranks. Some of you will have chafed under my poor guidance, and will be glad of the change.' He allowed himself a smile and turned to Conor. 'I myself will be glad for someone else to listen to the moans and groans of this ill-tempered pack of mongrel whelps.'

Conor stepped forward and, grasping Médon by the arms in a display of friendship, thanked him, then turned and said, 'The queen has chosen and I have accepted. Today, we begin to rebuild the warhost of the Brigantes. It is my hope to return it to its former superiority among the hosts of Eirlandia.' Médon's gracious speech had indeed smoothed over many of the rough patches on Conor's path. As the new battlechief, Conor could begin without having to fight his way to acceptance—that it would have been much of a contest, for he was already liked well enough.

Changes came thick and fast after that. Within the first few days, Fergal and Donal, alongside Médon, were appointed special advisors to the battlechief, and Galart was elevated to a position created just for him: master of the hall, the better to keep order and ensure peace and harmony within the ranks. By the time winter arrived in full, freezing bluster, the entire warband, to a man, acclaimed Conor's elevation to the titles of battlechief and warleader with steadfast approval if not outright enthusiasm. By the time spring rains arrived with the thaw, the older warriors' complaint that no one but a born-and-bred Brigantes should lead the Brigantes into battle had faded away like the last of winter's tired, sludgy snow.

And, by the time the summer sun began to raise the green heads of grain in the fields, the season of strife and skirmishes and swift, glancing enemy raids had resumed once more in blood earnest. The struggling Brigantes warband was hard pressed to adequately defend its borders and protect its outlying farms and fields. Yet, as the progression of summer stars made its slow-wheeling arc through the sky, strife along the southern border diminished; instead, raids among surrounding tribes and territories seemed to grow more numerous and more worrying by the day as the Scálda searched out easier prey.

The Brigantes warband faced its share of battles and helped out where it could. Conor and his small battle host fought well, suffering few wounds and fewer losses despite numerous conflicts. Other tribes and clans were not so fortunate. To Conor it seemed that surrounding tribes were harder hit and suffered more severe incursion. As the summer corn ripened in the ear, his suspicion was borne out: the tribes to the west were bearing the brunt of these continual lightning raids. Lughnasadh was only ten days away when the refugees began streaming across the land. The first to arrive at the gates of Aintrén were Cruithne from the western coastal territories: two score and six of them—women and children mostly, but a good few farmers, craftsmen, and a handful of warriors as well. The youngest among the displaced were babes in arms, and the oldest was a goldsmith fifty or so summers old, who told of the attack on the tribe's main stronghold that had overrun the defences and sent the terrified clansmen running for their lives.

'The Scálda were more interested in plundering the ráth than slaughtering the survivors,' he said, 'otherwise we would be standing here dead.'

Queen Sceana and most of the tribe had turned out to meet the refugees and hear what had happened; the Brigantes gathered in the yard in a wary circle around the shattered clutch of survivors. Exhausted, miserable, dishevelled, the desolate Cruithne huddled together in the warm sun as if braving an icy wind. 'Is this *all* who survived the raid?' asked Lady Sceana, indicating the close-clustered knot of people before her. 'Everyone?'

'Nay, lady, there are others.' The smith turned his gaze to his tribesmen clustered behind him. 'At least twice as many as you see here—maybe more.'

'Where are these others?' asked Conor; he stood beside the queen as head of her ardféne. 'Are they yet to come?'

The craftsman gave a shake of his head. 'I cannot say where they may be, lord. See now, we scattered in flight lest the Scálda give chase. We thought it would make pursuit more difficult.'

'Very wise,' replied Conor. 'I would have done the same.' He searched for a moment among the dishevelled group arrayed before him, then asked, 'Did any more of the warriors survive?'

The man merely shrugged. 'I cannot say, lord. They were fighting still when we made our escape. They may yet live, but I fear the worst.'

'These are very grave tidings,' said the queen. 'I will confer with my advisors and determine what is best to do. Until then, rest and recover your strength.' Turning to Galart, she said, 'The hall master will take you to a house where you can rest. Food will be brought to you there.'

The refugees were led to the larger of the two empty warriors' houses. Conor watched as the forlorn refugees shuffled away. 'What is your pleasure, my queen?'

'I do not see how we can support them,' Sceana replied, 'nor less yet how we can turn them away.'

'Then let them stay,' advised Conor, remembering another day, years ago, when Aoife had come into his life—first as a refugee and then as his beloved. 'It may be they will more than earn their keep—in the work they can do and the skills they bring. There are farmers among them, and herdsmen, and others—even a smith.'

She regarded the wretched tribesmen doubtfully. 'It is true that we have lost many over the summer. But they are Cruithne—how will they get on with us?'

'Touching that,' said Conor, 'I have a thought. Leave it with me for now.'

'As you will,' decided the queen. 'Let them stay.'

Conor had seen that among those seeking refuge there were four young men—only four: two farmers, a herdsman and, as his inquiries soon revealed, the son of the tribe's carpenter. Calling Donal, Fergal, and Médon together, he announced, 'I have it in my mind to make a school for warriors.'

'With those four Cruithne lads?' surmised Médon. 'They are too old to begin training.'

'Are they?'

'How old were you when you began *your* training?' asked Fergal. 'Eight summers? Nine?'

'Seven, I think,' replied Médon. 'No more than eight anyway.'

'Aye, that sounds about right,' agreed Fergal. 'Like you, I was no more than eight summers at the time.' He flapped a hand in the direction of Warriors' House and looked to Conor. 'These lads are twice that if a day. I agree with Médon.' He shook his head in disapproval of the notion. 'It would be like trying to cram seven whole baskets of grain into a single loaf. It cannot be done.' He turned to Donal. 'Tell him, brother, it is a harebrained idea and it cannot be done.'

'It *is* a harebrained idea, Conor,' agreed Donal. 'Yet, it may be there is a chance it can be made to work after a fashion.'

'What!' gasped Fergal in disbelief. 'You're every bit as foolish as Conor! Think what you are saying. You know well enough—or *should* know well enough—that you cannot make a man ready for battle in a single summer! Or even ten! To do otherwise only makes a fella ripe to join his fathers in the Red Badb's hall.'

'True enough,' agreed Donal. 'You may not be able to teach them all ninety-nine ways to kill and keep from being killed, but you might well train them up enough to defend a wall, or to serve those in the battle line by ferrying weapons and food and such from camp.'

'Exactly!' cried Conor. 'You have hit the nub of it there, brother. If we had men trained to serve in this way, it would release our more seasoned warriors to join the battle line.' Turning to Médon, he said, 'Is that not so?'

The tall warrior pulled on his moustache and glanced from Conor to Fergal and said, 'I suppose if we had men trained to serve the warriors during battle—carry spears and replace shields and such—then more could fight. Aye, so they could.'

Fergal, still shaking his head, replied, 'All you will be doing—mark me—*all* you will be doing is making those poor sheep fit for slaughter. It would be like growing grass for the scythe.'

'Perhaps,' allowed Conor. 'In better times, I would agree with you. In better times, I would never suggest such a reckless course. But these are not better times, brother. These are dangerous times, and we need all the help we can find. If you tell me there is somewhere else to obtain trained and seasoned warriors, I will be first on my horse to go and get them.'

'You know well enough that there is no such place,' Fergal huffed. 'And that is the whole pox-bitten point!'

'Then how else do you propose we build up our numbers?'

Fergal could not answer.

'I know it is chancy,' Conor said, putting his arm around Fergal's broad shoulders. 'Believe me, I know. But we do not have ten summers or more to build up our warband with trained and battle-hardened warriors. If we do not find a way to turn back the Scálda—and soon—we will *all* be refugees looking for shelter in an Eirlandia that is nothing more than a distant memory.'

Fergal kicked the toe of his shoe against the packed earth of the practice area and muttered that training farmers was a fool's errand and that Conor would only make them ripe and ready for an early grave. Donal shared this belief, too, but was willing to suspend judgement until he could see the results of the training Conor envisioned.

'As to that,' said Conor, 'I think you two will be best placed to judge the results.'

'Whatever would make you say a thing like that?' asked Fergal, suspicion shading his tone.

'Because, Fergal, chief among spearmen, you and Donal are going to oversee the training of our new men.'

Fergal squawked with disbelief and made bold to challenge the plan, but Conor was no longer listening. He told the two to begin by thinking through what they would need to proceed at once and to make a firm start. 'What will you do, Conor?' called Donal as Conor walked away.

'I will speak to your new trainees,' he called back. 'Come along, Médon.'

Both warriors watched Conor as he hurried across the yard. 'He is insane, you know,' observed Fergal.

'Ach, aye,' confirmed Donal. 'There can no longer be any doubt at all.' Glancing at Fergal, he added, 'That anyone would think *you* could teach even so much as a hungry dog to fetch a bone . . . it beggars all belief, so it does.'

15

The beleaguered Cruithne were but the first exiles to reach the gates of Aintrén. Before the Mabon celebration at summer's end, there would be two more groups seeking refuge within the sheltering walls of the Brigantes' principal stronghold. One moon later, there would be Laigini as well, and more. Indeed, the Samhain fires were still smouldering when the largest group of all arrived: Bréifne—three entire clans of them and, surprisingly, they came with their king.

Two riders appeared just as the last light died in the west on a gusty, blustery day; they begged entrance at the gate, saying that they merely sought food and a place to rest for the night in exchange for a promise to move on the next morning. Foremost of the two was a red-haired warrior carrying only a spear who greeted the gatemen and announced that he was in the company of the Bréifne king and asked to speak to someone in authority. The two were admitted and rode into the centre of the yard where they stopped to wait while the queen was summoned. Conor, having seen the strangers in the yard, marked their fine horses and, thinking them messengers, drifted over to hear what news they brought.

The Bréifne lord sat on his fine bay horse and cast an imperious gaze around the stronghold. He was a darkly handsome man fast approaching his prime, with bold, if slightly rough-hewn features; he had deep-set dark eyes under thick black brows and long dark hair that hung in heavy curls around his smooth-shaven face. At the appearance of the queen the monarch slid off his horse, approached, and knelt at her feet, his hands dangling at his side.

'My lady,' he said, gazing up into her face, 'I had heard that the queen of the Brigantes was the very vision of beauty—but I thought that must be the embellishment of the poet. Forgive me, for I see now that I was wrong. Your loveliness exceeds the bard's best efforts.'

Conor groaned inwardly at such naked flattery, but Lady Sceana appeared taken in by it, if not entirely delighted; and when she bade the Bréifne lord to rise lest he make himself less in the eyes of his people who were just then beginning to stream in through the still-open gate, the smile with which he beguiled her certainly charmed if not enchanted.

'You would think the Great Dagda himself had bestowed golden rings and bracelets upon her,' huffed Fergal, hugely unimpressed. He and Donal had witnessed the act and bustled over to join Conor. 'Such shameless fawning is repulsive—that's what it is.' He spat and shook his head. 'Well, he will not gain anything by it.'

Donal, observing the two thoughtfully, replied, 'I fear, brother, that he already has.'

'What?' Fergal scoffed. 'What has he gained?'

'Whatever he wanted.'

Fergal turned to his friend, and saw the far-off look in Donal's eyes. 'Ha! We'll see about that.' He turned and strode off. 'I'll find Galart and tell him we have more visitors.'

Conor stood gazing on, a frown of concern creasing his brow. When he had gone, Conor said, 'Tell me what you see, brother. Is this trouble?'

'Very likely.' Donal shrugged. 'It all depends.'

The queen conducted her royal guest to the King's House for refreshment. Donal walked away, but Conor stood for a while to observe the Bréifne refugees; the main body had now reached the ráth and were settling in the courtyard to rest. A group of three score, Conor estimated, they appeared harrowed and bedraggled from their recent ordeal, and Conor was once again minded of that day when, as a lad of nine summers, his father had welcomed such exiles into Dúnaird—his Aoife and her mother among them. Though he had hardly noticed his future betrothed then, he would, and soon, and the bond forged then was, so far as Conor was concerned, forever.

He made a good attempt to go about his business, but he found himself continually glancing across to the King's House and, when curiosity finally overcame his better judgement, Conor marched over and presented himself at the door and was duly admitted. As battlechief and head of the queen's ardféne, his comings and goings were never questioned. He thanked the handmaid and closed the door behind him. Lady Sceana and the Bréifne king were reclining at table, and the queen rose at Conor's entrance. 'Here is Conor now! I was just about to summon you.' She all but pulled him to the table. 'Lord Vainche, I present my battlechief and champion, Conor mac Ardan.'

The sleek monarch rose at once and greeted him pleasantly, then said, 'But I seem to remember a king called Ardan—from a small territory somewhere in the north, I think.' He smiled winsomely. 'Yet, Ardan is a common name in this place for all I know.'

'Lord Ardan, King of the Darini, is my father,' Conor told him.

'Not a Brigantes?' The fellow's shapely dark eyebrows rose in surprise. 'Well, it seems you have made a good account of yourself in any case. He must be very proud of you, your father.' Vainche paused, as if in thought, then said, 'Forgive me if I speak amiss, but I wonder why you are not battlechief for your father?'

Conor was taken aback by the audacity of the visiting lord. Not only was the question improper and unseemly, but he owed no explanation to a visitor passing through. In any event, it was none of his affair.

Conor was saved having to answer by the queen, who said, 'Conor was a trusted member of Lord Brecan's warband, and second only to Cethern, our battlechief.' She gave an embarrassed laugh and put her hand on Conor's arm, adding, 'After they were so cruelly killed, it seemed only right to make Conor my warleader.'

'Ach,' replied Vainche, openly dismissive, 'I am certain you know best. Who am I to question your decision?'

'Who indeed?' replied Conor, forcing a tight smile.

Lord Vainche returned to his place at the table, and Conor could not help but notice the comfortable, almost insolent slouch and the easy privilege—as one whose place was not only assumed, but assured. He was a guest behaving as an ill-mannered and indifferent host. Conor stared at the Bréifne monarch and his wine-red birthmark began to tingle.

'We were about to share a meal, Conor,' said the queen, her voice tight, nervous. 'I would be happy if you could join us.' She glanced at Vainche.

'Ach, to be sure,' the young man said, yawning. 'Although I imagine our tepid talk cannot hope to rival the robust banter of fighting men in the hall.'

He regarded Conor sleepily. 'I am sure you must have more pressing duties and I would not have you neglect them on my account.'

'As it happens,' replied Conor tartly, 'I do. It seems the queen's yard has filled up with a considerable number of people who require some assistance.'

'Yes!' affirmed Sceana quickly. 'By all means, Conor, do whatever is necessary to make them comfortable. They are only staying one night, after all.' To Vainche she said, 'It is the least we can do.'

Conor took his leave, heartily glad not to have to suffer the impudent stranger's rudeness a moment longer. Once outside, he paused on the steps of the house and looked out across the yard. The Bréifne were huddled together in tight little clumps, shoulders slumped, faces haggard in the fast-fading light of a dying day. Too tired to talk, most of them just sat and stared at their unfamiliar surroundings. Conor's heart went out to them. He hurried across the yard where the Brigantes store master—a garrulous old fellow with a red face and pot belly—stood before the storehouse and granary, guarding his supplies. Conor hailed the man and said, 'They will be needing something to eat,' he said. 'Give them some beans and bacon, oats or whatever, to make themselves a meal.'

This brought a mighty frown to the man's ruddy face. 'Under whose authority—if you don't mind my asking?'

'If anyone complains, you can tell them to speak to me,' said Conor.

'Aye, I will do just that.'

'It is only for one night, after all. They are moving on in the morning.' Conor turned and started away, adding, 'This time tomorrow they will be someone else's concern—them and their insufferable lord.'

Skirting the makeshift encampment, Conor made his way to the hall with a head full of thoughts and questions: why was the king with his people? Why was he here at all? Any king worthy of the name and rank would fight to the death in defence of his realm. How had Vainche come to abandon his warriors in the midst of battle? Why had he forsaken his kingdom?

These questions occupied Conor until he reached the hall. He summoned Médon and sent him to speak to the stable master and tell him to bring any Bréifne women with infant children into the stable for the night where they would be more comfortable. Then he dismissed the matter from his mind and moved to his place at the head of the board.

'So now?' asked Fergal, sidling up to lean on the table. 'What do you think of your man—this Bréifne lord?'

'An ill-mannered pig, to be sure,' replied Conor. 'But not worth a second thought. He'll be gone tomorrow.'

Fergal glanced at Donal who stood a little way off, a bemused expression on his broad face. 'Aye, so we hope,' murmured Fergal.

That hope died a swift death. The refugees did not depart the next morning. They were there when Conor and the warriors went out to take up their training in the lower field, and they were still there when the warriors returned. Nor, as the sun slanted toward sunset, did they show any sign of moving on. Night came and went, and the next day as well. Two days passed and the evening of the third day found them still idling in the yard.

Conor was standing on the narrow platform that ran along the front of the Warriors' House when the stable master approached. A short, flat-faced man with broad shoulders, a barrel chest, and bowed legs, he wasted not a moment on pleasantries, saying, 'They are still here.'

'Aye,' agreed Conor, eyeing the mass of people in the yard, 'so I see.'

'They can't stay.' He huffed, waving an arm in the direction of the refugees. 'They have to go.'

'Is there something you think I can do to move them along? If you know of anything, tell me, and I will do it this instant.'

'I want my stable returned.'

'Why? Where has it gone?'

'Those people . . .' He flung his arm at the displaced Bréifne. 'Those people have taken it. There's no room for my horses—it's all brats snivelling and mewling! There's women hanging clothes on my stall rails and babies sleeping in my feed troughs.'

'Have you spoken to anyone about it?'

'I am speaking to *you!*'

'Aye, so you are,' said Conor, 'but I don't—'

'Do something!' With that, the stable master turned and stormed off, calling down black thunder on anyone who crossed his path.

Unwilling to see the horse master upset any further, Conor decided to visit the King's House and take up the matter with the queen. Upon requesting an audience, he was informed by one of the queen's handmaids that Lady Sceana was not in residence. 'No?' he said, and asked where she could be found.

'That I cannot tell you,' replied the maiden.

Conor regarded the slim, fair-haired young woman. 'Breatha, isn't it? I must speak to the queen as soon as may be.'

'Aye, I know, but she went away with Lord Vainche and did not tell me where they might be going.'

'Went away?'

'Aye,' replied Breatha, 'I think I might have heard they were going down to the stream.'

'The stream,' repeated Conor. 'The stream where we wash—is that the one you mean?'

'I think so, sir. On foot they were.' She gave him a wan smile. 'That's all I know.'

Conor thanked the serving maid and turned to regard the flock of refugees. Some were already kindling fires for the evening meal, and others were sitting with their kinsmen or reclining in their cloaks. No one appeared to be getting ready to leave anytime soon. In fact, they appeared quite content and comfortable.

Conor delivered himself of a heavy sigh and crossed the yard, searching among the clusters of Bréifne for the red-haired warrior who had accompanied his lord on their arrival. He found the man with his wife and a young boy sitting in the shade of the storehouse nearest the gate. The fellow saw Conor approaching and rose quickly and came to meet him. 'I give you good greeting, my lord battlechief,' he said graciously. 'I commend you for the generous hospitality you and your queen have shown our people.'

'Touching that, our hospitality, generous or otherwise, has a limit. It has been three days. I thought your lord said you were staying but one night before moving on.'

'That is so,' confirmed the man, still smiling. 'But, as you see, we are still here.'

'I do see that. I want to know why.'

'Ach,' said the man with a shrug, 'that I cannot tell you. We have been given no command.'

'Nothing? No word at all?'

The fellow shook his head. 'My lord said only that the welcome here was good and better than he hoped.'

'I do not wonder.' A flush of frustration set Conor's ruddy birthmark tingling. He thanked the fellow and moved off, heading for the gate where he asked Dornach, one of the young Cruithne, who was on duty, when the queen and her guest had departed and whether he knew when they planned to return.

'They left around midday, I think it was,' replied the guard. 'I was up on the walk and did not speak to them. Maybe Laoire can tell you more, he was on the gate at the time.'

Conor was about to shout up to the walkway to ask Laoire, the other guard, when he heard voices out on the ramp leading up to the ráth. Stepping through the gate, he saw three people just then starting the climb: Lady Sceana and Lord Vainche on foot, and a dour, big-faced, thickset man on a stocky brown horse following along behind. All three were talking loudly and with some excitement.

Conor took one look at the light, mincing gait of the queen and the glowing expression on her face and he felt the ground shift under his feet. Clearly, something had happened and he knew in his gut and from the dull throb of the birthmark on his face that whatever it was that caused Lady Sceana's buoyant steps did not bode well for Conor mac Ardan.

He watched the three, resentment and misgiving warring within him: dislike of the louche and handsome stranger, distrust of the grim-looking stranger on the horse, and apprehension for the queen. As they came nearer, the queen saw him and lifted her hand to beckon him to her.

With slow, measured steps he walked down the long ramp to meet her. 'Lady Sceana,' he said, touching the back of his hand to his forehead, 'I hope you've enjoyed a pleasant day.'

'Indeed!' she gushed, and reached for Vainche's hand. He raised it and kissed it, sending a flood of revulsion and loathing through Conor and making his birthmark itch and throb. Had he a blade in his hand just then— or even a stout stick—he would have beaten the Bréifne upstart for his intolerable presumption. 'You have not been waiting for me long, I trust.'

'Nay, lady, only a moment or two.' He glanced from her to Vainche and could have sworn he saw a smirk playing on the lord's lips. Conor, his ruby birthmark kindling with the fire of anger, forced himself to remain calm. 'It is only that some of your people are asking how much longer our visitors will be with us. It was voiced about that they would be leaving two days ago.'

'There has been a change of plans,' Sceana said lightly. 'They will not be leaving at all.'

Vainche squeezed her hand and murmured, 'You are too kind. Your liberality is surpassed only by your beauty.'

Ignoring him, Conor said, 'They are to stay with us? All of them?'

'Indeed, I have asked Lord Vainche and his people to remain with us. They will make their home among us.' She turned adoring eyes on the darkly handsome lord. Conor could hardly believe the alteration in her character and demeanour. She seemed almost giddy.

'And has their lord given any thought where they might live? The court-yard is hardly suitable, and the horse master would have his stables back.'

'Lord Vainche will settle his people on Brigantes lands.' Glancing at Conor's expression, she said, 'I see my decision catches you unawares. But, if you will consider, it is surely for the best. You said yourself that the dis-placed more than earn their keep in the work they do and the skills they bring.'

'You are so very wise, my lady,' sighed Vainche.

'What is more,' continued the queen, 'twenty warriors come with him. We will double our warband at a single stroke.'

'Maybe so,' Conor allowed grudgingly, 'then again, maybe not. We know nothing of these twenty warriors save that they fled the field with their king rather than fight for their tribe and home. That does little to recommend them to me.'

'Who is this that dares impugn the skill and integrity of the Bréifne warhost?' demanded the hard-faced visitor from the back of his horse. His voice was rough as his mien and his hooded eyes smouldered with anger. 'Say the word, my lord, and this insolent milksop will regret he ever opened his mouth in your presence.'

Conor regarded the excitable fellow impassively. 'You take offense at what seems an obvious fact. Why is that?' Before the man could answer, he said, 'Could it be that I have thrust my finger in a raw and festering wound?'

Glaring fire, the blunt warrior threw his leg over his mount's withers and slid to the ground. He marched toward Conor and came within four paces before his lord put out a hand to restrain him. 'Calm yourself, Gioll,' said the king lightly. 'I am certain our friend's churlish behaviour is a result of ignorance rather than intention.'

Conor gave him a nod and an icy smile. 'I stand ready to receive what-ever wisdom you are able to impart.' Turning his eyes to the lumbering hulk called Gioll, he said, 'Enlighten me if you can.'

The tension between the two mounted and Lady Sceana, clearly uncomfortable, interceded, saying, 'It is not fitting to stand here quarrelling. I am certain all can be explained without rancour over a welcome cup.'

Lord Vainche agreed. 'A welcome cup is what is needed here,' he said expansively. 'My man Gioll has travelled far today and is in need of refreshment. Let us all sit down and hear his news together.'

The four entered the ráth and made their way to the guesthouse; passing through and among the Bréifne tribesmen encamped there. As they progressed, several of the refugees stopped their lord to speak to him and Conor seized the opportunity to pull the queen aside.

'They are to remain here?' whispered Conor, indicating the swarm of people around them. 'Truly?'

'Within the borders of our realm,' answered Sceana.

'What does that mean?'

The queen did not meet his eye. 'A place will be found for them—a holding or settlement, as I say. In time, perhaps, they will build a ráth for themselves. Other tribes have done the same.'

'That is true, lady,' affirmed Conor. 'But—'

'But what?' She turned on him. 'I sense your disapproval. There is no need to deny it.'

'I would be a poor advisor if I did not give you benefit of my considered opinion,' Conor countered. 'And just now, I am struggling to make sense of what you have told me.'

'I see no problem here.'

'No? Then let us ask ourselves what manner of king flees his kingdom, leaving his warband behind? Likewise, what chief of battle would abandon his warriors, leaving them to fend for themselves on the road? This troubles me greatly and it should at least concern you, Lady Sceana.'

'It does not,' she sniffed, 'because I believe the explanation is soon forthcoming and will prove entirely satisfactory.'

With that, she left him and hurried off to the King's House to arrange refreshment for her guests. Conor stared dully at Vainche and Gioll, his birthmark burning red hot on his cheek. There was much about the Bréifne lord and his battlechief he did not trust, and it rankled and gnawed at him like the persistent ache of a rotten tooth. Nevertheless, he entered the lodge when summoned and sat down with the queen and her guests as her ladies brought in food and drink.

When Sceana was seated at the low table, she began by saying, 'I was telling Conor that we have agreed that you and your people will have a settlement within Brigantes borders—to the south, perhaps. I believe there are suitable lands thereabouts.'

'That is so,' replied Vainche airily. 'It makes perfect sense. I believe the southern border requires protection in these difficult days. Those lands are closest to the Scálda and therefore require a powerful presence to deter raiding. The Bréifne warhost will do that and more.'

Lady Sceana smiled with approval. 'Is that not good news, Conor?'

'The Bréifne warriors would do this for our borders,' observed Conor, 'yet this powerful presence of theirs could not prevent the Scálda overrunning their own lands.'

'What do you mean by that?' demanded Gioll, slamming the flat of his hand on the table. 'I demand an answer!'

'Make of it what you will,' replied Conor evenly.

'There will be peace at my table and beneath my roof, or you will leave,' the queen announced, but looked at Conor as she spoke.

'Gioll is my warleader and battlechief,' offered Vainche by way of an explanation. 'And if he says that the southern borders will be better protected than they are now, then you can best believe him.'

Conor bristled at the abrupt dismissal of his own considerable, and largely successful, efforts to maintain the southern boundaries of Brigantes territory that bordered the lands the Scálda stole. The region fronting the deadlands was a perpetual worry, constantly under pressure from enemy harassment. Most of the skirmishes Conor led that summer arose from and took place somewhere along that contentious line.

'We were attacked by sea,' said Gioll the battlechief. 'Fifty ships of rabid Scálda scum if one. Every dún and ráth came under assault. We fought them off, held out as long as we could—long enough for our king to escape with any and all who could flee.'

'And yet you lived to tell the tale,' Conor said. 'How very fortunate.'

The overbearing Bréifne warleader leaned on the table and stabbed a stubby finger at Conor's chest. 'I don't like being called a liar, and I don't like you.'

'There is a ready remedy for that,' replied Conor. 'Leaving that aside, where is your vaunted warband, eh? These twenty warriors of your loud boast, where are they?'

'I rode ahead,' sniffed Gioll, 'to render an account of the final battle to our lord. The warband is a day's march away, I reckon.'

'Ach, well, now that you have rendered your account, I expect you will want to return to your warriors in all haste. They will be yearning for your powerful presence.'

Gioll's scowl hardened; showing a belated wisdom, he shut his mouth and said no more. But Conor had heard enough. 'I will leave you all to your well-earned refreshment,' he said, glancing at Vainche. 'The duties of a battlechief multiply if left too long unattended.' To Gioll, he said, 'I have enjoyed our little talk. In truth, I feel more enlightened than ever.'

16

'Your behaviour this night past was disgraceful!' fumed Lady Sceana. 'Disgraceful and appalling . . . ,' she said, pausing, searching for words, 'shameful and offensive! I was forced to apologise in order to win back their goodwill.'

'I heartily wish you had not done that, my lady,' Conor retorted. 'Why should you be required to win favour of someone who has done nothing but plunder your generosity since he and his beggar band arrived? And now he and his rabble have seized territory within your own lands. . . .' He shook his head in dismay, then tried a different approach. 'These people depend on your kindness for sustenance and survival—it is *they* who should be apologising to *you* for abusing your goodwill with their incessant demands.'

'The queen must uphold the honour of her tribe.'

'The honour of your tribe was never at risk, my queen. Only the insufferable vanity of these two preening magpies—men who are strangers to us. I tell you there was no need for any apology.'

'No need?' She arched a shapely eyebrow. 'No need? You as much as called them both liars.'

'That word never passed *my* lips—though Gioll was quick to reach for it. In my experience, it is the liar himself who first points the finger at others.'

'You insulted them beneath my roof, at my board,' insisted Sceana. 'You slighted and belittled them in my very presence. You are my champion, and I expect your support. I do *not* expect you to contradict me in front of esteemed guests.'

'I accept that, but I am also your chief of battle and your foremost advisor. I asked a few questions and made a few observations—as any royal advisor should do when seeking the measure of anyone who comes begging royal gifts and favours. If these two felt belittled by anything I said, it is because they hold themselves too grand. It hurts to prick a boil, aye, but afterward a body feels all the better for it.'

Sceana's pretty face bunched into an ugly glower. She had called Conor to her house to explain his quarrelsome attitude toward Lord Vainche and Gioll, but instead of contrition, she met resistance.

'You will apologise to them.'

'To apologise to a liar is to accept his lies. I said it before and I say it again, my queen—it is they who should be apologising to you, and to all of us, for their grasping pretention and arrogance. And for their continued drain on our supplies and, aye, our goodwill.'

Lowering her voice, the queen repeated, 'You will apologise and seek pardon for your discourtesy.'

'With all respect, my lady, I will not,' swore Conor. 'Indeed, I cannot— for I have done nothing wrong.'

'Then you make of *me* a liar because I told them that you would.'

Conor felt his blood warm and his birthmark begin to prickle with a sudden heat. 'That you should never have done,' he said bluntly. 'It does you no credit and will only work to your harm.'

Sceana stared at him for a long moment, then abruptly turned her back on him. 'You speak above your place if you think to upbraid me,' she said, her voice cold and hard. 'You will abide my decision, and apologise, or you will depart.'

'Think what you are saying,' Conor replied. 'You make this a point of honour when there is none to be gained—only honour squandered and lost. Those men seek only to use you and exploit your kindness for their own ends. A true friend would never do that. Lord Vainche pours empty words into your ear and spins shining promises out of thin air, but he has eyes only for your throne.'

Sceana turned on him with fire in her eyes. 'It is jealousy I hear speaking. And I thought you held yourself above that.'

'It is not jealousy. It is the truth. Vainche said they would stay but one night, but he gave no such order to his people. In fact, he came here planning to take as much as he could lay hands to and he has succeeded beyond any hope or expectation.'

'That is unworthy of you.'

'My lady, I accept that these are hard words and, believe me, I take no pleasure in saying them. But if you will not believe me, you have only to speak to his tribesmen. They will tell you, as they told me, that their lord gave no command to move on and, indeed, has still not done so. For all they know, they are to reside in our yard.'

'You blame them for trying to make the best of their sorry lot? What of the other clans and tribes we have welcomed? Do you begrudge them, too?' the queen countered. 'In any event, I asked them to stay.'

'Aye, you did. What did his lordship promise you to secure that invitation, eh?'

Sceana's eyes blazed, but she shut her mouth and turned away again.

A seething silence claimed the room.

Conor was first to speak. 'It was his promise to rebuild the warband with his twenty warriors and make the Brigantes great in Eirlandia once more,' he said gently. 'That was his promise, was it not?' The question hung unanswered. When the queen did not reply, he said, 'But where is this great and powerful band of warriors of which he boasts? Where is the mighty Bréifne warhost? I think when they arrive—if ever they *do* appear—they will be half that number of poorly trained and ill-equipped farmers and there will be some sad excuse given to explain the lack.'

'That is shameful, Conor mac Ardan. You speak of things you cannot possibly know.'

'I speak as your friend and true advisor, my queen. If the head of your ardféne cannot tell you the truth, then we are lost.'

'Anyone who speaks the way you do—shaming me, scorning me, defying me—is no friend of mine.'

'Lady, a friend would not allow you to be mistreated,' he said. 'I refuse to stand aside and watch you being molested by those sly rogues.'

'There! You see? You despise them and it obscures your judgement. Such counsel as you give is worthless to me. I will hear it no longer.' She turned back to confront him, and said, 'You will apologise at once. I command you.'

'And if I will not?' Conor held her gaze with his, refusing to give in to this unreasonable demand.

'Then I will have no further need of your service,' she said. 'For such service as you would render is useless.'

Again, Conor felt the ground shift beneath his feet. *How can things have changed so radically and so quickly in so short a time?* he wondered. *How is it possible?*

'You are telling me my skill and experience is of no further use to you,' he intoned in dull disbelief. 'Who will train up your warriors? Who will lead them in battle?'

'Gioll is Lord Vainche's battlechief and he will be mine. Lord Vainche has already suggested this very thing and I mean to accept his offer.'

'Already suggested it.' The words turned to ashes in Conor's mouth as the extent of their grasping reach became abundantly clear. The sudden realisation stole the warm breath from his lungs. *Already suggested . . . He had been right about them, but he had failed to reckon the sheer magnitude of the greed and ambition he had sensed, less yet the speed and audacity with which it could be employed.*

'Nothing to say now?' Sceana lifted her head in defiant challenge, and Conor understood that in the contest for the queen's affections—or even her rational mind—he had lost. He could but quit the field with whatever dignity he still possessed.

Finally, he mastered his voice enough to say, 'I will not remain in the same ráth where Lord Vainche is welcome. I will gather my belongings and go. I expect Fergal and Donal will go with me.'

'That is your decision,' replied the queen, uncertainty edging into her tone for the first time.

Conor squared his shoulders and gave her a curt bow, then turned on his heel and strode from the room. Once outside, he marched across the yard to the hall through the midst of the Bréifne refugees. From the corner of his eye, he saw Vainche and his red-haired kinsman, and the brute Gioll watching him, their heads together and, in that instant, understood that his eviction from the ráth had been their plan from the beginning. The knowledge made his gut squirm with indignation and his birthmark throb, but he did not allow them the satisfaction of seeing him weep or rage against his fate.

One day, he thought, *your fortunes will be in my hands and then we will see who weeps and rages. We will see that and all Eirlandia will bear witness. . . .*

Stopping briefly at the hall, he enquired where Fergal and Donal could be found, and was told that if he hurried he might still find them in the horse yard behind the stables where they were preparing to ride with the hunters. Picking up his cloak and sparán, and the kidskin bag containing his faéry clothes, he removed his weapons from the wall and stormed off to the horse yard where he told one of the grooms to prepare Búrach to travel. He hurried to the stable where Fergal and Donal were just then leading their horses into the enclosure. Galart was with them; the three were taking their mounts for an exercise run, but they had their spears with them in case they came across any game.

'Conor! Come join us,' called Galart.

'That will not be possible today,' he replied.

'You cannot be implying that your duties are so heavily taxing of your time that you cannot spare a swift ride in the hunting runs,' said Fergal. 'Your Búrach will not thank you for neglecting him.'

Donal, seeing the cast of Conor's mouth and the set of his jaw, said, 'I think our battlechief will ride, but not to the hunt. What has happened, brother?'

Conor did not know where to begin to explain, so he simply said, 'Go to the hall and gather your belongings. We are leaving Aintrén.'

Fergal glanced at Donal, who merely observed, 'So, it has come to this.'

'Come to what?' demanded Fergal. 'What has happened?'

'Get your things,' said Conor simply. 'Be quick about it.'

Casting sideways glances at one another, Donal and Fergal led their horses away. Galart, stunned, gaped in disbelief and watched them go. The groomsman brought Conor's grey stallion just then, haltered and with a clean horsecloth, and ready to ride. Conor thanked him, replaced Pelydr in the holder under the cloth, and slid Eirian into his belt. Then, gathering up the reins, he moved on to the Warriors' House.

'What about Médon?' asked Galart, hurrying after him. 'You should talk to him before you go.'

'Médon is riding the border with the scouts. He won't return until to-morrow morning and I'll not wait.'

'What should I tell him?'

'Tell him to guard his queen and see to her defence. With those two wolves in the sheepfold, she will be in need of a stout friend and defender.'

'What about the rest of us—your warband?' asked the young warrior.

'There is to be a new battlechief here now,' Conor told him. Raising his hands to his throat, he gently prized apart the ends of the slender silver torc, slipped it from around his neck, and handed it to the young warrior, saying,

'Gioll will soon take up the reins of authority if he has not done so already.' He started leading the stallion away.

Galart stared at the torc in his hands for a moment, then called after Conor. 'And you, my lord? Where will you go?'

'I am not your lord, Galart. I think Vainche is lord here now—or very soon will be. As for me'—he raised a hand in parting—'you need have no thought for me. A ready spear is always in demand now that the Scálda have stirred themselves to finish the destruction of Eirlandia. One way or another—whether here or somewhere else—I will do what I can to prevent that.'

Conor paused outside the Warriors' House to wait for Fergal and Donal to emerge, and Galart quickly rejoined him. 'It is not right that you should be cast out like this.'

'Ach, now, hear me. I am not cast out. I leave of my own accord.' He turned and put a hand on the young warrior's shoulder. 'Tell Médon and the rest of the warband that I wish them well and should we ever join one another on the battle line, I will be honoured to fight alongside them once again.'

Galart swallowed hard, but accepted Conor's charge. After a moment, the two Darini appeared; Conor swung himself up onto Búrach's back and bade Galart farewell. Fergal and Donal did likewise and the three rode from Aintrén without looking back.

Rhiannon

Even before the ship bearing our Dé Danann friends had disappeared from sight, I believe the change had begun. Though I cannot say what it was about that parting, I do know that it cast my father into a thoughtful, melancholy mood. On the morning of their departure, I stood with the king and watched the swift boat glide out across the bay; we waved our friends away and, even then, I sensed an alteration in my father's heart. 'Brave men,' Gwydion said, his hand raised in farewell.

That was all he said, but I heard in those two little words the seeds of doubt that would soon begin to sprout and grow. What is it that our bards say?

> Uncertainty, *the mother of Doubt*
> Doubt, *the mother of Reservation*
> Reservation, *the mother of Misgiving*
> Misgiving, *the mother of Unrest*
> Unrest, *the mother of Conflict*

Truly, that is how it was with my father. As the autumn passed into winter, I watched as the doubt worked away in the king's mind. Day by day, I watched him try to assuage his mounting unrest. I was not the only one to see it; my mother, the queen, observed his every mood and temper.

'Your father is distracted,' she declared one night as we walked to our bedchambers.

'He does appear somewhat preoccupied,' I replied. 'Perhaps he misses our

Dé Danann friends. He and Conor became very good friends—and Fergal and Donal as well. Indeed, I miss them, too.'

Arianrhod was shaking her head before I finished. 'It is more than that,' she told me. 'I know it.'

'What is it that troubles him, do you think?'

'His heart, of course. It is in conflict with his head.'

'In what way, Mother?' I asked. Though I was fairly certain I knew the reason, I wanted to hear her speak it aloud.

'It is obvious, is it not? It is because he has made a decision that will not rest,' the queen replied. 'He is still ploughing a field already twice ploughed.' She glanced at me. 'Did you know that he and Conor met at length before the Dé Danann left us. There was a disagreement.'

I knew, of course, but wanted to hear what she made of the matter. 'I thought they parted as friends,' I pointed out.

'They did—as friends who have quarrelled.'

'Have you spoken to the king about his disquiet?'

She gave me a knowing smile. 'This, I think, is one of those times when we must allow the fruit to ripen of its own accord, or it will not ripen at all.'

'Wise words, Mother,' I told her. Even so, I resolved then and there that, if my mother the queen would not speak to the king directly, then I would. I bided my time and chose my opportunity carefully. It was late one evening, after we had listened to one of our bards sing 'The Treasures of Annwfyn': a lovely song in its way, but also disturbing—at least on this particular night— for it relates the coming of a king who rises during an age of great upheaval to defeat a cruel oppressor and gains the treasures of the Otherworld for his people. As we left the hearth, I sensed my chance had come.

'An odd tale that,' I said. 'I am surprised you allow it to be sung anymore.'

'Why is that, my heart? It has long been a favourite of my court. Why do you call it odd?'

'It is a tale that celebrates and glories in warfare, is it not?' I replied. 'I think it odd that a king who holds combat in such contempt should revel in a song that extolls the virtues of war.'

Gwydion glanced at me and frowned. 'Truly? Is that what you think? If so, you misunderstand the song entirely. It is not about the glory of war, much less extolling any virtue armed strife may possess. The tale is about the necessity of defending the life and well-being of your people against a wicked and rapacious oppressor.'

'Necessity?' I challenged. 'Surely not, Father. Pwyll, the Righteous Prince, was never forced to take up arms. He could have simply made peace with his enemy. There was no need to fight at all—you have said as much yourself.'

He stopped walking and stared at me. 'When did I ever say such a thing?'

I stopped and turned to him. 'That is what you told Conor when he asked for your aid against the Scálda. So, then, it seems to me that our friend is just like Pwyll. Conor is trying to rise to the defence of his people against a wicked and rapacious oppressor. To do that he must take up arms and fight.'

'Armed conflict is not our way anymore.'

'Is it not? It was Pwyll's way—in this song you like so much.'

The king shook his head. 'You are too young to remember the terrible wars we fought against the Aes-sídhe of Albion. When those wars ended, we vowed never to fight again.'

'And yet you gave our Dé Danann friends charmed weapons with which to fight their hopeless battle,' I pointed out. 'This, dear Father, is the very thing I have been meaning to ask you—why *did* you give such splendid weapons to our friends if you did not intend for them to be used?'

'I merely wanted to . . .' he began, then gave up the effort to explain. 'You wouldn't understand.'

'You have said it there, my king. I do *not* understand. That is why I am asking. Of all the things you might have given them . . . what was in your mind to bestow a gift of weapons when you profess to oppose their use?'

He stared at me for a long moment and, in a chastened voice, replied, 'I see.'

I lay a hand gently on his arm. 'What do you see, Father?'

'I see that I have been a fool.' He sighed and looked away. 'Such a fool.'

Linking my arm through his, I resumed our walk down the long corridor—as if toward the decision I knew he wanted to make. 'Only a little foolish, perhaps,' I granted lightly. 'But only a genuine fool persists in his folly.'

He regarded me sharply. 'You knew this all along, yet you said nothing.'

'I know only that making peace with the Scálda—whatever that may mean—will not save Eirlandia. Conor and his people need help if any of us are to survive, and we are able to give that help.'

Gwydion considered this a moment. 'There are those among us who would not support such a venture. Though it pains me to say it, the Tylwyth Teg are not as strong as once we were, nor as numerous.'

'But if we allied with the Aes-sídhe both those deficits would be addressed at a stroke,' I replied. 'Come, Father, you cannot in good conscience counsel the Dé Danann to make peace with the Scálda if you refuse to make peace with King Lenos and the Kerionid.'

My father scoffed at the notion. 'Do you think I haven't tried that very thing? Lenos will not have it. Too much bad blood lies between us and the Aes-sídhe for any accord to flourish.'

'You may be right,' I granted, 'yet it may be that since King Lenos has suffered personally at the hand of Balor Evil Eye, he might finally be willing to reconcile with you in order to vanquish a common enemy. That would have an appeal for him, I should think.'

For the second time my father stopped walking, pulled his arm from mine, and stared at me. 'What manner of creature have I raised that you school me like this?'

I offered him a smile and put my arms around him. 'Only a daughter who loves you and has your best interest at heart.' I looked up into his handsome face. 'Will you do it?'

'I cannot promise so much.'

'But you will think about what I've said?'

'I will think about it,' he said, 'and I will do more. I will send to Eilean Céo to request an audience with King Lenos and his advisors—that much I can do.' He smiled. 'Would that suffice to make you happy?'

'It is not for *my* happiness, Father, but for the greater good. No one in the Land of the Everliving will be safe until we rid this worlds-realm of the Scálda curse.'

17

'I have just spent a wet night on a hard rock with nothing but a scrap of dry bread to ease my hunger and only thin water to relieve my thirst,' intoned Fergal as the three exiles sat warming themselves by their fuggy little fire and waiting for the mist and rain to clear so they could continue their journey. 'The least you can do,' he continued, 'is tell me why I did this.'

After leaving Aintrén the day before, they had headed west toward Coriondi territory, riding long and stopping for the night beside a stream at the edge of an expansive stand of white oak and ash. During the night the weather had changed; blustery wind streamed cold and wet out of the north, sharpening the desolation they all felt on waking.

'What more is there to say?' Conor poked the fitful flames with a damp twig. 'To remain with the Brigantes would be to accept the authority of that two-headed toad, Lord Vainche, and his toad-licking Gioll.' He snapped the twig as if disposing of a rival and tossed it into the fire. 'You, my long-suffering brother, may be able to endure such painful humiliation, but I am made of finer stuff. I do believe it would kill me.'

'This rain and the cold north wind will kill you the quicker,' Fergal grumped.

Donal chuckled and Fergal favoured him with a warning glance.

'Aye, well, far be it from me to force anyone to come with me. You are free to return to Aintrén any time you please,' Conor told him. 'In fact, you *should* go. I think Gioll likes you. Aye, he told me he considered you a fine figure of a fella.'

'Nay, nay,' Fergal shivered at the thought and pulled his cloak more tightly around him. 'It is too far to ride on a day like this, and we have this pleasant fire here.'

'Be that as it may, we cannot stay here forever,' Donal pointed out. 'Perhaps we should go back to Dúnaird and see if Ardan will speak to us. With all that has happened, I am certain he would be willing to hear us out.'

'Not if Liam had anything to say about it,' Fergal replied. 'I will not be crawling on my knees to get back what should never have been taken from me in the first place.'

Conor looked to his friends. 'I am sorry,' he said. 'You are paying a price for my poor judgement. Do it again and I would have told Mádoc to sell his mad scheme to some other butter-brained gull. Nothing but hardship has come from it.'

'Not so,' countered Donal. 'We have gained knowledge of the Scálda and the fact that it came at a high cost only proves how valuable it is.'

Conor gave a mirthless chuckle at the notion, and said, 'I doubt Aoife would agree with you—she has suffered, too.' He gazed into the spluttering flames of their pitiful little campfire. The memory of her tear-stained face when he told her he had been exiled came before him once more and the hopelessness of that parting pierced him through and through. In that moment, he wanted nothing more than to take her in his arms and make everything right again. The utter impossibility of that happening filled him with remorse and a longing akin to grief. Were they fated to remain apart forever? He murmured to himself, 'In her own way, she has suffered—and others as well.'

At mention of Aoife, a strained silence descended upon the unhappy group. It was endured for a time, but when the tension stretched to the breaking point, Fergal blurted out, 'Look at us here now—three men of woeful countenance, alone and friendless. What is that, eh? Cheer up! Let us go to Lord Cahir as we decided—and when we reach Dún Cruach, he will give us all welcome cup and a seat at his board. Aye, and he will also have a cracking great blaze in the hearth where we can dry our sodden carcasses.'

'And will he send a welcoming party to greet us and lead us to his ráth?' asked Donal.

'A grand notion, to be sure,' Fergal granted. 'But I will settle for a dry corner with a cup in my hand.' He glanced up at Donal, whose eyes were raised beyond the fire to the misty hills beyond. 'Why do you ask such a thing, brother?'

'Because we will be greeting just such a party very soon.' Donal nodded to the empty hills.

Both Fergal and Conor turned their gaze to where Donal indicated and at first saw nothing. Then, even as they looked, the head and shoulders of a rider appeared over the top of the hill. Another head showed itself, followed by a third and, by the time the head of the first horse became fully visible, the head and torsos of three more riders had joined the first. In all, five riders paused on the hilltop to search the broad plain and woodland below. Upon seeing the smoke from the fire, they resumed their ride, heading straightaway for the outcasts' camp.

'What do you think, Conor?' asked Fergal. 'Is it a fight they're after?' Fergal stooped and retrieved his spear and shield, then turned to face the oncoming riders.

'Sit down and try to stay pleasant,' advised Conor. 'We don't want to give them an excuse to quarrel. All the same, keep your weapons close to hand.'

'It is Médon,' intoned Donal in an odd, low voice. 'And Galart is with him.'

'How do you know this?' asked Fergal, still gazing into the hazy distance. 'I cannot make out any—'

'He's right!' said Conor, jumping up and cupping his palms to his eyes. 'It *is* Médon and Galart . . . and who is that with them . . . ?'

'It is Aedd and Calbhan—' Donal replied. 'And Dearg.'

'And Dearg!' cried Conor. 'So it is. The five of them. What can they be wanting?'

'They have come to beg us to return, maybe,' suggested Fergal.

Leaving the fire ring, Conor strode out to meet the riders. Fergal and Donal took up their spears and moved out from under the shelter of the trees to see how Conor was received. The five Brigantes, led by Médon, reined up in a line before them. As soon as his mount halted, Médon slid down and strode directly toward Conor, drawing his sword as he came.

'Bastard!' growled Fergal. He lowered his spear and started forward.

Donal snagged him by the cloak and pulled him back. 'Wait,' he said, 'and watch.'

Médon stopped a few paces before Conor, who, unarmed, stood waiting. The two spoke for a moment, but Fergal and Donal were too far away to hear what was said. Fergal, losing patience, pulled away and hurried out to stand beside Conor; Donal trailed a step behind. Fergal had crossed half the distance when Médon suddenly swung his blade sideways. He then dropped to his knees and, holding the blade across his palms, offered it up to Conor.

As Fergal and Donal took their places beside Conor, the four other Brigantes warriors climbed down from their mounts and arranged themselves in a row behind Médon. They likewise drew their swords and, sinking to their knees, offered up their naked blades.

'What is this?' said Fergal. 'What goes here?'

'Brothers,' replied Conor with a wide and handsome grin. 'These good warriors have come to join our warband.'

'We have no warband,' Fergal remarked, taking in the five offered blades. 'That is to say we had none the last time I looked.'

'We have one now,' Conor told him. 'Here they are!'

Turning, he spread his arms over the five young warriors and, in a solemn voice declared, 'You have offered your blades and with them your lives to my service. I accept your service and I accept you, laying only one condition—that you vow on your honour as a warrior in Eirlandia to uphold each of your brothers through all things, aye, even though it should mean your death.'

He paused a moment to allow those words to be understood, then said, 'Do you make this vow?'

'I do,' replied Médon. 'On my life and honour, I make this vow and that right readily.' His words were echoed by each of the other four men in turn: Galart, Aedd, Dearg, and Calbhan.

'Then get you up on your feet,' Conor told them. 'We are all swordbrothers from this day on.'

The five rose and, somewhat sheepishly, looked at one another and at Conor. Clearly, having done what they came to do, they had no other plan or thought beyond the moment and now that it had passed they no longer knew what to do with themselves. Conor, realising they must have departed Aintrén in the middle of the night, offered the bare hospitality of his camp, 'You have ridden far and the day grows no fairer for all that. Come, rest, and warm yourselves by the fire and we will think what to do next.'

'What are we going to feed them?' whispered Donal.

One of the newcomers, Dearg, a lean, wiry man of pale, milk-white, lightly freckled skin and fiercely red hair, overheard and spoke up. 'We have brought food with us. If you will permit me, I will make us all a meal to break our fast.'

'A man after my own heart,' said Fergal. 'So he is.'

Gathering the reins of their mounts, the five walked with Conor to the crude little camp at the edge of the forest. They had indeed come prepared to stay, bringing with them not only full water skins and bulging sparáns, but also fleeces for sleeping, cloth bags full of oats and other supplies, and, among other things, an iron pot for cooking. The new arrivals quickly unburdened the horses; then, while Dearg occupied himself with the food, Aedd and Calbhan made a picket line beneath the shelter of a spreading oak and tethered their horses beside the others, then set about rubbing down their wet coats and watering them.

Meanwhile, Médon and Galart sat down with Conor, Donal, and Fergal to discuss what had provoked their decision to leave the Brigantes warhost. 'Scarce two days have passed,' Conor said. 'What can have happened in the small space that you should embrace exile from your tribe?'

'We are not exiled,' Galart corrected, 'nor could we stay. The gate was not yet closed on your leaving when the rot began. As soon as Médon and his battle group returned from riding the border, Lord Vainche summoned us all to the yard to address us. He told us that he was to be warleader now, and that his man, Gioll, would be his battlechief.'

'Much as I expected,' Conor observed. 'The two of them had already reached that agreement with the queen before we left. Go on—what happened next?'

'Such a turn did not sit well with some of us, as you can imagine. Only a few knew you were gone, most did not. But Lord Vainche said that it was for the best that he took up the slack reins of authority and discipline—as he said—because things had grown too lax and lazy since Brecan's sad demise.'

Aedd and Calbhan, who had been taking care of the horses, joined the discussion. 'Vainche told us that under his rule the Brigantes and Bréifne would become a great warhost once more,' said Aedd.

'He said he would make of us warriors to be feared in all of Eirlandia,' Calbhan added.

'How ambitious of him,' scoffed Fergal. 'But is it Eirlandia we are trying to frighten now? Here was I thinking it was the vile Scálda we were meant to put the fear on.'

'Aye, and there was very much more like that,' Médon said. 'It was when that bloated braggart Gioll called us to begin our training—that was when the day slid into the midden heap.'

'Our new battlechief paired us off so we could spar and show him what manner of fighting we practiced,' said Aedd. 'He made us scuffle while he walked around yelling commands.'

'Nothing wrong with that,' Fergal observed. 'I might have done the same on any given day.'

'Ach, aye, so you would. But I think *you* would be having the good sense not to carp and complain of every last thrust and jab before you knew us better. Gioll said we held our weapons poorly, and that our feet were not placed correctly, and that our shield work was sloppy, and our blade work careless—and more like that.'

'He said we were the worst warriors he'd ever had the misfortune to lay eyes on,' put in Aedd. 'He raved and raged at everything we did.'

Galart joined in. 'He declared it was a wonder we were not all dead already. And this in front of our people in the yard. They watched the whole thing.'

'Bad as that was, it got worse,' said Calbhan.

There were aggrieved nods all around. Médon took up the tale once more. 'Aye, and the more he saw the angrier he grew, this Gioll. He told us he did not blame us for our poor training and lack of ability.' The young warrior raised his eyes from the fire and, looking at Conor, added, 'He said that it was a good thing Lord Vainche had dismissed you in disgrace—while there was still time to save the warband from your incompetence and stupidity.'

'Conor was not dismissed,' Donal said, 'in disgrace or otherwise. He left of his own accord and likewise Fergal and myself. It was our choice and ours alone.'

'Aye, I know it,' Médon said, 'but that is what Gioll said. And he told us we must unlearn everything you had taught us. He would teach us the proper way to fight.'

'That is when we lost all heart,' said Galart. 'He began to show us this better way of his and the more he talked and demonstrated, the more it became clear to those of us who have fought the Scálda that he did not know the first thing he was talking about.'

'Did he not?' mocked Conor. 'I am surprised.'

'Ach, well, so it seemed and most of us agreed. What Gioll showed us was how our grandfathers might have engaged an enemy, perhaps. I don't know.' Médon shrugged. 'But I came away with the strong suspicion that he had never swung a blade against a screaming Scálda on horseback.'

Dearg, who had been busy with the supplies, joined them at the fire ring with a large wooden bowl between his hands, and said, 'Aye, and if any warrior had done what Gioll said to do in a fight that sad fellow would not live to battle's end. Médon, here—what did you say, brother?'

'A most efficient way to make corpses of ourselves.'

'Aye, that was it—a most efficient way of making corpses of ourselves. That's what Vainche's man was showing us.'

'What did you do then?' asked Fergal, who was taking a wicked delight in the tale.

'After this training was finished, Gioll and Vainche retired to the hall with those few Bréifne men and a few of the warriors they liked and hoped to win to their side. The rest of us took ourselves to the Warriors' House to discuss what had happened out there in the yard. It was clear to most everyone that we could not follow this battlechief with good heart. To follow him at all would get us killed in the first clash. Something had to be done.'

'You went to the queen with your grievance?' suggested Donal.

'We tried,' said Dearg, kneading barley meal in the bowl with his hands. 'Médon and Galart and Aedd—they were chosen to go to her.'

'But she refused to hear us,' said Galart. 'She said she would not listen to any baseless complaints about Lord Vainche or his decisions. But, see now, Vainche was there with her when she said that. And he said that he expected such changes as he meant to introduce to sit ill with some who were too beholden to the old ways, but that this insolence was unseemly.'

'Nay, it was worse than that,' said Aedd. 'He told us that from now on such disloyalty would be rooted out and punished.'

Médon thrust out his chin. 'I told him that it was not disloyalty, but fear for the life and welfare of the tribe and its warband that concerned us.'

'Aye,' said Galart, 'and his high-and-mighty lordship leapt up shouting that any complaint against his rule was disloyalty in his eyes and an offense that would be met with punishment swift and stern.'

'What sort of punishment?' asked Fergal.

'He didn't say.' Dearg began to shape small lumps of dough into round, flat loaves, placing them on hot stones at the edge of the fire.

'We had no desire to discover what passed for punishment in his warped opinion,' Médon said; he poked the fire with a stick. 'We went back to the Warriors' House and told the others what had happened in the meeting. Ach, Conor, you could see the heart go out of them. The five of us decided to leave then and there and come find you. It was in our minds to ask you to return and take your place at the head of the warband again.'

'Aye,' agreed Galart. 'But if you would not come back, we came prepared to stay with you if you would have us.'

Calbhan, glancing around at his fellow Brigantes said, 'We came right gladly. That is the truth.'

'Yet, you left in the night with darkness to hide you,' Conor pointed out.

'Ach, well,' laughed Dearg. An amiable youth, he wore his red hair long and scraped back and in a tight half braid at the side of his head as if to emphasise his right to the warrior's rank. 'We are none of us as stupid as Gioll and his irksome lord make out. We thought it best to leave quietly lest they imagine riding after you an act of disloyalty. I had no wish to discover what manner of punishment they might devise.'

'Nor could we abide another day of Gioll's absurd training,' said Calbhan. 'Even Brotla knows battle better, so he does.'

'Brotla?' wondered Fergal, glancing around.

'My horse!' The dark-haired young warrior put back his head and laughed; and the mood around the fire ring, having grown sombre, began to brighten. The youngest of the group, his genial, light-hearted presence had a natural cheering effect on those around him.

Conor's fledgling warband did not move on that day, but remained camped at the forest's edge where they rested and made plans for the future. For, confidence restored, and emboldened by the spirit and conviction of his new followers, a new vision, like the sun rising after a long, cold night, slowly revealed to Conor the shape of fresh possibilities.

Of all those who sat around the fire, only Donal saw what was forming in his swordbrother's heart and mind. When the others went off to begin preparing a rough shelter for the night, he lingered behind to exchange a private word.

'We are not going to Lord Cahir,' he said. 'You have chosen a different path.'

'In truth, I believe I do,' Conor told him. 'Is it that apparent?'

'To me, perhaps,' Donal glanced over his shoulder where some of the others were cutting small branches and saplings to make a roof over their heads, 'but not to the others. Tell me, brother, what is in your mind?'

'I am thinking—it is not all planned, to be sure—but I am thinking we will become a roving warband.'

'A roving warband,' Donal intoned.

'Aye, a "fianna"—isn't that the old word?'

'Aye, I think so.'

'We will be a roving band of warriors owing no allegiance or service to any lord, and holding no king over us. We will answer to no one but ourselves alone.'

'What will you do with this roving band of warriors—this fianna of yours?' Donal asked, watching the light come up in Conor's dark eyes; in the shifting light of the campfire, the ruby-tinted birthmark that marred the side of his face seemed to glow with a fire from within.

'Our fianna will go where others cannot go, and do what others cannot do.'

Donal's eyes narrowed as he glimpsed something of the shape of Conor's design. 'Aye, and what is it that these others cannot do?'

'Seek out and kill Balor Berugderc,' Conor replied. Before Donal could begin to frame a reply to this audacious declaration, Conor continued, 'See here now, we sojourned in the deadlands before—and did great harm to the enemy.'

'Hardly that,' countered Donal.

'At the very least, we know our way around and can remain out of sight of the enemy.'

'More or less,' Donal granted. 'But our warband for all its zeal, laudable as that is, numbers only five blades—'

'Eight, including ours,' said Conor.

'Eight then—but that is eight against the entire Scálda warhost. Not the best odds a fella could ask.'

'Aye, but we do not have to defeat the entire Scálda warhost,' Conor countered, 'we only have to defeat one.'

'Balor Evil Eye.'

'Cut off the head and the creature will die, is that it?'

'Exactly,' Conor said, grinning. 'You agree with me then.'

'I did not say that,' Donal cautioned. 'If this plan of yours was a lump of bread, I would say it was not fully baked.'

'I said it was not complete in all particulars,' Conor replied.

'Fergal will hate it.'

'What will Fergal hate?' Fergal loomed up behind them just then to stand gazing down at them with his hands on his hips. 'You two are hatching something. What is it?'

'Conor has it in his mind to go and poke the bear in his cave,' said Donal.

'Dangerous business, that,' allowed Fergal. 'What bear? Which cave?'

'Balor Evil Eye in his ráth.'

Fergal stared at the two before him for a moment, then put back his head and laughed. 'Ha! What is it you are drinking—and is there any more of it?'

'We could do this,' Conor said quickly. 'We three—among all the warriors in Eirlandia—we three alone possess the knowledge and ability to do this. Moreover, we have been given the weapons to do it—charmed weapons, the gift of the faéry to be used in just this way. And now . . . now we have five more brothers in arms to support us in the task. All the threads are coming together—don't you see?' Conor wondered at his sudden insight. It felt as if his feet had been placed on a path leading directly to the place he needed to go—as if some unseen hand was guiding him, and it was right. 'This was meant to be.'

Fergal was shaking his head before Conor finished. 'Of all the mad things I've heard you say over the years, this must be the maddest ever.'

'Why?' said Conor. 'Think about it, brother.'

'Why? He asks me *why*? It is impossible, I say. Impossible, aye, and that is just the beginning. The region beyond the deadlands is a fair piece of territory—a realm all its own and one that happens to be under enemy control. Add to that your fella Evil Eye could be anywhere. How would we find him? Where would we even begin looking?'

'Finding him might not be that difficult,' Conor said. 'We know where we found him the first time.'

'Right so,' replied Fergal, he moved around to take a seat on the ground across from the other two. 'Even supposing we found him, there is the matter of getting close enough to plant a blade between his rib bones without anyone knowing.'

'I was close enough once, remember. And if I got close enough again, I would ply that blade—and I would not care who knew about it!'

'Even if you achieved such a vaunted feat, the Scálda would soon have your head on a stick. You'd never get out alive.'

'That would be a small enough price to pay for clearing the way to end the war.'

'On my sword,' breathed Fergal, 'I begin to believe you mean it.'

Donal turned his gaze from the fire to Conor. 'Ach, he is in earnest, brother. But I see a ray of light in this dark design.'

Fergal puffed out his cheeks and sighed with frustration. 'You, too? The pair of you are daft as two wet ferrets. Listen to yourselves! Do you hear what you are saying?'

'Nay, brother—*you* listen,' said Donal. 'We are a small band and that will be a strength. A small group can roam at will where a larger force would be noticed and action taken to remove it.'

'The Scálda cannot fight what they do not know to be there,' added Conor. 'We can make a virtue of that. Aye, so where others would have to use force, we will use stealth. We can travel through the lands the Scálda stole without being seen.'

'So we ramble around in hostile territory—as wonderful as that might be, it does nothing to help us find Evil Eye.'

'I can find him,' Donal said, his voice taking on that rare tone of authority. 'I *will* find him.'

Fergal stared, and Conor said, 'He has the Second Sight.'

'I knew it!' cried Fergal. 'I knew there was that different about him. Why am I always the last to know these things?'

'It was a gifting, so to speak, from our time with the faéry,' Donal explained. 'I did not care to make much of it until I grew more certain of it and knew I could trust it.'

'See now,' said Conor. 'We *could* find Balor. This plan is not so impossible after all.'

'Nay, perhaps not,' granted Fergal. 'But it is still mad. What if we do this and we fail? It will be the death of us.'

'Then at least we will go to our graves with honour and the knowledge that no one in this island realm could have done more,' said Conor. 'The Scálda must be driven from Eirlandia—if there is even the smallest chance we can succeed, then we would be cowards not to try.'

18

Fergal tugged on the end of his moustache and frowned. 'You are fearless, brother, no man alive can say otherwise. But tell me now, how do you imagine we will steal our way into Balor's fortress, slay him, and flee the filthy place without being seen? Had we Rhiannon's charmed belt we might have a slender chance to succeed. Without it, we will surely fail.'

'A faéry charm is a useful thing, to be sure,' granted Conor. 'Then again, I seem to remember that we have crept into an enemy stronghold before without the aid of fair Rhiannon's silver girdle. It is how we found the faéry in the first place.'

Having exhausted their arguments, both men turned to Donal, who was sitting on a nearby stump with his chin in his fist. He saw their expectant expressions and raised his head. 'Ach, now you are wanting to know what I think?'

'It would make a change from listening to our talkative friend here,' replied Conor.

'Tell him, brother,' said Fergal. 'This plan of his is no plan at all. It is a design for disaster.'

Donal pursed his lips and, for a moment, seemed to gaze beyond either of them and into the woodland shadows gathering around their forest camp. Then he gave a little shake—as if with a sudden chill—and, nodding slightly, said, 'The chances of success are very thin, it is true—and the chances of failure prodigious. Fergal is right, such an undertaking would likely end in disaster.'

'At last!' crowed Fergal. 'Donal agrees with me. Let us hear no more about this mad notion.'

Conor stared aghast at the two of them. 'Am I to believe what I'm hearing? Donal, is this so?'

Wrapping his cloak around him like a druid, Donal rose slowly in the dying light, but said nothing, merely stood gazing into the fastness of his own thoughts.

'Tell him you agree with me and let's be done with this,' insisted Fergal.

'Fergal is right in that death and disaster is likely. Conor is right in that we *have* done this before,' Donal replied at last. 'I see—'

Fergal rolled his eyes. 'Ach, aye, so we did—and Mádoc lost his life because of it, and little Huw—and you yourself were wounded to the death if not for the faéry saving you. If we go into that accursed place again we deserve every ill that befalls us and more besides.' He crossed his arms over his chest in staunch defiance. 'What our friend here proposes is a path to a swift and unpleasant death. It is a mad plan and I won't be hearing any more about it.' Thrusting out an imploring hand to Donal, he said, 'You said so yourself just now.'

'So I did.' Then, turning his gaze on Conor, Donal said, 'It could be done.'

'I knew it!' Conor jumped up from his perch. 'Aye, I knew it.' He stalked around the campfire, pounding his fist into his palm. 'Listen now—if we kept our wits about us and travelled at night, as we did with Mádoc, we could move about without attracting attention to ourselves.' A slow smile spread across his face for the first time that day—or many days. 'We will find Balor Berugderc, and we will strike him down in his fortress before anyone knew we were there.'

'Impossible!' protested Fergal. 'You cannot be making a plan that will only succeed by the enemy not knowing you were there. You must plan in such a way as it makes no difference whether the Scálda know or not.' He, too, began pacing around the little clearing. 'What if we made out that *we* were Scálda . . . but nay, I am never so ugly. It would never deceive them.' He gave his head a weary shake. 'Ach, what would I give for a bowl of ale just now. All this thinking has given me a powerful thirst.'

Médon and the rest of Conor's newly fledged fianna had spent the day foraging in the surrounding woodland. They now came trooping back with a small buck and several hares. While Médon, Galart, and Calbhan set about skinning and gutting the day's hunt, Aedd set to work building up the fire to begin roasting the hares and a haunch of the venison, and Dearg began mixing oats with some of the blood to make a porridge.

When all their chores were finished, they all gathered around the fire to watch Dearg cook their supper. While the meat sizzled on spits made from green oak branches, the evening faded and an early moon rose to shine through the scattered cloud cover. They fell to discussing how best to get the necessary supplies to keep themselves from starving: oats and barley, butter, cheese, salt, ale and the like—all the things they would need to keep themselves alive now that they had neither tribe nor home to call their own.

Dearg shared out the meal and, by the time the deer haunch had been pared to the bone and the bowls emptied, they had all convinced themselves that as they were the best and bravest of men they would thrive wonderfully well. Conor did not mention his plot to kill Balor Berugderc, nor did Fergal or Donal so much as hint that such a daring scheme might be under consideration. In truth, there was no real plan—merely an intention, and one that was rapidly hardening into a desire to strike a blow at the beating heart of the beast that had consumed so much of Eirlandia, its land, and its people.

Instead, Conor allowed his men to assume that they would be spending the next few days securing provisions for their impending adventures, never letting on what those adventures might be, much less that they would take place beyond the borders in the lands the Scálda stole. He hinted at daring raids, and taking Scálda horses and spoils, but never a word about wanting Balor's bloody head on the end of his spear.

They all went to their rest in good spirits and the next morning the newly formed fianna gathered their scant belongings and turned their faces to the south and the deadlands beyond. Riding easily, they worked their way through a region of low hills, steadily rising toward the rocky spine that cut across the island and marked the boundary limits of Dé Danann territory. They passed several Brigantes holdings—places where the Aintrén warriors were known, and where they were able to obtain a few supplies to bolster their paltry store. At one farming settlement, they traded half the venison carcass for oats and fodder for the horses and a bag of bósaill.

Two days later, the craggy spine of Druim Orchán rose before them; known as the Ridge of Lament, it served to divide Dé Danann territories from those under enemy control. Here they paused to observe the land and search for a suitable place from which to launch their audacious raid.

Donal moved up beside Conor as they rode along. 'You have to tell the fianna what we aim to do. You cannot begin as battlechief of this warband this way. It is a dangerous course we have set before us—'

'I have not yet decided on our course.'

Donal regarded him for a moment, his eyes narrowed. 'Aye, you have—and they should know. They are your fianna. They have sworn life and blood to you. It is not right to keep this from them any longer.'

'You're right,' Conor agreed with a sigh. 'I'll tell them tonight.'

Some little time later, they stopped to rest and water the horses and fill their water skins at a tiny rill trickling along a low rocky bed. 'Just over that great hump of rock there,' Fergal, pointing up at the jagged blue line in the near distance, 'lie the deadlands. Everything to the south is Scálda territory.' To a man, the fianna gazed up the rising trail to the jagged horizon. Dark against a white, featureless sky, the stark edge seemed a desolate and forbidding barrier. Aedd, the youngest of the warriors, asked, 'Why is it called the deadlands?'

'Ach, well, when we were here before, it was a blighted wasteland,' Fergal explained. 'The trees and brush all cut down—burned to sticks and stumps, the settlements and strongholds destroyed, farms and fields ruined, too, and all the wells and waters, loughs and rivers poisoned. Whatever the Scálda could not carry off, they burned.'

'You were here before?' wondered Galart. 'When was this then?'

'It was after that Oenach—the last one your lord Brecan hosted. The one where we caught the spy.'

'None of us were at that gathering,' said Galart. 'But, here now, I thought no one had ventured into Scálda lands since the Black Ships came.'

'They are *not* Scálda lands,' Conor told him. 'They are Dé Danann lands—lands the Scálda stole. Aye, and one day we will have them back.'

'Are Scálda strongholds very big,' asked Aedd, 'and well defended?'

'Do they really have walls of iron?' wondered Dearg.

'Ha!' cried Fergal. 'Who told you such a daft thing?'

The dark-haired young warrior shrugged and glanced around at his swordbrothers for their tacit confirmation. 'That's what we heard.'

'Neither walls nor gates of iron,' Conor told them. 'The walls of their strongholds are only timber—much like the walls of Aintrén or Dúnaird, or any others you have ever seen. And that is because many of the best ones they have were built by Dé Danann tribes driven out by the dog-eaters.'

'To be sure,' agreed Fergal quickly. 'Even so, there are some made by the

Scálda and these are never so strong. For all they are poorly made—with many gaps filled in with nothing but sticks and mud. We were able to walk right through those walls like smoke, and—'

Calbhan, who had been listening to all this, spoke up. 'You mean to say you entered a Scálda stronghold?' Dearg, standing next to him, added, 'With Scálda in it?'

'That we did,' replied Conor. 'And more.'

'If we told you the half,' said Fergal, 'you would take us for braggarts or liars. Ach, you would think us old wives reciting a tale grown large in the telling.'

'Yet, I would hear it,' Calbhan said; indicating the others, he said, 'I think we all would like to hear it.' He smiled as he added, 'Not to worry, we already think you an old wife.'

'Insolent pup,' muttered Fergal. Yet, cheered by the prospect of recounting his daring deeds, he drew breath to begin. 'This is the way of it. . . .'

'Hear it you shall—but not just now,' interrupted Conor quickly. 'We will let this old wife tell his tale tonight around the hearth. But if there is to be a hearth at all, we must first find a place to make camp before we lose the light.'

They spent what was left of the dwindling day on the ever-rising trail searching for a place near a stream or pool and a big enough patch of land for grazing the horses. As the sun dipped into the west, flaring briefly in a bright yellow blaze before sinking behind dark incoming clouds, they came to an outcrop of grey, lichen-covered stone—the base of which formed a rock wall half again as tall as a man. The outcrop faced the west and captured the sunlight and a thin little spring issued from a crease nearby to form a small pool before trailing off as a tiny burn that tumbled in fits and starts down the hill. To the south of this stone bastion grew a stand of slender rowan and hazel trees. Here, they would be sheltered from the harsh northeasterly winds and would not have to go far to refill their water skins and water the horses. A short distance down the slope gave onto a scrubby line of scrawny elder, stunted elm, and lonely hawthorn trees where they could get enough firewood to cook their food and warm themselves.

The fianna set to work at once, each man to his accustomed chore: picketing and feeding the horses, erecting the shelter, gathering firewood, and all things necessary to make life in camp bearable if not exactly comfortable. They laboured with the efficiency born of practice and soon a fire crackled in the fire ring and a roof of cut boughs and branches lashed to a willow frame formed a crude roof over their heads. When all was finished and the meal was over, they huddled around the fire to hear Fergal tell his tale.

He began by saying, 'Well now, as you know, Lord Brecan mac Lergath had summoned the kings to a special council. Conor, Donal, and I were not among our king's ardféne, but as it was to be a big gathering we had it in our minds to go and see what we would see.

'As it happens, we had fought running battles with the Scálda all summer and in one skirmish we won seven horses. Conor put it in our king's mind to make a gift of these horses to Lord Brecan and others as a show of goodwill—and it was in exchange for the care of these gift horses that we were allowed to attend. All swam along prettily enough until we fell foul of our battlechief's sense of propriety and pique and we were commanded to leave, which we did.' He chuckled, shaking his head at the memory. 'Ha! We left the Oenach, taking the water buckets with us.'

'As was only right,' put in Donal, 'seeing as they were *our* buckets.'

'Ach, who is telling this story—you or me?' demanded Fergal with a stern look. Donal apologised and Fergal continued. 'We left Mag Rí early the next day and had not travelled far before Lord Arden sent a rider to fetch us back, for it did seem our absence proved more irksome than our presence. We turned around and started back—only to find that good messenger attacked by Scálda raiders. We flew to his aid and the battle was both sharp and short. Four dog-eaters killed and one wounded.

'Back to the gathering we went, taking the wounded one with us to show the assembled lords that enemy spies were skulking about where no spies should be. Imagine our surprise when we presented the injured spy at the gathering only to be told by your man Brecan that it was nothing to worry about. Enemy spies at an Oenach and not a thing to cause a fella a mite of concern? Ach, well, that did not sit well with us, I can tell you. Our Conor took it on himself to challenge Brecan before the assembly and was called a liar and troublemaker for his pains.

'There was more pain to come, so there was. For, on the way back to camp, four Brigantes warriors—your own kinsmen, truth be told—attacked Conor and thumped him something fierce.'

'All that is forgotten,' Conor told them. 'We settled that long since.'

'Aye, well, if Donal and I had not come looking for him, Conor would not be sitting here right now,' continued Fergal. 'Up we jump and pull our swordbrother from the fight and carry him down to camp where he was in a bad way. Lord Cahir heard about the attack and sent his druid to bind and dress Conor's wounds and lend a crumb of comfort in his distress. When old Mádoc asked how he had come by his wounds, Conor told him—told him of his suspicions too.'

'What suspicions?' asked Aedd, speaking up.

'Did I not say?' wondered Fergal. 'Ach, well, it was in Conor's mind that the Scálda spies we had caught were sniffing about because someone had told the enemy about the Oenach and how the lords of Eirlandia would be gathered there. Who had told them? Someone who knew well beforehand when and where the gathering would take place. Who had this knowledge? Only Brecan Brigantes. Aye,' Fergal nodded gravely, 'and for him to deny the presence of spies when confronted with one in the flesh—and then attack the one who confronted him? Well, it raised a few suspicions as I say. So now, our Conor was not the only one to smell a rat in the granary. Old Mádoc nursed his own misgivings about Lord Brecan's designs on the high king's throne. He did more, did Mádoc—he hatched a plan to investigate the matter further.'

The fianna squirmed uncomfortably at this reference to their king's misdeeds and they glanced guiltily at one another. 'Believe me when I say we knew nothing about this,' said Médon, speaking for them all. 'Though we have heard much about it since. I can only say I am sorry.'

'Again I tell you that we put all that behind us,' Conor said. 'It happened. It is done. We moved on.'

'To be sure,' said Fergal, taking up his tale once more. 'Old Mádoc needed help to prove his doubts and since Conor shared his misgivings, it fell to Conor to help him. Woe to Conor! For Mádoc's plan was to show Conor up for a thief and get him cast out of the tribe. With Conor exiled, the two of them were free to go where they would and do what they could to discover the truth about King Brecan and his dealings with the Scálda. The best place to find rats is in their nest, as they say. So, it is to the Scálda that Mádoc and Conor determine to go.'

'This is where Fergal and I come into it,' offered Donal, breaking in again. 'Conor's exile sat ill with us, so it did. We decided to borrow horses and go after our swordbrother to lend him our aid if he would have it, and so—'

'Thank you, Donal, that was the very point I was making,' said Fergal.

'Well, we could in no wise allow Conor to go off into hostile lands alone with just a dried up old druid for company. So we followed him and caught up with them on the road—and that road led us here, to Druim Orchán.' He gestured to the rockbound ridge, now invisible in the darkness. 'Beyond that border lie the lands the Scálda stole, and it was into those lands we went.

'That first day's ride was a shock, I can tell you. I close my eyes and see it still . . . the strongholds destroyed, the farms burned to cinders and all the good, clean waters poisoned and foul . . . skulls and bones charred black, and not a living thing left alive to tell the tale—nor birds, nor fish, nor squirrels, nor hares, nor the least thing that runs or crawls about the earth or flies above it. Nothing at all but black and barren ground and desolation. We looked upon that sight and swore upon the blades in our hands to drive the Scálda into the sea whence they came and that vow is green as the day we made it.

'Old Mádoc, for all his obscure ways, was a canny creature. By means known to none but himself alone, he led us into that ravaged land to where the Scálda reside and we saw some sights along the way. We saw the dog-eaters making iron—cold hard metal for weapons and for round hoops for what purpose we could not guess.'

'Shield rims!' called Dearg. Drawn into tale, he could not stop himself interrupting.

'So we thought, too,' Fergal told him. 'But nay—not shield rims, but wheel rims. Slender wheel rims made of iron for the wheels of a thing we had never seen before—'

'What was it?' said Calbhan. 'Wagons?'

'Nay, not wagons, but war carts.'

'War carts!' cried several listeners all at once.

'Aye,' Fergal assured them. 'Carts made of wickerwork and leather and iron, and pulled by two horses. Fast and strong and big enough to carry two or three warriors into battle and away again. The Scálda are making hundreds of these war carts to complete the conquest of Eirlandia begun long since.'

'How do you know this?' said Médon.

'Ach, well, we know because we saw the ore dug from the hills and we saw the forges flare and smoke, and we saw the iron rims heaped high on wagons and brought to a Scálda ráth for keeping. Aye, and we took courage and stole silent as shadows into that enemy stronghold to see storerooms full of these wheel rims waiting for the wheels they were made for.' He paused, enjoying his listeners' rapt attention. 'And in one of those storerooms is where we found the faéry princess—'

'Faéry!' shouted the fianna almost to a man. They gaped at Fergal and exchanged astonished glances with one another. 'Truly?' said Galart. 'You have seen one of the faéry?'

'Aye, and not one only—'

'And are they as beautiful as people say they are?' Calbhan wanted to know.

'All that and more,' Fergal replied, 'all that and more. And if you would stop your chatter and hear the rest of the tale you may yet learn something. Well, then, we stole into the stronghold as I say, and in one of the storerooms we found two faéry women bound there with iron chains—as it so happens that iron is very poison to the faéry race. It steals their magic and does slowly kill them. By binding these faéry folk in chains of iron, the Scálda were trying to force them to reveal the secret of their magic. In gaining that, the dog-eaters would gain a potent weapon to wield against us—a weapon against which there would be no defence, a weapon to drive the Dé Danann to their graves for once and forever.

'But Conor up and says, "Brothers, we would be less than men if we did not free those suffering faéry folk from the wicked creatures who have made them captive." So that is what we did. We freed them then and there, and in gratitude for our rescue the faéry princess—aye, she is of royal blood— cast a charm on all of us to allow us to walk right out of the fortress full of enemies with no one being the wiser.'

'Except that is not what happened,' Donal pointed out.

'That is not what happened,' Fergal granted, 'for just as we rode from the ráth—'

'You rode?' said Médon. 'Where did you get horses?'

'The Scálda had taken our horses,' Fergal told him. 'Did I not say that already?'

'Nay, brother, you never did.'

'Ach, well, some Scálda hunters had found our horses where we left them in the wood nearby and took them up to the ráth. But, see, under the enchantment of the faéry charm of concealment, we were able to claim our mounts and ride from the fortress under the very noses of the vile and odious enemy. All the same, the charm was fleeting and began to fade before we could clear the gate, and one of the faéry was pierced by a thrown spear. She carried that wound to her grave, she did—for by the time we learned of her injury the poison of the iron had done its work and we could not save her. Donal, here, was wounded, too, by the selfsame spear and would have died if not for the healing arts of the faéry.'

'But you did save the other one—the princess?' said Dearg.

'We did that very thing. Rhiannon is her name, and it is her father who gave us the weapons we carry even now.' Fergal yawned and stretched. 'Ach, but *that* is a story for another day.'

Despite the howls of protest from his listeners, Fergal would not be drawn into telling more. Finally, Conor rose and called for quiet, saying, 'We have travelled far today and tomorrow will be here soon enough. I advise you to rest while you can.'

Galart jumped up and spoke for them all when he said, 'I hear and obey, lord, but I will go to my rest all the easier for knowing whether this tale of Fergal's is true, or has he made of it a story for children?'

Conor drew breath to reply, but it was Donal who answered. 'What Fergal said is true in the same way a view of a distant ráth is true—you see the hill and the walls and fields around it and know it for the fortress of a nobleman. And this even though you may not see every ring and road, nor how big the gates, nor less yet who owns the stronghold.'

Galart, somewhat dubious, looked to the others; Dearg and Calbhan were frowning and Aedd was shaking his head. Conor, stooping to his cloak, which was spread out on the ground, retrieved his sword. 'If any man still doubts what Donal and Fergal say, let him look at this.' Placing the naked blade across his palms, he offered it to Galart. The young warrior took the sword and as his fist closed around the pommel, he was instantly impressed by the quickness and supple vitality of the weapon. He gave it a quick flourish and was struck by the way it seemed to anticipate his movement and intention, making the stroke almost effortless. Awed and speechless, he passed the sword to Médon, who likewise experienced the uncanny sensation produced by the charmed weapon. The others clamoured for a chance to wield the blade and when everyone had tried it, Conor put out his hand and pointed to the curious figures engraved on the broad side of the blade near the pommel. 'This mark is the name of the sword, put there by its maker—a faéry artisan of the highest order. Fergal has a sword like it and

Donal, too—as well as a faéry spear and shield. These were given to us by Gwydion, Lord of the Tylwyth Teg and King of Tír nan Óg in the Region of the Summer Stars.'

Galart's eyes went wide and he said, 'You have been there? All three of you?'

'Aye, we have,' answered Fergal, 'and have I not been telling you the same?'

'Will we be able to see the faéry, too, do you think?' asked Calbhan.

'Ach, well, I don't know. Maybe,' replied Conor, taking back his sword.

But Donal, suddenly very solemn, turned his face to the bleak heights of Druim Orchán. 'You *will* meet the faéry,' he said in a voice that seemed to come from under a rock, 'sooner than you know. And fraught will be the meeting.'

19

Later that same night, after the fianna had rolled themselves in their cloaks and were asleep beside the low-burning fire, Conor came to Donal, who was sitting on a rock and gazing up at the night sky where gaps in the clouds allowed a patchwork of stars to shine through, casting the forlorn hillside in a thin and ghostly light. 'What was that back there, brother?' he asked. Donal edged over to make room for him on the rock. 'You saw something tonight.'

'Aye, I did,' he confided. 'Nothing good.'

'Tell me,' said Conor gently. 'Was it Rhiannon?'

'It was. There were others with her, I think, but it was her I saw. She was standing in a ruined ráth. It was dark—night I think, and she was crying. . . .'

Conor waited, but when Donal said no more, he asked, 'Why was she crying?'

Donal shook his head. 'I don't know. But her tears were not for grief, I think—or only partly that.' Donal, his face a dim, pale moon in the gloaming, seemed to turn inward once more to revisit the vision. 'It seemed to me that they were tears of desperation, of fear. She was afraid and . . .'

'Go on, brother, say it.'

'Conor, I think she is *here*.'

Conor looked at him in surprise. 'In Eirlandia?'

Donal shook his head. 'I mean here—in the deadlands . . . now, or soon will be.'

Nodding as he considered this, Conor asked, 'Anything else?'

'Only that.' Donal sighed. 'I wish I could see more, know more. But this gift is new in me still and I am never its master. I'm sorry, brother, that is all I saw.'

'No need to be sorry. You've done well.' Conor rose and stood for a moment looking up at the sky. 'We will go on as we intend.' He gave Donal a pat on the shoulder. 'Rest now, brother, tomorrow we start down a path from which there will be no turning back. We may have need of your Second Sight before long.'

Donal rose from his place on the rock and, pulling his cloak around him more tightly, said, 'You didn't tell them—about going into the deadlands to kill Balor.'

'I did not want them wakeful and thinking about it all night. Let them have their rest tonight. There is time enough tomorrow.'

'You must tell them, Conor. They have a right to know.'

'I will,' he promised. 'In the morning.'

The wind changed during the night and they woke the next morning to a low grey sky and a damp mist clinging to everything. They broke their fast on cold meat and porridge from the night before and then Conor called the men to gather around and hear what he had to say.

'We going into the deadlands and beyond into Scálda territories,' Conor told them bluntly. 'But our purpose is not raiding or taking spoils as I may have led you to believe.'

'What then?' said Médon. 'I think you did not bring us here for the balmy weather.' He drew his cloak more tightly around himself.

'We are taking the fight to the enemy in his lair,' Conor said. 'We go to find Balor Evil Eye and, once we have found him, we will kill him.' He passed his gaze around the others as they took in this news.

'A bold plan,' allowed Médon after a moment. 'We are very few against so many.'

'We are few, aye, and that is our strength,' Conor told him. 'Few as we are, we will be fewer still. Only Donal, Fergal, and I will go. The rest of you will remain here and keep the camp for our return.'

A round of disappointed murmuring greeted this announcement, and Médon undertook to speak for the rest of the fianna. 'With all respect, lord, we would go with you. I think we would be more use as blades quick and ready at your side than as idlers sitting here on the far side of a mountain.' The others endorsed this sentiment with nods all around.

Conor heard the resolve in Médon's voice and saw the determination on the faces of the fianna and his heart swelled with pride to see it. He motioned to Fergal and Donal to join him in consultation. 'They do appear resolute,' Conor said, glancing back at the fireside where the warriors waited. 'I'm thinking we should take them with us.'

'Ach, well, that will change things,' said Fergal. 'But whether for better or worse, I can't say.'

'Another spear or two could be a help,' suggested Donal. 'For tending horses and such if nothing else. I say we let any come who will.'

'I would not take more than three, mind,' cautioned Fergal. 'The fewer the better.'

'Then that is how it will be,' said Conor, making up his mind. Returning to the fire ring, Conor announced who was to go and who would stay behind. 'Médon, your counsel is sound,' he said. 'Three of you will come with us, and two will stay behind to keep our camp. Therefore, I have decided that you and Calbhan will remain here and await our return.'

Neither of the two warriors objected, but their disappointment was palpable. Conor put a hand on Médon's shoulder and said, 'It is a perilous journey we take and those who go may not return. I am trusting you to keep watch and, if necessary, carry a message for me.'

'A message, lord?'

'An important message.' Conor nodded gravely. 'If in the space of twelve days we have not returned, you and Calbhan are to go to Dúnaird and tell my father and my betrothed what has happened and that we will not be coming back. If you like the look of him, ask the king to take you into the warband. Otherwise, go to Cahir of the Coriondi. I have no doubt, you will be treated well in either place.'

To his credit, Médon squared his shoulders and returned Conor's level gaze. 'Trust it will be done.'

The six adventurers rode out a short time later. The two left behind watched their swordbrothers ascend the long slope to the crest of the ridge where they paused briefly for a last farewell, and then, one by one, disappeared over the top and were gone.

The deadlands were not dead anymore—at least they were not as lifeless as they had been the last time Conor had seen them. New growth had reclaimed much of the previously scorched and blackened ground, filling in the empty places in broad expanses of delicate new green. Grass had begun growing over the mounds of ráth and dún, and the woodland margins were edging into what had once been oat or barley fields; saplings of pine and larch, plum and elder, and tiny oak sprigs had sprung up where squirrels and birds had dropped seeds and pits and acorns. Thistles abounded in tight clusters where other plants could not thrive, and towering ranks of nettles lined the brooks and streams.

Here and there among the green-covered mounds, charred ruins of gate-posts or rooftrees could still be seen. And the stench of rot and decay still hung in the air, tainting every inhaled breath. Occasionally, they saw birds—crows and solitary kites mostly, and a few straggling flocks of geese and ducks as well; there must have been squirrels around, and hares—but no larger creatures; the ground was still too barren and open for fox or deer or other animals. The deadlands were deserted, but no longer desolate. Apparently, the Scálda did not renew their devastation with any particular regularity. Danu, the Great Mother, continually reclaimed her own.

These signs of healing in the land, hopeful as they might be, failed to cheer the travellers. For, the day, having begun grey and damp, did not improve, and by the time Conor and the fianna had reached the southern limit of the deserted borderland, a miserable cold drizzle was leaking out of the dull sky and the wind was a mournful whine from the northwest. The riders had crossed the open ground as quickly as possible, and entered the shelter of the southern tree line; here Conor called a halt to their journey for the day and told his men to search out a suitable place to make camp.

'I find myself wondering,' said Fergal easing the aches out of his lanky limbs, 'when it was that we were here before? Our time in Tír nan Óg has muddled my memory, I think. Was it two years, or three—or only last summer?' ·

'I hardly know what to tell you,' Conor puffed out his cheeks and shook his head. 'So much has happened since then if you told me it was twenty years ago, I would believe it.'

Donal, who had dismounted, stood beside his horse holding the reins and staring out across the barren land, looking back the way they had come. 'Someone is out there,' he said after a moment.

Conor and Fergal moved to join him. Both scanned the empty hills. At first, Conor saw nothing he had not already seen; then, out of the corner of his eye he saw a dark patch—like the shadow of a cloud scudding across the land, moving from the west to the east.

'There—I have it,' said Conor. 'What is it?'

Fergal turned to regard the two of them with a wide, incredulous look. 'What are you seeing that I cannot see?'

'That shadow,' Conor replied, stabbing a finger at a farther hill. 'There, at the foot of the far hills.'

Fergal looked where Conor was pointing and said, 'I don't see . . .'

'Just there—moving toward the far tree line to the east,' Conor said, following the movement with his finger.

Fergal stared until his eyes ached. 'I still cannot—' He broke off just as a small body of riders emerged out of the dim, drizzly mist. 'Ach! There!' He watched for a moment, then said, 'However did the two of you see them?'

Conor and Donal glanced at one another and shrugged. Fergal gave a small, guttural groan of frustration and turned back to watch the riders. 'Who are they then—since you can see so much?'

'Scálda,' replied both Conor and Donal at the same time. 'Eight of them, I make out,' added Conor.

'Nine,' corrected Donal. 'They have another with them—a captive, I think.' Both men exchanged a look. 'I feel like I have been here before.'

'Near enough,' replied Conor.

'What do you want to do?' asked Galart; he had joined them and stood watching the distant riders as they swept across the empty land. 'Should we follow?'

'An excellent idea,' said Conor. 'I was just about to suggest it myself. Mark where the dog-eaters entered the wood. We'll make camp there and follow on at first light. I'm thinking those riders might lead us to Balor.'

'If only,' said Fergal, still staring after the Scálda raiders. 'It is my present hope to spend as few days in the southlands as possible.'

Supper that night was a subdued affair with a too-small fire and not enough to eat. Unwilling to risk announcing their presence by way of a larger camp fire, or deplete already limited supplies with a bigger meal, they made do with as little as they could spare. After settling the horses for the night, they all crowded as close to the fire ring as they dared, wrapped themselves in their cloaks and went to sleep, waking before sunrise to another wet, grey dawn. They busied themselves to banish the night chill from their bones by tending the horses, broke fast on scraps of bósaill soaked in warm water, then rode on into the cold morning mist. They soon found and began following the trail of the Scálda riders they had seen the day before. Judging from the bent and broken branches, the hoof impressions in the churned-up earth, the dog-eaters had pushed a reckless pace, little heeding the path or any minor obstacles in their way.

'Someone was in a very fever,' observed Fergal. He rode at the head of the fianna with Conor at his right hand only a pace or two behind.

'Keen or desperate,' Conor replied. 'All the same, keep an eye on the trail ahead. I do not care to be riding into their camp.'

'We could do worse than to take them unawares,' Fergal pointed out.

'Aye, so we could.' Conor seemed to consider the idea for a moment before dismissing it, saying, 'But then we would not find their dún.'

'We don't even know if Evil Eye is to be found there in any case,' Fergal pointed out.

'We don't know that he is not. He has to be somewhere—why not there?'

'*Everyone* has to be somewhere,' Fergal replied. 'If not, where would *we* be? That is no answer at all.'

'I will make a wager with you. Balor will be where we find him, and not somewhere else.'

'Ach! And who would be fool enough to take that wager?'

'I was thinking you might,' said Conor. They talked like this for a while— as much to relieve the apprehension of following the enemy into his lair as for the easy camaraderie—following the well-marked trail through the wood, passing streams and dells and thickets of bramble and black currant heavy with fruit. At each approach to a place where someone might have made camp, Fergal slowed and moved ahead in a tense, cautious silence. But there was never any indication that the enemy riders had stopped . . . until at last they came to a river: wide, but shallow, and bordered either side by extensive reed beds. Directly across the river in the near distance, rising above the ground fog already seeping across the marsh, rose a fortress mound topped by the high timber walls of a Scálda dún.

Here Fergal halted and waited for the others to join him. Taking care to remain hidden among the foliage of the surrounding wood, the fianna sat for a moment to observe the enemy settlement. It was of a fairly substantial size—the peaked roofs of several large houses could be seen rising above the top of the wall—and but otherwise the place was unremarkable; and the fact that it lacked ringed ditches and watchtowers proclaimed it, in Dé Danann terms, less a fortress of a lord and more the dwelling of a minor nobleman and his clan. Even from a distance they could tell that the place was of the crude, slapdash construction employed by the Scálda, with high walls of rough, untrimmed timber and a long, narrow earthen ramp leading up to a wide, gated entrance.

'This is no place to linger or we'll be seen,' Fergal said, his voice little more than a low whisper. He gave a nod to the many muddy hoofprints along the banks where riders habitually crossed. 'Do you think they are in there?'

'We'll have to get a closer look,' Conor replied, then signalled the others to move on. They crossed the river and worked their way through the reed beds and onto the soft, soggy land of low marshes. Ground cover was sparse here, so they stayed close to the river, following it south and east as it coursed through bogs and hillocks until the land rose again becoming firmer, dryer, and able to support stands of larger trees. By the time they had worked their way back within sight of the enemy settlement, the sun had burned through the low overcast allowing washed-out blue to show through the gaps; the day had begun to fade around them and low clouds scudded in from the west.

Leaving Dearg and Aedd to guard the horses, Conor, Fergal, Donal, and Galart took up their spears and continued on foot along a lightly wooded path lined with beeches and hawthorn—young trees sprung up where the tall larch and plane trees had been felled to construct the dún. The grove ended at the edge of a haphazard sprawl of fields; filled with old, decaying stubble from a previous harvest, the fields had not been ploughed or planted this year, nor, perhaps even the one before. There were no animal pens to be seen, but there was a clutch of outbuildings huddled at the base of the mound and, from somewhere close by, smoke drifted skyward in a thinly threaded column. Clearly, some activity or another was taking place there and, above the trees on the other side of the field, smoke from at least two more fires signified additional labours elsewhere.

'There's folk around,' observed Fergal. 'I wonder what they'd be burning?'

'Charcoal maybe?' suggested Galart. 'Getting ready for winter. Same as at home, I expect.'

Conor was about to remind the young warrior that as a wandering fianna they had no fixed home, but thought better of it. Instead, he said, 'Let's get a closer look. I'd like to see what's going on beyond those trees.'

They faded back into the wood and, skirting the empty fields, worked their way closer to the Scálda settlement. They soon came to a little stream. The turgid water, like the pond, flowed with water tainted by the runoff from a reeking hillock of muck and manure they could see at the base of the dún. Beyond the manure pile, higher on the slope of the mound, a crude sort of cattle pen had been constructed. Wide at one end, it tapered down to a space no wider than a single beast; at its narrowest part a wooden ramp led up to a pair of posts separated by a stout crossbeam. The ground beneath the heavy beam was stained black and crusted thick with the dried blood of countless animals; yet there were no beasts to be seen, so Conor and the others retreated into the wood once more and made for a place around the far side of the dún marked by the two rising columns of white smoke. Though they crept as carefully as they could so as not to alert the enemy of their presence, there came no sound of any activity from the settlement. All remained quiet—but with a strained, unnatural silence that whispered of desertion and abandonment.

Directly ahead, the wood gave way to an open expanse filled with stumps where the trees had been clear-cut to make space for three enormous stone structures shaped like gigantic beehives. Each was made of unhewn stone, and partly dug into the side of the dún's earthen mound; each enormous hive had a small hole or doorway on one side near the bottom and, scattered about, lay stacks of split wood and heaps of white rock in chunks the size of a child's head. 'What . . . ?' began Fergal. 'They look like forge furnaces—but forge furnaces are never so big.'

'What else can they be?' said Donal. 'There is the wood to feed them, but where is the ore?'

'And where is the slag and cinders?' wondered Galart. His question went unanswered as, after a last look, they moved back into the trees to continue their circuit of the strange Scálda settlement. Around the next bend they came to another work area consisting of a mass of small hillocks. Leaving the others to keep watch, Conor crept out from the shelter of the trees to examine one of these little knolls and saw that it contained a large vat that had been sunk into the earth to form a pit of sorts. The vat was filled with a thick white slurry that stained the sides of the pit and the earth; it stank of singed hair and rotten meat. Between two of the pits lay a few mangled cow hides dry and brittle, but stained with the white slurry from the vats; a little distance away a series of rails—like horse pickets—had been set up, but instead of horses, each had a long line of square wattle frames tied to it. A well-beaten path led from the rail and around the base of the settlement hill.

Conor retreated to the wood to tell the others what he had seen, and their trek around the dún continued. As they came in sight of the rising columns of smoke visible above the trees, they became aware of a peculiar smell, slight but distinct, carried on the wind. Directly ahead, the wood gave way to an open expanse at the base of the dún hill and there, glimpsed through the trees was a pond made filthy with detritus, the water green and rancid; bloated fish rotted on the pond's surface amidst floating patches of grey-green scum. On the far side of this befouled pond was a clearing containing several large heaps of something grey and oddly angular which, on closer inspection, turned out to be animal bones: primarily leg bones, horns, and hooves. The haunches, ribs, flanks and other meaty portions had been removed and the poor cuts thrown onto piles to form three massive charnel mounds. At some time in the recent past, one of the mounds had been set alight and the embers sputtered still, the burning flesh and fat, sinew and gristle and bone sent threads of greasy, stinking smoke into the air. Smaller fires continually sputtered around the base of this heap, spewing dirty smoke across the clearing on the fitful wind. Though Conor would have liked a closer investigation, the filthy smoke, laced as it was with the stink of burning hair and bone brought tears to their eyes and he could not bring himself to creep any closer. So, deciding there was nothing more to be seen, the five spies backed away into the trees once more, and resumed their circuit of the dún hill.

Painstakingly working their way through the trees and brush at the edges of the cleared fields, they at last returned to the entrance they had seen upon their first sighting of the fortress. The road leading to the ramp was clear and the gates of the dún stood open; one of the gate doors seemed to have broken a hinge; there was no one in sight within. Still, they waited, observing the place and watching for any sign of movement. Finally, Conor said, 'I think it is deserted.'

'Aye, I'm thinking the same thing,' agreed Fergal, 'and maybe not so very long ago.'

'Whatever they were doing here is finished,' Galart added. 'What *were* they doing, do you suppose?'

'Who knows?' Conor replied. He looked to Donal who only offered a shrug. 'But, as you say, whatever it was it is finished, and the Scálda have moved on.'

'More to the point,' said Fergal, 'Balor Evil Eye is not here, and it is him we're after. Unless you want to go inside and search the—' Seeing the look on Conor's face he halted abruptly. 'Tell me you're not thinking of going up there.'

'We wouldn't all have to go,' Conor said. 'I'll go alone.'

'And leave us here wondering whatever happened to our old friend Conor when you fail to come back?' said Fergal, his voice rising in disbelief. 'I say we leave now and move on while we still have a little daylight left.'

'Wait here,' said Conor. 'Warn me if anyone approaches.'

'I'm not for staying behind,' said Donal, moving out from the cover of the trees. 'I'll go with you.'

Fergal looked at Galart and sighed. 'Come on, we cannot let them have all the fun without us or we'll never hear the end of it.'

20

Feeling every inch the intruders that they were, the four Dé Danann hurried past the field of vats to the long ramp leading to the entrance to the dún, pausing at the gate to watch and listen. They saw no sign of activity and the only sound they heard was the incessant clatter of crows from somewhere inside. Conor, satisfied that there were no Scálda lurking in the shadows, slipped in and pressed himself to the back of the gatepost. Donal followed and took his place next to him; Fergal and Galart joined them a moment later. As observed from the open entrance, the yard was silent and, save for a half-starved brindled cat that hissed at them as it disappeared behind a pile of rags, deserted. The surrounding buildings—four large houses, a wattle-and-daub hall with a high, pitched roof of haphazard thatch, a granary, several storehouses, and a small forge—appeared empty, too. Many of the doors were open and no sounds came from within.

There were more buildings half hidden behind the hall. Conor gave a nod and they proceeded to investigate, pausing at the open doors of the buildings they passed. All were vacant and empty but for rubbish and detritus—broken jars, scraps of cloth or leather, worthless furniture. The hall was the same. The board had been removed, and the benches overturned; the hearth was cold, the ashes of the last fire sodden from rain seeping in through the roof; the floors were covered with rushes rank with mildew and animal urine giving the great empty space a sour stink. One whiff, and Fergal observed, 'No one here but the rats . . . filthy rats.'

'It looks like they left in a hurry,' said Galart.

Just then a great squawking arose from somewhere outside. Conor, having seen enough, retreated to the yard to see a flock of rooks and ravens swirling over the dún. The screeching emanated from someplace behind the hall. 'Let's see what all the noise is about.'

Fergal rolled his eyes, muttering, 'And then let us be gone and be glad.'

Passing down the narrow gap of the close-set buildings, they slipped around to the back of the hall where they found several more storehouses, a large stable, and a fenced horse pen. The contents of that pen had drawn the carrion birds, and it drew the Dé Danann now.

The sudden appearance of the men sent a multitude of rooks and crows and ravens, squawking and flapping in all directions—and not these only: among the swirling gyrating flock were magpies and gulls, jackdaws and jays. A few larger birds—buzzards, red kites, and an eagle—glanced up and glared at the men, but did not take wing as they continued their grisly feast on the mound of bloated human corpses.

Conor started forward and then stopped to stare. The others stood frozen in place. Heaped in the centre of the cattle pen were the decaying remains of a score or more human beings. Men, women, and children, their bodies discoloured and swollen in the early stages of putrefaction. Some were naked but for the scrags and hanks of hair that still clung to their exposed skulls; many others still wore the tattered shreds of clothing that had covered their emaciated frames. Among the rags and scraps of cloth could be seen the distinctive checks and stripes of cloaks and siarcs, breecs and mantles, once colourful, now faded and grey with rot and decaying matter.

'Badb's breath,' coughed Donal, 'they were Dé Danann!'

Fergal muttered a curse under his breath and Galart stifled a cry.

Conor felt his crimson blotch of a birthmark throb and burn with a sudden heat like molten iron flashed through him, blinding him. *Dé Danann!* he shrieked inwardly, his mind reeling. *Dé Danann!* These were his countrymen, his people—and that they should be so abused and mistreated in life and degraded and dishonoured in death pierced him to the core.

Then the wind shifted and the full force of the stench hit them all at once—the sickly sweet feculent stink of rotten meat combined with the nauseating tang of burst entrails—that cloying, pungent reek of dissolution and corruption, the signature scent of death.

Fergal gagged and Donal spat; Conor felt the gorge rise to his throat and bile surged into his mouth; Galart puked in the dirt.

Many of the corpses had been worked over by the birds and vermin and were now little more than hollow husks of ruined skin stretched over bones; other bodies were still being torn to crimson strips as the birds greedily ripped gobbets of flesh and muscle from the dead. Most had their eyes and tongues plucked out and gazed in empty mute astonishment at their own demise and that of their doomed clan. Here and there the shocking white gleam of bone, picked clean, protruded from an arm or a leg, a skull or rib cage; the sinuous serration of a spine lay exposed to the air and elements, its covering of skin and muscle stripped away and devoured.

Sensing no danger from the men, the black, circling squall of birds began settling once more on the funereal heap, reviving the poor broken bodies with a kind of squirming, hopping, flutter of wings and clacking beaks. Soon the decaying mass was covered with a feathered cloak as the scavengers squabbled and scrapped over the choice morsels their dry, croaking calls and outraged screeches rising in a ceaseless clamour. Conor, unable to look away, took in the sight; slack-jawed, rendered silent and cold by the shocking brutality of the display he could but stare in shock and disgust, and a slowly mounting rage. For there was little doubt in his mind that these doomed wretches had all met death around the same time, perhaps even on the same day.

Galart, wiping his mouth on his sleeve, drew a long shaky breath and flung out his hands in a gesture of futility. 'Why?'

Fergal, seething at the atrocity, turned his gaze from the horror. 'Who knows why the Scálda scum do anything?'

'But why bring them here to kill them?'

Conor spat and turned abruptly. 'I have seen enough.'

Without another word, the three trooped back down the hill to the shelter of the woods where Aedd and Dearg waited.

'What did you see?' asked Dearg, hurrying to meet them as they came walking through the grove. One glimpse of their faces, however, brought him up short. 'What is it? What did you see?'

Fergal regarded him, his mouth worked, but no words came out and so he turned his face away.

'Not now,' Conor said, his voice husky and low. 'Not here.'

Aedd came running to join them. Struck by the change in his sword-brothers, he and Dearg exchanged a worried glance. 'What happened up there?' he wondered.

'Just do as you're told,' Fergal snapped. 'We're leaving this place. Now!'

Aedd stared at them and would have asked more, but Donal, coming next, said, 'Get on with you, lads,' said Donal. 'We'll speak about it later.'

They took their mounts and rode back through the wood to the trail, leaving the abandoned dún behind them. Once on the trail, they resumed their search and rode on without encountering any more Scálda settlements. When at last the sun began to fade into a bleached white sky and low grey clouds moved in from the northwest, they set about making camp in a little clearing near a nameless river where they would be well hidden, but could keep watch on the trail lest any enemy pass. It was not until later that night when they were all gathered around their fire—as much for the light against the darkness they felt in this place as warmth from the worsening weather—that anyone felt like speaking. It began with a simple question. 'Where do they get all the animals?' wondered Galart. 'The cattle and oxen and sheep—where do they get so many?'

'Hmph!' snorted Fergal. 'The same place they got the Dé Danann—from the farms and holdings they have raided all summer. That's where!'

'Animals?' said Aedd. 'Was it animals you saw up there?'

For the benefit of Dearg and Aedd who had not witnessed the degrada-tion of their countrymen, Conor said, 'It is not just a few cattle, mind—or even a few dozen. They were slaughtering animals by the score.' In a low voice, he added, 'And not just cattle. There were people, too.'

Aedd and Dearg glanced around at the grim expressions on the faces of the others. 'Many people?'

Fergal nodded. 'Too many.'

'Thirty or so,' said Donal.

'Fifty at least,' growled Fergal. 'Too many.'

'They were killed together and thrown onto a great, stinking heap,' Conor told them bluntly. He went on to describe the abandoned works surround-ing the dún and the deserted hall and dwellings. Then, haltingly, his voice breaking now and again, he told about finding the horse pen filled with birds feasting on the corpses of executed Dé Danann. 'Maybe as many as fifty, aye. And all Dé Danann from what we could see.'

'Men, women, and children, they were,' snarled Fergal. 'Murdered and then thrown onto a great heap like rotten meat. The stench reaches to the clouds and the sky is filled with all manner of corpse-picking birds. On my sword and shield and spear, I swear I have never seen anything like it.'

He shook his head fiercely. 'What were the bastard dog-eaters doing up there?'

The all gazed at one another in confusion. Finally, Conor said, 'Nothing good. That much is cert—'

'I have it!' said Donal abruptly. 'Why didn't I see it before?'

'Well?' demanded Fergal.

'It's leather.'

'Leather?' Fergal and Conor exchanged a wondering glance.

'They were making leather,' Donal repeated. 'Think about it . . . the vats . . . the furnaces . . . the animal bones . . . the charnel heap. . . . It is leather they were making, and I think I know why.'

'Are *we* to know at all?' said Fergal.

'Think you now. The vats were for flenching and washing the hides—which were taken from the animals.'

'Which accounts for all the carcasses,' mused Conor. 'And the furnaces?'

'For making the lime to put in the vats in order to cure the hides.'

'That explains all those wooden frames,' added Conor. 'For stretching the hides while they dried.' Conor considered this and decided it did make sense. 'And the human remains—the skeletons? What about those?'

Donal went very still. 'Slaves,' he said. 'Dé Danann slaves . . . they were the ones slaughtering the cattle, working the slurry vats, washing and scraping the hides. They also quarried the limestone and stoked the furnaces to make the quicklime.'

'Slaves . . . dozens of them.' Conor rubbed his burning cheek to ease the fiery tingling there, but it was no relief.

'But why do the dog-eaters need so much leather?' wondered Galart.

Before Donal could reply, Conor said, 'Armor—the Scálda arm themselves with hardened leather.'

'And harnesses for their horses,' added Fergal, 'and probably for those war carts we saw. They have no end of use for the stuff.'

'Then why abandon the settlement?' wondered Galart.

'Who can say?' replied Fergal. 'Maybe they have all the leather they need.'

'Aye, all they need to complete the taking of Eirlandia,' added Conor.

A sickly silence settled over them as the implications of this suggestion hardened into certainty. Combined with what they had seen of the wanton destruction of the deadlands and the constant need for vigilance in hostile territory, this latest revelation pushed the fianna to the edge of the abyss where they teetered, about to fall over into a churning welter of hopelessness and desolation. Conor knew. He felt it, too. But, as their leader, he also knew that giving into despair now would be inviting disaster.

Dragging together the scattered shreds of his own courage, he rose from his place and took up his spear. Raising Pelydr high, he brought down the butt of the shaft with a solid thump. 'Hear me, brothers. I know what you are thinking. Today, we have seen the bestial depravity of our pitiless enemy. Think on it. Think long and hard so you will remember. Today we have seen what the Scálda intend for all our race should they succeed in wresting Eirlandia from our grasp.

'Hear me!' He slammed the butt of the spear again with a sound like the crack of a bone. 'Before you, my swordbrothers, my fianna, I make this vow. I will neither rest nor cease from striving to free our land from the evil of the Scálda invasion. Though it cost my life and the lives of all I love and all I hold most dear, while there is yet breath in my body, I will not abandon the fight. I will see this outrage avenged. And I *will* see the day the Dé Danann rule this island realm in peace once more.'

Sleep was a long time in coming for Conor. He kept turning the image of the massive mound of corpses in his mind and hearing the cries of the rooks and ravens. When at last sleep came, he felt a light touch on his shoulder. Instantly awake, he sat up to see Donal bending over him. Pressing a finger to his lips, he handed Conor his spear and gestured for him to follow.

Into the night dark wood they went, quietly threading their way around trees and through the undergrowth, working their way along the river. As they neared a marshy fording place, Conor noticed the pale glow of a light shining through the trees. Donal saw it, too, and slowed; crouching low, they edged toward the ford for a better look. 'There is someone on the trail,' whispered Donal. They both stared through the thick-grown elder and scrub willow, trying to see into the path beyond.

'What is that light?' said Conor. 'Not a torch, I think.'

Donal, his face ghostly in the pale, unflickering light, squinted his eyes and gazed ahead. After a moment, he shook his head. 'Nay, nay, not that. It is something else.'

'Can you see who it is?' asked Conor.

'Nay, brother, I cannot.'

'I'll go see. Stay here and be ready with your spear if I shout.'

Dropping down on all fours, Conor crawled through the low-growing shrubs to the very edge of the wooded trail where, hunkered down behind a leafy elder bush, he parted the branches slightly and peered out upon an outlandish sight: a group of four tall figures shining with a spectral light. Whether the glow emanated from these beings, or whether they stood within it, was not at all clear, but Conor had seen enough. Rising to his feet, he pushed through the branches, stepped out into the clearing and strode toward the shining ones with strong purposeful strides.

Fergal, having been wakened by the furtive movements in the night, appeared at Donal's shoulder. 'What's happening?' he whispered, dropping down to kneel beside him. 'Is that . . . ?'

'Rhiannon!' replied Donal. Throwing back his cloak, he leapt up and started to run. 'The faéry have returned!' he called back, hurrying to join the shining figures on the plain.

Conor glanced around as Donal and Fergal arrived, and beckoned them into the glowing orb of light enveloping the group. 'Brothers, our friends need our help,' he announced.

One glance at Rhiannon and her companions left no doubt: the faéry were in a desperate, dishevelled state. Of the four, Rhiannon seemed in the worst condition: her lustrous black hair hung in limp tangles; her immaculate clothing was crumpled and smudged—her cloak frayed and ravelled at the hem, and her seamless green mantle torn at the shoulder and travel-stained; her usually pale skin was dull and ashen; there were dark circles under her eyes, and those eyes gazed out with the unnatural brightness of fever, or fear. Those with her were no less distressed and anxious; their flesh, like their lady's had a grey, waxy appearance, and all wore gaunt and haggard expressions—as if they had succumbed to a wasting disease. There was Olwen, the princess's handmaid, her gaze empty, her slender body swaying with fatigue; and Morfran, King Gwydion's brother, visibly shaken and distraught; and Eraint, the ship's pilot who they had met when on the return voyage to Eirlandia, mute, rigid, as if bearing great pain at enormous cost. During their sojourn on the Isle of the Everliving, the Dé Danann had met them all from time to time and knew them well; in their present state, however, they were nearly unrecognisable. All three stood stiff and unmoving, watching the Dé Danann with grim wariness—as if fearing some great evil was about to devour them.

'My dear friends,' Rhiannon was saying, 'I am overjoyed to have found you so quickly. . . .' Here she wavered.

Conor reached out and took her hand in his; the flesh was cold and clammy. 'What has happened? Tell us and trust that we will help you if we can.'

Clutching Conor's hand in a fierce grip, she reached out with the other and touched first Donal, and then Fergal as she said, 'The worst has befallen us.' Her voice quivered on a note of anguish. 'My father has been taken.'

'Taken,' repeated Conor. 'You mean captured.'

She nodded, dropping her head. 'Captured, yes.'

'Who's taken him?' asked Fergal. 'Was it Balor Evil Eye?'

The faéry princess put her face in her hands; her shoulders trembled as she nodded. 'I fear we may already be too late. I cannot . . . cannot reach him.'

'What happened?' asked Donal gently.

Eraint, the pilot spoke up, the words coming in a rush. 'The king and his advisors were sailing to Albion,' he said, his voice trembling with anger and violence. 'A Scálda ship found them and gave chase. They were overtaken and boarded. Lord Gwydion was captured and his men were killed.'

'But you escaped?' said Conor.

'Rhiannon and those with her were in a second ship with me. When the first was caught, we were able to fight free and escape.' He glanced at Rhiannon and added, 'We have come seeking your help to rescue our king.'

'How did you find us?' asked Donal.

'That could not have been easier,' Rhiannon replied and offered a sad, forlorn smile. 'As Conor will know.'

'Magic?' said Fergal, catching the implication. His eyes, lit by the mysterious faéry glow, sparked with interest and he looked to Conor for confirmation.

Instead, Conor merely said, 'And do you also know where to find your father?'

'I do. But now that we are here, I feel our strength is much diminished. All Eirlandia seems to conspire against us. It is the iron here—there is so much of it about.'

'The Scálda have been building mines and forges all over the southlands,' agreed Donal. 'Indeed, the stuff is everywhere.'

Conor announced, 'We will gladly help rescue your father. To that end, we will require your aid in concealing us from the enemy. If you can make a charm to help us elude capture, we will be that much further toward saving Gwydion.'

Rhiannon was already shaking her head before Conor finished speaking. 'I am sorry, my friends,' she said, 'but we have no magic.'

Fergal raised his eyebrows. 'No magic? None at all?'

'Our powers are not ours alone,' she said, and quickly explained that the mystical force of her race descended from on high through the reigning monarch, king or queen. 'The health of the king is everything to us. When the king suffers, we *all* suffer. Even the land derives its well-being from that of the king.'

'No magic, then,' said Fergal, stroking his moustache. 'That will make things more difficult.'

It was Rhiannon who answered. 'We may not have the use of charms and *caims*,' she told him, her voice taking on strength and fire, 'but we are not without some of our more subtle arts and the woodcraft that we have perfected and employed through the long history of our race.' She fixed her gaze on Fergal as she concluded, saying, 'These will aid your efforts if you will but trust us.'

'I am admonished, lady,' said Fergal, ducking his head in a small bow. Looking to Conor, he said, 'So then, it is decided. What next?'

Turning to Rhiannon, Conor said, 'Lady, we are ready to ride. Show us the way, and leave the rest to us.'

21

From the moment they departed the glen, the night took on a bizarre quality none of the Dé Danann could explain or later describe. Under Rhiannon and Morfran's guidance, the journey became a fevered blur of furious motion through darkened woodland and moonlit meadows, face-less figures half seen, strange sounds, imagined creatures looming out of the shadows and disappearing again—all visions, no doubt inspired by Re Ronea, Goddess of the Night and Horses and Dreams.

The frantic pace pursued by the company began to slow with the first glints of dawn brightening the eastern sky, and by the time the sun breached the horizon, they could hear the restless churn of the wave-washed strand on a deserted stretch of beach. Here the spent horses finally stopped, and their exhausted riders dismounted in the thick morning fog flooding in from the sea. Dé Danann and Tylwyth Teg alike stood swaying on their feet, stretch-ing aching backs, or slumping onto the damp shingle; Fergal and Galart scanned the surrounding cliffs and heights for any sign that their presence had been discovered.

Now, as the morning sun brought a thin measure of light to the land, Conor felt as if he had been moving mountains with his bare hands. Fa-tigued to the pith and marrow, he lowered himself onto a rock and cradled his head in his hands, his mind clouded as with the sea fog, trying, but fail-ing, to think how they had come here. He remembered setting off. With a faéry mounted behind each Dé Danann rider, he and Rhiannon had led the way. After that, his memory became a jumble of images out of turn: flying through the woodland, ducking tree boughs and low-hanging limbs, hearing vague sounds of a chase behind them, halting in a river and standing in the water for a time, and then riding at full cry over hills and along the reed-fringed shore of a lough while the moon came and went with the scattered, wind-driven clouds overhead. Mostly, he remembered glancing behind him every now and then to see how far behind the phantom pursuit might be, while at the same time trying to keep everyone together lest anyone become lost along the way.

Stirring himself, he rose slowly, stretched again, and walked down the strand where he knelt and washed his face—once, twice. He took a mouthful of cold seawater, swished it around and spat it out, licking the sharp, salty tang on his lips. Somewhat revived, he returned to where Rhiannon and Olwen sat staring dull-eyed at the grey sea—numb, expressionless, swooning with fatigue. Clearly, the faéry were all at the end of their endurance. Conor beckoned Aedd and told him, 'Make a fire. We will rest here a little and recover our strength.'

'Not here, brother,' countered Fergal. 'This shore is too exposed. We must find some better shelter.' He gazed down along the coastline to the south. 'There must be a cave or hollow somewhere nearby. We can rest there.'

'As we did with Mádoc,' said Donal. He, too, looked along the coast, and then back to where Dearg, having gathered the reins, was standing with the horses, steam rising from their broad backs in the early morning light. 'The horses must be fed and watered,' he added, 'but we cannot do that here. Fergal's right. We'll have to move on.'

Roused by the sound of their voices, Rhiannon stirred. She glanced around and, seeing the others standing around her, struggled to rise. Conor knelt beside her, put an arm under her shoulders and helped her to sit up. 'Bring a water skin!' he called, and Aedd hurried to his mount, returning a moment later with a half-filled skin.

Conor pulled the stopper and offered it to her. She thanked him and drank, then passed back the skin, saying, 'Please, give some to the others.'

Donal called Galart to gather the water skins and share them out among the faéry. As the skins were fetched and passed around, Conor, kneeling beside Lady Rhiannon, said, 'We are moving on to better shelter. Are you able to ride?'

She regarded him with eyes the colour of a troubled sky, bit her lip and nodded. A few moments later, all were mounted again and they moved on—albeit at a much slower pace than before—riding along the high water line, searching for a cave or secluded nook where they could make camp and rest before continuing their mission to save King Gwydion.

The southern coastline opened before them as a series of cliffs and collapsed rock stacks that formed numerous coves and crannies. They soon found a tiny bay secluded enough to afford protection from anyone watching the shore. Runnels carved in the shingle fed freshwater from the land to the sea, and sheer rock walls provided a low overhang to form a fair shelter from the wind and rain. Here they stopped and, after tending and tethering the horses, they built a fire of driftwood and dried seaweed, and slept—waking late in the afternoon to prepare a meal. Still tired from the previous night's exertions, they decided to stay the night and move on the next morning. Aedd and Dearg put the horses to graze through the remainder of the day, and took it in turn with Galart to keep an eye on the coastal pathways for any sign of Scálda raiders, fishermen, or a hunting party. Then, as the dwindling day's shadows gathered around them, Conor, Fergal, and Donal sat down with Rhiannon and Morfran in counsel while Eraint and Olwen and Dearg tended to the cooking chores for their meagre evening meal of porridge and bósaill boiled in seawater.

Rhiannon began by relating the chain of events that had led the faéry to Eirlandia. 'Some little while after you left us,' Rhiannon said, her voice soft in the twilight, 'what you said about the necessity of the Dé Danann and Tylwyth Teg uniting forces to vanquish the Scálda began working in my father's mind.'

Conor remembered that conversation—and the fact that it had not ended well—but offered a polite nod of acknowledgement and tossed another knot of dried seaweed to the fire. It fizzed and crackled and shrivelled before bursting into flames. 'I said a lot of things, as I recall.'

'Aye,' agreed Fergal, 'you always do.' To Rhiannon he said, 'Which of our friend's many misspoken words happened to catch King Gwydion's ear?'

'It was that inasmuch as we have a common enemy our interests are the same, and that if the Scálda succeed in conquering Eirlandia then Tír nan Óg will be next for destruction. And, as we know to our cost, they have acquired the ability to capture our ships.' She gave Conor a forlorn smile. 'My father told me what you said and I can almost see you standing before the king, pounding your fist into your hand, saying, "By standing together we can overpower the Scálda and drive them from this worlds-realm forever!" This, I think, is what finally began to work in Gwydion's heart.'

'Lord Gwydion heard my plea to join forces, aye, so he did,' Conor replied. 'But I was left in no doubt that the king believed a war with the Scálda could not be won and it was a cause he no longer chose to pursue. He said the faéry would leave the mortals to their own demise.' He shrugged. 'Something like that.'

'You are too harsh, I think,' Rhiannon countered gently. 'But you are right in thinking him opposed to any further involvement in the endless war with the Scálda.'

'Even so, the king changed his mind?' said Donal. 'He has agreed to help us?'

'He gave us weapons, after all,' Fergal pointed out.

Before Rhiannon could reply, the taciturn, wary Morfran spoke up. 'You misunderstand,' he said sharply. 'Our king has not agreed to any such thing. He has merely determined to put aside ancient enmities and seek peace with the Aes-sídhe.'

'What so?' wondered Fergal. 'Admirable as that may be, it does little to help us against the Scálda.'

'That was but the first step on the way,' Rhiannon said quickly, casting a disapproving glance at her uncle. 'It was my father's fervent hope to convince King Lenos and the Aes-sídhe to join us in an alliance with the aim of aiding the Dé Danann in the fight with the Scálda.'

'Was he on the way to see King Lenos?' asked Donal. 'Or on his way home from having seen him?'

'I am sorry to say, it was the former,' replied Rhiannon. 'Messages had been sent, and envoys received. The Aes-sídhe had agreed to meet at Eilean Ceó in Albion and my father was keen to make the first effort without delay. He summoned his advisors and several lords of our tribes to accompany him, and we all set out together.'

Morfran took up the tale, saying, 'We were hardly out of sight of Ynys Afallon when our ships were attacked. One vessel was sunk, one captured, and ours was badly damaged.'

'We were able to make landfall here in the south,' said Rhiannon. 'And we came to find you as soon as we reached the shore.'

'You knew where we were to be found?' said Fergal.

'Aye, Fergal,' she replied, a wistful note in her voice, 'I will always know where to find you.'

Conor nodded thoughtfully, recalling the charm she had used on him and her words at their first parting . . . *I have only to speak your name to know where you can be found—and you have only to whisper mine and I will be there.*

'You said you also know where to find Gwydion,' said Donal.

'We do,' answered Morfran curtly. 'He is here in the south, no doubt a captive in one of the Scálda fortresses.'

Fergal glanced at Conor. 'There are all too many of those,' he muttered.

'We may not know the name of the ráth,' Rhiannon added quickly, 'but so long as my father remains alive, we can lead you to the place where he is being held. I can tell you that we are closer now than we were last night. I can feel it.'

'Tomorrow we will be closer still,' Conor told her. 'And once we've found him, we will do our best to free him.'

Later, after they had eaten and the faéry were asleep, Fergal, spear in hand, pulled Conor aside to say, 'Brother, I am thinking you have been somewhat overhasty today.'

'Have I?' Conor regarded him curiously. 'In what have I been overhasty?'

'We are only six warriors to be attacking a Scálda fortress,' he said.

'Six? As many as that?' replied Conor, refusing to take Fergal's point.

'That is six blades against . . . how many? Sixty? A hundred? Two hundred and sixty?'

'Six Dé Danann blades are worth a dozen Scálda as we know,' remarked Conor.

'No argument there,' Fergal conceded, 'but that is still not enough. You know I do not shrink from a fight—'

'Nor do I.'

'It is not your courage I doubt. But I would be a poor advisor if I did not advise you to turn around and ride north where we can gather a proper warband to help free Gwydion.'

'Ach, that would be a fine thing indeed. If only we enjoyed the particular luxury of time,' Conor told him. 'Raising such a warband as you describe would take weeks—months, more like—and that is *if* we could even get anyone to listen to us. We are outcasts still, remember? And there are few who would credit a single thing we said, much less join us.'

'They would, you know.'

'My point is it would take time, and the faéry cannot wait. Look at them, man! They are wasting away before our eyes. Can it be you are forgetting how we rescued Rhiannon? Just us three. Nobody else. What we did once, we can do again. We'll find a way.'

Fergal's frown deepened.

'Fergal, hear me, the Lord Gwydion is suffering. How much longer he will endure we cannot know. Even if we left now and our horses sprouted wings, I fear the king would be dead before we reached the borderlands.'

'We do not know that,' Fergal pointed out. 'But I *do* know that getting ourselves killed will not help them draw one breath more. I think *you* are forgetting why we came here in the first place!'

'I have not,' replied Conor. He regarded his friend for a long moment, then put his hand on Fergal's shoulder and said, 'But isn't it just possible that where King Gwydion is, there Balor Evil Eye will be? Sooner or later, Balor will come to see his prize.'

'Are you sure about that?' demanded Fergal. 'No? Then why waste time thinking about it? If we are to succeed, we must have more men.'

Conor sighed. 'I thank you for your wise counsel, brother. You have done me good service.'

'Does that mean you will consider what I've said?'

'Aye,' Conor told him. 'I will think long and hard.'

'And then?' Fergal regarded him narrowly. 'Will you tell me yet?'

'Not yet.' Conor patted him on the back. 'But soon.'

Fergal, knowing he had pressed Conor as far as he could for the moment, contented himself with this answer, and watched as Conor returned to the fire ring where he wrapped himself in his cloak and stretched out to sleep. Fergal walked down the pebbled strand to stand at the water's edge where he stood for awhile, listening to the waves splash against the boulders out in the bay. The night was growing chill on a steady breeze out of the west, shredding the low clouds to allow a little starlight to peep through now and then. There was no moon to be seen. At least, he considered, that would make it more difficult for the Scálda to track them.

Thinking this, he went in search of Aedd, who was sitting up on the bluff above the bay, keeping watch on the trail. 'All quiet up here, brother?' he asked.

Aedd yawned and climbed to his feet. 'Nothing stirring tonight. There may be rain by morning.'

Fergal drew a long breath down into his lungs and tasted the fresh wetness on the wind. 'Most likely, aye,' he agreed. 'You best go down and warm yourself by the fire. I'll take the next watch.'

After the younger man had gone, Fergal sat down on the rock Aedd had just left. The lumpy perch was still warm. Fergal put the shaft of his spear across his lap and sat listening to the wind in the heights above and the waves on the shingle below. The fitful wind moaning through the night sky seemed to echo his disquiet. *Why uneasy, old lad?*

He had, on reflection, no reason for anxiety . . . other than the fact that here they were, a tiny band of outcasts with few friends and fewer resources, alone and wandering around in hostile lands with ailing faéry the enemy would stop at nothing to capture. The hopelessness of the thought made him smile. 'Not a reason in the world to be worried,' he murmured to himself.

He was still smiling a moment later when he heard footsteps behind him. He rose and spun around, sweeping the blade into fighting position in one swift motion. 'Be easy, brother,' came the voice out of the darkness.

'Donal, man, what are you doing up here now? I thought you were asleep.'

'Ach, I could not sleep for thinking,' replied Donal.

'Thinking was it?' Fergal wondered, taking up his place on the rock once more. 'And what was it you were thinking that kept you from your peaceful slumbers?'

Donal joined him on the rock. 'I was thinking that Conor needs our help.'

Fergal reared back and half turned to face Donal beside him. 'Is that what you were thinking now?'

'Aye, so it was.'

'And why would you be thinking a daft thing like that?' Before Donal could reply, he continued. 'All the world *knows* our Conor needs every last scrap and crumb of help he can get—all that and more besides!' He blew air threw his nostrils in a hearty snort. 'And here I was thinking you were going to say that we are in heavy mud and the waters are rising . . . or that we have bit off a chunk of gristle too big to swallow . . . or that our hut is on fire and the door is barred.'

'This is what you were thinking?' asked Donal, regarding him askance.

'Ach, aye. That is our very present predicament.' Fergal looked away. 'And is it that you imagine I am not helping Conor that you say something like this to me?'

'The thought occurred to me,' Donal confessed.

They were quiet for a time, listening to the wind and waves, content in one another's company. After a time, Fergal sighed, 'So, now, about this Second Sight of yours. What do you see coming down the path toward us?'

'Nothing good.'

Fergal accepted this dire pronouncement calmly. 'Well, it is no more than I know already. Can anything be done to prevent it?'

'That is beyond my poor ability,' replied Donal. 'I see only blood and confusion ahead.'

'Whose blood? Mine? You can tell me if that is what you see.'

'I would, brother, but I cannot. Even so, I have been in enough battles to know that when blood flows and chaos reigns, there is also opportunity to achieve greatness.' His voice took on an ominous tone. 'Brother, I think we are about to enjoy a rare opportunity.'

Fergal considered this. 'That is why you come up here telling me that we must help Conor as much as we can?'

'So it is,' replied Donal evenly. 'It is through Conor that our portion of greatness will be won.'

'Or lost?'

'Aye,' he agreed softly, 'or lost.'

Rónán

Many a word spoken in passion's heat is regretted by reason's cool regard. Thus, I held my tongue lest I say something I would later regret. Ach, I was that angry that I might have spit flames and daggers had Liam appeared before me then.

Druid bards are well schooled in the ways that excitements of any kind can cloud the keenest judgement. I may not be the wisest brehon to ever shake a staff, but having spoken at length to Aoife, I knew well enough to let my temper burn itself to cold ashes before confronting Liam with his foul behaviour toward that dear girl.

Accordingly, I sought out Tuán and spent the day roaming the rocky hills of Dúnaird's northern fastness. We watched the flocking birds and sought to discern from the patterns of their flight a meaning for our time. We gathered a few plants bearing roots or leaves beneficial for healing, and observed one of the Darini shepherds with his goats. Tuán knew my mood and did not press me to explain, but let me come to it in my own time. When I finally told him what designs Liam had on Aoife and how he was treating her he rolled his eyes and shook his head in disbelief. 'Does he loathe your brother that much that he would abuse the lady so?' he said.

'He is that jealous,' I replied.

'What will you say to him?'

'That is what I have been asking myself all day.' I shook my head and sighed. 'I will tell him what Aoife has told me and ask him to explain himself.'

'Poke the bear in his den.'

'A swift, sharp poke with a sharp stick is needed here, I think.'

'When?'

'We are to be leaving tomorrow, so it must be tonight.'

'In the hall?' he asked. 'With the warriors and serving men in atten-dance?'

'I will try to get him alone.' I shrugged. 'If not, then it will be in the presence of his men. So be it.'

Thus, I was resolved. I would speak and Liam would hear that this spite and unreasoning jealousy could have no place in a man who one day aspired to the kingship. But, as so often happens in the affairs of all who walk the world by day, intentions are overtaken by events. When I finally found my brother alone, I made bold to raise the subject of his unrighteous behaviour toward Conor, saying, 'A moment, Liam, I have something to say.'

'Well then? Say it, but be quick about it—the warriors are returned from the borders and the cups are waiting to be poured.'

'As you know, Tuán and I are leaving tomorrow. And I—'

'Tomorrow! So soon?'

'Samhain approaches, and we will be needed at—'

'Let Tuán go on without you,' Liam told me. 'I would have you sing at my wedding celebration.'

This simple declaration brought me up short. Who was to be the bride? For surely he could not mean Aoife. So long as she was convinced that Conor was alive she would never agree to marry anyone else—as anyone who knew her could have told him. I did not say as much to Liam, mind. I glanced around at the silent Tuán, who merely gazed ahead thoughtfully. 'I would be honoured, of course,' I told him, 'but I—'

'Good. It is settled.' He strode to the door of the hall and called for a serving maid, and when he told her to fetch Aoife to him so we could dis-cuss the ceremony and celebration he planned I realised the full extent of his delusion and the stormy waters we had entered.

The maid hurried away, and Liam returned to his chair while I tried to think how best to disabuse him of his plan. But even before the argument could form in my mind, the maid had returned with the report that Aoife had disappeared. Indeed, word of her disappearance was already flitting through the ráth. The explanation was shortly delivered by one of the tribe's elders: Inna, a stooped little woman of advanced age. She had been chosen, I suspect, because no one else dared risk their volatile prince's fearsome wrath. I watched Liam's face as he took in this news and saw the fire-born beast of rage flare up and seize him in its slavering maw.

Liam stared with hard eyes at the old woman for a moment, then curtly dismissed her to go about her chores and stormed back into the hall and hurled himself into his chair once more and slammed his fists upon the board so hard the cups jumped. A group of warriors who entered just then instantly discovered they had other things to do; Tuán gave me an encouraging nod and departed for the guesthouse. The hall was quiet, dark and cold.

I took a seat on the bench at the board and sat thinking what to say. I had just about decided when the door opened and Eamon appeared. He had heard that Aoife had gone and, good man, hurried to his prince's side. Thus, of all the tribe, only Eamon and I were left to attend Liam and quench his anger if we could.

'I will track her down and break her like the wild and wilful creature that she is,' Liam vowed. He wiped his hand across his face as if to rub away the insult. 'I will not rest until she is here beside me where she belongs. She *will* be my queen.'

These were not the sentiments of a lover for his beloved, but of a peevish and petulant child who had been refused the shiny ornament he desired and had persuaded himself belonged to him.

'Permit me to speak, lord,' said Eamon with a guarded glance at me. 'Perhaps she has only gone to—'

'Only what?' snarled Liam. 'Gone to pick flowers on the hills? Gone to collect walnuts in the grove? Gone to gather in the wayward calf?' He fixed his battlechief with a look of angry defiance. 'Since you seem to know so much, tell me—where, do you suppose she has gone, Eamon?'

Eamon had no answer to this, and looked to me for help.

'Nothing to say?' growled Liam. 'Ha! I thought not. You always take her part. Get out of my sight, stinking coward!'

'Hear me, Liam,' I said, entering the fray, 'Eamon is not to blame here. You speak out of anger like a thankless brat denied, and you wrong him to mistreat one who has been loyal through all things.'

'Wrong him? *I* am the one who is wronged here. No one considers the wrong done to me!' Half rising from his throne chair, he clenched his fist and thumped himself on the chest. 'I am a nobleman and warleader of our people! It is my right to choose my bride.' He flung the words in my face as a challenge. 'By my sword, I have chosen Aoife as is my right!'

I regarded him coolly, marshaling my thoughts. 'Do not presume to school me on the rights of nobility. No true sovereign builds his kingship on rights, but on the privilege of being elevated to lead his people. As prince and warleader of the Darini, you have no rights—only such honours granted you by your people. And, brother, you enjoy those honours *only* so long as your rule is true and just.'

Liam glared at me. 'How dare you speak to me like this!' he growled, spittle flying, his voice all but strangled with rage. 'False bard! How dare you!'

'I am your blood kin,' I replied. 'Moreover, I am a brehon in Eirlandia— and I speak to anyone I like in any way I choose. And as brother and bard, I tell you now that you are behaving in a manner most unbecoming a nobleman and leader.'

In some less fevered part of him, Liam knew I spoke the truth. He could not sustain his irrational argument and so looked away, his features a twisted rictus of frustrated fury. He longed for nothing more than to punish someone for the humiliation he felt at being openly spurned by Aoife. But there was no one to blame or punish. 'Leave me,' he moaned—as much a plea as a command.

'When you have regained your better judgement, we will speak again,' I told him. 'In the meantime, I will ride out in search of Aoife.'

'And bring her back?' asked Eamon softly.

'If possible,' I allowed.

'Then go,' said Liam, seizing on the opportunity to have the last word in this at least. 'Go now.'

Eamon walked to the entrance and stepped outside with me. 'When will you leave?' he asked, falling into step beside me.

'At once,' I told him. 'The sooner I find Aoife, the sooner we will resolve this problem. He must be made to understand that Aoife is not his to claim or command.'

'A problem of his own making,' Eamon murmured gloomily. 'Liam has his heart set on Aoife, but her loving heart is set on Conor—as it has been ever and always.' He paused, gave a quick sideways glance, and added, 'This is not the first time she has tried to flee our Liam's embrace. If you think to persuade her otherwise, save your breath. Never was a lady more devoted, nor more loyal to her man.'

'Even so,' I told him, 'she is alone out there and will not have an easy time of it. I cannot bear to think what Conor would do if anything should happen to her.'

'Do you want me to go with you?' said Eamon. Before I could say otherwise, he said, 'I am going with you.'

'But Liam will want—'

'Liam will be of a better mind if he thinks I go to help you bring her home.'

As soon as a few provisions and fresh horses could be secured, we departed Dúnaird and rode off in search of the runaway Aoife.

22

Conor and the fianna travelled with all the speed they could command—though it was not nearly as fast as need required. Traversing unknown terrain in territory seeded with enemy settlements—while riding double with ailing faéry—forced the company to go in halting fits and starts. They kept to the coastal pathways as long as possible, but eventually had to move inland. Conor sent Galart and Dearg ahead to scout the trailways in order to avoid any ráth or dún they might happen upon. Their food rations, already low, dwindled further; the fianna hunted when they could, making the most of their frequent rest stops to take whatever game they could find from the surrounding woodland trails. Once, they passed close to a Scálda holding and were able to make off with a yearling cow that had wandered too far away from the herd at pasture; that served them well for several days—but the supply of hardtack bread gave out, as did the bósaill and oats.

Rhiannon served as their guide and, though her strength was fragile and failing, she urged them along a determined southward course with unwavering resolve. The other faéry remained subdued and withdrawn, holding themselves apart—more out of habit and instinct, Conor imagined, than from arrogance or disdain. Then again, to have ventured so far into Scálda territory, and suffering as they clearly were, he did not begrudge them their distance. On the other hand, the fianna regarded the faéry with an awed but wary regard—fascinated by the exotic appearance of the enchanted race, and slightly fearful of them. Aside from Conor, Donal, and Fergal, who were easy in their company, the faéry were left to themselves and appeared on the whole to prefer it.

Still, the slow pace told on everyone.

'Would it not be better to leave Morfran and the others behind?' asked Fergal as he and Conor watched the fianna water the horses at the edge of a stream. 'They could rest and we would travel that much quicker. We could leave them in the care of Dearg or Aedd and the rest of us could then race ahead to Gwydion's aid.'

'There is much in what you say, brother,' Conor granted. 'But things may fall out such that we need every hand to help us.'

'A right ready hand, aye,' replied Fergal. 'But our friends are in no way fit for a fight, and only delay the help we aim to bring.'

'I wish we could move more quickly, too. I do. And I know that our slow pace goes hard against the faéry and chafes at us.'

'They grow more feeble as the days wear on—and that is a fact. You must have seen as much yourself.'

'Aye.' Conor puffed out his cheeks in a sigh, but would not relent. 'They must endure but a little longer,' he said at last.

'A little longer is all they have left.'

Having said what was in his mind, Fergal moved off to help with the watering, and Donal, who had been watching the exchange from a distance, turned away without comment. Later, as the sun began its sloping descent into the west, they paused at the edge of a grassy meadow to allow the faéry to rest and the horses to graze. Conor went to where Rhiannon and her handmaid, Olwen, were sitting beneath a spreading elm with her back hard against the trunk; Morfran and Eraint sat a little apart, heads resting on their knees. All four looked to Conor like warriors depleted after a long, losing battle.

'We have travelled far today,' said Conor, kneeling beside her. 'But the day is almost finished. We can rest a little longer and then find a place to shelter for the night.'

Lifting her head, Rhiannon pushed a strand of raven-black hair away from her pale face and gave him a brave smile, though clearly it pained her to do so. 'And our journey is soon at an end,' she told him. At Conor's alarmed expression, she put her hand on his arm. 'I mean only that the place where my father is imprisoned is near. I can feel it—though his strength is fading.'

'How near are we?'

She turned her head and gazed toward the rising woodland on the other side of the meadow. 'Within that wood is a river with a fording place. On the other side we will find a well-worn trail—a road. After a time, that road divides. One branch will continue north, and the other leads south and east to a small fortress on a rocky hill. . . .'

At her description an image flickered in Conor's mind along with the undeniable impression that he had been there before.

'. . . A strange little stronghold—walled with iron . . . a place of great violence,' Rhiannon continued. 'That is where my father will be found.'

'The Iron Ráth,' mused Conor. 'I think I know it.' He gazed at Rhiannon, a royal princess and loyal daughter struggling to remain brave and hopeful, yet the stresses of her ordeal showed in the taut lines of her face and the hot brightness of her crystalline blue eyes. His heart moved within him. Conor covered her hand with his and gave it a squeeze of encouragement; she returned the gesture with a weak smile. 'There is no need to ride further. We will camp here tonight,' he told her and rose. 'I will leave you to your rest.'

He hurried back along the riverbank to where Galart and Aedd had begun setting the horses to graze. He considered what Rhiannon had just told him about the ráth where her father was being held captive; it did sound very like the place King Brecan had been murdered, and not only the king, but Cethern, and Mog Ruith—as well as a fourteen Kerionid faéry. If indeed it was the same stronghold, then the princess was right: the Iron Ráth, as Conor called it, was indeed a place of great violence.

Galart, seeing the look of intense concentration on Conor's face, spoke up. 'Is something troubling you, lord?'

'Eh?' Conor glanced up, then shook his head. 'Nay—it is only that I am thinking I know this region and some of the land hereabouts. And I think I know where the faéry are leading us.'

'We must be getting close then,' observed Aedd. His easy acceptance of this fact cheered Conor somewhat. 'You were here before, then?'

'Aye—when I fled the Scálda ráth the night Lord Brecan was killed.' Conor regarded the wooded hills rising above the dell. 'Rhiannon tells me there is a river with a fording place just upstream a little way. The trail on the other side leads to the fortress.'

Fergal, coming up just then had overheard most of what was said. 'And that is where you think Gwydion is being held?'

'The very same,' Conor told him. 'Aye, and if I remember aright, it is where Balor and Brecan were wont to meet, and where I found Lenos and the Kerionid captives. Rhiannon tells me she believes her father is there now.'

'How far is this Scálda ráth of yours?' asked Donal coming up just then to join the others.

'Not far at all.' Conor observed the shadows lengthening through the valley, and said, 'We can easily be there by midday tomorrow if not before. But we must go quietly and with all caution. There will be Scálda lurking about—all the more if Gwydion is there.'

The rescuers spent a quiet, but restless night in their camp at the meadow's edge, moving on as soon as it was light enough to see. They rode in silence, every sense alert, through the early morning mist along pathways and trails that remained untraveled and untroubled by any sign of the enemy. As the sun quartered the sky, they came upon a wide, shallow river bounded by low banks overgrown with reed and rushes. A short ride upstream led them to the fording place Rhiannon had indicated; here they crossed and, after pausing to scout the immediate area and reassure themselves that they had the trail to themselves, they resumed their journey.

By midday they reached the place where the road divided, and took the southern branch, proceeding with renewed caution through a wood grown dense and heavy with older trees and impenetrable thickets of plum and bramble under overspreading limbs furred with thick green moss. The sun did little to dispel the shadows and the path grew damp and muddy. Judging from the hoof prints, many of them fresh, the little roadway had seen a fair amount of use recently. Finally, seeing the way ahead begin to rise, Conor called a halt and sent Fergal and Galart ahead to find a place where they could wait without being seen from the road. The two returned almost at once with the report that they had found the Scálda stronghold.

'Just around the next bend,' Fergal explained, 'the road descends to a reedy marsh. On the far side of the bog, there stands a great rocky hump of a hill and on that hill is a ráth.'

'They've thrown a wooden causeway across the bog that leads to the ráth,' Galart added. 'It looks wide enough for a horse or two men on foot—no more.'

'Did you see anyone about?' asked Donal.

'Not so much as a solitary hair on a single ugly head,' replied Fergal. 'Unless you told me otherwise, I would say the place was deserted.'

'My father is there,' Rhiannon said. Silent Morfran nodded in confirmation. 'I know it.'

'Good,' said Conor. 'Let's get off the road before someone comes. We'll find a place to wait.'

'The trees thin out as you near the marsh, but there is a lot of low scrub right to the banks of the bog,' said Galart. 'We can hide there easily enough and still keep watch on the ráth.'

'Show us,' Conor instructed, and Galart led them to where the road curved and the wood grew sparse. They moved off the road and sought cover in the brush growing along the banks of the bog. There they dismounted and tethered the horses. Leaving the faéry in the care of the fianna, Conor went with Fergal and Donal to spy on the stronghold and see what could be seen from across the marsh. Creeping through the low scrubby brush they came to the edge of the bog and there it was, sitting atop its steep-sided lump of a hill overlooking a sea of rushes in a quagmire: a ramshackle fortress of hastily erected walls made of nothing more substantial than hazel wickerwork hurdles bound together with rawhide straps and then lashed to iron hoops sunk into the ground; two timber posts supported a flimsy gate that opened onto a narrow ramp leading down to a wooden causeway across the soggy spread of the bog.

'Is this the dún you remember?' asked Fergal as they peered through the tall rushes at the hill with its flimsy little fortress on top.

'It is.'

'And is it as you remember it?'

'Aye,' affirmed Conor. 'Nothing has changed. As you can see, it is not much of a stronghold at all. It is made to keep the faéry in, I think, not to keep an enemy out.' Indicating the quagmire, he said, 'The marsh is the chief obstacle. Once across, there is nothing to stop us getting in.'

'What about watchmen? Guards?' asked Donal.

'None that I recall—at least not when I was here before. It seems to me that south of the deadlands the Scálda do not trouble themselves to maintain a watch or guard of any kind. That is to our advantage, too.'

'Think you now,' Fergal said, putting out a hand to the makeshift little dún on its rocky hump of hill, 'our tribes have never raided here.'

'Until tonight,' said Donal.

Conor smiled knowingly. 'Ach, aye. That changes tonight.'

Donal regarded the surrounding marsh again. 'Getting through the bog here will take some work—if it comes to that. Once the attack begins there will be no turning back.'

'The time for turning back passed long ago, brother.'

They watched the fortress for a while and then crept back to where the others were waiting and settled down to wait for night to fall. When at last the day's light began to fade in the west, Conor called the fianna to him to describe the plan he had been turning over in his mind. 'I will go in alone and free Gwydion,' he told them. 'I know where the Scálda keep their captives and I can work quickly. Once the king is free of his chains he or one of the others should be able to conceal us with a charm to make good our escape.'

'And if not?' wondered Galart.

'Then we will have a fight on our hands,' said Fergal.

'There may be guards up there, so I will wait for the darkest part of the night,' Conor continued. 'Everyone else must remain alert and watch for my signal . . .' He paused. 'If things go badly, you'll know it soon enough.' He glanced around at the ring of faces around him. 'If anyone has any questions, ask now.'

'What about Balor Evil Eye?' wondered Aedd. 'Will that great brute be there as well?'

'We don't know,' said Fergal bluntly.

'But that is a thing greatly to be wished,' added Conor. 'And if the Vermin King of the Scálda *is* there, then that crude fortress will become his tomb.'

'By the spear in my hand,' Fergal vowed, lofting the spear, 'if Evil Eye is there, the bony skull of his hateful head will become my drinking cup!'

'And his guts a feast for pigs,' added Galart. Others offered similar sentiments, rousing themselves to fighting pitch.

Conor felt his ruby-red birthmark begin to tingle as his blood warmed to the possibility of engaging the great adversary of his people in personal combat. Gazing at the faces now ringed around him, he said, 'Tonight is our first battle as a warband. Let each do all he can to make it a night of triumph.' The fianna pledged themselves to the fight, and Conor concluded, 'Go now and take your mounts. Be ready to move out on my signal.'

The fianna hurried to ready their horses and Conor went to Rhiannon and her companions and told them to be prepared to flee should the battle go against them. 'If you fail,' Morfran told him, 'we fail with you. There will be no flight for us.'

'So be it,' Conor replied. Hurrying to where Búrach stood waiting, he paused to stroke the stallion's head. The grey whickered and nuzzled him at his touch. 'Patience, my friend. There will be fighting before the night is through. Then you and I will show those dog-eaters what a Dé Danann champion can do.'

Pulling Pelydr from its strap beneath the grey's horsecloth, he brushed the design etched into the honed blade with his fingertips and felt the charmed weapon quicken in his grasp. Then, mounting Búrach, he raised the spear high as a signal to the others and set off, riding easily through wood in the quickly fading light, reaching the road a few moments later. The well-beaten track, sunk in shadow, led them through the dim and silent wood until they came in sight of the march and the hump of hill topped by the rude little stronghold of the Iron Ráth.

'To your places, men,' Conor ordered, his voice a strained whisper. The fianna scattered: Fergal and Aedd going off to take up a position on the left side of the track, and Galart and Dearg on the other. Donal joined Conor and they rode on to the end of the causeway where Conor led Búrach off the trail and into the wood; he found a place where they could watch both the causeway and the stronghold without being seen. There, he and Donal dismounted and, after tethering the horses a little way off, they settled back to wait for night to claim the marsh.

They sat for a long while in silence, listening to the quiet of the woodland around them and Conor was just about to doze off when Donal gave a jolt and sat up. 'Shh!' Placing a finger to his lips, he leaned close to Conor and whispered, 'Someone's coming!'

Rolling up onto his knees, Conor peered out through the brushy tangle to see a body of riders emerge from the wood and onto the wooden causeway. A fair-sized company—ten or more warriors, armed with swords and shields. Four of them carried torches to light a path already steeped in darkness. The riders clattered across the wooden causeway across the marsh and up the ramp leading to the dún. As the last of them disappeared through the gate, Conor turned to Donal and asked, 'Was Balor Evil Eye with them, do you think? Did you *see* him?'

Donal understood what Conor meant; he squinted as his sight turned inward. In a moment, he shook himself and replied, 'Nay, brother. He is not.'

'Pity,' Conor sighed. Would that his great foe had been among those returning to the ráth. That he might have had a chance to end the war at a single stroke—and that chance failed—left an almost bitter taste in his mouth and he spat. 'Too much to hope for, I suppose.'

They hunkered down again to wait and the wood round about soon echoed to the squawks and chatter of home-roosting rooks and crows; when those at last diminished, the nocturnal creatures began to stir: frogs in the marsh, and mice, ferrets, and rabbits in the undergrowth. From the hilltop fortress came neither light nor sound. All remained quiet within the walls. Still later, as the night air grew chill, clouds of misty fog began rising from the marsh, flooding the low, marsh-bound land, making an island of the rocky scrag of a hill. When at last the moon, which had long since risen above the treetops, began its descent, Conor decided it was time to act.

He gave Donal a nudge to rouse him, then rose, rolling his shoulders to loosen muscles grown tight from the long vigil. Unpinning his cloak, he handed it to Donal; sliding Eirian, his faéry sword, into his belt, he took up his spear and shield and said, 'Watch for my signal. I won't be long.'

Creeping quickly and quietly to the wooden causeway, Conor paused to thrust Pelydr's blade into the mire and stir it around. He pulled the muddy blade from the ooze and, satisfied that the razor-honed edge would not catch the moonlight, he sprinted quickly across the walkway, his footfall making a dull thump on the planks. He paused at the bottom of the fortress hill and looked at the narrow switchback path ahead; in the dim light of the waning moon the track could be seen as a pale thread winding its way up to the entrance. Anyone looking down from above would, perhaps, see only a vague shadow flitting up the hillside.

Halfway to the top, Conor paused again to listen and cast a glance at the rickety wall rising directly above him—no sound or movement could be detected. Drawing a breath, he resumed his climb. Once he gained the top, he moved off the track and started around the perimeter of the ramshackle fortress, keeping close to the wickerwork wall, halting every few paces to listen. Hearing nothing to alarm him, he moved on.

Slowly, slowly, Conor worked his furtive way around the fort. Within the walls, if memory served, he recalled only two buildings: a large, thatched-roof round house used for a hall where Brecan and Balor met, and a crude hut where King Lenos and the Aes-sídhe faéry had been imprisoned—as he discovered when held there briefly himself. Once he had located that hut—not difficult, even in the dark—he lay aside his shield and spear and, drawing Eirian from his belt, quickly sliced through the rawhide straps binding the top of two wattle hurdles together, then did the same at the bottom. Having loosened one section, he then cut through the straps binding the wicker panel to the half-buried iron wheel rim to which the hurdle was fastened.

He shifted the panel from its place, set it aside, and peered through the little doorway just created directly behind the hut. The rough-timber wall of the hovel blocked any view of the yard or round house beyond. He stopped to listen. Hearing nothing to alarm him, Conor ducked under the iron arch formed by the half-buried rim and stepped through the gap. Slowly, slowly, he edged his way around the hut to get a view of the yard. Clouds had begun moving in some little time ago, and the darkness was now almost complete. He stared intently into the shadows, but could discern no activity in the yard—no guards, no watchers; the compound appeared empty save for a line of horses picketed along the far wall on the other side of the hall. Even so, he crouched down and waited for a time to see if anyone emerged from the house. No one came or went and, save for the occasional murmur of voices and a burst of rowdy laughter issuing from the round house, all remained quiet.

Conor retreated to the back of the hut where, his mouth pressed against the timber cladding of the hut, he whispered, 'Gwydion!'

He waited a moment, then whispered again. He drew his sword and was about to tap against the wall when he heard the sound of movement inside.

'Gwydion, can you hear me?' He waited. 'Can you hear me? It's Conor.' He waited.

'Gwydion, is that you—'

'Conor?' The word was soft as a feather falling, lacking all strength—a mere sigh. 'You're here?'

'I have come for you, my friend. Your rescue is at hand.' He hurried around the building and, with a last glance across the quiet, empty yard, moved quickly to the rickety door and pulled the peg from the hasp to open the door.

Stepping into the darkness he was almost overcome by the overripe sour stench of urine and human waste. 'I'm here,' he whispered. 'Where are you?'

'Here, Conor,' came the reply in the fluttery murmur of an ailing creature. 'Over here.' Fumbling his way in the darkness, Conor moved toward the sound and saw a dark, formless shape bunched in a corner.

'Rest easy, my friend,' Conor told him. Kneeling, he extended a hand to the unmoving mass before him. He felt a body that quivered at his touch. He moved his hand around until he felt what he knew would be there: an iron chain. 'I will soon have you free.'

Hand over hand, Conor followed the links to where the end was fixed to one of the metal hoops that lined the walls of the hut—the iron wheel rims used in the construction of Scálda war carts; these overlapping rims formed the barrier of iron against which the faéry had no defence. As before, Conor found that the chain was fixed to the wheel rim by a large ring. Unlike last time, however, this ring was heavier and much more firmly attached. He tried prizing it open at the join using the point of his sword, but on contact with the iron he felt something of the charmed force go out of the blade and feared he might damage the weapon if he persisted in forcing it.

'This will take a little doing,' he told Gwydion. 'I must find something to loosen it.'

Moving to the faéry lord's side once more, he sought the end of the chain and found that it was attached to a heavy iron band encircling the captive king's stomach. For good measure, another length of chain secured the king's hands. Conor was still examining the links and fixings when he heard horses in the yard outside. Diving for the door, he peered out to see three more Scálda riders pounding through the gate; they were quickly joined by four more, two of which held torches. The horses were lathered, having been ridden hard, and the sudden appearance of the newcomers brought a few warriors out from the hall. Conor, his face pressed to the crack in the door, watched them dismount and one of them—a large, black-bearded hulk almost as wide as he was tall—summoned one of his men; the two exchanged a word and then the fellow called a command to the dozen or so warriors now gathered outside the hall. Three of their number took up the reins of the exhausted horses and led them away. Two other warriors stepped forward; one of these was handed a torch, and the two started across the yard toward the hut. 'Someone's coming,' Conor hissed. He stepped through the door and pulled it shut, saying, 'Don't worry. I won't be far away.'

'Conor . . . don't go.'

'I'll be back as soon as they're gone.'

'Conor, no. Don't leave me . . .'

But Conor was already through the door and out.

23

Conor quickly closed the hasp and replaced the peg then slipped around the side of the hovel and out of sight of the yard. He pressed himself against the back wall of the hut and clutched his spear to his chest.

The footsteps grew louder as the Scálda guards approached, then stopped as the two reached the hut. Conor heard the rattle of the hasp and the creak of the door as it swung open. Torchlight seeped through the many cracks in the cladding, and one of the guards growled a command in his despicable tongue. There came a scraping sound on the wall and then the dull chink of the iron chains . . . more commands . . . and the sound of the chains moving.

They're taking him to the hall, thought Conor. He edged along the side of the hut and peered around the corner to see the faéry king being led away. The rest of the newly arrived Scálda were filing into the hall. Gwydion, hobbled by his chains, limped and lurched, supported in a careless, haphazard way between the two guards; all three headed across the yard to the round house. Conor was not slow to recognise a gift when he saw one. Darting out from around the side of the hut, Conor streaked like a thrown spear to Gwydion's rescue.

At the rush of running feet, the guard holding the torch half turned, glimpsed a movement behind him and opened his mouth to shout. Conor's blade cut short the cry as the sword point found the guardsman's throat. Hot blood spurted into the cool night air. The torch spun to the ground as the Scálda grabbed his neck with both hands. He opened his mouth to scream, but blood bubbled from his throat instead. The second guard dropped the chain he was holding and reached for the knife in his belt as he turned.

Eirian flicked upward in a savage arc, catching the fellow just below the jaw, slicing effortlessly through the veins and tendons. The man tumbled like a lopped branch, his hand still fumbling at his belt.

Gwydion, limbs shaking, staggered backward under the weight of his chains. Conor leapt forward and caught him as he slumped. 'Can you walk?'

The faéry king gazed at him with glazed, unseeing eyes.

'Gwydion!' He put a hand to the king's face and forced him to look. 'Can you walk?' he rasped in a sharp whisper.

Before he could frame an answer, a shout echoed out across the yard behind them. Conor cast a quick glance back toward the round house. In the fitful moonlight he made out the form of a single warrior standing in the doorway of the hall; the fellow seemed to be scanning the yard. As yet, he had not seen the two escapees, nor had he seen the two Conor had slain.

Throwing an arm around the faéry lord's shoulders, Conor spun around and half carried, half dragged the faéry lord toward the wattle wall.

The warrior called out again. Likely, Conor reckoned, someone within the hall had begun wondering why the two sent to fetch the faéry captive had not yet returned, and this one had been sent to find out what could be taking so long. The warrior stepped out into the yard. He spied the torch, still faintly burning where it lay on the ground and started toward it, took a few steps and then, seeing the bodies, rushed to them.

Conor tensed, holding his breath. Gwydion shivered beside him.

The warrior picked up the torch and held it low over the corpse of the first fallen guard. Then, as Conor watched, the Scálda straightened and, raising the torch, turned his gaze slowly around the yard.

It was then he saw Conor and Gwydion huddled against the wall.

Rather, he saw something odd and started forth to find out what it might be, shouting as he came. He was but six paces away when Conor, sword ready, leapt up to meet him.

The sight of a Dé Danann warrior looming out of the darkness brought the Scálda to an instant halt. His free hand reached to his belt for a sword that was not there. Conor advanced to meet an opponent who had foolishly engaged without a weapon.

The Scálda gaped and opened his mouth to cry out—a cry that never came. One quick lunge and the keen-edged blade did its work, sliding up under the ribs into the heart. The guard toppled like a rotten tree.

Spinning around, Conor grabbed Gwydion and pulled him toward the gate. They crossed the yard and were but four or five steps from freedom when there came another shout from the hall behind them. Conor looked back to see three more warriors emerge from the round house hall—and one of them was the big battlechief Conor had seen arriving. The black-bearded brute glimpsed the two figures at the gate, and one of his men called a command. Another guard ran into the yard and stumbled over one of the bodies sprawled there. Regaining his feet, he started shouting to those behind him.

Conor took Gwydion's arm and gave him a shove to start him moving. 'Run for it!' he cried. 'My men are in the wood below and I am right behind you.'

The faéry king lurched forward, gathered himself and lumbered away. Wheezing and tottering like an enfeebled old man, he limped along, hindered by his chains and the enervating poison of the iron.

Conor spun to face the attack, cursing the fact that he had left both his shield and spear outside the wall. The warriors closed on him fast. Conor let them come, backing quickly through the gate and down the ramp; the angle would put him below his attackers, giving them the high ground, but on the relatively narrow ramp they would not easily be able to get behind him or surround him.

The first Scálda reached Conor in great bounding leaps, thrusting with short, quick jabs of his iron spear which Conor dodged easily. The warrior loosed a wild cry and lunged again. This time, Conor did not feint to the side, but stepped forward and, seizing the spear with his free hand, yanked it hard, pulling his attacker toward him. The Scálda, momentarily unbalanced, followed his weapon and Conor slammed the knob of the Eirian's hilt into the side of the warrior's face.

The Scálda fell sprawling. Tucking his sword into his belt, Conor seized the man's spear and swung it around in time to meet the second attacker, who made a great swipe with his shield to knock Conor's spear thrust aside and narrowly avoided being skewered. As the Scálda's shield swung out, Conor lunged in with the spear, opening a gash on the man's unprotected chest. The warrior yelped and scrambled back, out of range.

But two more screaming Scálda had reached the gate and two more rushed in behind them. Within three heartbeats, Conor had four blades waving in the air before his face. The first made a tentative stab at him and

Conor knocked away the halfhearted thrust. Another took its place and Conor knocked that one aside as well. A third drove in hard and Conor evaded the stroke and countered with a rapid sweep across the top that forced the attackers back—but only for an instant. There was more shouting from the yard behind them and the Scálda redoubled their assault. Conor deftly met each blow with a stroke of his own, but with each thrust and parry, he was forced to give ground. He edged farther down the ramp and, as he stepped backward, caught a glimpse of movement out of the corner of his eye and braced himself to take a strike.

Instead, a blade slashed out of the darkness catching the nearest attacker on the upper arm. The warrior yelped and dropped his weapon and suddenly Donal was at Conor's side, driving the point of his spear deep into the leather shield of the nearest Scálda attacker. In the sudden confusion, Conor dived forward to deliver a ferocious slash to an unprotected pair of legs and another attacker went down screaming. With Donal's shield between them, and Donal's deft spearwork, they were able to blunt the assault. The enemy retreated to the gate to regroup.

Donal cast a swift glance down the ramp and could just make out the lurching, lumbering form of the faéry king limping onto the wooden causeway. 'Time to go!' At the shout, Conor and Donal both turned and fled down the ramp. They caught up with Gwydion, still gamely hobbling as fast as his chains would allow, but struggling heavily, his breath laboured and coming in raking gulps and gasps. The sound of Conor and Donal's flying footsteps on the walkway planks brought Gwydion around, raising his hands as if to fend off the blows he feared were coming. Conor and Donal dashed forward and, each grabbing an arm, lifted him off his feet and carried him along.

High up on the ramp behind them they could hear cries and shouts as more angry Scálda boiled out from the Iron Ráth like wasps shaken from a poked hive. Running flat out, the two Darini and their charge reached the end of the causeway and streaked for the wood beyond. As they came within the canopy of the trees, Conor glanced around: at least four enemy warriors had reached the bottom of the ramp and three more were already on the causeway. Several more were halfway down the slope and, from what Conor could make out in the scanty pallor of the feeble moon, the black-bearded battlechief was among them, torch held high, shouting commands.

Conor and Donal, carrying the faéry lord between them, dashed into the wood. As soon as they passed within the shelter of the trees, they dived off the trail and hid behind the first big oak they found. Gwydion, wheezing like a wounded animal, lay on his side on the ground and Donal stood over him. The Scálda in blind pursuit behind them, unimpeded by any burden, raced headlong into the wood and down the road.

Here the frantic pursuit faltered. Uncertain where their prey had gone, the hunters paused and, with much shouting and cursing, began searching the nearby thickets and brushy undergrowth—frantically probing among the intertwined branches with their spear points and sword blades. They were thus preoccupied when the fianna, like the Hag Queen's avenging ravens, swooped out of the forest to wreak havoc upon their unsuspecting heads.

24

That thump of hooves and crash of breaking branches was the first warning the Scálda had that their lives were about to end. Out of the darkness of the surrounding wood, four charging horses burst through the undergrowth and onto the track. The enemy closest to the surprise attack were swiftly cut down or trampled beneath the churning hooves. Others turned and fled back toward the causeway where they were met by Conor and Donal. Two Scálda managed to escape by heaving themselves into the brush.

Having dealt with the first tranche of pursuers, the fianna turned to meet the second. Fergal wheeled his horse and took position in the centre of the road; Dearg, Aedd, and Galart filled in on either side. Fergal gave a shout and all lashed their mounts forward at once. They met the oncoming Scálda at the end of the causeway and cut them down. Any that tried to escape by running along the soft earth at the edge of the bog were met by Dearg and Aedd on one side, or Galart and Fergal on the other, and were quickly dispatched to take their places at Red Badb's grim feast in the Halls of Endless Night.

One by one, the attackers fell as they tried to force their way back onto the road. Against the mounted fianna, the enemy on foot could not form a serious threat, and when they realised their superior numbers gave them no advantage, some quit the causeway and leapt into the bog, floundering, splashing, wallowing their way through the mud and rushes to the safety of the mist-shrouded marsh and the night. The black-bearded battlechief and those with him on the causeway heard the sounds of the clash and the despairing cries of their kinsmen and halted. Standing on the causeway midway between the road's end and the ramp, the chieftain bellowed orders to those coming on behind him and within moments the Scálda had given up the fight and were scrambling back up to the stronghold.

'Get our horses!' shouted Conor, dashing onto the walkway.

Donal called after him. 'Conor, stop! What are you doing?'

'Get everyone mounted and ready to ride!' He put his head down and raced out across the bog, up the ramp to the ráth. Avoiding the gate, he ran around the outside of the walls to retrieve his Pelydr and Pared, his shield. From the Iron Ráth above, he heard the shouted commands of the battle-chief resounding across the yard as he prepared whatever remained of his warband to rally and form the pursuit. Quick as a shadow, Conor found the panel he'd cut out of the wall, scooped up his weapons; with Pelydr and Pared in his grip once more, he turned and fled back down the ramp and across the causeway to the road where Donal, ready mounted, was waiting with Búrach.

'Where are the others?' he shouted, snatching up the reins and vaulting onto the stallion's back.

'Gone ahead,' Donal said. 'We'll catch them on the way.' He glanced up at the ráth. 'Let's ride.'

'Hie!' Conor shouted and, with a snap of the reins, they were flying down the road through the wood. Trusting the instinct of the horses and any errant rays of moonlight that happened to reach the path, they soon came to the river ford and splashed across to meet Galart who was waiting for them on the other side. 'This way,' he said, and led them off the road and through a stand of young birch and hazel trees to a little clearing. Fergal was already working to remove the chains from Gwydion who lay lifeless on the moss-thick ground. Rhiannon and Morfran hovered at his shoulder, watching with mute anguish as Fergal, using the point of Galart's sword, struggled with the cold, killing iron binding the faéry king.

Sliding down from Búrach, Conor hurried to Fergal's side. 'These chains are heavier than those we saw before,' Fergal said as Conor came to kneel beside him. 'The links are bigger, stronger, better forged.' He looked around to Rhiannon. 'We can do nothing here. I'm sorry.'

'Help him, please—you must . . .' She pressed her fist to her mouth to stifle a cry. 'You must. . . .'

'We need a stout tool of some kind,' Conor said, glancing around. 'Find one! Hurry!'

'We *will* find a tool,' said Donal. Still mounted, he gazed into the darkness, his voice coming from a distant place. 'But not here, and not now.' He shook himself and glanced down at Conor. 'Now, we must hurry if we are to make good our escape. The enemy will soon be on our trail—if not already—and in greater numbers than we've seen tonight.'

Rhiannon fell upon the prostrate body of her father. 'He is dying! Please, you cannot leave him like this.'

'Lady, we will *all* die if we stay,' replied Fergal brusquely. 'There is no help for him here. We have to go.'

'I fear Fergal is right,' said Conor. 'We must leave now to have any chance to get away.' Rising, he called a command and said, 'Donal and I will ride ahead with Gwydion and Rhiannon. Fergal, you and the fianna come after and cover our retreat. Morfran and the others with you. Where the trail divides, follow the northern branch to the deadlands. If you do not catch us before that, make your way to Druim Orchán and we will meet you there.'

'I will take Gwydion,' countered Morfran, stepping forward. 'Give me a horse and I will carry the king. Eraint and Lady Rhiannon will ride alongside. There may be some comfort to the king in our presence. Olwen can ride with your man Donal.' He thrust out his chin at Conor. 'You will lead the way.'

Sensing it was futile to argue, Conor quickly agreed. Turning to the fianna, he said, 'Dearg, give Morfran your horse—you and Aedd can ride together. Galart, go with Fergal.'

'You heard him, lads,' said Fergal, clapping his hands for action. 'Do it.' He hurried to his horse, snatched up the reins and, as soon as all were mounted, called the fianna to follow.

Rhiannon, still kneeling by her father, seemed in a daze. Conor reached down and pulled her to her feet. 'We can do nothing for him here. Our best hope is to reach our camp on the other side of the deadlands.'

Morfran, mounted now, spoke a word in the faéry tongue and she replied in kind, then moved to where Eraint was mounted on Dearg's horse; Conor lifted her up and helped seat her, and then ran to Búrach. The seven set off at once. Conor led the way, followed closely by Morfran and the unconscious king with Eraint and Rhiannon close beside; Donal came next with Olwen. In this way, the party soon reached and overtook the fianna. 'Whatever happens, keep moving north,' called Conor as he passed Aedd and Dearg; he repeated the same message to Fergal and Galart then sped on with the faéry close behind.

The sky gradually lightened, greying as they went. The clouds that had been thickening through the night now formed a low, heavy roof above their heads and a fine mist began to drizzle over them. Along the forest pathways, the air smelled of damp and decaying leaves. As the light grew brighter, so, too, did Conor's conviction that this was indeed the same trail he had travelled when following King Brecan to his ill-fated meeting with Balor Berugderc. Certain now, he pushed on with greater urgency, pursuing a breakneck course through the heavy scrub and brush lining the track—until at last reaching the end of the wood where he paused to allow Búrach a moment's rest. When the others reined up, Morfran, on the horse next to him, asked, 'Is it much farther this camp of yours?'

'Aye, some way yet,' he replied. 'We must keep moving.'

Rhiannon, from her place in front of Eraint, lifted her eyes to the hills and sighed; and it fair pierced Conor to the quick to see how much more worn and haggard she appeared. The flight had exacted a heavy price on the faéry and it was not over yet.

'Take heart, Rhiannon. Just the other side of those hills—' He indicated the undulating line of Druim Orchán in the distance, 'my men are waiting for us. There will be food and warmth and help for your father.'

At his words, tears welled in her crystalline blue eyes. 'Truly?'

'Truly,' he assured her. 'We have but to cross over these blighted lands and we are saved.'

Eamon

Aoife had a fair lead on us. Near as we could reckon, she'd fled the ráth shortly after Liam confronted her with his demands. We set out from Dúnaird at once, taking only those things we might need for a day or two on the trail. I had my spear and shield, sure, and Rónán brought whatever druids carry in those mysterious big sparáns of theirs, and his druid staff, of course.

From Dúnaird there are only two roads, two ways to go: north, along the coast, or south. Aye, the southern road follows the coast a little way, too, before turning inland. The nearest settlements lie to the north in Robogdi lands, a sizeable tribe with close kinship ties to the Darini. The south path leads to Darini holdings and, beyond these, to the strongholds and settlements of the surrounding tribes—the Volunti first, and the Eridani, and finally to Brigantes territory. We chose the way north, thinking that Aoife would certainly find a ready welcome among the Robogdi.

In this we were wrong. The first few holdings we came upon knew nothing of any woman travelling alone. No one had sheltered her, much less seen her. We wasted almost two days in a futile search before turning our attention to the south. Even so, a lone woman on foot cannot travel as quickly as a searcher on a strong horse. Rónán and I still had every hope of catching her before she had gone too far.

To the south lay the Volunti and Eridani, as I say, and the Brigantes and Coriondi. Lord Cahir of the Coriondi was a good friend of our king and Aoife surely knew this. It seemed likely she might seek shelter under Cahir's roof. Then again, the Brigantes lands were closer and, after all, it was with

King Brecan that Conor had found shelter when he was made outcast. It stood to reason that Aintrén might be where he sought shelter now—and a place Aoife might go to find him. In the end, we determined that it was to the Brigantes we should go. So, we set our faces to the south, retracing our steps with renewed purpose, stopping at settlements along the way to ask after our runaway.

'She is a dark-haired young woman of upright bearing,' Rónán told them by way of description. Though that could have applied to any one of a thousand or so female folk.

'And she will be carrying a harp,' I added—and this seemed to impress those we questioned.

No one at the first three places we stopped had seen anything of our Aoife, but at the fourth stop—a small farm steading a stone's throw within Volunti territory, the head man sucked his teeth, thought a moment, and replied, 'Aye, she was here with her harp and all, so she was.'

'She played for us, and sang,' added one of the farmwives. 'Lovely she was, and so lively on the harp. Ach, I could listen all night.'

The farmer cast a sour glance at the woman—for filching his story, no doubt.

'How long did she stay?' I asked.

'Only the one night,' answered the farmwife.

'Aye,' added the farmer quickly, 'only the one night.'

'Did she say where she was going?' said Rónán.

'Nay, nay,' he shook his grizzled grey head, 'just that she had to move on.'

'Had someone to find, so she said,' volunteered a maid—one of the holding's daughters. 'We thought it strange, so we did, that a slight young thing should be all on her own like that.' The maid fixed me with a challenging glance, and asked, 'Is she your wife that has run off from you?'

'Me? Ach, nay, nay,' I spluttered. 'Never that.'

'She is betrothed to my brother,' said Rónán tersely. 'He has gone missing and she is looking for him—not that it is anything to you.'

They could tell us no more, so we thanked them and took our leave. Our shadows stretched long on the trail by the time we reached the next settlement—a Volunti stronghold on a hill overlooking the river Teffyn. A proper old dún, this, with high walls of good, solid timber, and a large gatehouse, and a well-dug ditch around the whole. There were various houses and barns on the flatland below the mound. Rónán begged hospitality for the night, and the chieftain—a stout, red-faced fellow with a squint—could nowise refuse a druid request and gave us places at table in his hall.

By way of thanks, Rónán sang the song of Becuma of the White Skin, and won the great approval of all who gathered in the hall to hear him. We drank with the chieftain and small warband then and went to our sleep. Next morning, as we prepared to take our leave, the chief told us Aoife had indeed been there. 'Two nights she stayed,' he said, 'she was that tired.'

'Did she sing for you, too?' I asked.

'Ach, aye, for a fact she did,' replied the round-faced fellow with a smile. 'Like a lovely bird, she sang. A right lissome girl.' He squinted at me. 'It's surprised I am you should let her get away from you.'

'She is betrothed to my brother,' Rónán said bluntly.

The chief nodded knowingly. 'Ach, well, these things happen.'

'He has gone missing and she has taken it on herself to go in search of him,' Rónán told him. 'If you've heard anything of her, we'd be in your debt.'

'Your brother, you say?' wondered the chieftain. 'Who is your brother, then? What is his name?'

'Conor mac Ardan,' I told him. 'Perhaps you will have heard of King Ardan of the Darini?'

'Aye, we know him right enough. Good king by all accounts. Always been fair by us and ours—that much I know for a fact.' He pointed to one of the warriors just then entering the yard. 'Céadach there—he has just come in from riding the border. Ask him if he's seen or heard anything of your runaway.'

He called to the warrior, who came over to join us. Céadach walked with a limp and had a nasty red scar at the base of his throat that disappeared down into his siarc. He listened politely as Rónán repeated his request. 'I've been out on the trails these last two days, aye,' he said. 'But I didn't see any women traipsing around. Mind, I *have* heard of this Conor of yours.'

The way he spoke the name gave me to know he did not hold Conor in the highest esteem. 'What have you heard?' I said, 'If you would not think me overbold in asking.'

'What did I hear?' The warrior shrugged. 'Only that he had turned traitor and got himself killed alongside Lord Brecan mac Lergath.'

Rónán bristled beside me. I put out my hand to him and addressed the warrior. 'Friend, I can tell you that did not happen. He is not dead. I have seen him with my own eyes, so I have. And I can tell you—one warrior to another—as a man of honour, Conor is no traitor.'

'I'm not lying,' insisted Céadach, 'that is what I heard.'

'Ach, I believe you,' I assured him. 'But now that you know the truth, you will kindly correct any who, like yourself, have laboured under that filthy lie this little while.'

The warrior nodded and accepted this reproof right manfully and begged his leave. We asked his chief if he knew which direction Aoife might have gone when leaving the dún. 'South,' he said, but could tell us nothing more—only that she had a way with a song and a good hand on the harp.

We bade them farewell with thanks, and moved on.

'Ignorant louts,' muttered Rónán when we had passed well down the road. 'Conor a traitor—is that what everyone thinks?'

'Only those who do not know our Conor,' I told him. 'I would not fret myself. Not even druids can prevent ignorant tongues from flapping. People speak all manner of nonsense when gossip gets hold of them. It means less than the air it takes to repeat it.'

We travelled on, passing two more Volunti settlements and a handful of Concani farmsteads before the day was half gone. At each of these places we found people who had seen Aoife and by the time the sun stood high overhead we were firm in our conviction that she was indeed heading for Aintrén, the principal stronghold of the great Brigantes tribe where Conor had taken refuge. It seemed that we were not the only ones with that self-same notion; for, as we came to a river ford and saw that great fortress on its hill in the distance, we saw, too, our runaway Aoife—surrounded by five unknown warriors; one of them had her arm in his grasp and another was pulling on her mantle.

'What is this?' muttered Rónán darkly.

'Nothing good,' I said. Lowering my spear, I urged my horse to speed and rode to our Aoife's defence.

25

The sun was well up by the time Conor, Donal, and the rescued faéry reached the low tumble of rocky humps that rose rank on rank toward the bleak heights of Druim Orchán. Beyond all hope and every expectation, they had crossed the deadlands—that wide band of territory bereft of trees or low brush to shield them, exposed to view, not a patch of shade or shadow in which to hide—and had detected no visible sign of pursuit. Before starting the long, arduous uphill climb, Conor paused to allow the horses a little rest and the travellers to regroup. While the others dismounted and refreshed themselves or tended the stricken faéry lord, Conor walked a short distance up the hill for a better view of the land they had just traversed to see how far behind Fergal and the fianna might be.

They rested and waited, watching the barren strip and, when Conor had the fianna in his sight, he called a command to remount and prepare to move on. Waving his spear to get Fergal's attention, he saw Fergal return the signal and then turned the grey stallion and started up the long, shelving slopes leading to the top of the ridge. Rhiannon and Eraint, Donal with Olwen, and Morfran with Gwydion, fell into line behind him and the fugitives resumed their flight. The long day wore on, step by step and rock by rock, sometimes on horseback, more often on foot.

The sun stood low in a bone-white sky when they finally achieved the summit of the ridge. Conor, with a last lingering look behind into the desolated valley stretching away below, crossed the dividing spine of the ridge and started down the other side. Before him lay the gently rounded mounds of more familiar, friendly hills. Heavy forest clothed the slopes, stretching toward the upper heights to form a thick green cloak spreading down into wide plains and valleys. Here and there, he could make out the thin, wandering silver-blue line of a river cutting through the wooded land; empty moorland opened out in the distance glowing with a dirty copper colour in the pale autumn light.

'My men are just there,' called Conor, pointing to a large stone outcrop at the edge of the tree line below. 'See that great heap of grey rocks? Médon and Calbhan are just under that cnoc.'

'I cannot see anyone,' said Rhiannon, riding at his right hand. Fatigue weighed on her shoulders dragging them down.

'They will be there,' Conor assured her. 'Come along at your own pace. I'll ride ahead.' With that, he urged the tired grey to a fast trot on the downward trail.

Conor reached the rocky mound well ahead of the others; he gave out a shrill whistle followed by a shout—to alert the waiting warriors. When, after a moment, he received no reply, he shouted again. Before he could call a third time, Calbhan's fair head poked up from behind the jumble of stone. The young warrior saw the riders and began waving his arms in welcome; scrambling around the boulders he ran to meet his returning comrades. Upon catching sight of the faéry accompanying Conor, he halted and stood staring at the otherworldly beings.

'Here! We need help,' Conor called as Morfran and Gwydion arrived, with Eraint and Rhiannon trailing just behind. 'Calbhan! To me! Listen, the king here is in a bad way.' Sliding down from the grey stallion, he clapped his hands to reanimate the awestruck warrior. 'Listen to me! Lord Gwydion will die unless we get these chains off him. We need a hammer and a wedge—something . . . anything. Go!'

Calbhan came to himself then and, with a last glance at the faéry, scurried off to find some tool with which to remove the iron chain binding the king and slowly sucking out his life. Conor hurried to Morfran's mount and led it the rest of the way to the little camp at the edge of the wood.

'This way!' he called to Rhiannon and Eraint. 'Just a little further. We're almost there.'

Soon, they were under cover of the trees and on the path made by Médon and Calbhan as they came and went from the site to their lookout place on the heights. The camp itself was greatly changed since Conor had last seen it. There was now a substantial lean-to shelter—a bothy of boughs and branches trimmed and set upright and thatched with pine and bracken fronds. The fire ring had been enlarged and built up—with a stock of fire-wood nearby and three fair-sized logs to serve as benches. A large earthenware cauldron had been procured from somewhere and was simmering away on a bed of glowing embers. Lastly, a picket line for horses was strung up in the wood—near enough to a sweet-running brook so they would not have far to go to water the animals.

Conor led Morfran's mount into camp and helped ease Gwydion down; he and Eraint then carried the insensate king to the shelter. Rhiannon moved quickly to join him and together they gently lay the king on the rush-covered ground. Gwydion gave out a weak gasp, but did not wake. The princess seized her father's hand and raised it to her cheek, her face twisted in anguish.

'We will soon have him free of those chains,' Conor promised. Turning his head, he shouted, 'Calbhan! Where are you?'

The cry was answered by a guttural groan and a soft thud. Conor spun toward the sound and saw that Morfran had fallen from his horse and was now in a crumpled heap on the ground. Eraint had seen him fall and dashed to his comrade's side. Conor rushed to join him. 'What happened?' said Conor. 'He was well enough a moment ago.'

Eraint pressed a hand to the stricken faéry's chest and let it rest there for a moment. 'It is the poison,' he said, shaking his head. 'He has yielded.'

Conor took in the pasty, grey face—beyond exhaustion, it now seemed drained of all vitality. 'I don't understand.'

'It was that metal—the killing iron,' explained Eraint. 'He was too near the poison for too long.'

'He never said anything,' Conor muttered. 'He should have said something. I could have taken the burden.'

Eraint dismissed this suggestion. 'He knows what he is about. He is next in line of succession. It is his place to carry the king, not yours.' The faéry lowered his head and put his ear close to Morfran's mouth, then sat back and said, 'The iron has been removed and he will rest more easily now. I think he will recover. I will stay with him.' He raised a hand toward the shelter. 'Please, see what can be done for the king.'

Conor left them where they sat and returned to the bothy where Rhiannon was trying to arrange Gwydion in a more comfortable position; together they straightened his limbs, placed a rolled fleece under his head, and covered him with a woollen cloak. While they worked, Donal and Olwen arrived; Donal helped the lady down and the two hurried to where Conor and Rhiannon knelt beside the body of the king. Conor had drawn some water from the leather bucket and Rhiannon was trying to get Gwydion to drink from a wooden cup. The water ran out of the sides of his mouth and down his chin; he swallowed none of it.

'Any change?' asked Donal.

Conor shook his head. Rhiannon said, 'He is very weak. I fear he will not survive the night.' She swallowed back tears as she spoke. 'Perhaps not even that long.'

Conor jumped up and dashed from the shelter. 'Calbhan! Hurry!'

A moment later, he saw the young warrior racing to him. In one hand he carried a small hammer and, in the other, a long iron spike. 'Good! Good—' Conor took the spike. 'What is this? Where did you get it?'

'We were using it to secure the picket line for the horses,' explained Calbhan. 'Médon found it. I don't know where he—'

Conor snatched the hammer and ducked back into the shelter. Throwing off the cloak covering the king, Conor proceeded to try prising open the centre ring on the thick iron band encircling Gwydion's waist; that ring held the band in place and also affixed the tether chain to the band. He plied the spike, working it this way and that, but could get no purchase secure enough to allow much leverage and, clearly, strength alone would not succeed.

'Here,' said Conor, 'help me roll him to his side.' Together, Donal and Conor eased the faéry lord over and onto his side which exposed the ring and brought it closer to the ground. After another attempt or two, he concluded, 'This should work.' To Calbhan, he said, 'Go find me a stone—this big. . . .' He showed him where he intended to use it.

'The fire ring,' he said, darting away. 'I'll get one from there.'

Conor turned back to his work. 'Now, hold him by the shoulders and keep him steady.' Rhiannon moved to kneel beside Donal; together they braced the unconscious Gwydion while Conor positioned the iron spike in the ring. Calbhan returned with three fair-sized stones and Conor chose one and wedged the stone beneath the exposed ring. Then, taking up the hammer, he struck the spike—once . . . and again. He examined his effort and saw that he had made very little impact on the ring: the two joined ends had not spread by so much as a hair.

He tried again, swinging the hammer harder and harder against the spike in an effort to force the two ends apart—just a little, just enough to allow the chain to pass through and free the band. Time and again the iron smashed against the stone. Sparks scattered with every blow. Conor started to sweat with the effort, but did not cease.

Rhiannon bit her lip and clutched her father's body, steadying it against the blows Conor delivered. With each hammer strike, the spike bent a little more . . . but so, too, did the fixing ring.

'It's working!' said Donal. 'Let me take over.'

'Wait!' said Calbhan. As Conor sat back, wiping the sweat from his face with his arm, the young warrior removed the battered stone and replaced it with another.

Conor relinquished the hammer and took Donal's place as Donal began to hammer at the fixing ring. Once more the blows rang out and sparks flew. Donal's shoulders hunched, the muscles bulged on his arms, and his eyes narrowed with the intensity of his concentration. Slowly, the ring spread beneath the relentless onslaught. Finally, Donal gave out a shout and brought the hammer down with all his might, shattering the stone beneath.

'Here,' said Conor, bending to hand him the third stone. 'Use this.'

But Donal turned, a broad smile spreading across his sweat-slick face as he reached down and pulled the chain away. The ring had broken in two.

'You did it!' cried Conor. 'Well done, brother.'

Calbhan grabbed up the chain and dragged it away. Rhiannon took up Gwydion's hand in hers; she kissed it, saying, 'Bear it but a little longer, my heart. You are soon free.' Then, turning to Conor, she said, 'Please, please, hurry.'

Through all this the faéry king remained unconscious, his eyes closed, his mouth slack, half open, his breath light and airy—only the slow rise and fall of his broad chest and the occasional breathy moan let them know that he remained in the land of the living.

The thick band of heavy iron that passed around Gwydion's waist, above the hips but under the ribs, was cinched into a tight ring the ends of which overlapped where the chain had been attached. Conor expected it to be a fairly straightforward affair to simply prize apart the overlapping ends to allow the band to be removed.

This proved to be much more difficult than anticipated, however; and, after a few unsuccessful attempts on his own, he called on both Donal and Calbhan to help. 'You two take that side and I'll take this.' All three grasped the thick iron band and tightened their grip. 'Ready?' Donal gave a nod. 'Pull!'

The three men reared back, straining at the metal band. It refused to bend. After the initial surge, they relaxed, renewed their grip and Conor cried, 'Again!'

They reared back with all their might. Muscles bulging, backs and shoulders straining, their faces red with the exertion, they heaved and pulled before falling back in a panting, chest-heaving sweat.

'It's no good,' muttered Conor. 'We need more help.' He looked around and, for the first time, realised someone was missing. 'Where is Médon?'

Calbhan said nothing, but appeared apprehensive.

'Where is he?' demanded Conor. 'Out hunting?'

Calbhan looked around as if he might see the missing Médon lurking among the nearby trees. Finally, with a shamefaced shake of his head, he admitted, 'Nay, lord, not hunting.'

'Do you mean to tell me that you are here alone?' demanded Conor. 'Where is he then?'

The young man lowered his eyes. 'He has gone to Aintrén, I believe.'

'Aintrén!' Conor exploded. 'Gone back to the Brigantes, you mean!'

The young warrior swallowed hard. 'He was to have returned long since. . . .' Calbhan looked around again. 'I cannot think but that something has gone wrong.'

'Something has gone wrong, aye,' growled Conor between gritted teeth. 'If he dares return now I will have the skin off him.'

'Aye, but see now he thought—'

'I won't hear it!' Turning to Rhiannon, Conor said, 'The iron is too strong. We need help to bend it. Run to the top of the ridge and see what has become of Fergal and the fianna. If you can see anyone, signal them to come running.'

The faéry princess nodded once, turned on her heel, and fled, moving with grace and speed that was wonderful to see.

Conor turned once more to the task at hand. 'Again!' he barked. And again the three men seized the cold iron; and this time—placing their feet sole to sole, their hands between their knees—they arched their backs and bulled their necks and pulled with all their strength.

To no avail.

When they could no longer endure the pain of their exertion, they fell back, lungs heaving, sweat streaming from red faces.

'Again!' said Conor after a moment's rest, and they returned to their fruitless labour.

Gwydion, if he heeded the struggle taking place over his body, gave no indication. He lay ashen-faced and still, only the lightest breath of a sigh escaping his slack mouth. Where his rich tunic had ridden up, his white skin showed angry violet welts and blackened streaks from its too-close contact with the lethal metal.

Rhiannon came running back to say, 'I saw them! I saw the horses. They are coming.'

'Did they see you?' asked Conor.

'I cannot say,' she replied. 'I hope so. They are picking their way up the mountain. But they are coming.' She glanced at the body of her father and stifled a gasp. 'Is there nothing I can do?'

'The iron is just too strong,' Conor told her. 'I think we must wait for help.'

By way of reply, she glanced toward the hilltop. 'I will send Eraint to summon them more quickly.' She spoke a lilting word to her handmaid who nodded and darted away, as light as a cloud shadow slipping over the rocky ground. A few moments later, Eraint ran to his horse, mounted, and rode off, disappearing up and over the crest. 'He will go and bring them as fast as can be,' Rhiannon explained, gazing at her father's lifeless body upon the ground, hands clenched beneath her chin.

Conor, Calbhan, and Donal returned to the task at hand. Once again the three warriors gripped the unbending metal and again they strained against it with every nerve and sinew and all that sheer brute force would provide, cursing the Scálda and willing the cold hard iron to yield. And, if will alone had been power enough, that encircling band would have bent like soft butter. In the end, it was their own flesh that gave out first when, with hands torn, the skin of their palms greasy with blood, they at last fell back on their elbows in defeat.

'It is no use,' said Conor, blowing on his hands to soothe the pain throbbing there. 'When the others get here, we'll try again.' Rhiannon rushed forward just then and threw herself down where Conor had been kneeling. 'Fergal and the others will soon be here,' he told her, 'and then we'll have strength enough to—'

'They will come too late,' intoned Rhiannon in a strained, unnatural voice. Her hands were shaking and her eyes were closed, but her head was erect and her shoulders straight.

'Too late?' Conor pushed himself up beside her. 'What—' he began, and then saw what Rhiannon already knew.

Gwydion ap Llŷr, Lord and King of the Tylwyth Teg, was dead.

26

Despite their strenuous exertions on his behalf, Lord Gwydion had succumbed to the slow toxin of the Scálda iron. Even as they watched, the king's once-regal body was already beginning to decompose in the bizarre and eerie way of faéry flesh. The pale skin withered and cracked like ancient leather worn thin through untold ages as the muscle and sinew beneath the skin desiccated, shrinking away into a thin, fibrous mass; here and there, rents opened to reveal the skeletal bones. Then these too began to melt away, crumbling into tiny, cinderlike fragments of ash.

Conor and Donal rose and stood bereft over the rapidly crumbling corpse, their throbbing hands limp and powerless at their sides. Calbhan gaped in disbelief, his expression one of awed dismay at the mystery transpiring before his very eyes.

The noble king's clothing disintegrated, rotting away to mere threads and then to fine dust. For a moment, the outward shell of the corpse held its rough semblance of form and then the fragile crust collapsed in a flurry of snow-white ash to scatter on the evening breeze. There was a muffled cry and the onlookers turned to see Rhiannon slumped upon the ground, her face pressed to the earth, her slender shoulders heaving with silent sobs.

Within moments, the transformation was complete. By the time Eraint and Olwen returned with Fergal and the fianna there was little left to see but a heavy iron band and a powdery body-shaped depression in the damp grass. The fianna stared at the telltale residue in bewildered amazement; the two faéry went to Rhiannon and the three knelt together, their arms around one another, their bent heads almost touching.

'Ach, well, that is a very pity,' observed Fergal, turning to Conor with a question in his eyes. 'If we had come sooner . . .' He sighed. 'A very great pity.'

'It is that,' agreed Conor, turning his eyes away from the chalky shape in the grass. 'And a grievous wrong, aye.'

'I'm sorry, brother. If we had been here, we might have saved him. We might have—'

Conor was already shaking his head. 'Without a blacksmith's tools and a blacksmith's craft, Lord Gwydion was lost—whether you were here or not. The fault is mine, not yours.' Conor lowered his head, and it seemed as if every one of Eirlandia's myriad troubles had settled on his shoulders, crushing him down beneath an intolerable weight. 'I brought him into this, and I failed him,' he muttered, shaking his head slowly. First Mádoc and Huw, and now Gwydion . . . was *everyone* doomed who trusted him?

An upwelling of rage flooded through him—rage at the injustice, rage at the futility of his best efforts, rage against the senseless brutality and wickedness of the Scálda. His ruby birthmark flared like a hot poker applied to his cheek. Stooping suddenly, he seized the iron band that had leeched away the faéry king's life and, with a growl of angry frustration, hurled the cruel thing away. It sailed, spinning slowly, into the trees at the edge of the wood.

Conor watched it disappear into the brushy undergrowth, and muttered, 'I failed him—and it cost him his life.'

'Never say it!' said Rhiannon breaking in just then. Lifting her head, she drew herself up, climbed slowly to her feet and came to stand in front of Conor. 'I will *not* hear you reproach yourself over my father's death. You did what you could for him. I know that.' She took his hand and turned the palm up to reveal the raw, bleeding wound there. 'I see the sweat and blood of your attempt to free our king from the death the Scálda decreed for him. You tried with all that was in you, my friends. No one could have done more—of that I have not the slightest doubt. And I will not hear any one of you reproach yourselves or regret offering your aid.'

Morfran, all but carried by Eraint, hobbled forward to take his place beside the princess, and Olwen moved to her shoulder. 'It is as the princess has said,' Morfran declared, his voice hoarse, his manner grave and solemn. 'We hold you and your people in the highest esteem. Nothing that has happened in these last days will change that. But I tell you now that the Tylwyth Teg will never be party to this hateful war of yours. It would be cruelty to allow you to think otherwise.' Placing an arm around Rhiannon's shoulders, he said, 'Our ship awaits our return on the eastern coast. We will go there now and board that ship, and that will be the last you shall see of us or any of our people in this worlds-realm.'

In Conor's sorrowful state, it took him a moment to fathom the significance of the faéry's words. 'You will not help us?' he said.

Fergal spoke up. 'You will not revenge yourselves on the enemy who killed your king?'

'There is neither solace nor comfort in revenge,' Morfran intoned. 'And this war between the Dé Danann and the Scálda has been nothing but a plague to our kind from the beginning. We will go our own way and leave you to go yours.'

Donal spoke up. 'Unless the Scálda are stopped, the attacks on you and your people will continue and in time increase. You must see that. In helping us, you help yourselves.'

'No,' replied Morfran bluntly. 'We are finished with all things mortal.'

Rhiannon, raising her voice, replied, 'That is neither fair nor noble, uncle. This is the second time these good men have put their lives at risk for ours. We cannot sever the ties of friendship so easily.'

'Our friendship with Conor and his people will remain intact and unchanged. Indeed, he and his men will be welcomed into our halls and celebrated in story and song as long as we have breath to sing their praises. But,' his manner, already grave, grew haughty as well, 'we will no longer place ourselves between these two enemies. In the end, the only outcome for us is suffering no matter which side gains the victory.'

With that, he gestured to Eraint. 'We will go now.' The faéry pilot, stunned by the loss of their king and Morfran's adamant stance, glanced helplessly at Rhiannon. 'Eraint! We are leaving,' Morfran said. The two hobbled away again. Olwen, standing mute beside her mistress, took Rhiannon's hands in hers and bent her head.

'Morfran is distraught,' Rhiannon said softly. 'He did not mean what he said.'

'We are all distraught,' agreed Conor sadly. 'But he knew well enough what he meant. Nor do I blame him. I, too, wish to be finished with this endless fighting.'

'I will speak to him again when he has had a chance to regain his better counsel.'

'Thank you, Lady Rhiannon.'

'What is done is done,' interrupted Fergal. 'But I think we will not be entirely safe until we put a fair bit of distance between ourselves and the borderlands.' He jerked his head to the high hills rising behind him. 'The dog-eaters may soon be on our trail. We should move on while we can.'

Conor accepted the wisdom of Fergal's counsel and ordered Calbhan to ready the horses to ride out. To Rhiannon, he said, 'Come with us at least as far as Mag Belach. It's half a day's ride and it will be safer for you. We will part company there.'

The faéry princess glanced uncertainly at her uncle. 'Conor is right, my lady,' Fergal told her. 'You ride on ahead with Conor. Donal and I will see to things here and follow when our horses have been fed and rested.' He hurried off to tell the others.

'We'll wait for you at Áth Brúagh,' Conor called after him. 'You know the place?'

'The Ford of the Brigantes?' replied Galart. 'Aye, I know it.'

'Then you go with Fergal. Calbhan, you will come with me.' Conor instructed Rhiannon to tell her people to prepare to journey on. She moved off to consult with Morfran and Eraint. To Galart, he said, 'We'll see you at the ford.'

Donal, who stood a little apart watching this exchange, opened his mouth as if he would speak, then thought better of it. Instead, he gave Conor a farewell wave and turned to the horses. Conor moved off to gather his weapon and prepare to ride and when Calbhan did not follow, called, 'Get your horse, lad, we're leaving.'

'What about Médon?' asked the young warrior, stirring himself at last. 'He won't know where we've gone.'

'Do not talk to me about Médon,' huffed Conor. 'He'll just have to fend for himself as best he can. If that proves a hardship for him, he has no one to blame but himself.'

'But—'

'But what?' he snarled. 'I should have both of you horsewhipped—him for disobeying, and you for allowing him to leave. Now get your horse. We're leaving.'

Calbhan's mouth squirmed into a frown, but he held his tongue and hurried off to retrieve his mount. Moments later, Conor, Calbhan and the faéry bade farewell to Fergal and the others and departed the ridgeway camp for

the safety of the lands beyond the river boundary. They journeyed in petulant and regretful silence, their progress slowing as they went; the horses
were tired and it was no good pushing the animals further, lest a sudden
burst of speed be required.

The sun climbed higher by degrees and was standing almost directly
overhead when they came to a wide, low plain called Mag Belach, a sprawling grassland within reach of a stand of oak and ash and elm along the
river, the wide Abafínd, that served as the southern boundary for the many
territories to the north and west. It was a good place, so they paused to rest
their mounts and let them graze a bit before crossing the river at the Ford
of the Brigantes some little distance downstream. While the horses browsed,
the faéry settled in the long grass to rest and confer; meanwhile, Conor
searched the backward trail for any sign of the rest of his band. Instead, he
saw a lone rider coming toward them, riding along the line of trees to the
north.

He called Calbhan to him and asked, 'See that rider there? Who is that?'
The young man squinted his eye as he gazed into the distance. 'Can you see?
That cannot be Fergal, can it?'

'Nay, lord,' he said, glancing at Conor, 'I think it is Médon.'

'Him!' Conor growled. 'Well, if nothing else it will be interesting to hear
what tale he spins to explain his disobedience.' He glanced at the young
warrior beside him and saw the frown and wrinkled brow. 'What? You
think me too harsh?'

'For a truth, I do. He only meant to—'

'I have not yet begun to be harsh with him,' Conor snapped. 'Wait and
see what punishment I devise—then tell me if I am too harsh.'

The rider came on and was still some way off when he reined to an abrupt
halt.

'Ha!' scoffed Conor. 'The rascal has seen us and realises the trouble he
is in.'

The words were still in the air when, with a sudden start, the distant rider
wheeled his mount and galloped for the river and the sheltering trees beyond.

'See there!' crowed Conor. 'He fears the punishment waiting for him.
His guilt is confessed.'

'I think it is not his punishment he seeks to outrun,' observed Calbhan.

Conor heard the tension in the young man's voice and glanced around to see him looking askance into the distance. 'It is the Scálda.'

Conor turned his eyes to where Calbhan was looking and his heart sank within him: a fair-sized enemy raiding party—at least twenty strong—was even now racing toward them.

27

'Quickly now! Rouse Rhiannon and the others,' shouted Conor. 'Tell them to hide themselves among the trees. Then arm yourself and hurry back.' Calbhan nodded and raced away. 'We will hold them off as long as we can to let the faéry escape,' Conor called after him. When the warrior had gone, he added to himself, 'There will be no escape for us.'

Conor ran to Búrach, retrieved his weapons. 'Come, Brother Pelydr,' he said, sliding the spear from its sheath under the horsecloth, 'let us teach these dog-eaters a trick or two.' Then, tucking Eirian into his belt, he thrust his arm through Pared's straps; exulting in the lively strength of one and the comforting weight of the other, and strode out onto the plain. The enemy raiders were close enough now that he could make out individual warriors. One look at the ugly scowls on their glowering faces, and Conor's crimson-stained birthmark began to tingle as his blood rose to the fight. Clearly, they had marked the presence of a victim and were racing to the attack.

Conor turned and called out to the stand of trees behind him. 'Calbhan! To me! Hurry, man!'

He listened for his swordbrother, but the only sound to reach his ears was the hush of the wind sighing over the long meadow grass and the drumming thump of fast-flying hooves. Conor shouted again but, receiving no reply, he tightened his grip on the spear shaft and adjusted the sword hilt at his belt. With a last backward glance toward the tree line in the vain hope of seeing Calbhan on his way to join him, he ran to take a position on a small rise nearby. He emptied his mind of all else but the fight before him and prepared himself to confront the Scálda raiders alone.

The sight of this solitary Dé Danann warrior striding to meet them on foot brought the entire raiding party to a churning halt and put a grim smile on Conor's lips. No doubt the raiders surmised an ambush or trap. Certainly, a bold trick of some kind. The winded horses stamped and snorted, the scowling raiders sat for a moment to assay the situation; several kept an eye on Conor while the rest surveyed the wood, searching for the disagreeable surprise they reckoned awaited them the moment they committed themselves to any action.

Then, out from behind the forerank emerged the leader of the battle group—a man so large he made the horse beneath him look like a hill pony—and Conor recognised him: it was the great brute of a battlechief from the Scálda ráth. Even uglier in the daylight, his swarthy face was almost obscured by a virulent black beard, the ends of which were braided into twin forks that reached halfway down his chest over which he wore the Scálda breastplate of hardened leather studded with iron rings; a large, two-handed sword swung from his wide belt. On his head he wore a leather helmet festooned with a horsetail; his feet were shod with heavy brócs laced to the knee and these, too, were studded with iron rivets. He sat for a moment, eyeing Conor with a cold and calculating grin, then barked a rough guttural command to those with him.

Three riders from the line wheeled their horses and rode for the tree line. The rest of the raiding party remained watchful, dark eyes agleam with menace as they waited for the command to strike. Nothing moved—save the horsetail plumes atop the pointed leather helmets clamped on their heads. All sat their lathered mounts in a tense, suspicious silence as they watched the three riders disappear into the wood.

Conor, anticipating the command to attack, began tapping the bronze shaft of his spear against the rim of his shield. The raiders tensed and glanced nervously toward the trees. Conor tapped louder and faster, rousing himself to brave the imminent assault.

'Come! Die with me!' he shouted, his blood-red birthmark kindling with its accustomed fire and felt the charmed spear quicken in his hand, as if eager to be about its work.

As if in reply to Conor's challenge, the big battlechief growled another command and two riders joined him—one on either side. Raising his fist, the chieftain pointed a fat finger at Conor and the two raiders drew their swords and swung their shields off their backs, preparing to charge.

Before either one had gathered the reins, however, there came a short, strangled shout from among the trees—as if someone's startled cry of warning had been sharply truncated before the words could properly form. All eyes swung instantly toward the wood.

Conor, too, held his breath and waited. The air was heavy with the pungent scent of sweating horses and men; and, aside from the snorting of winded animals and the nervous stamping of hooves, no further cry was forthcoming. Into the tense silence, Conor resumed beating on his shield rim once more with the slow, rhythmic thwack! thwack! thwack! Each blow louder and harder than the last, and each resounding slap a death-laden stab at the heart of the enemy.

The Scálda chieftain thrust out his chin, the long ends of his braided beard quivering; turning once more to the Dé Danann before him, he ordered his two men to attack. They lifted the reins and started forward, swinging their blades with a slow, circular motion as the horses quickened their pace.

The distance narrowed. Conor raised his shield and crouched low behind it, preparing to engage the enemy. But, just as the two came within striking distance, out from among the trees burst a riderless horse, running free, nostrils flared, eyes wide with terror. And there, bouncing against the frightened beast's broad neck, swung the severed head of its rider. The ghastly trophy had been tied to its mane by the reins. Fresh blood splattered a wide swash across the animal's throat and shoulder.

The two warriors advancing on Conor halted and stared as the runaway horse crossed directly in front of them, racing toward the open plain. The Scálda raiding party roared their outrage, which made their horses jig and jostle against one another, uncertain what was happening. The big battlechief shouted another command: two riders streaked off in pursuit of the runaway horse, and two more joined the two presently advancing on Conor.

Faced now with four combatants, Conor decided to strike the first blow. Crouching low, he waited until the first two were twenty or so paces away. Then, releasing a tremendous bellow, he launched himself at a run, driving in fast behind the point of his spear. He struck first not at the rider, but at the poor beast that had the misfortune to be under him. Staying low, Conor raked Pelydr's keen blade along the side of the animal's broad neck. The pain and shock caused the horse to rear and lash out with its hooves. Conor was ready. As the horse came up, the rider flung his shield arm wide to maintain his balance and Conor buried the head of the spear in his enemy's exposed thigh.

The charmed blade pierced clothing, skin, and muscle with the ease of a hot knife slicing ripe cheese. The wounded warrior yelped in pain and swung his sword at Conor's head, but Conor was already dancing away and out of reach, preparing his next thrust: up under the lower edge of the leather armour. Again he struck, and again felt the blade slide through the hard leather and into living flesh. He withdrew the Pelydr's blade quickly. The sharp, coppery scent of fresh blood bloomed in the air. The screaming rider reeled and plunged from his mount to lay writhing on the ground; his three comrades continued the attack. Two spread out to keep Conor between them, and the last circled around behind to prevent any attempt at escape.

Distrustful now of Conor's deadly feints and deceptions, all three advanced with caution. The remaining raiders, watching the fight from the backs of their horses, rallied their kinsmen with raucous shouts of encouragement, rattling their blades against their leather shields. Conor, whipping the point of his charmed spear in slow, lazy arcs likewise called words of encouragement for them, inviting them to allow him to introduce them to Red Badb, Hag Queen of the Tomb.

A sly signal passed between the two advancing toward him. Both charged together—shoulder-to-shoulder, intent on riding him down and trampling him beneath the hooves of their horses. Conor allowed them to commit to the attack, then darted forward—straight into the onrushing charge. At the last moment, he gave out a mighty shout and threw his shield high. The heads of both oncoming animals rose as one and Conor swept the spearhead across the throat of the nearest. Blood gushed in a sudden gout and the horse, screaming in pain and alarm, stumbled, throwing its rider. Conor was also knocked to the ground, but held on to his spear and was able to carve a nasty groove into the leg of the rider as he passed. Rolling to his feet, Conor spun and lunged at the second rider as he pulled up and wheeled his mount to make another pass. The spearhead missed by a hair's breadth.

Conor spun around and lunged again, slamming the flat of his shield into the wounded Scálda's bleeding leg. The warrior yelped and made a clumsy swipe with his sword over the top of Conor's shield, the blade skidding along Pared's rim; Conor easily stopped it midstroke with the shaft of his spear. Then, with his assailant's blade trapped between shield rim and spear shaft, Conor hurled himself against the side of the horse, then bounced back a step, dragging down the rider's blade. With a quick sideways jerk of the shield, he twisted the sword from the raider's grip. Then, darting out from behind his shield, Conor rammed the head of Pelydr's bright blade directly into the rider's chest. The blow penetrated the tough leather armour and carried the unbalanced rider from his seat. He fell over the back of the horse as, half rearing, half stumbling, the beast lost its footing and rolled onto its wounded rider. Conor dove forward to deliver a killing blow, but heard the rapid thud of hoofbeats behind him. He spun around to see the third Scálda bearing down on him, arm raised, blade poised to strike.

Conor barely had time to brace himself for the blow.

But a peculiar thing happened. Even as the warrior's arm swept forward, the blade seemed to jerk backward of its own accord—as if meeting a resistance in the air. The rider tried to finish the stroke, but the sword blade stubbornly refused to move.

Conor threw his shield high and ducked low behind it. Out of the corner of his eye, he glimpsed a flashing glint of light, as from an unseen blade. The light flickered and was gone; in the same instant, a gaping wound opened on the rider's upraised arm. The Scálda tried to pull away, but his arm appeared to be frozen in that awkward attitude; his horse, however, jogged away and the hapless rider was yanked from its back as if plucked bodily from the animal by a giant hand.

Conor was not the only one to observe this uncanny sight. The entire Scálda raiding force was now close enough to witness the extraordinary event and many of them stared in wide-eyed disbelief at what they had seen. Others darted anxious glances around themselves as if fearing a similar phantom assault.

The black-bearded Scálda battlechief appeared likewise disturbed by the weird turn, but drew his weapon—the huge, two-handed sword that he grasped and raised in his massive fist. Hefting this enormous blade, the brute advanced on Conor. He signalled his men to follow but, preoccupied and fearful, none made bold to join their leader in the fight.

Conor had no time to wonder about the weird event just witnessed; bloody spear level, shield high, he squared himself to meet the battlechief's charge.

'To me, you worthless cur!' he cried, and his birthmark aflame with a fierce and wonderful battle heat, seemed to glow with an inner fire. Conor felt a surge of strength and lofted the shaft of faéry spear. 'Come to me! Queen Badb demands fresh meat for her hungry company!'

The Scálda chief surged ahead, teeth bared, the scowl beneath his black beard a grinning rictus of hate. Conor, loose and ready, watched for an opening. The battlechief, however, was not to make the same mistake that his men had made. Before he closed on Conor, he slipped a leg over and slid down from his mount, never taking his eyes off his opponent.

Nor did Conor allow his attention to waver. He made a quick backward feint to draw the attack, but the big battle leader did not rise to the bait. He advanced with a slow, cautious tread. Conor tried another feint—to the left this time. But that also failed to avert the Scálda's blade from its determined path. After another unsuccessful attempt to draw the battlechief, Conor steadied himself and took up his stance and prepared to meet the first blow.

When it came, it was delivered with a ferocity Conor could not have imagined. The bulging muscles tensed as the sword arm came up and the heavy shoulders rolled forward. The great sword fell like a bolt of thunder from a clear sky and the clash of the stout iron blade square on Conor's upraised shield sounded like a thunder blast as it resounded over the plain, echoing in the nearby wood.

The stroke would have carved a chunk out of an ordinary shield, but Pared was no ordinary shield. True to its nature, the faéry-crafted weapon not only took the blow, but did not so much as dent. Even so, Conor felt the shock to the very marrow of his bones. Before he could recover, the second blow, more devastating than the first, sent Conor reeling backward. He kept his feet, righted himself, and made a desperate lunge with his spear—which the battlechief easily knocked aside with his shield even as he raised the great sword to deliver yet another bone-shattering blow.

Again, Conor saw the bearded battle leader's arm swing up, and the blade commence its downward stroke. Again, Conor threw his Pared high to meet the blow . . . but it did not come.

Out of the corner of his eye, Conor glimpsed an uncanny glimmer in the air and seemed to see the shape of a knife blade—a mere thickening of the air and light. Just a flash and then gone. In the same instant, a bright crimson crease opened beneath the Scálda battlechief's upraised arm.

The huge chieftain grimaced and cried out. He tried to swing the great sword, but the weapon resisted—as it might if hung up in the thorny branches of a bramble thicket. As it wavered there, a second slash sprung open below the first—this one deeper and more severe. Releasing his mighty sword, the battlechief made a grab at the gaping wound.

Conor watched, peering over the rim of his shield, and saw the fork-bearded battlechief's head whipped to the side and down as if someone had tugged hard on his beard. A moment later, a thin red line appeared along his jaw, loosing a sudden spill of hot, dark blood. The lumbering brute groaned; his eyes rolled up into his head and he sank to his knees, his fierce expression giving way to a look of bewildered wonder. Then, like a rotten elm, the giant body slewed sideways and crashed to the ground. After a feeble effort to rise, the Scálda warleader relaxed into death and lay still.

Conor leapt onto the battlechief's chest. He lofted his spear and jeered at the enemy. 'Come, you stinking vermin horde!' he shouted. 'Who will be next?'

The fear-rattled raiders, seeing the body of their warleader dead on the ground and surrounded by the corpses of their swordbrothers, declined Conor's invitation. One warrior in the rear ranks broke from the pack and galloped away, and that was all the encouragement the others needed. A moment later, the entire raiding party—what was left of the leaderless lot—was in motion and fleeing for their lives from the unnatural display of combat performed by the lone Dé Danann warrior.

Conor stood for a moment, watching the Scálda scatter across the plain of Mag Belach as if all the dogs of the Bitch Queen Mórrígan were baying for their blood. Within moments, Conor was alone again.

Turning once more to the wood, he called, 'Calbhan! Where are you? Show your face if you dare.'

The reply came, not from the forest, but from only a few paces away.

'I am here, lord.'

Conor spun around behind him and saw that same glimmering movement in the air—a sudden shiver that seemed to congeal and then solidified into the shape of a horse and two riders: one of them Calbhan, and the other the faéry Eraint.

Conor gasped for sheer relief. He dropped his shield and spear and began kneading his aching arm. 'You might have told me you were with me,' Conor said. 'It would have saved me a deal of fretting.'

'I am sorry, lord,' replied the young warrior, sliding quickly from his mount and hurrying to join Conor. 'We could say nothing without alerting the enemy.'

Eraint turned the horse and rode back to the wood. 'How did you know about the faéry concealment charm?' Conor asked. He picked up his weapons and started toward the wood.

'The princess Rhiannon—she told me,' replied Calbhan, falling into step beside him. He went on to tell how she had described her use of the charm to make good their escape when Conor had rescued them from Balor Berugderc's dún. Raising his hand, he signalled toward the tree line where Lady Rhiannon, Morfran, and Olwen were just then emerging from their hiding place among the trees. 'The lady said she thought it might work again if I was willing.'

'Fortunate for me that you were willing,' Conor replied. He looked around at the dead on the ground and the riderless horses standing some way off. 'Get their horses and bring them to the wood,' he told Calbhan. Then, still rubbing his arm, Conor walked back to where the faéry were now gathered. He thanked Eraint for the skilful application of his charm and turned to Rhiannon. 'And thank you, too, my lady. Your quick thinking surely saved me. But, I sent Calbhan to warn you so that you could make good your escape.'

'Warn us he did,' Rhiannon replied. 'But we could not leave you standing alone against those vile creatures.' She moved close, reached out, took Conor's hand in hers, and stroked it gently. 'This is the third time you have put your life at risk for us,' she said this to all, but seemed to direct her glance to Morfran. 'Our life debt to you grows greater each time we meet.'

'I reckon no debts,' Conor replied. Then, he, too, glanced at Morfran who stood stiffly a few paces away. Though clearly still suffering the ill effects of his contact with Scálda iron, the ailing faéry had joined the princess and lent his aid in maintaining the charm of concealment that enabled Calbhan and Eraint to strike unseen. Conor could not help asking, 'Does this mean that you have changed your mind about helping us?'

'I have not. Consider what we did a parting gift,' Morfran intoned in a dour voice. 'Or, perhaps, a way to repay some portion of the life debt we owe you and your men.'

'I am disappointed,' Conor told him. 'I tell you that plainly. I am heartily disappointed.'

'Please know that you will always be welcome among us,' Rhiannon told him. She glanced uncertainly at her uncle, but said no more.

Morfran folded his hands across his chest and announced, 'A ship has departed Ynys Afallon. It is coming for us. We must go now if we are to meet them on the way.' He made a gesture of salute with his hand, and then turned and started away without another word.

Rhiannon bit her lip. 'I am sorry, Conor,' she whispered. 'Forgive our haste.'

'Eraint! Olwen!' Morfran called in a tone of command that fully indicated what manner of king he would be. 'Escort Lady Rhiannon to the ship. We depart at once.'

'Wait,' Conor called after him, 'we will accompany you. How far is your ship?'

'Our welfare is no longer any of your concern,' replied Morfran haughtily.

'At least let us lend you horses to speed your journey,' Conor countered. 'Calbhan could go with you.'

Morfran appeared ready to shun the gift, but Rhiannon quickly agreed, saying, 'Again, I thank you, dear friend. We accept the loan of the horses, but we will travel the quicker if we travel alone. In the forest we will not be seen.' The austere Morfran opened his mouth to object, but Rhiannon silenced him with an imperious look. 'I will see that the horses are returned.'

'Keep them,' Conor told her. 'A last gift for friendship's sake.'

Morfran stiffened at the suggestion and said, 'We will return them.'

With that, he stalked off. Rhiannon watched him for a moment, then turned and placed her hand on Conor's arm. 'Words alone cannot express my thanks for all you have risked and done for us. I *will* find a way to repay.'

Conor gazed at her, shaking his head sadly. 'There is nothing to repay. I am only sorry we could not save your father. Gwydion was a good friend to me and I will miss him greatly.'

'Death is but a change—a passing from one life to another.' Rhiannon put her hand to Conor's face and gazed at him with sympathy in her pale blue eyes. A moment passed, and then 'Farewell, my friend. May your fortunes increase.'

Conor gave her a forlorn smile and shook her head. 'My fortunes run only one direction—from bad to worse.'

Rhiannon reached down, took his hand and, pressing it, said, 'When one of the faéry wishes you good fortune, it means good fortune is yours for the taking. Think on that.' Turning away, she bade him farewell once more, then hurried to join Morfran.

Calbhan helped the faéry with the horses and then returned to Conor and the two surveyed the remains of the recent skirmish. He looked around at the dead enemy, lying where they had fallen. 'The faéry took two horses,' he observed, 'but we gained three.' He looked to Conor who, though he stared at the enemy dead, appeared not to see anything at all. 'What would you have me do now, lord?'

'I am no lord,' muttered Conor, moving off. 'Strip the dead—anything that might be useful.' As Calbhan started away, he added, 'See if they have any gold on them—or any food!'

They were still at this loathsome chore when Fergal, Donal, and the rest of the fianna arrived. Fergal reined up as Conor was cutting the armour off the corpse of the big Scálda battlechief. He gawked at the oversized body, then turned his gaze to where Calbhan was piling the warriors' weapons. 'It looks like someone has been busy here.'

Donal, reined in beside him and, taking in the Scálda dead, asked, 'What did we miss?'

Aoife

A woman travelling alone can expect to face hardship, at least, and any of a hundred perils if she is unlucky. So far, Danu's good fortune was with me and I had not suffered anything more perilous than fatigue and aching feet. I was welcomed and made much over at every place I begged a crust and a bed.

In truth, my harp was largely responsible for my kindly reception. The high regard enjoyed by the bards carried to me as well. Because of the harp and the music I coaxed from the strings, people considered me kin to a druid bard and, as everyone knows, it is bad luck—or worse!—to insult a druid in any manner whatsoever.

Even so, I expect it was also the music as well. Music is a sacred thing and those who practice its enchanting ways often gain high and valuable esteem. Folk who rarely see a druid, or hear music other than that of their own making, most always covet the chance to hear more, preferably something they have not heard before. The esteem of the bards has been extended to me and I try never to abuse it.

So it was that after the first days of my sojourn among the ráths and little farming settlements, I grew in greater confidence that I would eventually hear of Conor and learn where I might find him. My hope was that he had returned to the Brigantes where he had found refuge before. Unless I heard otherwise along the way, my plan was to make my way to Aintrén and see for myself whether he was there.

True, I did not know exactly where to find the Brigantes' foremost ráth— Aintrén as it is called—but I knew it was somewhere in the south no great distance from Tara's sacred hill. I also knew that sooner or later, I would meet someone who could tell me how to get there. That is exactly what I was thinking when I first saw the warriors on the road ahead. There were five of them—a small hunting party, perhaps—all mounted, riding easily toward me.

Perhaps they had come from Aintrén, I thought. If so, they might well have news of Conor—or at least point out the way. Oh, but I was sorely mistaken.

At first, they were friendly enough in the coarse way many warriors seem to believe is the chief requirement of their caste. The leader of the little band, a sandy-haired fellow with a patchy scrag of beard on a well-shaped face that had not seen a razor for some time, asked me where I was going and why I was alone on the road.

'I am on my way to join my betrothed,' I told him. 'I would be grateful for any help.'

'Has he a name, this lucky fellow?' he asked.

'Aye, he would be a strange one if he hadn't. His name is Conor mac Ardan of the Darini. Do you know him?'

'Nay, nay,' he replied shaking his head. He glanced at the rider next to him and a subtle look passed between them. 'We know only what people say of him.'

'Is that so?' I said, trying to keep my tone pleasant, though I did not like the sly insinuation of his knowing glance.

'We have heard that he is a traitor and a murderer who has sided with the Scálda and now serves Evil Eye himself.'

'Then what you have heard is a lie,' I told him. 'And the one who told you is a liar—as are all who lower themselves to repeat it.'

The rider next to the leader spoke up then. 'I am the one who told him,' said he, a slow menacing smirk playing on his lips. He had a shock of dark hair gathered in a knot atop his head and a recent scar, still pink, on his left cheek. 'How can you call me liar? You don't know me well enough for that.'

'I may not know you,' I granted, 'but I know Conor. And I know that he is wrongly accused. He has betrayed no one. Anyone who says otherwise is either a fool or a liar.' I looked him in the eye and asked, 'Which are you, then?'

'Did you hear that, brothers?' said Topknot. 'I do not care for the way this woman speaks to her betters. I am thinking it time someone taught her proper respect.'

With that he threw a leg over his mount and slid down. I held my ground to show I was not afraid of them. When the sandy-haired leader likewise dismounted and approached, my heart began beating faster. Unslinging my harp, I clutched it to my breast as if to shield me from what I feared was about to take place. Still, I did not give ground.

'You are a pretty thing,' said Sandy-hair, approaching slowly. 'If you were my betrothed, *I* would never let you out of my sight.'

With that, he reached out and took me roughly by the arm and tried to pull me to him. I resisted.

'Perhaps this Conor is a faithless bastard as well as a traitor,' said Top-knot, moving closer. 'Perhaps it is time someone schooled *him* as well. When I see him, I will make a point of it. Just as I mean to make my point with his woman.'

So saying, he made a clumsy grab for me, but I swatted his hand away. He made another lunge and snatched my mantle, winding it in his fist and pulling me closer. The other remaining warriors began hooting and making obscene noises—though none climbed down to join their leaders.

'If you knew who it was you have laid hold of,' I said, forcing venom to my voice, 'you would not be so bold. Release me at once and I will pardon your insolence.'

'Pardon? I seek no pardon from a milkmaid who does not know how to keep a polite tongue in her mouth.' Sandy-hair grinned and looked back at his fellows. 'I think I shall put a better tongue in her mouth—and maybe more besides. What do you think, brothers?'

I tried to pull away from his grasp. 'Release me at once!'

He turned back to me and the sloppy grin disappeared from his face like water poured from a bowl. The next voice I heard was one I knew well.

'Are you deaf, friend? The lady demands release. I'm thinking it would be in your best interest to obey.'

Casting a quick glance over my shoulder, my heart leapt. 'Eamon!' Behind him came Rónán, trotting up.

'And I am thinking this is no concern of yours, old man,' replied Top-knot carelessly.

'I know this lady well and that makes it my concern, sprout,' said Eamon. To Sandy-hair, he said, 'Take your hand away or prepare to lose it.'

I saw Eamon's spear come down over my shoulder as he directed the point to the young warrior's chest. Sandy-hair hesitated, then slowly released my arm. Topknot, too, let go of my mantle and I moved back a few steps so they could not easily seize me again.

'It seems to me that when blades are drawn,' said Topknot with a defiant thrust of his chin, 'a fellow would do well to count the blades against him.' He raised his hand in a signal and the mounted riders drew their swords. 'I make that five blades against one.'

'Five against one—*and* a druid,' said Rónán, speaking up at last.

The renegade warriors looked up and, as if seeing him for the first time, took in his appearance. His robes, the distinct cut of his hair, and the wide intricately patterned belt and overlarge sparán and rowan staff tucked under the horsecloth marked him out as a bard of considerable distinction. Suddenly abashed, all shifted uneasily, looking to one another for help.

'Put away your weapons,' Rónán ordered, sliding down from his mount. 'There will be no blood shed here this day.'

When no one moved, he roared, 'Put those blades away! Now! Or find out what a druid's curse can do!'

'We meant no harm,' said Sandy-hair, his tone pleading and pathetic. He backed away a step.

'We thought she was someone else,' added Topknot, convincing no one.

'Aye,' scoffed Rónán as he came to stand beside me, 'no doubt you thought she was a stray sheep you could abuse for your pleasure and no one would ever know or care.' His lips curled in a grim smile. 'But I can tell you that one day soon, Conor mac Ardan will be king, and if he ever finds out you chose his betrothed for your rough sport he will surely demand the honour price. Aye, and the day he comes to collect it will be the last day you look upon the world as healthy men.'

'We meant no harm,' insisted Sandy-hair. 'We will beg the lady's pardon and go our way. No more need be said of this to anyone.'

'You would beg her pardon?' said Eamon. He looked to me and I nodded. 'Then do it. Do it now before she changes her mind.'

Sandy-haired swallowed, then said, 'Lady, we do beg your par—'

'On your knees!' roared Rónán. 'Beg as if your life depended on it, for I tell you now it truly does!'

Gritting his teeth, Sandy-hair sank down on his knees in the dust of the road. He cast a quick glance to Topknot, who with a dark glance at the druid, knelt beside his fellow.

'We do heartily beg your pardon, lady,' said Sandy-hair. 'We regret this lamentable incident and wish nothing more than to go our way in peace.'

He looked to me pleadingly. It was all I could do to keep from spitting in their stupid faces. Yet, seeing as no real harm had been done, I granted the pardon they sought—though Danu knows they did not deserve it. 'Pardon is granted,' I said. 'But if I ever hear that you—or anyone like you—has molested another woman, I will lay your offense at the feet of my Conor.'

'But, see here—' Topknot began to protest.

'Count on it,' Eamon told him. 'For if she does not, then I will.'

'Go your way,' Rónán said, his voice assuming the druid tone of command. 'We will hear no more from you.'

They wasted not a moment, but scurried for their horses and departed hastily without another word or glance.

'That was well done,' said Eamon, swinging down from his mount. 'And you, Aoife—are you well?'

'I am,' I told him, and then thanked both of them for coming to my defence. 'Sorry as I am that you had to defend me, I am glad you are here.' I looked to Rónán and asked, 'Why *are* you here?'

'We have come to take you home,' replied Rónán simply.

'Ach, then you have come for no purpose,' I told them. 'I will not go back to become Liam's queen.'

'But lady, we must think how best to—' began Eamon.

He still held his spear loosely at his side. Reaching out, I took hold of the naked blade and placed it against my breast. 'If you mean to take me back, then it will be my lifeless body that goes with you.'

I looked them both in the eye, my voice steady with the fierce determination I felt surging through me. 'I tell you the truth, I will die today rather than become the wife of that man.'

Eamon thought to object again, but Rónán raised his hand. 'Peace,' he said softly. 'I hear and understand. We will not force you against your will—on that, you have my word.'

He placed his hand on mine and drew the point of the spear away from my heart.

'The king will have our heads,' sighed Eamon. 'Mine, at least.' Raising his eyes to the sky as if he would find an answer there, he said, 'What are we to do now? We dare not return to Dúnaird without her.'

'Leave that to me,' Rónán told him. 'We will go back, but I will lay a geas on Liam that will cool his ardour.'

'A geas,' repeated Eamon, wholly unimpressed. 'That's all?'

'I will bind him with a geas that will forbid him to so much as touch Aoife,' Rónán explained. 'A taboo he dare not break at the cost of the kingship he hopes one day to achieve.'

Eamon stared for a moment, then gave a little snort and stalked away shaking his head and muttering, 'Druids.'

Rónán watched him for a moment. 'We both know Liam cares far more for obtaining the kingship than he does for marriage—to Aoife or anyone else. Believe me, once I pronounce the geas he will be bound to observe it.'

He gave a decisive nod then looked to me. 'What is in your mind, Aoife?'

The thought was already on my lips before I knew it. 'Is Conor really going to be king?'

28

'Was it that bad, then?' asked Donal. The corpses of the enemy had been accorded the dignity they deserved: a shapeless heap on the grass open to the sky to feed the scavengers. The three Scálda horses, along with the fianna's mounts, were now tethered and grazing on the green plain of Mag Belach. Bits of food—hardtack for the trail and a couple bags of oats—had been found among the enemy dead's belongings. The hardtack they threw away, but Dearg made a porridge of the oats and, added to the last of their own provisions, they shared it out among them. The measly meal finished, Galart and the others went off to tend the horses, leaving Conor, Fergal, and Donal to confer.

'If not for Rhiannon's quick thinking, that would be me you're seeing among the dead.' Conor rubbed out the throbbing ache in his arm where the Scálda battlechief had bashed his shield. 'I was that close to a place at the Hag Queen's board.'

Fergal regarded the pile of corpses. 'It seems you made good account of yourself all the same.'

'Was it the charm of concealment, then?' asked Donal.

'That, or something very like,' Conor said, and went on to explain how Calbhan and Eraint had helped him with the aid of faéry magic.

'With charms and enchantments like that, just think what we could do if the faéry could be persuaded to join us on the battlefield,' mused Donal.

'And is this not what I've been saying all this time?' said Conor. 'Aye, but nothing happened here to change their minds. Morfran holds me to blame for Gwydion's death and they want no more of us.'

Out on the plain, carrion birds were already circling and beginning to alight and feed. 'Nor do I blame them,' he added gloomily.

The three fell silent, contemplating a future that, despite the bright sun-filled day, seemed bleak and cheerless as the depths of unending winter. They were still sunk in this bitter mood when a shout hailed them from out on the plain. Conor glanced around, started, and then leapt to his feet. Fergal and Donal noted his reaction and rose to stand beside him.

'Who is it?' asked Fergal. 'Donal—can you tell who it is?'

Donal squinted his eyes a moment, then said, 'It is Médon—with two more besides.'

'Calbhan and I spotted him earlier,' replied Conor, exasperation edging his tone. 'He hid in the forest when the Scálda attacked. I wonder what he has to say for himself?'

Skirting the woodland, three riders advanced at a pace. When they had come close enough, Conor strode out to meet them. Médon threw himself from his horse and ran to greet Conor, but before he could speak, Conor called out, 'So, here you are at last, friend Médon. Or should I say Médon the Disobedient? Or, Médon the Disloyal? Perhaps, it is Médon the Cowardly?'

The young warrior dropped to his knees and bowed his head. The two warriors with him reined up but remained mounted a little way off. Fergal and Donal moved to join Conor, one on either side. 'Well? Which is it, Médon? We are wanting an answer.'

'We saw the Scálda raiders out on the plain,' replied the warrior. 'We took to the forest and lay low, but if we had known you were here, we would have engaged them—even though they had the larger warband.'

Conor gave a snort of derision. Disgusted as he was, however, it did oc-cur to him that the wayward warrior's claim could well be true. 'Leaving that aside,' said Conor, determined to hold Médon to account, 'you disobeyed my command and quit the ridge camp, leaving Calbhan to fend for him-self. Did it ever occur to you that we were counting on you to be where you promised to be—that this is the very least one should expect from a sword-brother?'

'I am sorry, lord—'

'Sorry?' Conor scoffed. 'Not as sorry, I think, as you soon will be. Do you know how the battlechiefs of old punished a man who broke ranks, retreated, or disobeyed a command?' Conor glared at the man kneeling before him. 'You would be killed with your own sword, your head cut off, and nailed to the gate of the ráth for the crows to feast on your eyes.'

Médon, his head still bowed, replied in a low voice, 'You must do what you think necessary, lord.'

Fergal opened his mouth to speak, but Conor silenced him with a warning flick of his hand. 'I have already slain three men today, and I find that I have little appetite left for killing. Yet, I am curious, Médon. Aye, that you linger in the Land of the Living with the light of life still burning in your faithless eyes you can thank my curiosity. I yearn to know *why* you disobeyed the command you were given and had vowed to uphold? Answer me if you can.'

When Médon did not reply, Donal said, 'Perhaps you would allow me to take him aside and—'

'Nay, brother. I will have an answer.' To Médon, he said, 'Well? Speak up. It is time to settle accounts.'

Only then did the young warrior raise his eyes, and only then did Conor and the others see how very tired he was: his shoulders sagged beneath the weight of fatigue, his flesh waxy, his hair matted, and his cloak filthy.

'I disobeyed—it is true,' mumbled the young man. 'You must do as you will with me.' He lowered his head again.

'That is no answer,' growled Conor. Fergal and Donal exchanged a look of concern. 'Tell me why you disobeyed!'

It was one of the new arrivals who spoke first. 'A moment, my lord.' The stranger—a young man not yet twenty summers old—dropped down from his horse and moved to the kneeling Médon's side.

Conor stared at the youth with a vague sense of recognition. 'Do I know you?' he asked.

'Aye, lord, I am Maol mac Morna of the Brigantes. I beg your mercy on our swordbrother.'

'What is this to you, Maol mac Morna?' enquired Conor, his voice dark with menace. 'Speak quickly. I grow tired of waiting.'

'Médon went against your command, lord. That cannot be denied. But he did so out of loyalty to you.'

'That is true,' called the second stranger. He also jumped down from his horse and stepped up to join the other two.

'And who are you to intrude in this affair?' Conor looked closer. 'I know you, too, do I not?'

'I hope so, lord. I am Caol mac Morna.'

'The brothers mac Morna,' said Donal, moving to take his place beside Conor. 'Ach! I remember now.'

'We were among those you helped to train,' replied Caol. 'And friends of many years with Médon and Galart and the other Brigantes who have already joined you to fight the Scálda.'

Conor considered this and turned back to Maol. 'You said Médon disobeyed out of loyalty to me? This is something new.' He glanced at Fergal, 'Disloyalty out of loyalty. Fergal, have you ever heard of such a thing?'

Fergal shrugged. 'With you, brother, I see and hear new things every day.'

'All I meant, lord,' Maol continued, 'was that Médon acted with the best intention. He came to Aintrén to persuade more warriors to join this fianna you are raising.'

Conor looked at Médon. 'Is this true? You went to Aintrén seeking warriors to join the fianna?'

Médon nodded. 'So it is, lord. The more I thought about it, the more certain I became that there would be many of the Brigantes warhost who might be anxious to escape that blowhard Vainche and his repugnant rule. Truly, I thought you would be away longer.'

'He would have returned to the place where you left him and we with him—long before your arrival, lord,' said Maol, placing a hand on Médon's shoulder. 'But on our way back we encountered some Volunti and the Ulaid as well.'

'What so? You stopped to engage them in a skirmish to sharpen your skills and this is what delayed your return?'

'Never that, lord. The Volunti and Ulaid are our allies. Nay, it is that when I told them of the warband forming under your rule, they asked to be allowed to return to their ráth and beg of their lord to join the fight.'

'We told others,' added Caol, 'and they are even now on their way to join us.'

'We could only get two horses,' explained Maol. 'The rest are coming on foot.'

Conor looked to Médon. 'How many?'

'Thirteen,' he replied. 'At least.'

'Thirteen.'

'Maybe more,' said Maol. Reaching down, he pulled Médon to his feet and the three stood together. 'Now that word has gone out that you are rais-ing a warhost to challenge the Scálda in their own lands, I expect more will be eager to join you.'

'All along the way,' Caol said, 'we spread the word that there is a rising in Eirlandia.'

Conor stared at the three young warriors then turned around and, mo-tioning Fergal and Donal to join him in consultation, moved off a few paces to confer. 'What are we to make of this story, brothers? Do we believe it?'

'A bold lie, if lie it is,' replied Fergal. Shaking his head, he added, 'Leav-ing his duty like that—what was he thinking?'

Donal stroked his stubbly chin a moment, then said, 'I find it an unlikely tale to tell when the truth or falsehood can be so easily discovered. All we need do is wait. If more warriors are on their way to join us we will know the truth the moment they arrive. If no one appears, then we will know Médon was weaving a tale to save his sorry skin.' Donal smiled. 'Truth or lie, we will find out soon enough, so we will.'

'What are we to do with them until then?' asked Fergal. He jerked his head toward where the three stood awaiting Conor's judgement.

'Tell them to see to the horses and—' Conor began, then stopped him-self. 'Nay, nay. Rather, tell them to go and bathe. They smell like animals. When they are done with that they can go help with the horses.'

Fergal hurried away to deliver Conor's command and Conor regarded Donal, who was gazing across the plain, but clearly, was seeing something else. 'What is it?' asked Conor. 'What do you see?'

'I see a man's foot upon a stone,' he replied.

'Whose foot? What stone?'

Donal squinted as if by dint of will he could force the future to deliver the answers; then he sighed and shook his head. 'For this, too, we must wait.'

29

Maol and Caol, the brothers mac Morna, were not twins, but like enough to be taken for such. Both were lithe, dark-eyed men with broad shoulders and long limbs; they were young—like most all the others in Conor's burgeoning fianna—not above twenty-two summers, if that. And both carried their arms with the easy confidence of warriors well trained and proficient in the killing craft—which, for most of that, they had Conor, Fergal, and Donal to thank. The similarities did not stop there: both wore cloaks and siarcs of pale yellow and russet breecs the colour of autumn leaves, and both wore torcs and armbands of rolled and burnished copper, and both wore their hair hard shaved on the side and long in back and braided tight. Easy of temperament and calm of manner, they were well liked by kinsmen and friends and, because they knew Conor as a battle-seasoned warrior, seemed happy enough to cast their lot in with him and their Brigantes swordbrothers who had already joined the fianna.

By the time they and Médon had bathed and washed their clothes, they had already made a favourable impression on Fergal, who observed, 'Good men, those two. A few more like them and we'd have true warband.' He saw the frown forming on Conor's face and quickly added, 'A shame Médon betrayed his duty to get them.' He clucked his tongue. 'A very shame, that. But if more are coming, perhaps his lapse can be put aside this once.'

Conor gave a dismissive grunt and, ignoring the comment, said, 'The day is still with us. We should move on.'

'Aye, or we could linger here awhile and wait for Médon's stragglers to arrive,' Fergal suggested. 'There is good grazing to be had around here and, after the last two days, I think we could all use the rest—the horses included.'

Conor considered the notion and decided. 'Well said. Let's put this miserable sight behind us and find a place near the river. We can hunt a little today and shelter in the forest tonight. We'll travel on tomorrow.'

'Where are you thinking we should go?'

'To Lord Cahir is what I'm thinking. If there are more warriors joining us, we'll be needing mounts for them. Maybe we can persuade him to give us some horses in return for helping protect his borders,' Conor replied, turning his eyes to the animals grazing on the plain. 'If not, we may be able to trade one or two of our mounts for food and fodder.'

They fell to discussing which of the horses they might willingly trade and which would be worth keeping, and how best to go about negotiating the animals' value. A little while later, the troop moved on, hunting as they went, and following the arc of the river to a nearby bend on the spreading plain known as Mag Belach, a water meadow lined with willows and alder trees. Here, they stopped to make camp and Conor sent the newcomers out to hunt while he and the others rested. Through the day, they kept a close watch on the many approaches to the plain. But no one came and as twilight crept slowly over the broad greensward, it appeared they would enjoy a peaceful night. Firewood from the surrounding forest was readily hauled into camp and three small fires lit among the trees at the river's edge.

The yield from the day's hunt—three fat hares and two squirrels—along with the last of the oats and some bósaill that Maol and Caol had brought with them were prepared, but everyone went to sleep hungry.

In the morning, it was Conor who woke first and roused everyone else with orders to water the horses and prepare to ride. He saw Médon sitting by the fire ring lacing up his brócs and asked him, 'So! Where are these thirteen warriors of yours, eh? Where are they?'

'I cannot say, lord, but they are surely coming.'

'Surely . . . surely,' Conor scoffed, shaking his head.

The young warrior lowered his gaze to the spent ashes of the previous night's fire as if at his own demise. 'No doubt they will meet us on the way.'

'Up with you!' Conor barked. 'Help ready the horses. We are leaving.'

Médon jumped up and, without another word or glance, hurried off. Conor watched him go, shaking his head, and slowly became aware that he himself was being watched. 'Another day or two of that,' Donal said, 'and his spirit will be broken. If that is what you want, it was better to have slain him yesterday.'

Conor sighed, still watching his disobedient follower run to fetch his horse. 'It is not his death I desire. But he must learn—and the others, too. If we are to survive we must be able to count on one another.'

'He was trying to help. He brought back two men, after all.'

'Two, aye, and that may be all.'

Donal crossed his arms and thrust out his chin. 'We shall see.'

As soon as their mounts were ready, they set off riding north on the trail that ran alongside the river. The sun rose above the rim of the world, causing the mist to rise from the water and flow across the land in low banks of damp fog. They had not gone far when Galart, who was with Aedd at the head of the fianna, halted and came flying back to where Conor and Fergal rode in the rear. 'Someone's coming, lord! A warband, I think.'

'Médon's missing men?' wondered Fergal. 'Or another Scálda raiding party?'

'I cannot tell—the fog is too thick, and they are still some distance away. But I think they are on foot.'

'Then it must be Médon's missing thirteen.'

'Or hunters,' suggested Conor. 'We'll go have a look.'

Conor and Fergal followed Galart up the trail where Aedd sat waiting and paused to gaze through the ever-shifting billows rising up off the water, trying to get a glimpse of the travellers Galart said he had seen. It took a moment, but then the fitful breeze wafted across the trail and the low-lying banks thinned and parted, and there, moving stealthily along the riverside trail, two solitary of figures emerged from the fog—two only, but quickly followed by another, and then one more.

'Four? That's all?' said Fergal. 'But how did—'

'Shh!' Conor hissed. 'Wait.'

The shifting haze stole the four figures from view once more. When the fog thinned again a few moments later, they were closer. Four men, each of them carrying spears, and running with the easy loping gait of men keen to cover distance.

'Four I make it,' said Conor, disappointment edging his tone. 'Only four.'

'Not Scálda at least,' said Fergal. 'We might as well ride on. I'll go back and tell the others.'

'Stay a moment,' Conor said. 'I would speak to them first.'

They waited until the little group jogged closer, then rode ahead to meet them. 'Good hunting today?' called Fergal as the men came within hailing distance.

The fellow at the head of the group raised a hand in greeting and slowed to a walk as he approached the horses. 'No luck yet,' replied the fellow. 'That is unless you know where Conor mac Ardan can be found. It is himself we are hunting.' His eyes flicked to Conor and the light of recognition dawned on his open, affable face. 'I don't suppose you'll have seen him at all?'

'We might have,' replied Fergal. 'What sort of fellow is he—this Conor of yours?'

'Ach, well, you would know him if you saw him,' said the second of the four. 'His reputation goes before him. If that is not enough, you would identify him for the garnet mark on his face just there—' The fellow drew a hand over his own smooth cheek and jaw. 'If you see him could you tell him we're looking for him?'

'I might do. But it would depend on who was asking and why.'

The first stranger's smile grew wide as he said, 'Ach, now you have hit on it there, friend. I am Diarmaid mac Aodh, a warrior of the Volunti. My swordbrothers and I have heard that this Conor is raising a warband—a fianna as of old.' The warrior indicated the two others standing a half step behind him. 'We've come to join this fianna.'

'And why would you be wanting to do that?' asked Conor, speaking up then.

'Easily told that is,' replied Diarmaid with a slight bow of acknowledgement toward Conor. 'For the reason that we are sick to the back teeth of watching these bastard dog-eaters burn our fields, steal our cattle, destroy our farms, and carry off our people. We want to take the fight to the Scálda in their own territories—'

'Burn some of *their* strongholds for a change,' said one of the group, speaking up just then. 'Maybe take some of their cattle and all.'

'Aye, so we would,' affirmed Diarmaid. He glanced at Conor again, and said, 'We were told this man Conor was a warleader who knows how to do this very thing. If that is true, we want to pledge our swords to his service.'

'So, if you know where he can be found, please oblige our request and tell us,' said the third stranger with a wink to the warrior beside him. 'Otherwise, we will bid you good day and trouble you no more.'

'Ach, well, my impatient friend,' replied Fergal, 'I know the very man you speak of and I think I know where to find him.'

'And will you tell us yet?' asked the second warrior. 'For we are hard pressed to be on our way.'

Fergal turned his gaze on the fellow. 'What do men call you when they want to call you?'

'They call me Niall—for that is my name.'

'You are not Volunti, I think,' said Conor, noting the triple slash mark on the fellow's arm below the sleeve of his faded red siarc. 'That, as I recall, is a Nagnati mark—is it not?'

'Aye, so it is—the mark of a Nagnati warrior.' He smiled, a flash of white teeth below a voluptuous brown moustache. 'You know your tribal marks, I see.'

'I also know that you are a long way from home, Niall of the Nagnati.'

'So I am,' said Niall. 'So are we all, I think.'

'And you there,' said Conor, turning his attention to the other two men. 'You do not wear the mark of the Nagnati—nor, from what I can see, the Volunti, either.'

'It would be a rare thing if I did,' replied one of the pair, a narrow-hipped, deep-chested young man. Slightly shorter than the one next to him, but with a bull neck and well-muscled shoulders, he wore his hair in a long braid down the side of his head. Extending an arm, he opened the neck of his siarc to reveal his upper chest bearing a woad-stained spiral with a barbed line through it to represent a spear. 'I am of Cael mac Colla, and this one here is my swordbrother, Tréon mac Enda. We are Ulaid, born and bred.'

'Ach, well, your luck is with you today,' said Fergal. 'As it happens, the man you seek is closer than you know. He will be found riding a grey stallion and carrying a sword on his hip and a shield on his back. He will be travelling in the company of a tall, handsome warrior of vast renown and prowess. Next time I see your man, I will tell him you are looking for him.'

'If you would kindly do that, friend,' said Diarmaid. 'We would be much obliged.'

Fergal turned to Conor and said, 'Brother, there are four men looking for you. They claim to be warriors.'

'So we are!' cried Diarmaid, laughing. He moved to stand before Conor. 'I knew you, my lord, the moment I set eyes to you.'

'The stain on my face is difficult to miss or mistake,' conceded Conor.

'With all respect, lord, it is not the red mark of Danu on your cheek that warriors speak of when they speak your name,' volunteered Niall. 'It is your battle craft and skill with a blade'—his eyes flicked to Galart, who was silently enjoying the banter—'as the bold Brigantes never tire of telling us.'

To Conor, Diarmaid said, 'We would be honoured to join your fianna—if you will have us.'

'Tell me, what does your king have to say about this?' said Conor. 'No doubt he will be sorry to lose good men to another's warband.'

'Our lord may be many things, but he is not a man to waste a stray thought to warriors who are no longer content to remain under his rule,' replied Diarmaid simply. 'Since we are unhappy, he has given us leave to search elsewhere for our hearts' desire.'

'Why unhappy?' asked Fergal. 'Could it be you are contentious men who are easily dissatisfied with your lot and portion in life?'

'Nay, brother, never that,' said Cael. 'It is that we are no longer satisfied to hide behind the walls of our strongholds and wait for enemy raiders to come and burn us from our homes. We want to see the Scálda driven back into the sea.'

'Spoken like a man after my own heart,' Conor told him. Looking to the other three, he said, 'Is this also your desire?'

'So it is,' answered Diarmaid, and Cael, Tréon, and Niall nodded as one.

'And was it Médon Brigantes who told you where to look for me?'

'Him and no other,' Cael answered. 'Some of us met him on the way to Aintrén and he bade us take word back to our ráth and gather any who wished to join us.'

'He said there were thirteen of you,' Fergal said. 'Where are the others?'

The newcomers regarded each other uncertainly. 'Ach, well, maybe there were thirteen to begin with . . .'

'But not now?' said Fergal.

'Nay, lord . . .' Diarmaid glanced around at the trail. 'There are many more than that now.'

'How many more?'

Diarmaid turned and gestured at the trail behind him. 'Three tens at least. But you need not take my word alone. You can count them for yourself, for here they come now.'

Both Conor and Fergal lifted their eyes to where Diarmaid indicated. From out of the fog emerged the first rank of warriors—a body of eight or so men jogging easily along the river road. A moment or two later, another group, just as large, emerged out of the mist and these were followed by two more ranks of eight or ten—at least two of which were leading pack ponies—their forms all but obscured by the shifting curtains of fog. Thirty warriors! Instantly, and without so much as a blade lifted or a single word spoken, Conor had acquired one of the largest warbands in all Eirlandia.

'Look there, brother,' said Fergal, shaking his head in disbelief. 'It seems you are to have a fianna worthy of the name.'

'So it seems,' replied Conor, still taking in the sight of all those warriors streaming toward him on the path. 'The question now is what are we to do with them all?'

30

'How many?' said Donal, both voice and eyebrows rising in astonishment.

'Thirty-one all told,' replied Fergal. 'Brigantes and Volunti, mostly—but also Nagnati and Ulaid.'

'Probably some other tribes as well,' said Conor. 'We did not speak to every one of them.'

Donal glanced to the trail ahead, still obscured by fog and mist. 'Where are they?'

'Not far,' said Fergal. 'I expect they'll be here soon enough.'

'What will we do with so many?'

'The very thing I'm asking myself,' Conor replied.

'You know what this means?' said Donal. 'We will have a warband to rival the biggest in Eirlandia!'

'That's what *I* told him,' said Fergal. 'A right fair warband—only one or two tribes can boast larger.'

'This is a new thing. Has anyone ever seen such a thing?' wondered Donal, and then: 'How will we support so many?'

'My very thought,' said Conor. 'We'll make camp hereabouts—somewhere near the river.' He looked to Fergal. 'Find a place and make a start.' To Donal, he said, 'Wait here for the warriors to arrive and then we'll decide what to do.' With that, Conor gave Búrach a light slap of the reins and the grey trotted off. He rode back to where Galart and the others had dismounted and stood waiting beside the trail. 'Médon!' called Conor, while still a little way off. 'A word.'

Médon jumped up and hurried after Conor, who had dismounted a little farther down the trail where they would not be overheard by the others. 'It seems we have come to an impasse.'

'An impasse?' Médon's voice held a resigned tone and his eyes searched Conor's face as if he feared judgement for his disobedience had come at last.

'So it is,' said Conor. 'For we can no longer continue as we are, and yet we cannot go back to what we were before any of this happened. Something must be done.'

'You must do what you think best, lord.'

Conor nodded, then smiled. 'Well, then, the best I can think to do is to forgive your lapse of obedience. Your wild and reckless risk has borne fruit in wild and reckless abundance. Thanks to you we are now forty-one blades strong. And *that*, brother, is a warband to match any in Eirlandia.'

Médon's demeanour changed in that moment; the pinched, haunted expression he had worn for the last day fell away and a smile spread across his face: the relief he felt made manifest for the world to see. 'Forty-one,' he repeated, glancing around as if to see them trooping into sight, but all he saw was the mist-wrapped track passing out of sight around a bend in the river.

'They are on their way even now,' Conor assured him. 'The warband you sought to raise will soon arrive and, as Fergal says, we are now a fianna worthy of the name.'

Extending his hand for the young warrior to take, the two clasped arms in the age-old acknowledgement of friendship and acceptance. 'Your disobedience is forgiven, Médon mac Cerna, and we will speak of it no more. Instead, we will consider it foresight and ingenuity. I return you to your former place in the fianna.'

Releasing Conor's arm, Médon touched the back of his hand to his forehead and said, 'You are most gracious, lord. I am yours to command.'

'As to that,' said Conor, 'it is also thanks to you we now have many more mouths and bellies to fill, and we must have food and shelter—for tonight, aye, and all the days and nights to come hereafter. I would have you sit down with Donal and Fergal and myself to consider what is best to do.'

'Food and shelter may be closer than you know,' replied Médon happily. 'Brigantes lands lie across the river to the north and east of here. There we will find a few farming settlements. We might do well to go to these and see what manner of aid they can offer us.' He looked around at the surrounding countryside. 'Even if very little, it would be better than camping in the wood.'

Conor considered this for a moment and agreed. 'It is a place to start.' The two rode back together to tell Donal and Fergal and, while Dearg and the others tended the horses, the four sat down beside the track to discuss how to traverse the new landscape that had suddenly opened before them.

Fergal was first to speak aloud what had already occurred to the others: maintaining a roving warband might be more challenging than first imagined. 'There are few enough kings who can keep a warband as large as our fianna—and those will have a ráth with farms, and fields, and pastures to support and supply their men,' he pointed out, adding, 'and we have none of those.'

'Then perhaps we should have those, too,' suggested Donal.

'A ráth of our own,' Conor mused.

Fergal stared, then started to laugh. When neither Conor nor Donal joined in the mirth, he stopped, looked again, and said in a voice ripe with disbelief, 'Do I believe what I am hearing? You are in earnest! But this is surely the strain of our ordeal beginning to tell on your weak and feeble minds.' He shook his head wearily. 'Ach, well, I have been fearing something like this would happen, so I have. Why not go down to the river and bathe your heads in cool water until your better sense returns—if it ever will.'

'Be easy, brother,' chided Conor. 'It is merely an idea just now.'

'Aye, a *bad* idea. Where do you imagine you would find land to establish this stronghold of yours? Even if you found such a place, who would farm it for you? These things take time and cannot be done overnight. We need food and shelter now, and tomorrow, and the next day, too, come to that. We are meant to be a *roving* warband—a *fianna,* if you care to recall. We don't even have horses enough for everyone. I expect we will find it somewhat wearying to be a roving warband without them.'

They then fell to discussing how they might beg, buy, or borrow enough horses to supply their needs; they were still at it when Calbhan arrived to tell them that Diarmaid and the fianna had been sighted some little way off and would soon be arriving.

'Ach, well,' sighed Conor, 'it seems we have decided nothing.'

'Give it time,' replied Donal. 'You can't build a ráth in a day.'

'True enough, but maybe you can take one,' said Conor. Turning to Médon, he said, 'How far are these Brigantes holdings you mentioned?'

'The closest might be a half a day's ride, more or less.'

'More than that for men on foot,' Fergal pointed out needlessly. Recognizing Conor's thoughtful expression, he added, 'What so? You cannot be thinking of taking over an entire settlement, now.'

Conor, still thinking, made no reply, so Donal offered, 'A few of us could ride on ahead to prepare a place maybe. That way we would be assured of a welcome.'

Conor nodded absently.

Donal said, 'Médon and I will go on ahead then. The rest of you can follow on.'

'We'll all go together.' Conor rose abruptly and started for his horse. 'Forty warriors appear at your gate, you do not dare turn them away.'

'Sure about that, are you?' Fergal called after him, but received no answer.

Fergal sat for a moment longer and watched as Conor strode off. 'We cannot be taking over every ráth and holding we come to.'

Donal rose, too, and stood for a moment. 'Ach, well, not *every* ráth, perhaps. Just this one for now.'

'And you, Donal mac Donough,' muttered Fergal, rising to his feet, 'you are getting to be just as bad. You should know better than to encourage his insanity.'

'You wound me, brother. Anyway, his insanity needs no encouragement from me. He is more than able to maintain it all on his own.'

'But you stand idly by and let him run away with himself, so you do.'

'Not so,' Donal protested. 'I stand by and hold his cloak while he runs.' Donal smiled at Fergal's exasperated expression. 'Cheer up, brother. We do not know how this will turn out. But it does no harm for a man of Conor's temper to dream a little. Something good usually comes of it.'

Fergal rolled his eyes at the notion, then sighed. 'Ach, well, it is not as if we had any better choice. I like a hearth and a roof over my head as much as the next man, so I do.'

Once the greatly expanded fianna had assembled and was welcomed by

Conor, they moved on. Médon knew the region well and knew where the nearest holdings were to be found. The nearest, as it happened was no great distance from the river that formed the southern border of Brigantes lands. Even so, with so many afoot, the fianna arrived at the farming settlement late in the day. The head man of the holding was not best pleased to see such a large warband trooping into his tidy yard. The place was home to sixty-three farmers, their wives and assorted children, several dogs and fair-sized herds of cattle and pigs, some sheep and a few scraggy goats. Judging from the tepid reception offered by their head, none of the farm folk particularly relished the idea of hosting forty-one hungry warriors and twelve horses. Yet, to refuse the request outright would be to damage the honour and standing of his clan within the tribe, not to mention earning the displeasure of his lord if it was voiced about that he had denied hospitality to foot-weary warriors, some of them Brigantes.

Conor understood the chieftain's dilemma and sympathised. Feeding and lodging so many men and beasts, even for just one night, would put a considerable dent in the community stores of grain and supplies of foodstuffs. Conor felt for the man—all the more since it was not just one night that he asked to stay. 'Three days and nights,' Conor told him, 'and then we'll move on.'

'Three days . . .' The fellow scratched his rough jaw and spat onto the ground. He glanced at the white-whiskered man beside him, one of the farming clan's elders. 'A fella could wish it was just two, now.'

'And *I* could wish it was ten,' Conor told him. 'But we need those three days.' His tone left no doubt that he was in earnest. Time and need was against him, and it was not as if he could simply move on down the road and hope for a better reception elsewhere. There would be no lavish welcomes for his fianna—enthusiastic or otherwise—save, perhaps, on the field of battle. Reluctant though they might be now, when the Scálda came screaming into the yard with spears and torches, these same reluctant settlements would be eager enough for the protection of these same warriors.

Médon, standing next to Conor, grew impatient with the farmer's dithering. 'What is the name of this place?' he demanded.

'This is Aghabhall you've come to, as anyone will tell you.'

'And what is your name, friend?' he demanded, displeasure colouring his tone a darker shade.

'They call me Blai,' replied the head man. 'And this one here,' he nodded to the grizzled elder at his side, 'is called Aonghus.'

'And was not Lord Brecan a good king for you?'

'Fair enough. We never had cause to complain overmuch.'

'And how many times have the Scálda burned down your barns, killed your wives, and stolen your cattle?'

'Not any at all,' said the elder. 'And you, a Brigantes, should know this.'

'Aye,' answered Médon. 'I do know it right well—for the reason that the two you see standing on their legs before you were in Brecan's warband and we protected settlements and strongholds like this while our king was alive. Now that he is gone, we find ourselves pressed hard to continue that protection without the help of people like you.'

'I don't think we've ever seen you or your men around here before,' remarked the white-haired elder. 'Not in my time anyway—and that stretches back a ways, so it does.'

'What is your place here?' Médon demanded.

'I am stockman and keeper,' answered the white-whiskered one, thrusting out his chin. 'I've worked the herds since I was a lad in bare feet.'

'Well, Aonghus, my man, you can call yourself fortunate that you have not seen us before. That means we have kept trouble away from the gates of Aghabhall these many years. And if you have a care for that protection to continue, you will cheerfully grant my lord Conor's request to host our fianna these next three days while we work out how best to make our way in this Scálda-worried world.'

The two farmers shuffled their feet and sucked on their teeth, but still hesitated.

Médon, increasingly incensed by their reluctance, drew himself up. 'I hope you are not contemplating turning away warriors of your tribe? That would be a grave mistake, friend—and one you and your clan would long regret—if you value remaining in your home here.'

'Turning away?' the fellow spluttered. 'Turning away? Have you heard anyone say such a thing? See now, I will not have it said that I turned away a warrior of the tribe who asked a meal and a bed.' He raised his eyes hopefully. 'For three nights only it was—so you said, aye?'

'Three nights only,' Conor assured him. 'And then we will leave you in peace.'

'Aye, that's all right then,' said Blai, relenting at last. 'Three nights it is.'

'In any case,' volunteered Aonghus, 'I expect you will be wanting to reach the gathering before it begins.'

'What gathering is that?' asked Conor.

The two farmers glanced at one another. Aonghus said, 'There's an Oenach at Tara—all the kings and kinglets are summoned. There's talk of a new high king coming to the throne.'

'There is always such talk,' Blai said. 'It doesn't mean anything.'

'Ach, there may be more to it now that Brecan is gone and the dog-eaters have grown all the bolder for it. We need a high king they say, and that is the truth of it.'

'I agree,' said Conor. 'That was your Lord Brecan's ambition, too.'

'Aye, so they say,' replied Aonghus, 'and it's the new Brigantes lord leading the pack now.'

'The new Brigantes lord?' wondered Médon. 'Queen Sceana is ruling our people as you should know.'

'No more she is,' Aonghus the herdsman told him. 'This new lord—the Bréifne fella—'

'Vainche, you mean,' said Médon.

'Aye, that one. He is king now—same as summoned the gathering.'

Conor glanced at Médon and, judging from the fierce scowl, the warrior was not taking the news at all well. 'You did not know this?' wondered Conor.

Médon shook his head. 'I did not,' he spat. 'Mind, I only spoke to a few of the warriors at their training down in the field and did not go up to the ráth at all—the better to avoid being seen by Gioll or Vainche. No one told me about the marriage. Then again, maybe the deed had not yet been perpetrated.'

'This gathering you mentioned,' said Conor, turning back to Blai, 'when is it to be?'

The chief conferred with Aonghus for a moment and together they decided, 'At the next full moon. That's . . . what? Maybe eight . . . ten days away.'

'Ach, well, I thank you for your kind offer of hospitality, friend Blai,' said Conor grandly. 'I will be sure to mention it to your lord when I see him at the Oenach. No doubt he will be eager to repay you in kind for any shortfall you may sustain in hosting us.'

The two farmers fell to discussing how best to shelter and feed so many men and animals on such short notice. Leaving them to work out the details, Conor and Médon rode back to the fianna who were waiting on the road. The two had just left the yard when Médon asked, 'Am I right in thinking that you mean to attend the gathering?'

'I am thinking it would be imprudent *not* to attend. We can reach Tara in . . . what? Three days? Four? Though you would likely know best.'

'Possibly two even—*if* we stir ourselves and do not dally along the way,' Médon told him. 'Mind, it will take longer for those on foot. Then again, the entire fianna would not have to arrive at once.'

'Better if they didn't appear at all, in fact. We don't want to incite the ire of the more peevish lords and lordlings with a show of force like that. We could ride ahead and the rest of the fianna could come along in time.'

'We?' asked Médon hopefully.

'Ach, aye,' replied Conor, a grin spreading across his face. 'A lord cannot attend an Oenach without his trusted advisors. If I am going to take my place at an Oenach, I must have an ardféne of my own. And you, Médon mac Cerna shall be among them—if you will accept the duty.'

'I would be honoured, lord.' Médon beamed his good pleasure. 'You will not be disappointed in your choice.'

They began discussing who else should be included in the group to support Conor at the gathering when Fergal came riding up to meet them. 'Will they be having us?' Fergal called while still a little way off.

'They will,' answered Conor. 'But for three nights only.'

'Well, that is something at least.'

'Three nights is all we can spare if we want to reach the gathering in time,' Conor replied and, seeing the question forming on Fergal's lips, quickly explained what he'd learned about the Lord Vainche summoning the tribes to an Oenach.

'This is Vainche's doing?' He looked to Médon for confirmation. The young warrior nodded and Fergal shook his head in disbelief. 'That flatulent swine must hold himself very grand indeed if he imagines he has any right to summon a gathering, much less plant his pale skinny arse on the high king's throne. Can the man really be so deluded that he thinks anyone would support him?'

Before Conor could reply, Fergal added, 'The very idea! It's an outrage, that's what it is—an outrage against sense and nature. And it cannot be allowed to go unchallenged.'

'You speak my mind, brother,' Conor told him. 'And that is why we're going to the gathering.'

'Aye, we'll go and put a stop to that insolent upstart before he up and starts.'

31

For the next three days the ordinarily peaceful beaten-earth yard at the little farming settlement of Aghabhall was transformed into a mock battlefield with groups of warriors training by day and gathered around five separate fire rings by night. The warriors of the fianna took their meals by turns in the holding's modest hall, and slept in the barn and storerooms, and anywhere else a roof could be found. There was not a corner within the low, banked-earth walls that did not echo to the clatter of clashing weapons by day, nor their roisterous voices lifted in song or laughter by night. Both day and night, the inhabitants of little Aghabhall were fully stretched to meet the constant demands of their guests.

On the first day, Conor had summoned his new ardféne, consisting of Fergal, Donal, Médon, Galart, Dearg, and Aedd, of his earliest supporters, and Diarmaid from among the new arrivals. As the warriors went about their chores and training, Conor and his advisors walked among them, assessing each man's strengths and noting any apparent weakness. When each practice session was over, the fianna trooped down to the river to bathe and shave while some of Aghabhall's women washed their clothes. On their return, Conor and Fergal, in his role as Chief of Battle, made a point to spend time with each man individually to get to know him and discover any talents or abilities that might prove useful for the fianna as a whole.

This process continued on the second, third, and fourth day, along with a series of sparring matches arranged by Conor to test the mettle of various pairs in order to determine who among the new group might become the leader of a branch. 'A battlechief can only be one place at a time,' Fergal had said. 'Your father always chose one or two to lead a separate branch, if you recall. And I always thought it a fine thing.'

'No doubt because you were often chosen to lead a branch and it pleases you to give orders,' Conor quipped.

'None of it,' sniffed Fergal. 'The place fell more often to Eamon if you care to recall.'

So, while the fianna sparred for Conor and Fergal, Donal took it on himself to organise an essential requirement that had so far been overlooked and underperformed: cooking and preparing meals. To this end, he called Dearg aside and told him, 'You have proved that you have a cheerful way with a pot and a skewer, brother. The fianna has had the benefit of that these past many days. For that we are grateful and you are to be commended.'

The young warrior grinned, but shrugged off the compliment, saying, 'I like to eat, and cooking is the best way to ensure a mouthful now and then.'

'Even so, it is a skill in which you excel and I commend you,' Donal told him. 'But, see now we are forty-one knives at the board and that will require more of everything—more work, more food, and much more preparation. And we will need someone to take on that task, at least until we are better established than we are at present.'

'Are you about asking me to be the cook now?'

'I do ask it,' replied Donal. 'And not only that. As well as food, you will also oversee the provision of shelter.'

Dearg's brow wrinkled with concern. 'Food and shelter . . . for a warband this size?' He puffed out his cheeks in a sigh. 'A job and a half, that. You won't be wanting a man, you'll be wanting a whole ráth.'

'You've said it there, brother. Ach, but we must start where we find ourselves, and that is why I propose to make you master of the hearth. The work should not fall on your shoulders alone, so your first duty will be to choose three men to help you, or four if you think you need another. These men will be yours to train and command—in the hall and cookhouse, at least. These men will be excused any duties that conflict with your orders for them.'

'The fellas I am to choose,' said the redheaded Dearg, 'must they be warriors from among the fianna?'

Donal pursed his lips in thought. 'I suppose not,' he concluded. 'It is merely that warriors is what we have ready to hand. Why do you ask?'

'Only for the reason that I have a friend, a kinsman, who was a warrior wounded in a battle a year or so ago and can ride with the warband no longer. Fíoldhla is his name, and what I know about cooking, I mostly learned from him.'

'This kinsman of yours you say? Where is he?

'He resides at Carnabhan where he served in Lord Toráin's warband.'

'Lord Toráin . . . ? I don't know the man. What tribe?'

'He is of the Concani,' Dearg told him. 'One of King Brecan's client lords. That was how Fíol came to be there. I could go and ask him to join the fianna if that is agreeable to you.'

'We have more need of you here just now,' Donal said. 'I will tell Conor and have him send someone to fetch Fíoldhla if he is willing. Until he comes, I would have you choose three men to help you with the chores, and then we will discuss what to do about supplies and provisions.'

Dearg took his leave and went away smiling. 'Master of the hearth,' he said to himself. 'Master of the hearth . . .'

On the third day, Conor and the ardféne walked once more among the sparring warriors, arranging various pairs and evaluating the shieldwork and blade craft of each man. Then they met together to arrange the battle groups. There would be four branches; Conor would lead one, Fergal another, and likewise Donal and Médon, each of whom would choose a second from among the men under him. In this way, the warband could operate as a single unit or four separate smaller units acting in close coordination. The four commanders spent the remainder of the day in their deliberations and, when the sun began to set and the chill fell upon the yard with the evening shadows, Conor assembled the warband. He called out Dearg from among them and confirmed that he was now master of the hearth, and asked Dearg to name the men he had chosen to aid him in his duties. Then, one by one, Fergal, Donal, and Médon stepped forward to call out the names of the men they had chosen for each warrior branch, and these sat down together in their groups.

Satisfied with this arrangement, Conor then took his place before the ordered ranks, and lifting his voice so that all could hear, he said, 'Tonight we become a true fianna. Take this moment and look into the eyes of the man sitting next to you. Then, look into the faces of those around you. Take a good long look, for from this night these men are your swordbrothers.

'Hear me, all of you! We are the fianna, and we have foresworn allegiance to the kings and lords of our past. No tribe or clan has any claim over us. Our loyalty is to each other and to our kind. In the battles to come we fight not for tribe or clan, we fight for the Tuatha Dé Danann. From this night, when we take up our spear to enter the fray we fight for all Eirlandia.'

He paused, allowing this thought to take root, then moved on, saying, 'Word has gone out and the kings have been summoned to an Oenach. To-morrow we leave here and travel to Tara where we will take our place among the warbands. We have not been invited, for few know we exist. But soon *everyone* will know that a new power has arisen in Eirlandia.'

These words met with the hearty approval of all gathered within the sound of Conor's voice. Then he and the members of his ardféne walked among the warriors, confirming each one in their place within the branch of the fianna into which they had been placed. Supper that night, though a simple meal, became a revel—such that Fergal induced Blai to open a few casks of ale. 'See here, my man,' he cried from halfway across the yard, 'tonight a new tribe has risen in the island and we must celebrate. Hurry! No time to lose.'

The noisy zeal of the fianna proved infectious and Blai and Aonghus and some of the men brought out a vat and began filling it, while the women gathered up every bowl and cup they could lay hands on. Meanwhile, fire-wood was stacked in the centre of the yard and a bonfire lit. The long board was removed from the hall and set up nearby, and the food that was to have been served inside was carried out, and soon the entire settlement converged on the yard to share the impromptu celebration with the warriors. When everyone was settled and all the cups and bowls filled, Conor raised the first cup to his hosts, praising Blai and Aonghus and all the folk of Aghabhall for their hospitality and care. There followed round after round of healths drunk, food shared, and stories told. Even the weather seemed to smile on the glad occasion: the rain that had threatened all day held off; the clouds parted to reveal a patchwork of stars and a late-rising moon that cast a sil-very glow over the revellers below.

Some of the warriors, after trading friendly taunts and ridiculous insults, challenged one another to feats of strength—such as lifting the ale vat and seeing who could carry it the farthest. Others engaged in tests of skill: pierc-ing a turnip with a spear thrown from fifty paces; champions were declared and the winners lauded with impossible attributes and cups of mead. Some of Aghabhall's wives and maidens even allowed themselves to be talked into dancing with the warriors to the accompaniment of rowdy singing and the stamping of feet.

As the celebration reeled on, Donal noticed Conor sitting by himself in the shadows at the far end of the board, far away from the fire and the dancing. 'You look like the man just thrown from his horse and trodden on,' he said, sliding onto the bench across from him. 'Why the woeful look, brother?'

Conor took his time answering. 'Ach, well, I was just thinking that we have seen little of music and dancing in this last year or so,' he said at last. 'And that put me in mind of Aoife's harp. . . .' He broke off and gazed down into his half-empty cup.

After a moment, Donal concluded, 'And that put you in mind of fair Aoife herself.'

'So it did,' Conor sighed. Still gazing into his cup, he murmured, 'I do miss her so.' Glancing up to meet Donal's concerned gaze, he said, 'Is she well, do you think?' He gave an embarrassed shrug and said, 'Ach, I might better ask the moon, eh?' Raising his cup, he quickly drained it, then stood abruptly and, bidding Donal a good night, stalked off to find a quiet place to sleep.

The merrymaking lasted long into the night and the next morning, while others were picking up the pieces and clearing away the remnants, restoring the yard to its former state, Conor called his advisors together and told them to gather their weapons and prepare to ride—all save Médon and Dearg, who would lead the rest of the fianna travelling on foot to Tara. 'I place the men in your care, brothers,' said Conor as he swung up onto Búrach's broad back. 'Bring them along as quickly as you can.'

'Give us good weather and you won't be missing us,' replied Médon, and Dearg echoed the sentiment. Taking up the reins, Conor bade them farewell and he and his new ardféne departed for the Oenach.

The six rode quickly through a land draped in autumn's many-coloured cloak. Every farm and settlement they passed was busy preparing for the winter to come: cattle were being fattened, pigs slaughtered, sheep brought in from the remote hills, grain stored, straw stacked to dry. On the evening of the third day, they entered a region of low, gently rounded hills and wide valleys that opened onto a broad heartland of rivers, loughs, marshlands, and meadows—and, at last, the woodlands bordering the storied plains surrounding the sacred hill of Tara. These plains, celebrated in song, were where the lords and lordlings of Eirlandia would camp while attending the

Oenach. Conor had thought best to approach from the southwestern edge of Mag Coinnem, the southernmost plain. Though rougher and fringed with elder, whitebeam, and elm—and therefore a somewhat less desirable location than the others—on this, the Council Plain, they would encounter, perhaps, less opposition to their presence. They chose a place at the foot of a low hill well away from the nearest encampments, but close enough to allow a lone watchman on the hilltop to see when the kings began assembling at Tara's council ring. A stand of beeches grew along a tiny burn; a small grove of slender young trees, it would afford a scrap of shelter while allowing them to observe the southern approach for the eventual arrival of the unmounted fianna.

Leaving Galart, Aedd, and Diarmaid to make camp, Conor, Donal, and Fergal walked to the top of the nearest hill and gazed out over the broad green sweep of Tara's sacred precinct, the whole spread out before them in the dwindling daylight. Directly ahead stood the looming, flat-topped eminence of Teamhair, Tara's sacred hill, surrounded by its storied plains: to the west, Mag Teamhair, the Plain of Tara; to the north, the Royal Plain of Mag Rí; to the south, the expanse of Mag Coinnem, the Council Plain. The sun had only just set, but there were campfires already aglow here and there, sending threads of silvery smoke drifting on the freshening north-westerly breeze. Upon taking in the sight, Conor expressed a twinge of uneasiness, to which Fergal replied, 'It is not as if we could be taking the whole fianna up to the council anyway,' he pointed out. 'We'd only get ourselves banished.'

'Or start a riot,' added Donal. 'We'll be doing well just to get a hearing at all.'

'Very true,' allowed Conor. 'As to that, I mean to have my say and I will not be denied because some lord or other decides to make a fuss.'

'Why would anyone be making a fuss?' said Fergal. 'We're only a rebellious band of lawless exiles and outcasts showing up where we're not wanted to stop a vainglorious pretender overreaching himself. Why should that upset anyone at all?'

Conor laughed—a sound rare enough that it made Fergal and Donal smile. 'Ach, well, just for a moment I imagined there might be trouble.' They fell silent, contemplating the various encampments, each with its king or lord together with some of the best of Eirlandia's warriors.

'Nothing has started yet,' mused Fergal. 'I don't see anything happening up at the council ring.' He indicated the flattened plateau of the sacred hill; there were no torches burning or cooking fires to indicate a feast or reception of any kind.

'That's as well,' replied Conor. 'We have work to do down here, first. If we're lucky we might have a day or two yet before the council begins. I want to speak to my father and some of the other lords—if they'll hear me. They should be warned lest anyone consider trusting Lord Vainche.' He scanned the scattered campsites and wondered aloud where the Darini delegation might be camped.

'Do you want me to go and see if I can find them?' offered Donal.

'Nay, it'll be dark soon, and we've travelled far today,' Conor replied. 'We'll rest tonight and then go look for them in the morning.'

They enjoyed a calm and restful night and, after bathing and shaving and a meal of leftover porridge and hard bread softened in water, Conor, Donal, and Fergal prepared to set off on their search for the Darini delegation. Leaving their weapons in the care of Galart, and charging Diarmaid and Aedd to watch the camp, the three rode to the top of the nearest hill where they looked out across the three plains; the last, lingering patches of morning mist and fog, slowly dispersing in the sunlight, drifted across the flat, green expanse below. The ancient mound of Tara itself had yet to shake off the few remaining shadows of night around its northern base, but the bright sun's rays illumined the top well enough to see, even from a distance, that the council ring remained deserted.

Upon reaching Mag Coinnem, the three pursued a leisurely course that took them near the various encampments, passing close enough to guess whose camp it might be, but not so close as to disturb anyone or call undue attention to themselves. They moved across the level green, pausing now and again to ask of warriors on their way to wash or fetch water whether any knew where the Darini were camped. None of those they asked had seen the Darini or knew where they might be found. Along the way, however, they did locate the Coriondi camp and paused to exchange a word with Lord Cahir, an old friend and ally of Conor's father.

The Coriondi king professed himself astonished and pleased to see them and invited them into his tent to refresh themselves with a bowl of ale. From the first, the lord was more than solicitous, almost fawning over them—especially Conor, who grew uncomfortable under the lord's fulsome welcome. 'Come in! Everyone, come in!' Standing at the open flap of the tent, he shouted to one of his men. 'Earchna! Bring the jar and bowls for our friends here!' Turning to his guests once more, he gestured to the low, three-legged stools along one side of the tent and said, 'Sit down, friends. Rest yourselves. Look at you, Conor! The last man I expected to see and yet here you are. Have you seen your father? Ach, what am I saying? Of course not—otherwise why would you be looking for him? But here you are!' The king lowered himself into his camp chair and sat beaming at them.

Conor smiled back and said, 'It is good to see you, too. I would have come to you sooner, but things do not always follow the straightest course.'

'Why would you seek me?' asked Cahir. Just then, the king's steward, Earchna, entered with a large jar of ale and four wooden bowls. Handing the jar to the king, he passed out the bowls and then departed, closing the tent flap after him.

'To tell you how sorry I am about Mádoc's death. You must have heard long since how he died and what we—'

'Stop right there!' Cahir raised a hand. 'I will not hear it. You are not to blame for Mádoc's death. If anyone should be sorry, it is me and none other—sorry for allowing myself to get carried away with the old druid's schemes. I should have known better. But there it is. Water passed. And here you are!'

The king raised the jar and bade his guests to extend their bowls, which he filled to overflowing. 'We will drink to better times ahead, aye?' They all echoed that sentiment, raised their bowls, and drank. When they finished, Cahir turned to Conor and said, 'Last I heard you were an amais with the Brigantes.'

'True enough. And did you also hear that I betrayed King Brecan to the Scálda and got him killed?' Conor put aside his bowl and looked the Coriondi lord in the eye.

'Something like that came my way,' admitted Cahir. He gave a belated shrug and added, 'But the same also said how you were killed along with him and his druid—that old . . . what was his name?'

'Mog Ruith,' answered Fergal. 'But here is Conor alive and well and so you know the truth of the matter. Conor is no traitor, and that's a fact.'

Cahir raised his hands. 'A fella cannot help the birds from flying over his head, you know. That is just what I heard and, as I say, I never believed it.' He looked to Conor again, 'But what *did* happen to greedy Brecan, then?'

'Evil Eye killed him and I was there—that much is true, at least. The two of them were meeting together to discuss a plan Brecan had conceived that would gain him the high king's throne.'

'A mad and dangerous plan, if you ask me,' scoffed Fergal. 'The man was an overambitious fool.'

'Is this not what I always thought?' Cahir nodded forcefully. 'I knew it must be something like that got Brecan killed—and I told your father as much, so I did. Ardan has never given up hope that you are still alive, you know. He still believes.'

'He'll know by now that I've returned,' Conor told him. 'I only wish I could say the same for Mádoc and little Huw. I'm sorry for the loss of them. I want you to know that if I could have saved them, I would have.'

Cahir sighed. 'Ach, well, water passed, as I say. It was Mádoc's meddling that stirred all this up anyway. So there's no one to blame but himself alone.' The king reached for the jar and splashed more ale into the bowls, and said, 'What do you know of this Lord Vainche who's made himself king over there at Aintrén?'

Fergal was first to answer. 'We know enough to know that he is not fit to rule a pigsty full of young swine much less a tribe like the Brigantes. He's a preening, mutton-headed magpie and anyone who allies with him is a goose ripe for plucking.'

Conor was quick to apologize for Fergal's outburst, but the Coriondi lord slapped his knee and said, 'I like a man with bold heart and ready tongue, so I do. Well, and was I not thinking the very same thing myself? I've only seen the fella once or twice at some gathering or other, and found little enough to impress me. Then again, I've never said two words to the man.'

'We have had dealings,' allowed Conor, 'and I can tell you that Fergal's judgement is accurate as far as it goes. However, I would add that Vainche is also a wily schemer of considerable resolve and much appeal. It will not surprise me if there are many among us who would succumb to his flatteries. That is why I must speak to my father—and anyone else who will listen— before the council begins.'

They discussed the Oenach then, and who might be susceptible to Lord Vainche's blandishments. Then, having drained their cups, they rose to take their leave. Cahir walked with them to their horses and sent them off, saying, 'For myself, I welcome your timely warning—and I'll spread the word. But as for your father, I don't think the Darini are here yet. No doubt, they will arrive today or tomorrow when the Oenach begins. Soon as I see him, I'll tell him you're here and looking for him. Where are you camped?'

'Hard by the Council Plain,' answered Conor and, thanking Cahir for his hospitality, the three collected their mounts and rode on in search of Ardan and the Darini. As soon as they were away from the Coriondi camp, Conor turned to Donal, who was riding at his left hand, and asked, 'Nothing to say back there, brother?'

'Nay,' replied Donal, 'but I think deep thoughts.'

For the second time in as many days, Conor laughed; and the sun seemed to shine a little brighter for a while.

32

After searching for their Darini kinsmen among the tribes encamped on the two farthest plains, the three gave up and returned to the grove and set their mounts to graze alongside the others. They rested through the day, keeping watch on the council ring, but evening closed in around them without anyone making a move to convene the Oenach. A peaceful night passed beside a pleasant fire and the gentle rattling of the dry beech leaves allowed them to rise the next morning rested and ready for the confrontation that lay ahead. A freshening breeze from the north and a sky the colour of a slate gave them to know the weather was on the change. 'There will be rain before day's end,' was Donal's appraisal. As before, they broke fast on little more than crumbs and water and, leaving Galart, Diarmaid, and Aedd behind, rode out once more to look for Lord Ardan and the Darini camp, hoping to have a private word before the council began.

They passed by the Coriondi camp, but did not stop this time, and quickly moved on. The three were halfway across Mag Coinnem when Donal halted abruptly. Conor reined up and turned around. 'What is—?'

'Listen!'

Fergal, hearing the sharp tone in Donal's voice, stopped and looked back the way they had come. 'I don't hear—'

'Shh!' hissed Donal. They both listened for a moment and then Donal said, 'There—did you hear that?'

Fergal shrugged and shook his head. Conor said, 'Nay, not a—'

Just then a shout reached them from somewhere across the plain—a small sound carried on the wind, distinct and clear despite the obvious distance—a cry of alarm. Instinctively, the three turned in the direction of the sound and waited. The first, frantic cry was followed by a second shout and then others; they seemed to be coming from one of the camps at the western-most region of Mag Teamhair at the very perimeter.

'Something is going on out there,' observed Fergal as the distant shouting increased, growing perceptibly louder by the moment. He pointed toward the far tree line and there, streaming out from among the fringe of trees, emerged a line of mounted warriors. Fergal's stare hardened into anger, and Conor muttered a curse under his breath, but it was Donal who called them to action. 'Scálda!'

The word was still reverberating as two more enemy battle groups burst out from among the trees and onto the plain. The first wave of attackers streaked toward the outlying Dé Danann camps and the alarmed cries sounded clear in the air. Conor lifted the reins and lashed Búrach forward—only to be called back by Fergal. 'Wait!' he shouted. 'We have no weapons!'

Without a word, Conor wheeled the stallion, slapped the reins, started back the way they had come. Within four heartbeats, the three were galloping across the empty expanse of Mag Coinnem, shouting warnings to any they passed, but not stopping until they reached their beech grove encampment. Galart and Diarmaid, who were tending their mounts, jumped up as they thundered in.

'Arm yourselves and get ready to ride,' shouted Conor, throwing himself from his mount. 'We're under attack!' He raced to the fire ring and snatched up Eirian, sliding the sleek blade under his belt; he grabbed up Pelydr and, slinging Pared, his impervious shield onto his back, he raced back to Búrach and vaulted onto the grey's back, shouting, 'To me! Everyone! To me!'

Fergal, armed and ready, was first to join him, followed by Galart, Donal, Aedd, and Diarmaid. 'The attack is coming from the western edge of the Royal Plain,' he told them. 'We'll make for Tara Hill and take the high ground.'

'How many?' asked Galart.

'Sixty at least,' replied Donal. 'Maybe more by now.'

'For Eirlandia!' Conor shouted, lofting his spear, and with that they rode out, quickly gaining the top of the hill where they could see that the attack had progressed swiftly. There were not only more enemy than before, the various battle groups appeared to be coming from several different locations along the western border of both Mag Teamhair and, now, Mag Coinnem as well. Of the three plains, only Mag Rí to the north had yet to feel the assault, but the Dé Danann encamped there had raised the alarm and were now speeding to the fight.

Conor did not pause, but turned the stallion toward Tara Hill and gave Búrach his head and let him run. Over the flat turf of the plain they flew, the horses' hooves biting into the soft earth, flinging clots of turf behind them. As they neared the base of the sacred mound, they passed a group of four Auteini warriors making for the hilltop. Conor paused long enough to shout, 'Where were you camped?'

'Back there,' answered a warrior, shouting as he ran. 'Near the centre.'

'Who was with you?' called Conor. 'Have you seen the Darini?'

'Nay,' came the reply. 'Not a hair.'

Conor led his ardféne onto the winding track leading to the flattened summit of the hill. The climb was steep and even Búrach struggled at the end, but they gained the top to see that they were the first. Conor wheeled the stallion and turned to look back down upon the surrounding plains. From this high vantage they could hear the sounds of the clash echoing up from below: men shouting, horses whinnying, the crack and clatter of wood and iron—all merging to form a muted roar like that of a distant windblown sea crashing onto a rocky shore—a score of small clashes dotted all across the plain, isolated skirmishes, scattered combats, each a tiny island of conflict.

'We cannot fight them like that,' growled Fergal. 'They'll cut us to bloody rags.'

As if hearing Fergal's judgement, Dé Danann warriors began breaking away and making for the high ground—some mounted, others on foot. Soon, the entire plain was on the move: from the west where the enemy attack was concentrated, and from the north and south as well, Dé Danann warbands were in flight. The retreat to Tara Hill had begun. Dismounting quickly, Conor gave Búrach a slap on the rump and set the stallion free. He took a position on the western rim of the hilltop where the path from below met the crest. 'They're coming. We'll form the battle line here!' he called. 'To me!'

Fergal dismounted and took his place at Conor's right hand with Diarmaid and Aedd beside him; Donal took his place on Conor's left with Galart beside him. The first to join them on Tara were the Cruithne who had been camped nearest the base of sacred mound. There were seven of them—three mounted, soon followed by four on foot.

'Who else is coming?' Conor shouted across to the Cruithne battlechief as he leapt down from his horse and directed his men to take their places on the line.

'The Laigini were not far off,' came the reply. 'They should be right behind us.'

Indeed, only a few moments later, the Laigini warband appeared over the southern edge of the hilltop: six warriors, all on foot; they quickly added their number to the growing defensive line. Next came the Cauci, three on horseback followed by three on foot; breathless but unbloodied, they hurried to take their places. Dé Danann warriors were now streaming up—alone and in pairs, or groups of three or four—some, the remnant of their tribe's ardféne and others, on horseback, leading their comrades on foot. By the time the first wave had abated, eighty Dé Danann warriors were assembled on Tara Hill, raising a great clamour as men hastened to form the battle line: those on horseback dismounted and joined the ranks; those on foot, breathing hard from the climb, filled in gaps in the line; weapons were shared out: those who had been forced to flee without weapons were given blades by those who had two; men called out for their swordbrothers and re-formed their battle groups, shields were planted for the shield wall, extending the battle line across the western quarter of the hilltop.

Fergal, growing impatient, muttered, 'Where are the rest? There should be more. What's happened to the rest?' Conor told him to go and see what he could see, and Fergal ran to the northern edge of the hilltop and stood for a time gazing down onto the plains to the north and west.

'What do you see?' shouted Conor, raising his voice to be heard among the clamour of weapons and warriors on the line.

'There are more coming,' he shouted, racing back to the line. 'But they are having to fight their way through to get here. There are Scálda on the way, too!'

With a last look at the plains below, Fergal ran to his place once more and soon, from beyond the edge of the hill, could be heard the muted rumble of horses charging up from below. At the sound, Conor's blood-red birthmark began to itch and burn and Pelydr seemed to quicken in his hand with that ardour he had come to expect of the spear—as if the charmed weapon yearned for the clash. 'Here they come!' someone shouted, and the cry was answered by the stuttered clatter as late-arriving warriors slammed the bottom edges of their shields into the soft turf to close any remaining gaps in the shield wall.

The rumble of hoofbeats slowed as the enemy riders neared the top of the hill where the slope was steepest. The defenders crouched low behind their shields as the first wave of Scálda appeared over the rim of the hill. It was the first close look Conor had of their attackers, and it was a sight calculated to invoke terror: the dog-eaters had shaved their heads, save for a single hank of hair into which had been woven the skull of a bird or vole or ferret; their faces were smeared and caked with mud; the flesh of their cheeks and upper arms had been slashed in the symbolic drawing of first-blood wounds to banish fear; their hard leather armour had been crudely daubed with white lye in weird signs and symbols. Up over the rim of the hill they came—only to encounter the Dé Danann shield wall. Those leading the attack attempted to leap over the top of the wall, but speed and momentum were not with them and these were cut down or turned back before they reached the line. The rest, pinched in the narrow margin between the slope and the interlocked shields, looked for a gap or weakness to exploit. That brief hesitation was all the Dé Danann spearmen needed.

A score of spears flashed out, their blades tracing a dull gleam in the sunlight. Many struck home before the enemy knew the spears had been launched. Scálda riders fell from their mounts, some with a startled cry and others with a dying groan and, suddenly free, the charging horses turned and fled back down the hill just as a second wave of enemy riders reached the top. They saw the horses flying past them and, thinking a retreat was in progress, turned tail and followed them—to the cheers and jeers of the defenders.

As the last Scálda rider vanished over the edge of the hill, the defenders gave out a jubilant shout and those without spears ran to retrieve their weapons and any discarded by the enemy, pausing only to make certain the fallen were accounted for; those still breathing were swiftly dispatched and given a push to roll them down the slope. That done, the defenders hastily returned to take up their places in the shield wall. More Dé Danann began arriving from the northern plain. Having skirted Mag Teamhair and the battles there, the lords and warleaders of the tribes camped on Mag Rí now reached the summit to join the defence of the sacred hill. Lords and battle-chiefs shouted commands down the line and ordered their ranks; others cried out to shore up the line and for a moment nothing could be heard above the shouts of men desperate to protect a tenuous advantage against an implacable and merciless foe.

The noise quickly abated as the Dé Danann braced themselves for the next assault. They waited, listening to the wind whine as it gusted fresh out of the northwest. 'What are they doing down there?' muttered Fergal. 'Where are they?'

'We've made them wary,' suggested Donal from his place in the line.

Time slowed to a maddening crawl. Still, they waited.

'Maybe the dog-eaters have given up,' mused Galart from his place beside Conor. 'Do you think they've given up?'

His question was answered a moment later by the dull drumming of hooves pounding up the hillside track. Tightening his grip on the Pelydr's shaft, Conor braced his shield against his side, muscles tense, ready to strike.

This time the enemy charge was better coordinated: the raiders appeared over the edge of the hill, their progress slowed by the steep upward climb. Once they reached the hilltop plateau, the horses fanned out, allowing each rider a little more room to manoeuvre. This gave the attackers a little more time to choose their best point of attack. Nevertheless, the result was much the same as before: the spears flew and the foe fell hard to earth. Only a handful of Scálda even reached the battle line to exchange blows, and the rest retreated after a feint or two.

Thus, the second attack degenerated into confusion and, like a furious wave surge pounding on the shore, it swiftly withdrew, its force diminished, energy spent. As before, the last fleeing horseman disappeared below the rim of the hill and Tara's defenders raced to retrieve weapons and send the wounded to the Hag Queen's hall. The Dé Danann worked with swift, brutal efficiency and returned to the line once more, exuberant in their success.

From then on, the pattern was set: a glancing attack followed by a swift retreat. In between one assault and the next, straggling Dé Danann warriors used the lull to hasten up from the plains to join the battle line with the other defenders. Gradually, the numbers of defenders grew; but though Conor searched each battle group as it arrived, he never caught sight of his father, Liam, or any of the Darini.

So it went throughout the day. Each Scálda onslaught was met by fierce resistance and was duly rebuffed. Every now and then, however, an enemy blade would claim a victim—often at the assailant's cost, but a casualty nonetheless. And each failed assault tired the defenders and wore down their resistance.

As the lowering sun stretched the shadows across the table-flat hilltop, the clouds gathering through the day, closed in and the wind sharpened, swinging directly out of the north. Donal turned his face to the wind and sniffed the air. 'Smell that?' he said.

Conor sniffed and caught a damp scent on the air. 'You said it would rain.'

'Aye, and it will be here before dark.'

'Will the Scálda abandon the attack?' wondered Conor. 'Can you see that happening?'

Donal merely shook his head. 'Truly, I only see more Scálda joining the fight.'

'Then it is going to be a long night,' murmured Conor.

The last lights of day vanished in a murky haze, and two Luceni warriors came along the line offering water from water skins hung around their necks and over each shoulder. Every warrior, desperately thirsty, was given a drink and the skins were passed along; they had not yet reached the end of the line before the next attack commenced.

As every time before, the Scálda appeared over the rim of the hill, their horses labouring up the steep slope. Even as the defenders tensed for the impending collision, a blinding white flash of lightning seared across the sky followed a heartbeat later by the resounding crash of thunder booming across the hilltop and echoing across the plains below. A churning curtain of rain swept in on the wind and Tara dissolved in a veil of drenching rain; the shriek of the wind blended with the wild cries of the enemy even as the storm removed the charging horsemen from sight.

The foremost rank of Scálda struck at the centre of the Dé Danann line near where Conor stood. He had but a fleeting glimpse of a dark form looming out of the rain, and lunged instinctively. The charmed blade slashed through the darkness, met a slight, yielding resistance and then slid home. The rider gave out a startled cry and toppled from his mount as his horse shied, turned, and sped away. The wounded Scálda rolled and lay writhing at Conor's feet and Conor, reaching over the top of his shield, delivered the killing blow, the charmed blade sliding in and out as easily as a scythe through grass. Conor prepared himself for the next assailant. Working with Donal and Galart, three more riders were slain in quick succession. And then the attack was over.

The enemy retreated and the defenders removed the dead Scálda and did what they could to arrange the bodies so as to create impediments to attackers climbing the hill. Meanwhile, the Dé Danann wounded were carried away and any gaps in the shield wall repaired. Conor heard a shout behind them and glanced around to see a fresh troop of Dé Danann warriors hurrying through the rain to join them; they had come up the northernmost path from Mag Teamhair, avoiding the western approach to stay clear of the battles there. Upon reaching the shield wall, they took their places behind those in front, forming a second rank of support. When they got close enough, Conor called out and asked if there were more defenders on the way. The reply came back, 'I cannot say. The dog-eaters are everywhere. The plain is thick with them. We were lucky to get through.'

The initial burst of rain settled into a steady downpour, forming shallow pools in the low places and running in rivulets down the long slopes. This, Conor considered, was no bad thing. For if the Dé Danann must fight in the rain, so, too, the Scálda—a proposition that made holding the high ground all the more critical. Huddled against the wind and rain, the defenders stood their bleak vigil. While waiting for the next wave to break upon them, Conor searched the rain-streaked darkness for his father, or brother, or Eamon, or any of the Darini warriors; but, with the darkness and rain blurring his vision, he could make out nothing past the next two or three warriors along the line.

The next assault foundered before it even reached the hilltop. During the previous attacks, the horses' hooves had churned up the soft, wet earth, making the hillside treacherous; the horses could not gain any solid footing and the belaboured beasts slid and stumbled as they neared the top; few even reached the crest before they, too, turned and slid back down. From his place in the line, Conor watched all this and a ray of hope cut through the gloom: Tara's slope was just too steep to allow a climbing horse to reach full speed; by the time a rider attained the brow of the hill, progress had slowed so much that he was easily picked off by a waiting spear. Rain and darkness and Tara's steep rampart united to lend the defenders a slender fighting chance. The Dé Danann were still woefully outnumbered, but they were in no way outmanned.

The abrupt collapse of the latest assault brought a raucous chorus of jeers from Tara's defenders. Many were for seizing their imagined victory by giving chase and pulled their shields from the wall and raising a cry to pursue and punish the enemy. But these voices were quickly shouted down by more sober calls to "Stand firm!" and "Hold the line!" The overeager warriors eventually ceased their shouting and settled into a restive silence. The rain beat upon Tara's solitary hill and the wind snaked up and over its muddy slopes. The world was dark and wet and growing cold for the men hunkered behind their shields. Lightning flared again and again, and thunder trembled the nearby hills.

The next attack on the hilltop surprised everyone. The Scálda, having at last abandoned their horses, struck out of the storm silently and on foot, advancing by stealth until they were within a spear cast of the Dé Danann shield wall. Then they launched their weapons. The ploy succeeded in catching a fair number of defenders off guard.

Breaches opened along the line as warriors succumbed to the sudden offensive—an errant throw here, a lucky stab there, and a hole in the shield wall would appear. The Scálda made the most of this weakness. With screams and shrieks, they hurled themselves at the nearest opening, trying to hack their way through on brute force alone. The clattering clash of weapons echoed from a dozen places down along the line, and all along the line tired warriors fell.

'Close up!' shouted Conor. 'Close the gaps!'

The nearest warriors heard and obeyed. Those in the second rank leapt forward to drag their wounded comrades out of the way and fill the breach, driving the screaming Scálda back with the points of their spears. The fighting lasted longer than any of the previous skirmishes but, unable to gain an advantage, the surprise attack eventually waned and the enemy fell back to regroup.

That should tell us something, thought Conor, as the last Scálda warrior faded into the darkness. *Horses are no use to them, and their footmen cannot break the shield wall unaided.* This hopeful thought was followed by another, altogether more sober realisation: *This could go on all night—aye, if not longer.*

The next enemy offensive commenced almost at once—and followed much the same pattern: striking fast, killing a few, and then withdrawing in haste and disarray—only to be followed by another attack . . . and then another. Each time there seemed to be more Scálda footmen than before and, instead of simply trying to break the line by force alone, they halted just out of reach and, with their habitual screams and wild gyrations, taunted the Dé Danann, daring them to break ranks and fight. Conor, crouching low in the front line, could dimly make out enemy spearmen a few steps behind those making all the noise—waiting, no doubt, for the pursuing defenders to give chase. 'Hold the line,' he cried, pounding the butt of his spear against the wet ground. 'Hold! Wait them out.'

The Dé Danann warhost stood in the rain and watched the enemy display, adding to the din with taunts and abuse of their own. The commotion so occupied their attention that no one saw the Scálda horsemen who, having circled around the back of the hill to the more difficult ascent of the southeastern side, were at that moment bearing down on them from behind. It was only when the enemy spears began cutting down the men around him that Conor realised how they had been distracted and deceived.

33

Swarming out of the storm they came. Conor, his cries all but drowned by the wind and rain and the wild ululations of the enemy, began pulling men around to face the attack from behind. As defenders began falling around them, the Dé Danann finally realised what was happening and all along the battle line the defensive wall buckled as warriors pulled up their shields and fell back, forming individual battle groups. Within moments, the united defence of Tara's hilltop crumbled in a tumult of chaos and confusion.

Enraged Scálda came screaming through the rain-streaked darkness: the smeared mud melting on their faces, their gashed cheeks and arms bleeding anew, the white lye daubed on their shields and breastplates running in milky rivulets down their armour gave them the look of creatures loosed from nightmares and set to wreak havoc on the world of men. They struck hard, and darted away again. Each glancing charge aimed at dividing the battle groups, driving them into isolated clusters dispersed over the hilltop where they could be picked off one by one. The stalwart Dé Danann stood their ground and in some places succeeded in forcing the enemy back. But at a cost. Every advance was paid in blood.

Wave after ferocious wave broke upon the defenders, each time the enemy inflicted hurtful blows before dashing away again—only to regroup and strike again somewhere else. It soon became clear that the Scálda had no intention of engaging in a pitched battle, but meant to swoop in and pick off the defenders one by one until none remained.

Conor cupped a hand to his eyes and scanned the battle plain as desperation closed its suffocating fist upon him. There were clustered knots of defenders scattered over the hilltop now, driven ever farther apart. *We're being cut to shreds,* he thought. *We've got to move.*

'Fergal!' he shouted, straining to see through the dark and rain.

'Fergal here!' came the reply from down the line.

'We can't stay here like this! We've got to move!'

'Lead the way!'

'The Pillar Stone!' cried Conor. 'Regroup at the ring.' He shouted the instruction to Donal and the message was repeated to everyone within hearing distance. Without waiting for a response, Conor lofted his spear and started for the council ring at a run.

The ring itself was the remnant of an ancient dún from the time when high kings ruled Eirlandia. Though the fortress was long since gone, the deep grooves formed by the three concentric ditches remained—in the centre of which stood a great yellow stone—the Pillar Stone. A timber platform had been erected nearby that served as the meeting place for the council gatherings. On the eastern edge of the plateau stood a large round house flanked by two small storage huts; nearby stood an ancient barrow said to house the remains of Eirlandia's last high king. Some little way past the barrow tomb was a stone circle where, on occasion, feasts and such were sometimes held. There were no defensive structures on the hilltop, but the platform and the ditch offered what little advantage could be had.

Blinded by wind and rain, Conor made a dash for the place; by instinct alone, he made it. Upon crossing the innermost ditch, Conor turned to see whether anyone had followed. The rain pelted down and the wind howled. A blast of forked lightning momentarily illuminated the hilltop and Conor made out clots and clumps of defenders racing to take their places inside the ring. Darkness flooded back instantly, but the muted sounds of men hastily making ready a last stand could be heard: the swish and thud of shod feet through the soaking grass, the errant clink of a blade against a shield rim, the soft muttered curse of a warrior tripping over a rock or stepping in a water-filled hole unseen in the dark. Group by group, the defenders appeared out of the rainy dark to join their swordbrothers in the ring and rebuild the shield wall. They were still shouting commands to one another when the next Scálda surge loomed out of the storm. The weak and unfinished defence crumpled, giving way in several places. Good warriors fell and the resulting gaps grew wider. The Dé Danann fought back with a ferocity born of desperation and at last succeeded in repelling the enemy assault. The Scálda retreated, leaving almost as many Dé Danann defenders dead and dying on the rain-soaked ground as remained standing on the line.

Conor did not have time to assess the damage done to the line before the enemy, sensing victory at last, sped back to the fray. Keen to exploit their hard-won gain, they came screaming—on foot and on horseback, they came and, by dint of superior numbers, succeeded in breaking through the Dé Danann line and forcing the defenders once again into smaller battle groups. Conor saw what was happening and a rush of helplessness swept over him. Glancing around, he glimpsed a small force of men bunched together in a beleaguered clump and shouted to Donal. 'Take command!' Shoving his hand through the Pared's straps, Conor raised the shield and ran to join the beleaguered warband. 'Here! Here! Let me in!'

'Who is it?' demanded one of the warriors, squinting through the rain; his torc marked him out as either lord or battlechief.

'Conor mac Ardan,' Conor announced. 'I must speak to your king.'

'Let him in!' shouted the battlechief.

Conor shoved in beside him, recognising him as one of the Auteini he had spoken to the day before. 'Your king, where is he?'

The nearby warriors looked away and the battlechief wiped the water from his face and frowned. 'You want to see our king?' He pointed with his sword to a sodden, cloak-covered heap on the ground. 'There he is.'

Conor turned to the warleader. 'The Scálda are carving us to pieces. If we do not combine forces once more, none of us will see morning.'

Turning his face into the teeth of the storm, he scanned the lightning-fretted darkness and could just about make out the nearest battle group some little distance across the soggy turf. 'Who is that over there?'

'The Ulaid, I think—or what's left of them,' came the reply. 'Lord Garbha and his men were beside us when the line broke.'

'We'll go to them,' Conor said. 'Tell your men to get ready to move.'

The battlechief pointed at the cloak-shrouded body of his lord. 'And leave our king behind? That we will never do.'

'Then you will soon join him,' Conor replied. 'Listen to me—all of you,' he shouted, raising his voice. 'Dead, you can do nothing for your lord. Stay alive and you can avenge him.' Conor could see them waver and pressed harder. 'You must think of your people now. They will need you in the hard days ahead.'

The reluctant warleader bent over his lord's body, knelt, and placed his hand on the breathless chest. Then, after a moment, he rose, stood, and said, 'We'll do as you say.' The battlechief looked to his waiting men. 'Move on his command.'

Conor turned again, marked the place he aimed for and shouted, 'Now!' Crouching behind their shields in the lashing rain, the defenders trudged across the battleground, lurching over the bodies of the fallen, and calling for the Ulaid battlechief to make himself known. Out of the lashing rain, a lone voice answered their call. They hurried toward the sound and the combined warbands quickly folded in and blended together. Conor then led his growing band of warriors back across the chewed-up ground to the council ring. On the way, he found a band of Luceni warriors surrounded by Scálda footmen, trading blows and fighting for their lives. Conor and his gathered warriors rushed in, forcing a path with the points of their spears to the Luceni front line. 'Conor mac Ardan here!' he shouted. 'Follow me to the Pillar Stone!' The Luceni needed no convincing, but fell into step behind him and thus the warbands of two more tribes were added to the defenders. The triple ring of ditches was now forming shallow loughs; the Dé Danann sloshed across and joined their swordbrothers on the innermost ditch's upper rim. They no sooner took their places on the line than Conor was away again.

Back into the storm he ran, every sense alive and alert. Somehow, above the wail of the wind, Conor heard the metallic ring of blade on blade—no great distance away, yet unseen in the rain-drenched dark, another solitary Dé Danann warband was fighting for its life. Conor marked the place and levelled his spear and ran toward the sound of the clash. Through the shifting curtain of rain, Conor glimpsed a cluster of warriors completely cut off by a horde of howling Scálda. The defenders were frantically trying to mount a defence against a sustained and frenzied onslaught. Conor raced into the hot heart of the desperate fight and hurled himself upon the unprotected backs of the Scálda. Four enemy warriors fell before they realised they were being taken from behind. Two more fell as they strove to disengage and turn to meet this unexpected challenge. Driving in from behind Pared, his impenetrable shield wall, Conor, wielding Pelydr like a butcher hacking at a haunch, carved a killing swathe. Like a creature bred to war, his blood-red birthmark aglow with the fiery heat of battle, he gave himself up to the fight. Bodies dropped and fell away with every exchange of blows. Shouting strong words of encouragement, Conor urged the defenders to join him in his bloody work.

Slick with rain and gore, Dé Danann spears thrust and Dé Danann blades rose and fell. The soft earth churned to blood-rich mud beneath their feet, the enemy struggled to stand against the sustained ferocity of the Dé Danann until the Scálda broke off the attack. The moment the Scálda turned tail and ran, Conor called out, 'To the Pillar Stone, brothers! Fall back to the council ring!'

Back across the broken field they ran to join the defenders at the council ring redoubt—all except Conor, who sped away again, disappearing into a storm that had grown to fill the night with gales of icy wind and stinging rain that seemed, like the enemy, to gather new strength with every assault, scouring the darkened, corpse-strewn plain where terrified horses, their riders thrown or killed, ran this way and that; and lightning seared the turbulent sky, and angry thunder roared in reply; and lone Scálda, lost or wounded, crouched waiting to strike. Heedless of the risk, ignoring it all, Conor ran toward the resounding shouts and clash of weapons and quickly came upon a lone warband encircled by mounted Scálda.

He halted and, crouching low, looked for an opening. It came when a Scálda rider came near, charging blindly out of the darkness. The horse was almost upon him when Conor saw that the beast was none other than his very own. Leaping up, he shouted, 'Búrach! Here, fella!'

The stallion's head swung toward the sound, saw his rightful owner and stiffened his forelegs, skidding to a halt and pitching the surprised rider headlong over its neck. Conor seized the bridle, and swung himself onto Búrach's back. He rode over the dazed rider, and flew to the aid of the hard-pressed Dé Danann. Holding Pelydr low, he drove into the unsuspecting enemy. His first few blows opened a way, but it closed again just as quickly when the Scálda turned and began swarming their lone mounted assailant, stabbing wildly with their iron spears.

Conor whirled this way and that, countering the strokes of the enemy with swift shieldwork, the blade of his charmed spear shearing into hard leather armour with the ease of a scythe through standing grain. Even so, it was all he could do to keep from being pulled from his mount and struck down. Faces contorted with rage and bloodlust, bloodied, mud-streaked, snarling like dogs or shrieking like the Bean Sídhe loomed out of the darkness, spears and swords struck and struck again. The counterattack was instantly so ferocious, Conor accepted that his last fight was upon him. The next stroke might be his last. He knew it, and yet he fought on. Despair clutched him close in its numbing fist and fear seemed to stream in on the wind; he manfully resisted both and, though anyone could see he was only a spear thrust away from certain death, he gripped the Pelydr's blood-slicked shaft and redoubled his effort.

The more hopeless his predicament grew, the bolder Conor became. Having given up trying to save himself, he hewed and hacked at the close-gathered thicket of blades before him with an abandon that was wonderful to see, each blow of the faéry spear striking sparks from the soft enemy iron. Determined now to go to his grave fighting, he put back his head and, raising his spear high, taunted his attackers. 'Come, little ones, loathly ones!' he cried. 'Red Badb is hungry! The Hag Queen awaits!'

And in that moment, as if in answer to this challenge, the sky blazed white and a blinding blast of lightning scoured the storm-riven sky, like an earth-flung star, like swift destiny streaking home to its mark, a searing gash of blue-white fire stabbed down through the turbulent air, striking the up-raised spear and scattering tongues of flame in all directions. Pelydr rang like a struck bell. The answering thunder drowned all other sound, filling the night like a judgement of doom from the lips of Great Danu herself. Conor felt the jolt like the blow of a hammer to his skull and his vision dimmed. Bright fire seemed to spread through each and every sinew in his body. His sodden cloak steamed, and his siarc and breecs dried instantly. His skin remained unscathed, but his facial blemish flared with a deep crimson glow like live coals in a forge, kindling with a weird and glorious warmth that strengthened and spread out in a heated bloom to envelop both horse and rider entirely.

The lightning bolt removed all fatigue, all fear, all doubt. Conor felt the ravenous, scorching desire of the Dé Danann long oppressed, the frustrated yearning of a people longing to be free from the threat of death and destruction. It seemed to him that he embodied the hopes and fears of his countrymen and knew in his bones that he held the power to free them at last. In that moment, Conor felt his strength reborn and knew he could dare anything, do anything.

More: in that moment, Conor mac Ardan, son of the Darini, Lord of the Fianna, became invincible.

Lofting Pelydr once more, he gave out a roar that rattled the blades ranged about him; the spear in his fist, its blade and shaft agleam with a keen and deadly light, seemed to come alive in his hand. The enemy, stunned beyond sense by the blast, fell back in terror at the sight. Conor pulled hard on the reins, Búrach, no less terrified by the lightning strike, reared, lashing out with his forelegs. 'Búrach! Hie!' cried Conor, and the stallion leapt forward. The Scálda in his path shrank from this flame-touched apparition that lightning could not consume, and thunder did not destroy. Conor, gripping his spear with a grasp as tight as life, lunged again and again and again, each stroke delivered another guest to Red Badb's hall. Unable to defend themselves against such terrible magic, the Scálda turned and ran, fleeing in disordered ranks before him.

The sight of this solitary rider dispatching Scálda with every cut and thrust of his faéry spear emboldened the beleaguered Dé Danann and they took to their weapons with renewed vigour. Any advantage the Scálda possessed to that moment melted away in the heat of the exchange and they abandoned the fight, streaming back into the darkness as from which they came. With them went the otherworldly gleam that had illumined Conor and his grey stallion, dimming as the last of the Scálda disappeared into the rain-riven night.

Silence claimed Tara's Hill then. Slowly, slowly, the storm died away; its wrath spent, the rain dwindled and ceased and even the wind seemed to sigh and hold its breath. Conor, dizzy now and a little dazed, came to himself once more to the slack-jawed, openmouthed expressions of awe of those around him. Some of the warriors nearest him backed away; the rest stood in flat-footed amazement at what they had just witnessed. Then the storm closed in once more; the rain renewed its onslaught and the icy wind wailed. Conor, suddenly cold, and shaking uncontrollably, slid from his horse and sank to his knees. In days to come, there would be other battles, greater battles, but this one, at least, was over.

Eamon

The dead . . . Badb take me, there were so many! Sodden corpses lay strewn in all directions! Corpses of friend and foe alike, aye, and all mired in the blood-tinged mud. Riderless horses stood forlorn, proud heads bent low— and I felt like one more of those poor, tail-draggled beasts, so I did. My siarc and breecs were black with blood—some of it my own. Never had I seen such a battle, such a night. How we survived, I believe we will never know.

Ach, but there were so many who did not survive . . . so very many. The decision to take and hold the high ground aided us and hindered the dog-eaters. True enough. But in the end, it was the fury of the storm that decided the battle's outcome.

Word came to us that the way was clear to the top of Tara's mound. The tribes were uniting up there to make our stand. My lord Ardan gave the command and we all ran for the high ground. But before we even reached the foot of the hill, we were cut off by a wing of mounted Scálda and were forced to fall back and rely on our own defence. As the battle fell out, this was to be our portion in the fight. For, each time there came a chance to climb the hill, another assault would steal the chance away.

'They're at us coming and going,' called Ardan. 'Attacking or retreating, we're in their way.'

Aye, and he was right. Whether riding to attack the hill, or retreating to regroup, the Scálda passed us on the way, preventing any attempt we made to mount the long slope. The best we could do was work ourselves out of the direct approach and maybe find another path to the top. This we did, moving farther by steps and lurches away from the main course of the battle. But we got no farther.

Though I tried three times to scout out a side trail, if the darkness alone had not made it difficult, the storm made it impossible. Down there on the Mag Teamhair, we could not even see the top of the hill, so we fought the battles that came to us—and those were enough to keep us sharp-eyed and ready—and we waited for either a break in the storm, or a lull in the fighting to allow us to join our swordbrothers holding the hilltop.

Now, the sorry sun of an ill-favoured day crept toward dawn and I stood stiff legged on the wasted battleground and witnessed what the night had left behind: the dross and squander of war flung across the churned-up ground like flotsam heaved up on the beach and left there to rot when the squall passed on to plunder other lands. The night's raw gale had gone, leaving only a desolate calm and the dead: Scálda and Dé Danann alike, fierce enemies in life but alike in death. A spear to the gut brings all men to the same level.

As soon as it was light enough to see your hand in front of your face, the miserable few of us who remained in the Land of the Living began search-ing among the bodies for fallen friends and any still clinging to life. I had not seen Lord Ardan since he commanded me to go and search out a clear trail to the hilltop. Allowing for darkness and the confusion of battle, our separation did not alarm me, but as our lord was not to be seen among the survivors working the battlefield, I did feel a pang of concern as I turned over the bodies.

I had just rolled the ninth or tenth corpse—an Eblani battlechief, judg-ing from his heavy braid and thick bronze torc—when I heard someone call my name. I raised my head and peered through the mist to see Liam, some little way off, bending over a small heap of bodies near the foot of Tara's slope. I answered, my voice rough and hoarse from shouting all night, and picked my way over the chewed-up turf to where I found him stooping over the body of his father.

'He is still alive,' whispered Liam as I joined him.

One glance at the pale, waxy flesh and dull eyes, and I shook my head. 'Not much longer, I fear.'

'Help me get him on a horse,' said Liam, bending low over his father.

'Liam, he is beyond—'

'Go! Hurry!'

With little thought or care, I went for the first poor beast I saw—a mud-caked mare nearby—and brought it back. Liam, on his knees beside his father, said, 'I am here, my king.' He clasped his father's bloodstained hand to his breast. 'We are taking you home.'

Ardan's eyelids fluttered and a faint smile touched his lips. 'Too late for that. Listen, my son, I want—' He coughed and could not continue.

'Here, get him up on the horse,' said Liam, taking Ardan by the shoulders and raising him into a sitting position. That was as far as we got him. Panting from the exertion, his breath coming in gasps, Ardan still had a thought for his people. He said, 'You will be king now. . . .' And, raising a shaky hand, my lord of many years touched the slender twist of silver at his neck. 'Take this . . .'

'Father, I—'

Ardan gave a slight shake of his head. 'Take it . . . make it your own, my son.'

Unable to speak, Liam simply nodded.

Ardan closed his eyes for a moment and then roused himself once more. 'Liam?' he said, growing frantic. His hand flailed, reaching for something he could no longer see. 'Liam?'

'I am here, Father.' He took his father's searching hand.

'Let Conor come home,' Ardan said, his voice fading to a dry, hushed whisper.

'Father? I did not hear—'

'Conor . . . let him come home . . . it is time.'

Liam clutched his father's hand the tighter. 'But, Father—'

Ardan struggled up, his eyes wide, but unseeing. 'Promise me,' he said with renewed force. 'End his exile . . . promise me . . .'

Liam glanced at me and I nodded my encouragement. Finally, he said, 'I promise, Father.'

My poor grieving heart moved within me. Our good king's last thoughts were of his outcast son. More than that, Liam had heard the request and made the promise. It was right and good.

Ardan slumped back once more and we lowered him to the ground. 'Is Eamon here?'

'I am here, my king.' I reached up and pressed the hand of my friend, kinsman, and lord. 'I am with you.'

'You will be battlechief,' Ardan whispered. 'Accept Conor back into the warband. Give him my sword.'

'With pleasure, lord.'

The flicker of a smile flitted across Ardan's dry lips. 'Then all is well. . . .' He closed his eyes once more.

'Come, let's get him somewhere dry and warm where he can rest.' Somehow, we lifted the all but lifeless body up onto the horse and, taking up the dangling reins, Liam led the bedraggled beast away. I walked alongside, keeping my hand on the king's side to keep him from sliding off his mount. We had gone but a few paces when Liam called over his shoulder, 'Tell the ardféne we're going home. We'll make a start and the rest of you follow.'

'Liam,' I said, 'there is no need.'

He heard the note of sorrow in my voice and stopped. 'What? Why is—'

'He is gone, Liam.' My voice sounded flat in my ears and my tongue numb as I spoke the fateful words. 'Your father is dead.'

It took Liam a moment to realise what I had said: Ardan mac Orsi had breathed his last and his cup and throne would know him no more.

We sat for a long moment in silence, gazing at the body of our lord and contemplating what we had lost and what was now to be done. Finally, I turned sad eyes to Liam and said, 'Sorry as I am to lose him, it is well he lived to tell us his last request. It will be good to have Conor back among us again.'

Liam's mouth squirmed into an ugly sneer. 'You always take his part.'

Reaching up, he carefully spread the ends of the kingly torc and gently removed it from around his father's throat. Holding the silver ornament in both hands, he extended it to me. 'Would you so honour me?'

I gazed at the torc and, after a moment's hesitation, said, 'Perhaps we should wait until we've returned to Dúnaird for a proper kingship ceremony. Rónán could perform it for you.'

'You gainsay me already?' said Liam sharply. 'Is this how we begin, *old friend*?'

'Nay, nay,' I said, taken aback by the sharpness in my new lord's tone, 'only that our kinsmen would want to participate in the king-making.'

'Our people will have their day when the druids come to affirm the decision,' Liam pointed out. 'Aye, and Rónán can make the ceremony. We will celebrate then.' He looked down at the body of his father and his voice took on a softer tone. 'But the people also need a king *now*—not in ten days' time when we lay Ardan with his fathers.'

Again, he thrust the torc at me, insisting I take it. 'Will you honour me, or must I do it myself?'

With no little reluctance, I placed the torc around Liam's neck and closed the ends—for better or worse, sealing the fate of our tribe. Then, without a word, our new lord started off once more. 'Bring the men.'

'Where are you going? They'll be lighting the funeral pyres soon.'

'Not my father,' Liam snarled. 'I'll not be leaving him to the flames. We're going home.'

34

'I think I saw Médon and some of the others out on the plain,' intoned Galart in a voice that sounded like it came from inside an empty shell. 'The fianna should be here soon.'

Conor put out a hand to the exhausted warrior. 'Rest now and take some food if you can find any. We'll have need of you later, so restore your strength while you can. Tell the others.'

Fergal—his hair matted, cloak and breecs spattered with mud and blood, a rent in his siarc revealing an ugly gash in his upper chest—leaned on the shaft of his spear too exhausted to move. 'No sign of Ardan and the Darini? Nothing at all?' he asked, his voice shattered from shouting.

'Maybe they were never here,' suggested Donal; head in hands, he sat beside Conor on the rim of the inner ditch of the council ring. 'That, or they are still on the way.'

'Lucky them if they are,' said Fergal. He made to turn and staggered backward, almost falling into the ditch.

'Sit down, brother, before you collapse,' Conor advised. Looking out across the battlefield—the once sacred ground now a foul morass strewn with the corpses of men and horses, of friend and foe alike. A dazed few survivors searched among the dead, stumbling on unfeeling feet like sleep-walkers. Conor shook his weary head, trying to clear it of the thick buzzing noise only he seemed to hear. 'There will not be a single tribe that has not lost their most esteemed warriors—kings and warleaders included.'

'Except the Brigantes,' put in Donal. 'It seems they had not yet arrived either.'

'No doubt Vainche the Vain wanted to make a grand procession of it,' grumbled Fergal. He turned red, tired eyes toward the plain stretching away to the west. He sighed, too tired to raise any spite at the thought. 'Ach, well, I expect we should go back to our camp and wait for the others. There is nothing to keep us here.'

Slowly, like enfeebled old men, the four rose on stiff and wobbly legs, took up their weapons, and started across the devastated ground, pausing here and there to speak to those who were searching among the fallen for friends or kinsmen, and collecting valuables and weapons to be shared out among the living. They had just started down the slope path leading to the plains below when they heard someone call out, 'Wait, lord! We would speak to you.'

Conor paused and turned around to see three Auteini warriors stumbling toward them. 'I know you,' said Conor. 'You are the battlechief who lost your lord—'

'And you saved us,' said the warrior. Before Conor could reply, the warrior added, 'That is why we want to join you.'

'Join us?' wondered Fergal. 'Why would you be wanting to do that?'

The man looked to Conor and answered, 'We have no one else.'

'What about your tribe?' asked Conor. 'Now that your king is dead, your people will be needing you all the more in the days to come.'

'I will not lie,' replied the Auteini battlechief. 'Our tribe is in a bad way. We can no longer defend the coast. We came to the gathering hoping to find a lord who would agree to help resettle us.'

'We have discussed it,' offered another of the three, 'and we believe our people will fare better with you to lead them than anyone else we know.'

'Especially after what we saw last night. Truly, lord, you have no equal in battle,' said the third warrior—the first person to mention Conor's extraordinary transformation. Not everyone had seen it, but enough had that word had begun circulating among the survivors that a new champion had appeared among them.

'Will you have us?'

Conor looked at the three of them and felt their need. Though they hardly knew what they were asking, how could he turn them away? 'I will,' he told them. 'You and your people will be welcome to join us.'

The Auteini battlechief pressed the back of his hand to his forehead in the ancient acknowledgement of fealty. 'Thank you, lord. We are yours to command.'

'Then go and tell your people what is in your mind to do. If they all agree—'

'They will,' said one of the warriors.

'If they *all* agree,' repeated Conor, 'then make ready and return to us in the spring. Bring with you whatever you can carry.'

'That we will,' said the battlechief. They took their leave then, and started away. One of them turned back and called, 'Where shall we come to?'

'Here,' Conor told him, spreading his arms to take in Tara Hill. 'You will find us here.'

The three Auteini went away and as soon as they were alone once more, Fergal said, '*Come to us here in the spring?* We cannot be staying here, brother.'

'Why not?' asked Conor. He turned and started down the path to the plain once more.

'Because . . . ,' began Fergal, then, unable to conjure a coherent argument, looked to Donal. 'Tell him, brother. He'll listen to you.'

'Because,' said Donal, falling into step behind Conor, 'there is nothing here—no food, no shelter, no stronghold.'

'Once of a time, there was.' Conor stopped again, his eyes narrowed as if peering far into the distance to discern the shape of a thing moving toward him through the morning murk. He turned to face his questioners. 'You say we cannot stay here, but I say that is exactly what we are going to do. Brothers, we are taking Tara for our own.'

'Taking Tara . . . ,' Donal repeated slowly. 'Here is a new thing.'

'New, maybe—but that does not make it wise or good,' blustered Fergal. 'You cannot be claiming Tara for your own. The lords will take a dim view of that. They'll never allow it.'

'How many men were killed last night?' asked Conor, defiance edging into his tone. 'Answer me that, brother. How many?'

'How should I be knowing that?' replied Fergal, somewhat tetchily. 'Do you know?'

'I do not,' replied Conor, 'but I know that every last one of those warriors shed life's sweet blood to save Eirlandia—and he did it here in this place.' He flung a hand wide to take in the entire hilltop. 'Hear me, brothers, Eirlandia lost a great many of its best warriors last night—aye, and many of them kings and battlechiefs. Not so?' He looked to Fergal, who offered a sober nod.

'You said the lords would not look well on my taking this hill,' Conor continued, 'but I ask you which lords do you mean?' He gestured across Tara's plains below, strewn with the corpses of slaughtered defenders and a few shattered survivors picking through the carnage of last night's catastrophe. 'Who among them will make bold to forbid us taking Tara for our stronghold?'

'The tribes will never stand for it. They will rise up against you,' Fergal insisted. He threw a pleading look to Donal for help. 'Tell him.'

'Nay, nay, brother,' countered Donal, his eyes lifted to the cloud-shrouded sky. 'Conor is right. I see it now. This is where it begins.'

Fergal stared at both his friends as if he had never seen either one of them before. 'Listen to the both of you,' he said, stubbing the butt of his spear against the turf. 'You said it yourself, Donal—there is nothing here. Look around. Take a good long look. A stronghold needs walls, so it does. It needs houses for people to live in, and stables for horses, and storehouses, and such. It needs fields and farmers to work them. It needs flocks and herds and pens to keep them. A stronghold needs a tribe of folk to people it, to work the land and make a life—men and women, aye, as many women as men, come to that. We have none of these things. Are we to raise walls and build houses and plough fields and breed cattle overnight?' He shook his head fiercely. 'Put this folly right out of your heads the both of you.'

'You call it folly?' said Conor. 'Think you now! Many of the lords and kings who clung so tightly to their small portion of power, who held their pride so high that they could never bring themselves to unite under Brecan Brigantes were swept away last night with the storm. Today the sun rises on a new day and with it a new chance to gather up what remains and bind it together, unite it and make it whole.'

Conor, his birthmark tingling as the vision sparked to life in his mind. 'Eirlandia is broken now. But it could be that breaking is what we needed in order to bring us together, bind us together, and make us strong.'

'Or weaken us for the killing blow,' suggested Fergal. 'Does that not seem the more likely?'

'There is another way to see it.' Conor began walking again in his excitement, causing Fergal and Donal to hurry to keep up. 'It seems to me that Balor Evil Eye and his dog-eaters achieved in one night what Lord Brecan could not accomplish in ten years of trying. The old opposition has been carried away on the wings of the storm, and now we have a chance to put our broken land back together stronger than it was before, stronger maybe than it has ever been. And Donal is right, this is where the saving of Eirlandia begins.'

'Ach, it is a grand scheme, I'll give you that, brother. Very grand,' said Fergal. 'You may have found a fleck of gold hidden in these ashes. But where are the *people*, eh? Where are the people to put flesh and bone to this handsome dream of yours?'

'Many of the tribes who were here for the Oenach have lost kings and lords, they've lost their warleaders—'

'They'll choose new ones to take their places.'

'Aye, they will. But I mean to offer them a choice. They could choose us—'

'Like the Auteini up there just now,' Donal pointed out.

'Aye, the Auteini are but the first and there will be others—perhaps many others. These tribes, weakened as they are, still have farmers and carpenters and weavers—women and children, elders and bards. Each will have an offering to make and it is just what we will need to support our fianna. We will make Tara's hill and plains the beating heart of Eirlandia. It was once of a time, and it will be again.'

'A new tribe with a new king whose stronghold is here,' mused Donal approvingly. 'It will be as it was in the days when Ros Ruadh ruled as high king and Eirlandia was the envy of the world.'

'Perhaps these lordless clans will not so readily leave their ancient homelands, brother,' said Fergal. 'It may not be so easy as you imply.'

'We'll see,' Conor. 'We'll see. But there are more pressing matters just now, duties we must discharge before anything else. We must help bury our swordbrothers and see them properly honoured.'

'While we are about it, we can tell our swordbrothers about our new tribe, ask about their people, and offer them a place at Tara,' suggested Donal, and stopped on the path so abruptly that Fergal almost tripped over him.

Fergal opened his mouth to object, but the strange look on Donal's face drove any such notion right out of his head. 'What is it? Have you seen something?'

'Remember when I told you about seeing a foot on a stone?'

'After the battle on Mag Belach when Médon returned with the first of the fianna?' answered Conor. 'Aye, you said you saw a man's foot upon a stone.'

'And you asked me then . . . you said, "Whose foot? What stone?" Remember? Well, I see it now.' Donal gazed at Conor, a clear and certain light in his eyes. 'It is *your* foot, Conor mac Ardan.' He gestured back toward the hilltop. 'And the stone is there.'

'The Pillar Stone?' said Fergal.

'Also called the Lia Rígad,' Donal told him. 'The Stone of Kingmaking.'

Fergal, unable to overcome his incredulity, rubbed his hand over his face. Perhaps, this was merely exhaustion taking hold of their better judgement. He decided not to press them further. 'What are you thinking, Conor?'

'Only this—that if I am to be king, then I must have a queen,' he replied, and started down the path again. 'And I am thinking that I have kept that lady waiting long enough.'

35

Even from a distance, Dúnaird appeared quiet. The late autumn sun was bright in a cloud-dappled sky, shimmering on the silvery sweep of sea visible beyond the rock cliffs to the northeast and turning the stubble in the hillside fields a rich golden brown. Conor savoured the sight, drinking it in through every pore. After the horrific battle at Tara, a little calm in this peaceful corner of Eirlandia was a healing balm to a battered soul. So many dead . . . far too many dead: the funeral fires across Mag Rí were still burning when they left. The smoke rose in a forest of black columns and ash fell like snow from a black sky.

The fianna had missed the battle, but reached Tara in time to help prepare the pyres and collect the weapons and valuables. What with the sudden surplus of horses that had lost their riders—both Scálda and Dé Danann—Fergal claimed, confiscated, and appropriated enough to mount Conor's entire warband and a few more besides. No more sore feet for Conor's men; from now on the fianna would ride.

Only when the last pyres had been lit did Conor give the order for the fianna to wash, gather whatever food they could find, find their mounts, and ride with him to Dúnaird. No Darini had been seen at the battle, nor afterward among the dead, and Conor was impatient for news of his father and brother. More than that, he was eager to see Aoife and tell her his plans for their future together at Tara; and for that he wanted to approach her in strength and with force.

Now, as he gazed upon his childhood home, a feeling of acute disquiet stole over him, for despite the apparent serenity and light, he sensed distress; misery seemed to flow from the stronghold like the troubled currents of a dark, invisible stream.

'Dúnaird is in mourning,' observed Donal, reining to a halt beside him.

'You feel it, too?' Conor glanced at him out of the corner of his eye. 'What do you see?'

'I see only that the board and bench in the king's hall is empty,' he replied, squinting his eyes as if to peer in through a darkened doorway into the next room. 'And the yard as well. Nothing more.'

Conor nodded and lifted the reins and made to continue on.

'Stay, brother,' called Fergal as his horse trotted up to join them. 'You are still an outcast here, remember. Let me go down and talk to them and see how things sit. If all is well, I'll summon you and the others.'

Conor dismissed the notion with a shake of his head. 'We'll go together.'

'Just us three, then,' said Donal. 'If we bring the fianna, Liam may think we've come for a fight and give us one.'

'He wouldn't,' said Conor.

'He might,' Fergal countered. 'You know what he's like.'

'He wouldn't,' insisted Conor. 'My father would never allow it.' He looked down at the stronghold, uncertain what his reception would be. Fergal had a point, he concluded, and decided, 'Right, then. We'll go together, but leave the fianna here until we see what manner of welcome the king will give us.'

'Very wise,' allowed Fergal. Wheeling his horse, he rode back and commanded Médon to wait with the fianna but remain ready to join them when summoned; then, returning to Conor and Donal, the three started down the long slope to the trail leading to the Darini stronghold. The sense of desolation that Conor felt upon seeing his home grew stronger the closer they came. They reached the ráth and stopped to observe. All was as quiet as it appeared from a distance; no sounds of activity could be discerned from within. The gates were closed, but there was no guard on the walkway.

'Where is the watchman?' muttered Conor.

'Let's see if we can rouse them.' Fergal urged his mount ahead a few steps and called out a greeting. Receiving no answer, he shouted again. When that brought no response, he glanced back to where Conor and Donal sat watching, shrugged, then dismounted and walked to the gate. Drawing the knife from his belt, he gave the timber a few good thumps, shouting,

'Anyone in there? Open the door, it is Fergal mac Caen come home! Who is guarding this gate?'

He was about to renew his assault on the door when a voice called out from within, saying, 'Hold your water! I'm coming!' There came a scramble on the wooden ladder leading to the walkway and presently a round head looked over the breastwork. 'Fergal! What are you doing here? We thought you were killed.'

'Who is that up there that would be thinking such a thing?'

'It is Cermod mac Riorigh,' came the reply.

'Cermod, lad. What are you playing at? Leaving your watch like that? Liam will have your skin off you. Open the gate and let us in.'

'I would do that right readily, but the king has made a stern command not to let anyone into the ráth.'

'Has he now?' Fergal rolled his eyes and sighed. 'I recall we've had this kind of talk before—and I can tell you it never ends happy.'

'Ach, well, I don't know about—'

'No matter, lad. You just hie up and tell the king that we've come home— Conor, Fergal, and Donal—all three of us, and we want to come in.'

The young warrior gazed at him and, with a backward glance over his shoulder as if fearing he might be overheard, he said, 'I would tell him right readily, so I would—but the king is not here.'

'No? Then where is he? Be quick! We've come a long way.'

'Lord Liam has gone to the entombment ceremony,' answered Cermod. 'Him along with near everyone else. There are only six of us here just now.'

'Where is everyone—' began Fergal. 'Wait! Did I hear you say *entombment*?'

'Aye, so I did.'

'Who has died?' demanded Conor. He swung down from his mount and hurried to join Fergal with Donal right behind.

Cermod stared at him in disbelief, then answered, 'Ach, Conor, it is you! Your father, King Ardan fell at Tara. Seven days ago. Did you not know this?'

Conor let out a groan and sank to his knees before the gate.

'Lord Ardan was at the Oenach with the ardféne and the Scálda attacked—at night it was, and they—'

'We were there!' snapped Fergal. 'Just shut your fool mouth and give us a moment. This is Conor's father we're talking about!'

'Conor, I am sorry, brother,' said Donal, squatting down beside his friend and putting an arm around him.

'Full sorry I am, too,' said Fergal. He rested a hand on Conor's shoulder for a moment, gave it a squeeze, then turned back to Cermod on the walkway. 'How long ago did they leave the ráth?'

'This morning just. If you hurry you may still see some of the ceremony.'

'Did you hear that?' said Fergal. 'We can still—'

Conor was already on his feet. 'Go and summon the fianna,' he said, striding quickly to Búrach. 'Meet us at the cairn. Come with me, Donal. I don't want to arrive alone.'

Vaulting onto their mounts, Conor and Donal galloped on to the Darini burial cairn: a low chambered tomb sunk into the cradling earth. Only the top three tiers of stone slabs and the massive domed covering showed above ground; all the rest remained below. The multiple chambers and niches contained the bones of Darini nobility: kings and queens, princes and champions, the great and the honoured. On a mound nearby stood a dolmen of vast antiquity. Together the two venerable structures formed the tribe's funereal precinct.

Wrapped in his best cloak, Ardan's body had been placed on a low wooden bier outside the entrance to the dolmen. At the culmination of the rite, the corpse would be consigned to the little hollow beneath the massive stone slabs of the dolmen where it would lie until the birds and beasts had consumed his flesh, and the passing seasons made decomposition complete. Then, at some auspicious time, there would be another ceremony and the necessary bones would be gathered up, the great chambered tomb would be unsealed, and Ardan's remains would be tucked into one of the many niches to mingle with those of previous generations of tribal rulers and worthies.

Conor and Donal reached the burial site on its high cliff overlooking the sea to find the tribe gathered around the dolmen listening to a funeral song for a fallen hero; sung by a druid, the song was one of the last parts of the funeral rite performed just before the first entombment. In this case, the druid was Rónán, and Conor could hear his brother's clear, strong voice before he could see him. Donal and Conor stopped a short distance away, dismounted, and hurried up the rise to the dolmen. Their sudden arrival did not go unnoticed; word of the newcomers spread quickly through the throng so that by the time Donal and Conor reached the dolmen, a strained silence had fallen over the proceedings. As the two approached, the crowd parted to let them through.

Rónán, his hands and voice raised in declamation, saw his exiled brother and ceased abruptly. Those closest to him turned and stared as Conor and Donal—freshly shaved, their hair combed and braided, arrayed like kings in their splendid faéry finery—strode to the low wooden bier on which the corpse of Lord Ardan mac Orsi lay wrapped in a long brown and yellow checked cloak—gathered over his face now and fastened by the large silver stag's-head brooch he wore at celebrations and when performing kingly duties.

Conor stood for a moment; head down, his hands limp at his side, he groaned. Then, with every eye on him, he knelt beside the bier and, stretching out his arms, rested his head and chest on his father's body; a moment later, his shoulders began to shake gently as the hidden tears fell. Donal, mindful of his friend's grief, took his place beside and a little behind Conor, affording him a portion of privacy and protection from intrusion.

'How dare you!'

The challenge came sooner than expected.

'How dare you show your face, traitor!' Liam charged up to the bier, pushing people out of the way as he came.

Donal put out a hand to stop him. 'Peace, Liam. We want no trouble here.'

'Then you should not have come!' shouted Liam, his face red and contorted with rage.

'Can you not allow your brother a moment for his final farewell?'

'I have borne his arrogance, his defiance, his treachery until now, but I will bear it no longer.' He whirled around and shouted, 'Eamon! Do your duty and take him!' Turning, he pointed at Conor. 'If he resists . . . kill him.'

Donal squared off, placing his hand on the pommel of his sword. 'Touch him and you will forfeit that hand.'

Rónán stepped forward then and, in a tone of absolute authority, cried, 'Silence!' He moved to the head of the bier and, holding his rowan staff sideways as if to place a barrier between the two opposing parties, declared, 'I will not have this sacred rite defiled by petty contention. There will be no blood shed on this day.' To Liam, he said, 'Step away!'

'And if I refuse?' he challenged, throwing back his head and thrusting out his chin in defiance.

'Refuse and I will denounce you to the four winds and satirise you before the Oenach. Your days as king will be finished before they have begun.'

At this Conor raised his face, the twin tracks of tears glistening on his cheeks. 'King Liam, is it?' he said and, with a last embrace of his father's body, stood to face his brother. 'It seems you gained the kingship that was ever your desire. Whether you deserve that honour or not, we shall see.'

'So! You come to challenge me for our father's throne—is that your plan?'

Conor shook his head. 'Nay, brother mine. I did not come to take your throne. I came to say farewell to my father and—' Stepping away from the bier, he turned and scanned the crowd.

Liam moved around the bier to put himself in Conor's path. 'Now you have done what you came to do, you think to ride off without paying the price for breaking the ban of exile? There is a price to pay, *brother mine.*'

Rónán rushed forward to occupy the space between them, putting a hand out to either side. 'That is enough! I have given you stern warning, Liam. I will not warn you again.' To Conor, he said, 'Step back. Go on—move aside and stay there.'

'He has broken the ban!' insisted Liam. 'He must pay the price—the honour of the tribe demands it.'

'That ill-conceived ban was nothing but a lame ruse and well you know it,' said Donal, taking his place beside Conor.

'I know of no such thing,' declared Liam. Livid with anger, he turned and gestured for Eamon to join him. 'Obey your king and seize them. Seize them both.'

Eamon, frowning mightily, remained rooted to his place.

Conor shook his head slowly. 'I did not come here to fight with you. I came to say farewell—'

'Liar,' Liam snarled. 'You came to claim the throne. But I say you shall not have it!'

'It is not your throne I mean to claim,' Conor told him again. Turning away, he passed his gaze around the crowd now pressed close about them. 'I have come to claim my betrothed.' He put out a hand. 'Aoife!' he called. 'Aoife, where are you?'

'Here, Conor,' came the reply. 'I am here.' With that, she stepped out from behind Eamon and flew to Conor's outstretched arms. He gathered her in and held her to him.

'I have returned for you, beloved. Will you come away with me?'

She put her hands on his face and kissed him, saying, 'After I have waited all this time, you ask me that now?' She kissed him again. 'Have I not already gone to you a thousand times a day in my heart?'

Liam, smouldering with rage and humiliation, could only stand aside and watch as his brother kissed the woman he wanted for his own. Holding her as if afraid of losing her if he released his grip even for a moment, Conor turned to Liam and said, 'I am leaving now, and will never trouble Dúnaird again. Do not so much as think to prevent me, or come after me.'

Liam heard a challenge in that and drew himself up, saying, 'Who is there to stop me?' Indicating Donal, he said, 'Him? Is *he* all you could find to stand with you?'

'I stand with Conor, aye, but I am not alone,' Donal replied. Raising a hand, he pointed through the crowd to the hillside beyond. 'I can assure you that Conor's warband will stand with him, too.'

At these words, the crowd turned as one to see Fergal with thirty-six mounted warriors riding slowly down the hill toward the burial site.

Liam stared, the colour draining from his face. When he finally found his voice again, he shouted, 'Eamon! Assemble the warriors! Get the people away—'

Rónán stepped close and took him by the shoulders. 'No! I told you there will be no blood spilled on this sacred ground. Tell your men to stand aside and let them go.' To Conor, he said, 'I will see the ban extinguished and let you go free if you promise not to attack Dúnaird.'

'Do you imagine I would attack the only home I have ever known? How little you know me, brother. Still, lest there be any who doubt it, I will do as you ask.' He lifted his head and called out to all those who stood looking on. 'I came in peace and leave in peace. Never will I attack Dúnaird, nor suffer any harm to come to anyone here so long as I have power to protect you. On that you have my promise.'

Stepping close, Rónán embraced his brother and took the opportunity to whisper, 'Take Aoife and go now, brother. I will come to you in a few days.'

'You will find me at Tara,' Conor told him.

'Tara of the Kings, is it?' said Rónán, stepping back in surprise. 'If that is so, then we have much to talk about, I think.'

With a last glance at the body of his father on the bier, Conor took Aoife's hand and led her from the burial site. He climbed onto Búrach's back and Donal helped Aoife to a place in front of him. Rónán came running up with a large leather bag. 'Your harp, Aoife. You'll not be wanting music where you're going.' Aoife smiled and thanked him, and cradled the instrument in her arms. When she was settled, Conor raised his hand to give the signal to ride out, but Fergal said, 'A moment, brother—the fianna would like to pay their proper respects.' He turned his eyes to the bier and the body of the king he had served since he had taken a warrior's vow. 'And I would make my farewell, too.'

Conor nodded and then watched as his fianna dismounted and formed a long line at the bier behind Fergal and, one by one, each warrior stepped forward, paused, then touched the back of his hand to his forehead in a final acknowledgement of nobility. Conor marvelled to see it. 'They didn't even know him,' he murmured, 'how is it that they should honour him so?'

Aoife, looking on, tightened her grip around Conor's waist. 'It is not for him, my love. It is you they honour. They want to show you what manner of king they want you to be.'

'Like my father,' Conor said.

'If you are half the ruler he was, you will be a king worthy to be remembered.'

Taking her hand from around his waist, Conor raised it to his lips, kissed it, and pulled her close. 'I care nothing for being remembered,' he whispered. 'But with you beside me as my queen, we will build a kingdom this worlds-realm will never forget.'

Eamon

Ach, well, skin me for a lizard if I told you I saw that coming. Truth, no one was more surprised and amazed than I was to see Conor and Donal appear in the midst of Lord Ardan's frithchor. There we were in solemn observance of the funeral rite when here comes the two outcasts—looking like very kings in regal finery, so they did. Bold as bronze, they went striding right up to the body and Conor claiming a son's right to a last embrace of his father . . . and Liam! Ach, our spiteful king beside himself with envy and angry as a wasp in an ale jar.

It is no secret to anyone now that our new lord is jealous of his brother and forever afraid that Conor will yet come to take away the throne he has worked so hard to gain. Be that as it may, I believe Conor when he said he had no interest in the Darini throne. Liam did not hear that—*could* not hear that, maybe. Yet, the arrival of Fergal with this large warband that Conor has gathered should have told, I think. It was plain to me, and plain enough to anyone who had wit to see it that our Conor has a greater plan in mind.

It never serves anyone well to get between two brothers when they fight. So, I stood aside and let them wrestle with it. When Liam called for me to step in, I ignored the command—a failing, I know, and I own it. But I would sooner cut off my own hand than lay a naked blade to Conor. Also, there was sweet Aoife to think about and the first thought in my head was to shield her lest she get pulled into an unseemly tussle. But, as I say, I do believe Conor had a greater plan in mind. He had come to honour his father, aye, but he had also come to claim his bride, and it did a heart good to see the two of them together at last. I ask you now, who would laud the name of Eamon mac Áine if he stood in the way of something like that?

Ach, but Liam let me know what *he* thought.

'You snivelling cur,' he snarled in my ear as we watched Conor and his bold fianna ride away on their fast horses. Where they got those horses, I cannot say. But, mark me, that is a warband yet to be reckoned.

'Why angry, lord?' I asked, knowing full well why he raged. 'Conor has taken nothing from you and has not impugned your dignity in any way. Nor has he challenged your authority. You were king before he came and you are king still now he's gone.'

'He is outcast and banned from returning on pain of death!' Liam growled, his face dark with the awful grudge that was in him. 'He has defied the law!'

'You know that exile was unjust,' I told him. 'Aye, and I think Mádoc, that addled old druid, had your help to get Conor cast out of the tribe in the first place.' Liam drew breath to shout me down, but I stayed the course. 'If that weren't enough of a mark against you, I knelt beside my king and heard him beg you with his dying breath to welcome Conor back into the hearth home of his people. No! I will not hear you deny it.' Liam glared raw hate at me. 'I heard the king demand your promise, Liam, and you gave it.'

Rónán, who had been watching Conor and his fianna ride away, joined us then and heard this last part. 'Is this so, brother? You gave your word to the king?'

'He was dying,' muttered Liam. 'He did not know what he was saying.'

'He knew right well, so he did,' I declared. 'And so did I.'

I might have said more, but Rónán realised that others were looking on and this argument on sacred ground was unbecoming. 'We will speak about this again later. Of that you may be certain,' he concluded. 'The funeral rite is begun and must be completed before the sun sets on this day. We will continue with the ceremony.'

And that is what we did. We concluded the frithchor for our king and then returned to the ráth to talk—and how we talked! Ach, aye, for days and days to come it was the only thought in anyone's head and the first word on the tongue: Conor—and him a king with a warband of a size not seen since High King Nuada Arteglamh ruled Eirlandia. Some of the younger warriors are even talking about going to join him and, aye, I will go myself if Liam will not change his ways, so I will.

But Liam, now . . . Liam is making noises like a man who will no longer be satisfied with his portion at the feast. It is in his mind, I'm thinking, to find another who will join with him and form a rival faction to oppose whatever it may be that Conor has planned.

Nothing good will come of this, I can tell you. As I said before, it serves no one well to stand between two brothers in a fight.